Beneath the Lion's Wings

Acclaim for ***Beneath the Lion's Wings***

"...Good escape reading in this tale of love and tough decisions in Venice...In her well-researched debut novel, Nardin does a fine job evoking Venice's atmosphere, culture, and history. The particular practices and customs of gondoliering, along with women's efforts to enter the profession, make for absorbing reading."
– *Kirkus Reviews*

"A love story as seductive as Venice itself, with a bi-continental romance, an appealing heroine, a hunky gondolier, sweet and surprising twists, and an insider's authentic details. The next best thing to sipping a Bellini on a sunny balcony overlooking the Grand Canal. Pure delight." – *Dianne Hales*, author of *La Bella Lingua* and *Mona Lisa – A Life Discovered*

"...a charming, moving romance...Venice—impossibly beautiful, mysterious, demanding—is a third character in the novel. A delicately nuanced love story." – *Elizabeth Jennings*, author and co-founder of the Women's Fiction Festival, Matera, Italy.

"Ohanesian Nardin knows of what she writes...It requires a long-time resident to understand the sense of place and history in a unique world such as Venice...the author's finest touch is her cultural understanding of an outsider wanting to fit in...she has tenderly handled true stereotypes and has avoided the touristic view while weaving a romantic tale through the waterways and narrow alleys of Venice, Italy." – *Pamela Sheldon Johns,* author of sixteen Italian themed cookbooks including *Cucina Povera* and *50 Great Pasta Sauces.*

"A fun escape to Venice…A love story with twists as captivating as the city's canals." – *Kathy Ayer,* founder of Food Lover's Odyssey Culinary Vacations

"Grab a spritz and lose yourself in the *calle* of Venice through this captivating tale of personal growth shrouded in secrets and mystery."—*Michelle Fabio*, author of *52 Things to See & Do in Calabria*

Marie invites you to visit her website:
www.MarieOhanesianNardinAuthor.com

Beneath the Lion's Wings

A NOVEL

Marie Ohanesian Nardin

W
L
Waterline
Publishing

ISBN 13: 9791220025881
Cover Art Design by Sally Spector

For

Roberto, and the gondolier trade he proudly belongs to;
Giorgia and Rebecca, who inspire me every day;
and Venice,
the extraordinary city that led
us to each other

Acknowledgments

MY DEEPEST THANKS: to Amy Dorta McIlwaine for her professional support when this novel was a budding idea; to Deb McIntyre, and the *allora group* of writers I met at the Women's Fiction Festival in Matera, Italy, for convincing me that this story merits being written and read; to Marlene Adelstein for her editorial guidance and encouraging notes; to Connie J. Strause, and the Rancho Del Oro Book Club members in Oceanside, California, for making the manuscript one of their monthly reads, and critiquing it with kindness, enthusiasm and honesty; to Kim Wiley for her helpful final edit, and to Kim Boykin for putting us together, and for her support and advice; and special thanks to the talented Sally Spector whose beautiful artwork illustrates our mutual love and respect for Venice, Italy, and with her permission dresses this book's cover; to Carole, for her steadfast optimism and friendship. Most of all, thank you to Roberto.

"If you recognize that the person you love deserves your love, will your soul to suffer some."
Carlo Goldoni – *The Lovers*

"Se conoscete che la persona che amate meriti l'amor vostro, disponete l'animo a sofferir qualche cosa."
Carlo Goldoni – *Gli Innamorati*

Chapter 1

THEIR BMW RENTAL car sped down the Italian *autostrada*, and the autumn breeze chased clouds around the soft blue sky. Victoria closed the *Best of Europe* guide book and peered through the windshield at a row of rusted boats docked in petrol-stained seawater—a part of Venice the guide book wisely didn't mention. She had insisted they include Venice in their vacation itinerary, not Portofino. They didn't have time to see both seaside towns.

"This must be the port." Seated in the passenger seat, Victoria turned to Jackie. "We should be there soon."

Jackie kept her eyes fixed on the road ahead. She tightened her grip around the sporty steering wheel and dominated the highway like a local. She followed the sign indicating VENEZIA, and then glanced at the on-board navigation screen. "7.8 kilometers."

"What's that in miles?"

"A 10k is a little more than 6 miles...so less than that. You'd know that if you ran."

"I have enough trouble getting my butt to yoga class, thank you."

Sinking deeper into the luxurious passenger seat, Victoria tossed the dog-eared guide book on top of the tourists' debris littering the backseat: a mix of plastic Evian bottles, a boxed vintage desk clock from the Swiss Alps, a tiny Chanel shopping bag holding an even smaller bottle of Coco perfume, a porcelain doll for Jackie's niece, a beauty case that didn't fit in the overloaded trunk, and crumbs from the fresh baguette they'd bought in Nice, the day before. She lifted her iPhone from the leather console and scrolled down the music list to Ed Sheeran's *Thinking Out Loud.* She tapped the screen with her well-manicured finger, and sent words of love pouring through the car-stereo speakers.

"This song is getting on my nerves." Jackie rolled her blue eyes. A simple beauty, she hid her attractiveness under bulky running pants and a faded U.S.C. sweatshirt—a style contrast to the gingham sundress and sandals Victoria wore.

"He's one of the agency's top clients."

"I went to two weddings last month. Both couples chose this song for their first dance."

"That's why he's one of the agency's top clients."

"Well I'm tired of hearing it."

"I haven't played it since we left Monte Carlo."

"That was this morning."

"It's sweet."

"The brioche I had for breakfast was sweet. This song is gooey."

"What's wrong with growing old with someone?"

"Well look at you." Jackie shifted her eyes from the road ahead to Victoria, and then back again. "Europe is turning you into a romantic."

"It's not Europe."

"Hello. Where did Victoria go?"

"She's sitting home alone on Sunday nights with her MacBook, and a tray of take-out sashimi."

"Sounds like my every-night. Only I take my take-out to the office."

"A few nights ago, I was answering emails, and then, there I was scrolling online dating sites."

"Paying to get laid, now?"

"I didn't sign up. But…well, I felt lonely."

"Lonely for sex is normal."

Victoria cleared her throat. "I'm starting to doubt what I preach."

"Which sermon might that be?"

"That my career is enough."

"You're allowed that sentiment *only* because we're on vacation."

"Oh please! You're a weekend disciple of wedding-planner reality television."

"I like wedding dresses! I never said I wanted to wear one."

"Whatever you say, counsel." The corner of Victoria's eyes crinkled.

The young women fell silent as the car left the high speed road and the vapor-billowing industrial port of Marghera behind, and merged onto a narrow, two-lane bridge surrounded by an immense gray-green lagoon. The lone road, fenced in on both sides by shallow water, connected the mainland to a patchwork of islands and tiled-roof edifices that cropped up from the sea.

"Is it *really* floating?" said Jackie.

"That's the myth. But the tour guide book says that it's built on more than a hundred small islands, and the buildings are set on foundations made up of wood stilts and stone."

"Well, I sure hope it doesn't sink while we're here. Whoa . . . look at the muscles on those men." A line of sleek, bright-colored gondolas, manned by duos in matching shirts, glided through the lagoon, heading toward the city.

"They must be the regatta teams I read about," said Victoria. "Each color represents a different zone of Venice."

"Then I want to visit the *yellow* zone. Look at the arms on those boys. Wait, *violet* is better." Jackie shifted her attention between the road and the rowers, and back again. "Then again, *red* has always been my favorite color."

The fire engine ringtone blasted through the car stereo speakers silencing the love song, and pulling their attention away from the rowers' athletic bodies. With each loud honk and ring, the iPhone vibrated and danced on the console.

"Damn." Victoria's dark eyes widened. The name Chloe Anders glowed across the onboard computer screen.

Jackie glanced at the screen, too. "You chose an emergency alarm ring for your boss's number?"

"She said she'd only call if it was an emergency."

"Then answer it, before the people in the other cars start pulling over."

Victoria reached back and gathered her long brown curls, and then twisted them on the top of her head. She cleared her throat.

"Getting ready for an interview? Answer the damn phone."

Victoria took a deep breath and touched the green handset icon on the screen. "Hello, Chloe?"

"*Buon giorno!* Your itinerary tells me you should be in Venice." Chloe's voice rolled into the car like crisp taffeta.

"Almost there. We're in the car. I've got you on the speaker."

"I miss Venice, and I was just there for George's and Amal's wedding."

Everyone who reads People magazine or watches E! Channel knows that World Talent Agency's top Hollywood agent attended George Clooney's and Amal Alamuddin's wedding, thought Victoria. "Is anything wrong?"

"No...no, you left the office organized and in tip-top shape. Still, it's amazing that anything is getting done around here without you. The temp was a disaster, had no executive assistant skills, and thought Larry the Cable Guy is top box office news."

Victoria wanted to remind her boss that in the four years since she'd become her Executive Assistant her life consisted of six day work weeks and ten hour days. Her job had become her social life, and having a love life had become so complicated that she'd set that aside. But she couldn't tell her. She wanted to become an agent, too, and not simply assist one. "I'll come home, if you need me to." She looked out the car window, her forehead creased. Docked in the distance, cruise ships as tall as skyscrapers looked down at Venice—their smokestacks spewing black clouds into the crisp autumn air.

"No. A new temp arrived this morning. At least this one can properly answer the phones."

Thank goodness. Victoria sighed in silence.

"But I'm not calling to tell you that. When I was in Venice last month, I bought two dozen embarrassingly expensive champagne glasses from the exquisite *Cenedese* Murano glass boutique in Saint Mark's Square. I need you to go there, and ask them why

I haven't received them yet. I understand that they're hand-made to order, and that we *are* dealing with Italy. Seems God gave that deliciously beautiful and stylish country good taste in architecture, fashion, film and food, but took away its understanding of time and speed. It's got to be the slowest nation on the planet—well besides Mexico. So do be firm with them. I gave them my business card, but do remind them who I am. And make sure they send the package here, to our Beverly Hills office, not to our New York office. Tell them if I don't have my glasses before Thanksgiving, I don't want them."

"It's late afternoon here now. If it's okay, I'll do that tomorrow."

"I have to go now. Miley is on the other line…God knows what she's gotten herself into…I hope not jail! Ciao, ciao...enjoy."

The line went silent and Ed Sheeran's voice spilled into the car, once again. Victoria turned down the volume on the car stereo.

"Would you have gone home if she'd asked you to?" said Jackie.

"I would have had to." Victoria raised her eyebrows. "Do you mind if we stop by the glass shop tomorrow afternoon?"

"That's fine."

At the end of the bridge, a high-rise parking structure held an enormous neon CAMPARI sign perched on its top story. Jackie turned off the main road. Their BMW's car tires squeaked up the slick spiral ramp where they waited for the attendant to stroll up to the car.

"*Quanto tempo vi fermate*?" he mumbled.

"Excuse me? Sorry, we speak English," said Jackie.

"How long . . . you be in Venice . . . parking?"

"Two days."

"Leave keys in car . . . park behind white car . . . I move it after."

Victoria turned and looked at the cars parked behind them. All but three cars were white. She turned to see Jackie doing the same, and when their eyes met, they broke out laughing.

"Excuse me Sir," said Jackie. "Which white car?"

"*E' lo stesso*." He walked away.

"What's *lo stesso* mean," said Victoria.

"*It doesn't matter*. . .you choose," said the man.

"And all our stuff?" said Jackie. "Can we leave some things in the trunk?"

"No good idea . . . you never know." He shook his head, and stepped back into his cramped glass office.

Jackie pulled the car into its spot. "Can we trust this guy with the keys?"

"I hope so. The rental agreement is in my name." Victoria stepped out of the car, twisting and stretching her back and legs.

Jackie popped open the overloaded trunk. "We should have packed lighter."

They unloaded the trunk, hoping the attendant would show a chivalrous streak and give them a hand with their six suitcases. Instead, he gave them a look of disbelief and pointed to a tiny elevator that could hold no more than three slender people.

"You go first and wait for me downstairs." Jackie blocked the elevator doors open while Victoria wrestled with her bags.

"Could they make these elevators any smaller?"

"Don't worry. If you get stuck between floors, I'm sure our friend over there will come to your rescue. Bye, bye."

Victoria hit the ground-floor button. The elevator jolted shut and began its slow descent. Forced to stop on the sixth and third floors, she flashed an apologetic look at the waiting patrons who scowled back at her when they saw they had to either wait or use the stairs. Upon arrival on the ground floor, she avoided the anxious looks of the locals who, at the end of their day, had lost their patience and didn't want to wait for another tourist standing in the way.

"Sorry . . . just a minute . . . I just need to get my last bag . . ."

"*Signorina* . . . Miss . . . you need help?" A tired-looking old man dressed in soiled overalls and a cap, pushed a luggage cart toward her.

"Yes, but I'm waiting for my friend. She's upstairs."

"No problem." The man tossed her bags on his cart.

Quicker than expected, the elevator returned carrying Jackie and her cargo. "Oh, my goodness . . . That was an adventure. Here, take this bag of Trail Mix." She rolled it shut.

Victoria placed the bag in her purse and gave her friend a critical smile.

"What? I got hungry after lugging all this stuff around, and I wasn't about to leave it for our friend upstairs to eat."

"These bags, Miss?" said the baggage handler.

"Thank you Mother Mary." Jackie looked skyward. "He's going to carry our bags."

Victoria chuckled at Jackie, and turned to the man, "Sir, we need to get to the Splendid Hotel. Can you take us there?"

"No, *signorina*. Splendid in Venice center. I take you to water taxi. You follow me."

They followed him across the busy, U-shaped thoroughfare, trying not to get mowed down by a flood of motor scooters, cars and buses that had no intention of stopping for pedestrians. At the extreme end of the parkway they passed stands bulging with cold drinks and souvenirs, and descended an asphalt ramp that swerved toward a taxi landing occupied by a high-gloss, polished wooden motorboat.

"Splendid." The baggage handler passed the suitcases one by one to the driver.

"Miss . . . water taxi take you from here. *Diciotto euro. . . eitin* euro."

"Eighteen." Victoria handed him a light blue banknote. "Thank you. You can keep the change."

"*Grazie,* miss. *Arrivederci.*" He tipped his hat and headed back toward his next run.

"Watch your step." The taxi driver extended his well-manicured hand and helped them board the boat—his Armani polo shirt and jeans, a stark contrast to those of the baggage handler.

"Your boat is beautiful," said Jackie.

"For beautiful customers like you," he said through a pair of Persol sunglasses.

Jackie blushed.

Victoria smiled to herself, and bit her lip. Jackie could argue and win tough juvenile court cases in the Los Angeles County Courts, but take her away from the judge's bench and drop a man with a charming smile in front of her, and she turned into that clumsy girl she'd met in gym class in Junior High School.

"Your English is good," said Jackie.

"I work with many tourists...my favorite are Americans. Is it your first time in Venice?" He prepared the boat, and made no excuses for looking Jackie up and down.

"Our first time in Europe," said Jackie.

"I could show you Venice . . . tonight."

"Oh, I don't know . . . we . . . I," said Jackie.

"We have dinner plans." Victoria sensed her friend's indecision.

He slipped his sunglasses down the bridge of his nose. His eyes looked like bottomless tar pits, calm and still, waiting to pull-in their next victim. That, and his suave demeanor, read like a warning sign. "No problem." He looked at Victoria, and then turning back to Jackie "Another time." His confident smile balanced the angles of his tan, chiseled features. "What's your name?"

"Jacqueline, but everyone calls me Jackie." She pulled the elastic band from her ponytail and let her hair fall to her shoulders.

"Jacqueline . . . beautiful name . . . beautiful woman . . . beautiful boat . . . beautiful long hair...you call me . . . tomorrow."

Victoria could tell he thought Jackie would call—she could see it in his eyes. He pulled a business card from his pocket, with it came a gold wedding band. The ring, lodged in the fold of his Gucci business card holder, fell to the floorboard. Clinking, rolling, it circled around, and landed at Jackie's feet.

"Lose something?" The glare in Jackie's eyes sent embarrassment across his face. She bent down and picked up the ring. "Keep it on your finger, or next time it could fall in the water."

The look on her face needed little translation. Surely the man realized that he had messed with the wrong woman. Further pursuit was useless. All he could do was take the women to their hotel.

"If you like, there is a good view from the back of the boat."

Without further addressing him, they ducked into the elegant cabin and made their way through to the open-air seating in the back. The boat's motor rumbled and churned the whitewater behind them. The driver glanced over his shoulder to assure they were seated, then pulled the sleek vessel away from the landing and veered right onto the Grand Canal.

"What an ass," said Jackie. "*You* think there's a Mr. Right out there? I think they're all the same, no matter where you go in the world."

Victoria smiled. "I was waiting for you to throw him overboard."

"If I knew how to drive this boat, I would have."

"Admit it, you were his."

"Oh, shut up and start taking photos. This place is amazing."

"And you wanted to go to Portofino instead."

"Alright, go ahead. You're dying to say it."

"What? That I told you Venice was the better choice."

"Do you feel better now?"

"Yeah. I do."

It was true. They were in awe. Never had either of them seen anything like it. The Grand Canal bustled with water traffic: motorboats and waterbuses coming and going, gondolas lazily slipping by, carrying love-struck couples or groups of tourists cradled in their hull. The water taxi passed in front of the sterile façade of the train station and approached the Scalzi Bridge. The mountainous marble structure towered above their boat, obstructing the last of the day's sunlight. Its imposing shadow followed them, arching toward the waterside cafés, deepening the hue of the multicolored lanterns that reflected on the water below. The water taxi journeyed on and was diminished to insignificance by the collage of waterfront palaces nestled shoulder to shoulder. Byzantine, baroque, Gothic, and Renaissance overlapped each other and adorned the waterway with a cornucopia of architectural achievements. Each, at first glance, gave the illusion of being depthless, a mere semblance of edifices that were too magnificent or complex to be real.

"I know it sounds dumb. And I'm really doing my best to appreciate all the culture and art, but doesn't it look like we're on a back lot in Hollywood?" said Jackie.

Victoria laughed. "I hate to admit it, but it does. It's inconceivable. The buildings appear to be rising up from the water."

"Okay, so…let's say . . . that one…with the cloverleaf marble balconies." Jackie pointed across the canal, at Ca' d'Oro—one of Venice's finest Gothic palace. "The one that looks like it's made out of lace. Let's say that's my house. How do I get there?"

"If that palace was your house, you'd find a way to get there."

"I'm serious. How do they get home . . . without getting their feet wet? I mean, look," Jackie pointed to the water lapping over the marble pavement of the exquisite portico "the entrance to the house is all wet."

"By boat, silly. That's why the gondola is a symbol of Venice."

"So everyone gets their feet wet," said Jackie.

"I guess . . . unless there's another entrance that we can't see, on dry land. Why don't you ask your friend up front?"

"It's not that important," said Jackie. "Look at that gondola! Hurry, take a picture."

Victoria took a snapshot of two gondoliers transporting more than a dozen people standing, packed like sardines, across the canal with the ease of acrobats. "If I had to stand up in that boat, I'd be in the water in a matter of seconds. Look at all those people in it. How does it stay afloat?" She watched through the smartphone screen and then snapped the gondola's arrival at the foot of a large, square portico draped with blood-red awnings.

"I smell fish." Jackie wrinkled her nose.

"We must be by the fish market. That building with all the arches resembles the picture in the tour guide book."

"Thank goodness for the tour guide book. Otherwise I'd never have known we were by the fish market."

"It doesn't smell that bad."

"No, it's lovely—if you like fish."

The water taxi pressed onward. They soon left the open market's pungent aroma behind and followed the Grand Canal's soft bend to the right, until they were brought face-to-face with the Rialto Bridge.

"Oh my goodness...alright, you win. I don't care if it smells like fish—this is what I was waiting to see. Hurry, take my picture with the bridge in the background." Jackie stood up straight, and posed.

They came to a smooth halt before the bridge. The boat engine rumbled to a purr, gliding under the lyrical sound of an accordion serenading a group of gondolas exiting a small canal. The taxi driver performed a series of sweet maneuvers to keep the boat steady and waited until the last stripe-shirted gondolier motioned that all was clear. Then he turned the boat down the narrow canal, proceeding with caution. He came within centimeters of docked boats, algae-lined walls, and footbridges, never once endangering the health of his boat. Regardless of his issues with maintaining fidelity, Victoria had to admit to herself that he had meticulous navigating abilities.

The taxi took them through a labyrinth of waterways until once again the driver limited his speed so as not to disrupt the delicate balance of a gondola heading in their same direction. The water taxi crept up beside the gondola. The sleeves of the young gondolier's red-and-white-striped shirt, rolled up to his shoulders, exposed a pair of taut, tan arms and matched a red bandana tied through waves of golden hair. He turned, and locked eyes with Victoria—his were as green as the water beneath them. They gave each other a smile only fate could have arranged.

Victoria's heart danced, and her face flushed and glistened. The gorgeous gondolier's smile made her eyes sparkle, and brought about that nervousness she tried to hide whenever a handsome movie star arrived unannounced in the office. Unexpected, his good looks attracted her like no man had in a long time. She blushed and fumbled with the smartphone, and then hid her embarrassment by snapping a photo of the attractive young man. She turned and watched as their water taxi slipped by and left him, and his shiny black gondola behind. The corners of her mouth still turned up, she leaned back against Jackie, and said, "I think I'm going to like Venice."

Chapter 2

ALVISE CROSSED THE mist-covered campo, thinking about the woman's captivating smile and the look she had cast him the day before. The crisp autumn morning air and the possibility that he might see her once again gave his light-hearted mood an extra boost.

His fifth year as a gondolier in Piazza San Marco neared its end, and it had been one of his busiest. So much so that he had seldom cracked open a book, much less attend his Master's Degree classes or begun writing his thesis. He had attempted to make up his missed exams during the off-season, but nonetheless had fallen far behind. The passion he felt for literature, poetry and the theater still lit up his heart, yet time and again he justified his increasing detachment from his literature studies, quietly admitting the real reason: he liked being a gondolier.

His birthright alone permitted him to participate in his family's trade. He was six years old the first time his grandfather placed an oar in his hands. Now, after five years of working in the Molo traghetto with his father, the same gondola station where his grandfather and great-grandfather had served, he had earned the privilege bestowed upon him.

He strolled past the church, over the footbridge, and down Ruga Giuffa. The shops on this wide street already open for business, swarmed with customers. The usual crossfire of morning pleasantries were exchanged along the busy alleyway, as were ample invitations to join friends and neighbors for a cup of coffee at the local bar. If Alvise accepted all of them, he'd be fortunate to get to work before lunchtime. He continued on without stopping for anyone.

Taunted by the fragrance of fresh-baked bread spilling through the alleyway, he entered the Milani bakery—a small shop that had served his neighborhood as far back as he could remember.

"*Buon giorno,*" he said.

His salutation interrupted the elderly shop owner, who, busy sharing the latest town talk with a group of matronly regulars, looked up. "*Buon giorno,* Alvise." She tucked a lock of gray under her hair net and scurried behind the counter. She filled a paper bag with bread rolls—one raisin, one olive, and one with fresh bacon bits. All hot out of the oven. "Ladies, excuse me for serving him first, but I never keep a good-looking man waiting." She folded and taped the paper bag shut, and placed it on the countertop. "I confess, Alvise, if I weren't already married." Her puffy eyes squinted into a smile "I wouldn't let a catch like you get away."

Used to their teasing comments, Alvise stepped forward to pick up his bag. He set a handful of coins on the counter and exited the *panificio.*

"*Signore . . . arrivederci.*" Bowing his head with jovial respect, he stepped into the *calle* and laughed to himself when he overheard one of the ladies ask another if he had a fiancée.

He left the wide thoroughfare behind him, and made a right turn down Calle Corona and then an immediate left at the Osteria al Vecio Canton. His fast-moving stride echoed through the narrow alleyway's curves. The walls amplified the noise from the upper-floor offices and, shouldered by low-lying palaces, created stereophonic sounds that bounced off them.

Damp, musty smells seeped out from the open-barred windows of each building's ground-floor storage rooms and penetrated his lungs. A small, ornate iron bridge arched over the San Provolo Canal and led him to an open walkway, home of his former elementary school. Children dressed in white school smocks skipped and scattered canal side. Their fluttering about reminded him of the butterflies he'd chased around his grandfather's vegetable garden as a child.

"Zio Alvise." A young girl called him. She ran toward him from the group. Her long hair, braided with a pink ribbon, swung at the nape of her neck.

"*Ciao,* Susanna." He swept his niece's petite frame into his arms. "Where do you think you're going?"

"Susanna." Her mother called the child.

"I don't want to go to school. Can I come with you?" She hugged him tight and twisted his sun-streaked locks of hair around her small fingers.

"No way. You want to get me in trouble with both of our moms?" Tickling her, he flipped her onto his shoulder and carried her toward his sister.

"*Ciao,* Alvise." Gina gave him a kiss on both cheeks. "You, little lady, off to class. Your teacher is waiting."

"Do I have to?" Susanna tightened her grip around her uncle's neck.

"Yes. Now *presto* . . . hurry along." Gina's chestnut colored eyes commanded her daughter from behind stylish eyeglasses. "I need to get to work,"

"Okay, little one, you heard your mom." Alvise kissed her on her forehead, gave her a gentle flip back over his shoulder, and put her down. "Be sure and draw something for me."

"I'll draw you and me on your gondola, and next time I come to Nonna's, I'll bring my toys so we can play." Waving good-bye, she ran to catch up with her classmates.

"Do you have time for coffee?" said Alvise to his sister.

"No, but thanks. My cleaning lady is sick, and I've got three couples to tend to at the bed and breakfast."

"Why don't you ask Mamma to give you a hand?"

"Are you kidding? Every time I let her help, she reorganizes all my stuff and then I can't find a thing."

"Sounds right."

"I don't know why she thinks there's only one way to do things—her way. You'd think she'd let up now that I've got my own family. Instead, it's as if she needs to remind me she's still the boss."

"Ah, come on, Gina . . . . let her believe she is, and then do whatever you want."

"If only it were so easy. Listen, *frattellino*, I got to go. Say hello to Papà, and remind him to come by after work. He promised he'd install the new bulkhead on the canal door before we get hit with high tide again."

"He's as dangerous with tools as Mamma is with a broom."

"At least he listens to me." She rushed on smart heels in the opposite direction.

Alvise moved on, his thoughts back on the pretty young woman in the water taxi. His polished skills at identifying nationalities made him speculate she was South American or perhaps Spanish. He pondered over her radiant smile and dark eyes, and slowed his step as he approached the marble wall shrine of the Virgin Mary and Child. Fingers crossed, he paused in the drab portico and glanced up, and solicited the Mother of all mothers to put him back on the young woman's path. He smiled at the thought, and then at the shrine which appeared cheerier than usual.

The morning foot traffic had thickened, slowing him down before he crossed another bridge that landed him steps away from Campo San Filippo e Giacomo. He waved to a group of waiters setting up umbrellas and preparing rows of outdoor tables with burnt-orange tinted tablecloths. In the middle of the campo, he turned down Calle dei Albanesi, an alley no wider than the shoulder widths of two men.

Through the Bonifacio pastry shop's glass door he saw his colleagues crowding the counter. All dressed in uniform: striped shirts, black pants, and sunglasses. A few gondoliers sported tattoos, and all had enviable suntans. They filled the small shop with boisterous laughter accompanied by a few one-liners and heavy slaps on the back. He observed them, noting the contrast between their rough, intimidating appearance and their playful manner. He understood how easy it was for them to incite fear in wide-eyed onlookers.

Alvise spotted Ciano looking up at him, and heard his loud laughter bellow out onto the street. The smile spread across his face was as wide as the devil's grin tattooed to his forearm. Ciano motioned for Alvise to join them, and waited for him to step inside the pastry shop to land him a right hook straight to the chest.

"Man did you miss out last night. Her friend was *piccantina*," said Ciano.

Alvise saddled him with a playful slap on the back of the head. "I stopped trusting your taste in women years ago."

"No man…you gotta believe me. This girl makes the last one I set you up with look like a dog," said Ciano. "What was her name…Daisy or Iris?"

"That was a long time ago. All I remember is that she was strange."

"What do you care if they're weird? They're tourists you're never gonna see again."

"You know the only reason I've never told you that you're a complete ass is because you're my best friend." Alvise laughed and shook his head. "Let's go, and I'll tell you about the real beauty I saw yesterday."

The men exited the tiny *pasticceria* and made their way down the tight alleyway toward their work station. Colorful striped shirts and straw hats trimmed with red or navy-blue ribbons were their mark of identity around town, and made heads turn. At the top of the Ponte della Paglia—the landmark bridge joining Castello and San Marco—a thick horde of tourists, struggling to catch glimpses and snapshots of the Bridge of Sighs, stepped aside to let them through. Alvise paused and looked down from his vantage point. He searched the unfamiliar faces swarming around the ancient *Molo* pier. *She could be in the crowd.*

Alvise and Ciano grasped onto the poles that protected their gondolas from banging against the wharf and jumped inside their boats to prepare for the day ahead. They followed the same routine that gondoliers had used for centuries. They bailed out and dried up the water that had seeped into the hull the night before, and then removed the tarp to air out the seat cushions. They gently wiped down the boat with a chamois dipped in seawater, polished the gold-plated seahorses, and rubbed the iron *ferro* at the bow until it shined. With forceful hands, they used delicate strokes to massage each surface of their boats, preparing the vessels as a trainer would ready an athlete before a sports event. Yet, while Alvise performed his tasks with care, thoughts of the young woman he had seen the day before consumed him.

"I swear I've never seen a woman as beautiful as her."

"Hotter than that Brazilian model...the one in those underwear ads?" said Ciano.

"This woman isn't *hot*, she's beautiful."

"Big tits...great ass?"

"Come on man. I'm telling you...when she smiled her face... her eyes...dark brown...maybe black...and shiny, like her hair. I couldn't take my eyes off of her."

"If her body doesn't meet specifications, there's no reason to waste your time."

"I got past her smile and her eyes, too."

"And?"

"I've got to find her. I've got to talk to her before she leaves Venice."

Their boats ready *da giorno*—for the day, the gondoliers put their straw hats on and headed for the gondola station. They flipped their assigned number *in volta* on the wooden work board, showing they were present, and waited their turn.

He searched past the agitated merchants who rolled their heavy portable souvenir stands through the crowd. Their loud voices and hand gestures gave the impression—to anyone who didn't understand the Venetian dialect—that they were fighting, and not simply discussing local politics, as they unlocked their carts' side panels, and set out their wares. Further down the square, smooth-looking *intermediari*—go-betweens—dressed in tailored slacks and starched pastel shirts solicited tourists to send onto the Murano Island glass factories. Alvise watched as they scanned the crowd for tourists like hawks hunting prey. He, too, scanned the faces of those same tourists, hoping one would be hers.

For many Venetians the tourist trade had become their city's contradiction—an inevitability to be criticized, envied, or sought after. Instead, Alvise considered the Piazza to be the most beautiful office a man could have. Its rhythm of business and confusion, framed by majestic marble archways, was a continuation of his city's centuries-old merchant tradition. Working there was a privilege that earned him a dignified living and, now, it gave him the best opportunity to meet the girl he'd seen the day before. No one came to Venice without visiting St. Mark's Square.

The morning and the afternoon slipped away like the tide. Hour after hour, he waited in the traghetto for his next run. When he rowed his gondola filled with tourists down quiet canals and under bridges, he searched for the girl, too. Then near the Rialto Bridge, his heart jumped, and his stomach fluttered. He was sure it was her walking along the water's edge. He rowed forward and closer, and slowed canal side, and then saw it wasn't her.

Used to seeing female tourists traveling through Venice, attractive women from the far corners of the Earth, none had ever struck him the way the allure in her smile and the glimmer in her eyes had. Reason told him otherwise, still he felt as if he had known her before.

Now, the late afternoon autumn sun sat low in the sky, and pulled shadows over the Piazza's marble facades and stone pavement. His shift was almost over, and he hoped to get one last ride in for the day—one last opportunity to find her.

A gray-haired couple, arm in arm, walked toward him. He noted their polite manner and unpretentious attire. *British,* he thought. But experience had made him cautious. He didn't want to address them in the wrong language, and chose to greet them in Italian.

"*Buona sera* . . . gondola?"

"Yes, please," said the lady, her accent British. "Could we take a ride through the city and then be dropped off at our hotel, near the Rialto."

"Yes, madam, that is no problem," said Alvise. "But we are required to come back here at the end of the ride. You understand if I leave you at the Rialto, the price will be the same because I need to return to Piazza San Marco."

"Will we pass under the Bridge of Sighs?" said the gentleman.

"It's one of the first bridges we'll cross under."

"We've heard that couples will be granted eternal love if at sunset, while in a gondola, they kiss beneath the Bridge of Sighs. Is that a local legend?"

"To be honest Madam, that's a film version. The legend my grandfather taught me says that kissing in a gondola beneath the Bridge of Sighs *any* time of day as the bells of St. Mark's bell tower ring will bring eternal love."

"Then we should be fine," said the gentleman.

The woman nodded in agreement and they followed him toward his gondola. Alvise turned and took one last look over his shoulder—and surprised the customers when he stopped.

Steps away, a young woman stood, her back facing him, admiring the Doge's Palace. Was it her? He had to find out, and couldn't let her get away, or worse, risk that one of his colleagues had his same intentions. He turned toward the traghetto and the dense group of gondoliers seated, waiting for their turn.

"Ciano, *vieni qua*...come here. *Fai presto*."

Ciano jumped down from the bench and rushed over. "*Cosa c'è*...what's up?"

"That girl I told you about...I think that's her. Look, over there."

"You mean the one wearing tight jeans?"

"Yeah, if she'd only turn around," said Alvise. "Listen, you've got to take this couple for a ride, leave them at their hotel near the Rialto. If I go, I'll never see her again . . . What if she's leaving tonight, or another guy sees her . . ."

"Take it easy, man. I got it . . . I'll take 'em. Ask her if she's gotta friend."

Alvise excused himself and reassured the British couple that Ciano would take good care of them. All the while, out of the corner of his eye, he watched her distance herself. She moved to the entrance of the Doge's Palace courtyard, but then he lost her in the crowd. Desperate to talk to her, he ran the distance from the traghetto, weaving through the stream of excursionists and around the palace's stocky, robust marble columns. He stretched his neck, searched for her over the cloud of heads, and pushed his way forward until he stood near the *Porta del Frumento* courtyard entrance, and could see the 16th century bronze wellhead inside.

"*Permesso*," he said. "Excuse me."

"*Dove pensi di andare?*" The young ticket collector straightened his museum uniform.

"I'll just be a minute. Someone I need to talk to just went inside."

"You gondoliers *think* you own this town, but this door is mine."

Alvise sighed and bit his tongue. His immediate future depended on the ticket collector. "I don't want to visit the courtyard...I've seen it a million times."

"Then get a ticket, and make it a million and one."

Alvise inhaled, and cooled the anger simmering inside him. He looked to his left, at the ticket line wrapped around the palace perimeter. "Look, there's this girl, and she'll be gone before I get to the front of that line."

"I could lose my job."

"You let me in, and I'll get a ticket and bring it back to you after I've talked to her."

"Not in the rules...sorry."

"Come on…this is serious…you could be messing with my fate."

"Maybe me not letting you through is your fate."

"Come on…don't you have a girlfriend?"

"What's she got to do with this?"

Alvise scratched his head, and blew out his cheeks. "If you let me through I'll take you and your girl for a gondola ride…on me."

The young ticket collector stopped tearing stubs from tickets and stopped letting their holders step past Alvise. "Whenever I want?"

"Yeah, whenever." Alvise's eyes filled with hope.

"Her birthday is coming up…and she's always wanted to take a gondola ride."

"I work right over there." Alvise pointed back at the traghetto.

The ticket collector looked around as if assuring none of his colleagues were watching. "It's a deal. But if anyone asks, I didn't see you. And don't let my girlfriend know that the ride is for free."

Alvise slapped the young man's back, and rushed through the entrance door. He didn't stop until he'd crossed the craggy marble pavement and reached the center of the grand courtyard. Searching, he lifted his eyes up from the porticos which, like a frame around a masterpiece, bordered the courtyard. He rolled his gaze over the gothic columns on the upper loggia, scrutinizing those standing beneath each pointed arch. Then he saw her standing between the massive marble statues of Mars and Neptune at the top of the Giants' Staircase. She held her camera up to her face, and pointed it in his direction. He raised his hand and opened his mouth to call her, but she stepped into the shadows of the upper portico before the words left his lips. He ran the remainder of the courtyard and climbed the imposing staircase, two steep marble slabs at a time. He scaled the last worn step and stood inches away from her. His heart raced, and he caught his breath. "*Signorina*," he said "excuse me."

She looked over her shoulder, and then turned and traded a smile for his.

He swallowed hard and looked into the young woman's eyes. They were brown, but not the sparkling dark eyes that had looked at him the day before. These thin lips cut straight across crooked teeth. They weren't full like the lips that had turned up at the corners and into a brilliant smile. "I'm sorry." He felt his smile slip away. "I thought you were someone else."

"I'm sorry I'm *not* someone else."

He gave her a polite nod and, feeling foolish, descended the Giants' Staircase. At the bottom, he heard a symphony of bells ringing from the *campanili*—bell towers—around town. He glanced up at the courtyard clock. Six o'clock. His shift was over, and he was out two gondola ride fares—one for the British couple, the other for the ticket collector.

Back in the traghetto, he closed up his boat for the night, and then sat on the green bench and waited for Ciano to return. He listened to the swaying, bobbing, splashing, and creaking of the gondolas lined up at the water's edge, and checked the piazza for the thousandth time. The crowd had lessened and made seeing to the opposite end easy. He thought about the young woman's captivating smile and the look she had given him the day before. He'd never see her again.

Ciano was standing at his side. "*Niente?*"

"No, nothing," said Alvise.

"She's just a babe, so don't get all weepy on me. Come on, I'm thirsty. Let's go to *Al Todaro*."

Alvise stood and looked down the piazza, past the towering marble columns which held the statues of the city's patrons: Saint Teodoro, and Saint Mark—the winged lion. He searched past the bell tower and the church, and under the distant clock tower. The lamplight's amethyst glow added to the evening's arrival as if coaxing him to give up. He followed Ciano out of the traghetto, and up the café steps.

At the top of the café steps, and outside the bar, he stopped. At the opposite end of the portico, wearing a white dress and leather sandals, the girl from the water taxi was exiting the *Cenedese* glass shop. This time, he had no doubt—it was her. He ran across the marble checkerboard pavement, erasing the distance that separated her from him. "*Buonsera*."

She looked up from her iPhone, and blushed. "Hello."

"Good evening." He repeated in English.

Her smile lit up her face, and the velvety tone of her voice combined with her American accent made her even more attractive. Now, more than the day before, he was convinced she was the most beautiful girl he had ever seen. Her brown eyes sparkled like pools of coffee, and like a magnet to metal, he couldn't break away from them.

"I'm Alvise." He restrained an incredible urge to kiss her. "Alvise Moro."

"My name is Victoria Greco."

"*Buonasera, Vittoria Greco.*" Softly, he repeated the words. "You're Italian."

"American-Italian…from Los Angeles. My great-grandfather was from Calabria. You're Italian, of course?"

"I'm Venetian," he said. "Do you remember me…from yesterday?"

"Of course I do." She bit her lip, and smiled. "My water taxi passed you on your gondola."

Victoria drank in his sweet smile, and pleasing features. Even more handsome up close, he looked at her like no one had ever looked at her before. She felt her heart race and her complexion warm. An unexpected shyness came over her. His presence set off sensations she had kept guarded for a long while. At a loss for words, she motioned for him to follow her down the portico steps, and waved at Jackie to join them.

Alvise's strong handshake greeted Jackie first, and then rushed and lingered when Victoria's hand met his. Beneath the surface, she trembled like a school girl. His beautiful eyes and tall athletic build made it difficult for her to concentrate on their small talk. His kind manner and gallant ways enticed her.

Jackie stepped away and toward two marble columns. She held up the camera, and gestured at them to move closer together. Victoria felt her heart tumble when Alvise slipped his arm around her waist. Like a strong vine holding precious fruit, he kept it there until Jackie turned the camera away from them, and up at the winged lion.

"May I offer you an espresso or an *aperitivo*?" He gestured toward the *Al Todaro* café.

"We're on our way to Harry's Bar."

"Harry's Bar?" He raised his eyebrows.

"Isn't it a nice place? We were told to go there."

"It's very nice. But my friend is waiting for me inside this other bar."

"It's one of the places Jackie really wants to go to. So..."

"We could meet afterwards...for dinner."

"Dinner?"

"You do have to eat. And I know the perfect place."

"I promised Jackie we'd go to the Casino this evening."

"I see."

Dinner with you would certainly be better than going to a stuffy casino she thought. "But give me a minute."

"Sure."

She stepped away, and felt his soft stare on her back. She caught up with Jackie down the waterfront pathway that, now, resonated more beautifully.

"Did you see his dreamy green eyes?" said Victoria.

"Did you text your boss about her glass order?"

"I did. She's happy they'll arrive before Thanksgiving." She looked at the water. "His eyes are as green as the sea."

"Geez, you're so easy."

"Jealous because you didn't see him first?"

"How could I have missed him? I gotta be at least a foot taller than everyone here."

"He's not short."

"Let's just say he's taller than most of the men I've seen."

"He wants to meet us for dinner. He'll bring a friend."

"Did you see his friend?"

"No, but I'm sure he's cute, too." Victoria slipped on her new pair of Dolce&Gabbana sunglasses to block the triangles of sunlight bouncing off the water. She had purchased the designer frames shortly before. Not because she needed another pair, but as a consolation gift for not being able to buy an exquisite ring she had seen in a jewelry store window.

The kind jewelry store salesman had helped her slip on the blood-red ruby and diamond ring—its band of yellow and white gold woven together like lace. The gems sparkled under the shop lights, and she held her hand up for Jackie's approval. The salesman explained that its design was Renaissance inspired, and then quoted the price. She wasn't surprised. *One day,* she thought, *when I'm a successful talent agent, not simply an assistant to one, I'll come back to Venice and buy this ring.* She admired the gems a moment longer, and then took off the ring. She handed it back with a smile of determination, and asked for directions to the *Cenedese* Murano glass shop. She and Jackie followed the salesman's directions down the designer alley to the Piazza, and past the Dolce&Gabbana store window. Beneath the mannequin wearing black lace, and next to the jewel-encrusted hand bag and ballet flats, sat a pair of black cat-eye sunglasses. Buying them satisfied her desire for something *Made in Italy*—for now.

"Go stand over there." Jackie pointed toward the thick marble banister on the water's edge.

"But the gondolier...Alvise...he's waiting for an answer."

"He can wait. I want a picture of you with that big white church in the background."

Victoria leaned against the cool stone divide, and tucked her sunglasses in her thick hair and posed for Jackie's camera, setting up the shot as if she, alone, stood there with San Giorgio Island in the background. "Hurry and take the photo. He's waiting."

"Stop talking and I will."

Victoria glanced over her shoulder, and smiled at Alvise. He looked anxious, and she felt the same. She'd never gone out with a man she'd met on the street. But vacations were different. Weren't they? Didn't they give license to do things, within reason, that one didn't do every day? Why not enjoy the company of a handsome gondolier? Why not indulge in a little vacation pleasure. Dinner was reasonable. She and Jackie would pay their own way, so nothing more would be expected. Dinner, that's all, and then *arrivederci.* "Well, do you want to meet them for dinner?"

"You said we were going to the casino tonight," said Jackie.

"That's her friend, Jackie." Alvise nodded toward the girls. "They want to go to the *casinò* tonight."

"*Aspetta un attimo.*" Ciano planted himself at the top of the café steps. "I'm not goin' to the *casinò.*"

"Man, don't do this now."

"Sorry, but I ain't got that kind of money to throw around."

"I'd do it for you...I've *done* it for you."

"Not with a new gondola to pay for."

"No, I was paying for college."

"And I still don't get why you wasted all that money." Ciano leaned against a marble column. "At least that night turned out to be worth the expense." He stretched his neck to get a better look at Jackie's tall, slender frame. "She's a looker all right. Just no tellin' if she'll make my time, and my money, worth it."

"I'll pay."

"Entrance fee, gambling chips and all my drinks," said Ciano.

"For all of us."

"You're crazy, man. That's a shitload of money."

"*Merda,*" said Alvise. "Are they leaving?"

"*Allora?*"

"*So?* They're headed for Harry's Bar."

He ran down the café steps, wove in and out of the crowd and clipped the corner of an artist's easel and scattered a stack of pastel paintings across the stone pavement, landing some in the water. He slowed for an instant, apologized and assured the mad-as-hell artist that he'd make up for his loss, and then continued running the short distance to the girls.

"Vittoria," he shouted. He saw her look up and smile back, and gently place a hand on Jackie's arm, stopping her. "What about dinner?"

"Jackie wants to go to the casino on the Lido."

"Right, well...sorry Jackie," said Ciano, joining them. "That's the summer *casinò*...and it's closed this time of year."

"*Signorine*, this is Ciano," said Alvise.

"Closed?" said Jackie.

"Yeah, it's been closed…since…I don't know—awhile," said Ciano.

"We must have misunderstood the brochure in the hotel." Victoria smiled, hopeful the closed Casino would convince Jackie to go to dinner with the young men instead.

"No, I understood," said Jackie. "It says it's open until the end of October."

"Pfft…," said Ciano. "This is Italy, where something is said and another is done. It's closed."

Knowing Ciano had lied about the casino being closed, Alvise watched Victoria send a soft, silent plea to Jackie, then look at him, and then back at Jackie. "What do you say? Will you have dinner with us?"

Jackie looked at Ciano, and then at Alvise. "Where?"

"A great seafood restaurant…the best in Venice," said Alvise.

"I don't eat fish," said Jackie.

"You can order anything you want," said Alvise.

Jackie shrugged her shoulders, and rolled her eyes. "What time should we meet you?"

"We'll pick you up at your hotel…Splendid, right?" said Alvise.

"How did you know?" said Victoria.

"It's the only hotel on the canal where I saw you yesterday," said Alvise. "Is eight thirty okay?"

"Fine," said Victoria.

Jackie checked her watch. "We better get going."

Alvise rested his strong hands on Victoria's shoulders and gave her a gentle turn, indicating the direction of Harry's Bar. He stood behind her, breathing in her soft perfume. He let his hands slide down her arms, and drifting to her fingertips, he gave them a soft squeeze. He let go only to catch up with Ciano, who had headed off in the opposite direction. But before turning the corner he looked back, and called out, "*A presto, bella . . .*"

Soon he thought *couldn't come soon enough.*

Chapter 3

THE SUN CUT through rain clouds and dropped sunshine here and there, and around Stockholm, Sweden. Zinnia stared out the hospital window, and waited until the nurse left. She set her bare feet on the cold linoleum floor, pulled herself out of bed, and felt reality weigh on her shoulders. At the wardrobe unit, she stepped out of the hospital gown, and into a pair of jeans and an oversized sweater. She fixed a leather belt another notch tighter around her waist and cringed at her reflection in the wardrobe mirror. The last round of chemotherapy had turned her eyes and skin a shade lighter than the yellow hospital room walls, and made her tall frame weaker. She studied the circles under her eyes, tied a scarf around her bald head, and then grabbed a stick of lip balm from her purse. She soothed her cracked lips, and hushed the doctor's voice whispering in her head: *Two, maybe three months*. A sigh rose from her ribcage, and made her tremble. The lip balm dropped from her hand and rolled across the floor, and hit the chair where her dear friend Magda had slept the night before. Not yet thirty years old, Zinnia turned her back on the sick woman in the mirror, picked up the lip balm and remembered what her mother would say when teaching her a moral lesson or when anger toward Zinnia's father surfaced: *As you sow, so shall you reap.* Life seemed to be applying that to her now, as it had to her mother and father.

Four years earlier, and months after Zinnia's son was born, her parents died in a car accident. She'd known her father to be a cautious driver. Never certain, she imagined her mother's ire against her father's gambling had lit another argument. Zinnia's imagination saw her dear dad lose control of his temper, too, and then lose control of the car. She wondered if her mother had seen the semi-truck coming, before it hit her side of their station wagon.

"So be it, if it's my turn to reap." She turned back to the mirror, and argued. "But when I'm gone, my son will suffer the most."

Zinnia pulled thick socks over her cold feet, and stepped into leather boots. Sitting back on the plastic chair, she caught her breath, and remembered holding her mother's hand as a child, and strolling the few city blocks from their apartment to the Stockholm Public library. While her mother browsed the murder mystery books section, she'd hurry to the children's corner, and select three books from the shelf—three being the number her mother permitted. *You don't want to deprive the other children their share.* Zinnia obeyed the rule, yet faced with shelves stuffed with books, she never understood why.

Books in hand, she'd plop herself onto a wooden bench, sift through the pages, and lose herself in stories about cats and old farmers, and red-head orphans with crazy pigtails. Cover to cover, she read them before handing her library card to the woman with black rim glasses and a bracelet of books tattooed to her wrist. Once again, she'd take her mother's hand, and take her checked-out books home, and read them to her dolls.

Zinnia knew then that one day she'd work surrounded by books, and be a mother. A Library Sciences degree got her a job in a countryside library, and a casual fling got her pregnant with her son, Thor. Except for her parents' marriage, matrimony never concerned her. Theirs only did for fear it wouldn't last. When asked, she explained she'd met Thor's father while studying abroad. She didn't give details, but clarified being a single mother was her choice, and a sign of the times.

Now, after two years of needles stuck in her arms, vomit burning ulcers in her mouth, losing weight and every hair on her body, and exhausted by the doctors' insistence she succumb to another last chance cure for an incurable disease, Zinnia had had enough. She signed the *refusal for further medical treatment*, and then checked herself out of the hospital. Prescription pain pills in her bag, she demanded Magda take her home.

Snug in the passenger seat of Magda's old Saab, Zinnia said goodbye to Stockholm's city streets. The car's muffler echoed down blocks of brick-red and orange row houses, and they headed to the fertile countryside. She wanted to spend her final days with Thor, at their farm cottage. A home Magda and her boyfriend Izak had rented to her since her parent's had died.

Outside the city, the rain clouds turned white, and acres of yellow flowers stretched from the road to the green hillside. Zinnia rolled down the car window, and leaned her head out. The warmth of the sun and the chill of the wind against her face reminded her she was still alive. She reached for her smartphone, and snapped a photo, and then another. The sea of yellow etched in her brain, she tapped the NOTES application on her smartphone. Silently, she read the list of things she'd accomplished in the last six months:

1. plant an apple tree—because Thor likes apples
2. take Thor fishing for salmon
3. watch the sun rise and set on the same day
4. dance barefoot at midnight under the full moon
5. take Thor on a hot air balloon ride at dusk

She added:

6. paint field of yellow canola blossoms

I've never painted before. Her eyes teared up. She put the smartphone down, and placed her gaunt hand on Magda's arm. "Then you're okay with it?"

"I want to."

"What did Izak say?"

"He's worried. He let go another farm hand."

"Thor can't end up in an orphanage."

"I promise you he won't."

Zinnia flashed a pleading look. "He has no one else."

The Saab rattled through town, past the general store and Pitcher's Pub, and public buildings with herbs and vegetable gardens planted on their rooftops. Magda accelerated the car across town, and down a narrow road toward the red farm house. Up the dirt driveway, surrounded by green fields and trees, a bicycle with training wheels lay on its side.

"Come, lie down." Magda fluffed the bed pillows, and helped Zinnia onto the soft mattress. She pulled the duvet up from the foot of the wood bedframe, and tucked it around the frail body of the woman she'd met in college.

Zinnia could see in Magda's eyes that she wanted to remember her as the beautiful young woman she'd been. Her long blonde hair and steel blue eyes had turned the heads of men and women. Now, with each hospital stay, she left her model looks, and another five kilos, behind. She watched Magda choke back the sadness, and then turn to the night stand. She heard her sniffle, saw her blink back her tears, and then set a plastic water bottle and prescription painkillers in a neat row, and within her reach.

"Izak asked me if I knew…financially…what you have."

"Of course, it's time we talk about that too." Zinnia pointed to a chest of drawers. "I keep my important papers and my jewelry box in the bottom drawer."

Magda opened the drawer, and lifted a rectangular leather box. "Oh, I remember this. You bought it while we were studying abroad. Those were fun times, weren't they?"

Zinnia shook her head. She was a different person then. Someone she no longer recognized, nor cared to remember. "Open it. Everything in there was my mother's. Rings, necklaces, bracelets…they should be worth a few thousand krona." *If only*

Mom hadn't had such expensive taste and Dad hadn't loved playing cards. I wouldn't have had to sell the apartment in Stockholm to pay off their debts. I would've had something more to leave to Thor. "There's cash in an envelope, too. It's from the sale of my car, and what was left in my savings account." *I wish it were more.*

"What if I foul things up?"

"You won't. You always land on your feet," said Zinnia.

"Are you going to contact his father? Do you want me to?"

"It's too late for that."

"He's Thor's family."

"No. You and Izak are Thor's family."

"And you know what our friendship has meant…how much I love you."

"I do…so please don't say anymore. If you break down now…It will be harder to face this. Please. You'll be fine. Now call Thor in here."

"I'll brew some tea, too." Magda stepped to the bedroom door.

"One more thing."

Magda stopped and turned, facing her friend.

"Books…make sure they stay in Thor's life."

"Every day, I promise." Magda's eyes welled up, and then she disappeared into the sunny corridor.

Zinnia leaned back against the linen cased pillow. Her legs stretched out under the duvet, she glanced around the room, and then out the broad window. The rain clouds had followed her from Stockholm, and turned the evening gray. She thought about Thor living a life without her. The idea hurt more than the pain that had returned, and gnawed at her body. She clenched her teeth against the agony, and took a deep breath. She reached for the painkillers, and glanced at the instructions: Take as needed. Not to exceed three pills in 24 hours. Pressing and twisting, her hands trembled and struggled with the plastic child proof cap. She swallowed what little saliva wet her mouth, and then inhaled against the misery pressing her bones and the spasms that made childbirth seem like a jog in the park. She bit her bottom lip, and made it bleed, and struggled with the plastic cap. At last, she twisted it off and let it fall to the wood floor. She emptied the pills in the palm of her hand, and shoved two in her dry mouth. She washed them down with water, and let the remaining fall on the duvet. She licked the blood from her lip, gripped the corners of the pillow, and begged the pills to chase away the pain.

When she heard Thor enter the bedroom, his teddy bear tucked under one arm, she opened her eyes. The pain had somewhat subsided, but she had no sense of how long she'd been asleep. She extended her hand out, but Thor stepped back. His mouth dropped open, fear and shock crossed his face.

"Mommy, you're yellow."

"It's not my best color. Is it?"

Thor shook his head. "Are you better?"

"I'm okay. But look at you. You're getting tall. You need a pair of big boy jeans. I want people to see how grown up you are."

"These are the ones you tell me to play in."

I won't need to worry about you remembering what I told you. "Come here." She gave the mattress a weak tap.

Thor clung to the teddy bear, and his eyes filled with tears. "I don't think there's room."

"You mustn't be afraid." She was terrified.

"Are you dying?"

His sweet voice and angelic lips sent the question ripping through her heart. She'd never lied to him, not even about who his father was—she just never told him the whole truth. She searched for words to explain her own death, and couldn't find them.

"Uncle Izak said you are."

"He told you that?"

"He told the man who picks up the milk." Thor wiped at his tears, and squeezed his little frame and his teddy bear onto the bed, next to his mother.

"The doctors gave me a lot of medicine, but it didn't work."

"Can they give you more?"

"It wouldn't help." She rustled his blonde wisps from his eyes, wiped a tear from his cheek, and then kissed his forehead. "I love you. Remember that. One day you might doubt how much. Instead, remember that nothing on earth or in the heavens is more important than you are to me."

Thor snuggled closer to Zinnia, and wrapped his pudgy arms around her thin neck. "I love you too Mommy."

Zinnia's eyes glistened and her chin quivered. "I love you more...so very, very much more." She held him so close she felt his little heart racing against hers, and inhaled the scent of the outdoors and farm animals from his unwashed blond hair. She missed him already.

Madga returned with the tea, and set a mug on the nightstand next to the pill bottles.

Zinnia wrapped her weak arms around her son, and felt her soul melt in his warm hugs and kisses. She kissed him on the neck, in a way that made him giggle. *That's the boy I hold in my heart.* "Remember to laugh and to love," she whispered in his ear. *It's what makes life worth living, even if only for a short time.* She sighed at Magda.

Tears fell across Madga's face, and she lifted Thor into her arms. "I'll give him a bath, and then I'll be back."

Thor wiped the tears from his eyes with his little hand, and blew Zinnia a kiss with the other.

Zinnia threw a kiss back, and didn't think her heart could take much more or be any sadder. The scent of ginger tea filled the room, and she watched the door to close.

Chapter 4

ALVISE HURRIED HOME to shower and shave. He knotted a silk tie around his white shirt collar to complement his navy suit. Anna, his mother, picked at the nonexistent lint from the back of his jacket.

"*E' una turista?* she said.

"Mamma, please." He talked to their reflections in the full-length mirror. "It's just back from the cleaners."

"*Allora*...are you gonna answer my question? Are you going out with a tourist?"

"Just some girls we met today." He buttoned and then unbuttoned the jacket. *Which way looked best?*

"We...meaning you and Ciano?"

"*Sì*...Mamma."

"Why don't you find a nice Venetian girl instead of wasting your time with all those other women?"

Alvise remained silent, but thought: *Because asking a local girl out is like inviting her to walk down the aisle.*

"I swear, when I get my hands on Ciano," said Anna. "I'll show him real hellfire—him and all your gondolier friends. I was right. It would've been better if you'd continued your studies."

"What has university got to do with me going out tonight?" He left the jacket unbuttoned.

"It means you'd be teaching at the University, and have your eye on the local girls instead of mixing with those tourist women you don't know."

His mother distrusted the unfamiliar, and he understood why. She'd been orphaned as an infant, and then brought north to Venice from the southern Italian town of Sorrento to live with her aunt and uncle. She'd lived with them until the day she married Alvise's father, when she moved into their home, only a mere three bridges away. For sixty years, she'd been living in the small Castello neighborhood. Except for family funerals, births or weddings Anna never left Venice. Now, Alvise found it best to give her as little information as possible about the evening ahead.

He lifted a money clip off the top of the dresser, and counted out a stack of bills. "Here's this month's rent, and the last installment of the money I owed you for my college tuition." He handed her the sum his father insisted he pay them as long as he continued living under their roof, and then some. "It feels good to pay off the rest of my debt, now that I'm working fulltime."

"Lower your voice," said Anna. "Your papà still doesn't know that I gave you that money for university. I'm in trouble if he ever finds out about that, or if he discovers the stash I hide in the coffee tin."

"Okay and this will be my last month's rent, too. I'll finish fixing up Nonno's old house in the next few weeks. All it'll need is some paint, and then I'll move the rest of my stuff in."

A cool gust swelled the bedroom curtains like fuel to a windjammer's sails. Anna moved to the open window, and pulled the curtains across the rod, opening them. She leaned over the window ledge, frightening a cluster of cooing pigeons off the neighboring rooftop, and grabbed the shutter handles pulling them shut. "You made a mistake, giving up the Master's program." She latched the shutters, closed the window, and then drew the drapes, again.

"Papà doesn't think so." He put the money clip in his pants pocket.

"That's 'cause you're doing what he wants, and what Nonno wanted." She turned on the bureau lamp, and a cone of soft light splashed against the damask wallpaper and white corniced ceiling.

"I'm doing what I like to do."

"Don't tell me what you like." The click of her house slippers against the marble floor followed him around the bedroom. "I put you in this world and I know you better than anyone."

"And you know gondoliers make a good living."

"You could make just as much money or maybe more doing something you studied to do. Ciano . . . he's perfect for that job... he drinks too much and has the foulest mouth I ever heard . . . even for a gondolier."

"There's nothing easy or dishonorable about being a gondolier. I'm proud to follow in my family's footsteps, and I enjoy showing the world our special city." He finger combed his hair. "So if the job was okay for Papà, Nonno, most of my uncles and my great-grandfather, then why can't it be okay for me, too?"

"Because when they were your age winning regattas and following the family tradition was all they knew…all they could do."

"You're right. I have a choice." He glanced up at his father's regatta victory banners hanging above the desk, their gold-ink inscriptions glistened in the light.

⁂

"Come on, man, don't be a fool," said Ciano. "They met other guys."

"You're such a cynic." Alvise didn't want to heed to his own mounting doubts. "They'll be here."

Alvise berated himself for not having gotten Victoria's last name. *At least that way I could call her room.* He shifted his weight on the velvet lobby chair, and focused his attention on Ciano and the elevator doors. He didn't hear his own foot tapping on the chair's wood frame, until the concierge cleared his throat and shot him an irritated look.

"We've been here more than twenty minutes. I'm not waiting any longer." Ciano headed for the door. "Can't you see that they ain't coming? He pushed on the revolving glass door, and exited the hotel lobby.

"Wait." Alvise followed Ciano, grabbed onto his arm, and stopped him.

"Hey man, you're gonna wrinkle my jacket."

"Listen." Alvise let go. "If they don't show up in five minutes, then we'll leave. I promise. Give them five more minutes."

"You think girls that can afford a hotel like this are interested in guys like us?"

"What's wrong with us?"

"Nothing, but look at them...no doubt they got a slew of rich guys waiting in America."

"Maybe, but those guys haven't got our Italian charm. And they're not here now."

"We're wasting our time out here." Ciano walked away. "They're not showing up."

And, as if that was all that needed to be said, the girls exited the elevator at last.

"Ciano, they're here." Alvise watched his friend stop, and reluctantly turn back.

The girls, chattering away, apparently didn't notice that they'd kept their dates waiting close to thirty minutes.

Alvise didn't mind waiting. Not for her.

He fell speechless when she looked back at him through the lobby window. The classically cut black leather pants she wore outlined her soft curves, and her matching silk camisole's simple neckline revealed a sprinkle of freckles on her chest. Captivated, he waited for her to exit the spinning door, and greeted her with a kiss on the cheek. His senses, seized by the delicate touch of her hand and the soft citrus smell of her perfumed skin, brought him to step back, and look at her.

"Let's go," said Ciano. "I'm starving."

Nightlife buzzed through the Ristorante Antico Pignolo's outdoor patio. Their elegant table—set with pristine white linens and dishes, fine silverware, a flickering candle nestled next to a vase of white dahlias, and a mismatched splash of jewel-hued Venetian glass stemware—held a reservation card with the name *Moro* written in black ink. The dinner, orchestrated by the dapper-looking owner, introduced the young women to Northern Italian cooking's sumptuous aromas and flavors. Each exquisite course flowed from the kitchen with impeccable timing: fresh seafood appetizers from the Adriatic, simmering scallop gratin on the half shell, and a steaming plate of creamy *risotto* with scampi for the fish connoisseurs at the table. And for Jackie, oven-baked porcini *crespelle,* followed by a beef filet *tagliata* spread across fresh arugula leaves, and sprinkled with aged balsamic vinegar from Modena.

The busy restaurant's sounds went mute. He felt his senses raising their arms to her in surrender. His increasing desire to kiss her lips pulled him closer and she leaned into him without saying a word, letting her hand brush against his.

Glasses of sparkling Prosecco continued to be enjoyed as much as the foursome's laughter and smiles. In the rare moments when Alvise pulled his eyes off of Victoria, he watched Ciano and Jackie relax in each other's company. Ciano's rough ways softened around her, and she seemed entertained by him. Still, Jackie was a hard read. Alvise didn't understand if she liked Ciano or if she simply liked his jokes.

"Here's another one," said Ciano. "A group of old guys are sitting on a park bench. One says: *They keep investing more money in Viagra research than in Alzheimer's research.* The old guys nod, chew their gums. Then another one says: *At this rate we'll all have a hard on but we won't remember where to put it.*"

Alvise laughed, shook his head, and Victoria chuckled and rolled her smiling eyes. Jackie and Ciano burst out laughing, so hard she spilled her drink. The patrons at the tables around them seemed to like the joke, too. They were all laughing.

"I knew you'd like that one," said Ciano.

"I've got a better one. One I heard from a judge at work," said Jackie.

"You work with judges?" Ciano's smile left his face.

"She's a lawyer," said Victoria.

"Then you're the first lawyer I've met who has a sense of humor," said Ciano.

"There are a few of us around," said Jackie. "But thank you."

"She works with kids, on Juvenile Court cases," said Victoria.

"A lawyer with a sense of humor and a heart," said Alvise.

"I heard this one from a female judge. Here it goes: *Do you know what the lightest thing in the world is?"* said Jackie.

"No," said Victoria.

"A penis," said Jackie.

"Not mine," said Ciano.

"Sorry, Ciano….this applies to all penises," said Jackie.

"Are you asking me to prove it?" Ciano's devilish smile lit his face again.

"No." Jackie laughed. "Just listen."

"Yes, your honor," said Ciano.

"She's a lawyer, not a judge," said Alvise.

Ciano leaned his elbows on the table. "A penis is the lightest thing in the world, because all it needs is the power of thought to make it rise."

Laughter and applause flooded the table, again, and Ciano gave Jackie a quick squeeze.

"Damn it! You stole my punchline," said Jackie.

"I should've warned you," said Alvise. "You're sitting next to *the* master joke teller in Venice."

"Okay," said Jackie. "You win. But only because I'm in your country."

"What do you do for work?" Alvise turned to Victoria.

"I work at a talent agency. My boss is a partner at the firm, and an agent to movie stars and celebrities."

"Anyone we might know?" said Alvise.

"Jennifer Lawrence."

"She's a babe," said Ciano.

"She's nice and talented and smart," said Victoria.

"Bradley Cooper," said Jackie "who my best friend still hasn't introduced me to."

"*I* only speak to him when he calls Chloe." Victoria turned to Alvise and Ciano "Chloe is my boss."

"How about Stallone?" said Ciano.

"He's with another agency."

"What exactly is your job?" said Alvise.

"I'm an Executive Assistant. I answer calls...actually I screen most of them. Chloe only takes calls from the A-list actors. The others have to wait for her to call them back."

"You do more than answer phones," said Jackie. "She schedules meetings, manages her boss's calendar, answers emails, books travel arrangements...makes sure expensive Murano glasses her boss ordered last month in Venice arrive before Thanksgiving."

"That's why I saw you leaving the Cenedese shop earlier today," said Alvise.

"Uh-huh."

Alvise raised his glass of prosecco. "Then cheers to your boss for buying Venetian glass." Alvise watched Victoria's cheeks turn pink. He hoped he hadn't embarrassed her. He brought his glass to his lips, and emptied it. "You were telling us about your job. What do you like most about it?"

Victoria rested her hands on the table. "Meeting with new talent…and recently Chloe asked me to read a script. She usually asks the Junior Agents to do that."

Alvise was taken by the way she tilted her head and straightened her strong, feminine shoulders. "Is that what you want to do? Be an agent?"

The pink had left her cheeks. "That's my goal."

"Impressive." Alvise nodded.

"It's taking longer than I'd hoped. I was twenty-two when I started working in the agency's mailroom, and just out of college."

"How long ago was that?" said Alvise.

"Eight years ago."

That makes you a year younger than me, he thought.

"But you've only been working for Chloe for the last four years," said Jackie. "And you said that the woman you replaced worked for her for…what was it?

"Close to six years," said Victoria.

"…before she became a Junior Agent," said Jackie.

"Yeah. So, fingers crossed," said Victoria.

"*In bocca al lupo*," said Alvise.

"Wait, don't tell me. My father taught me that *bocca* means mouth..."

"Her grandfather was from Calabria." Alvise looked at Ciano.

"Great-grandfather," said Victoria. "And I know that *lupo* means wolf. But *in the mouth of the wolf* doesn't make any sense in English."

"We say it to wish someone *good luck*," said Ciano.

"Then, thank you."

"It only works if you respond *crepi il lupo*," said Alvise. "It's a wish that the wolf dies."

"A metaphor, obviously, but what's the wolf got to do with good luck?" said Jackie.

"Some say its origin comes from the days when hunters would track down and kill wolves to protect their families and livestock. When they'd go out on a hunt, they had to get close to or face the wolf. Metaphorically, put themselves in the wolf's mouth—which is a challenge and an act of courage."

"Then...*crepi il lupo*," said Victoria.

Alvise and Ciano laughed.

"Did you always want to be gondoliers?" said Jackie.

"I did," said Ciano.

"We both come from a family of gondoliers," said Alvise.

"Four generations," said Ciano.

"Now *that's* impressive," said Victoria. "Outside of kings and politicians, not many can say their family has been doing the same thing for four generations."

"It wasn't a simple choice for me," said Alvise.

"Oh, listen to *el Professor*," said Ciano.

"Professor?" said Jackie.

"My nickname."

"He's got a degree in Italian Literature gathering dust somewhere," said Ciano.

"It's at home in a frame, not gathering dust. And I'd do it all over again."

"Do you regret not finding a job more in line with your degree?" said Jackie.

Alvise shook his head. "There's no other job I'd rather do."

The dessert and espresso dishes were cleared away, and Ciano asked the waiter to bring four tall, narrow glasses and a bottle of *grappa*.

"Ladies, this is an excellent digestive." Ciano removed the loose cork from the slender bottle and poured them each a dose of the transparent liquid. "You gotta drink it in one gulp . . . like this." In an instant, Ciano tossed back the Venetian *acquavite,* squinting and tightening his lips, and then he swallowed. He raised his empty glass, and gave a wicked smile, inviting them to join in. Jackie took a small sip and quickly set her glass down, her eyes wide.

Alvise, too, lifted his glass and drank. Victoria inhaled the alcohol's strong fumes and hesitated. She followed her date, and took the entire shot. At once, the clear liquid swelled her eyes with tears, and turned her face red. She put the glass down, held her fingers to her temples as if halting an explosion in her head, and then grabbed a glass of water and smothered the blaze.

"Good, isn't it?" Ciano laughed. "Want another one?"

"I don't think it's a good idea." Alvise turned to Victoria. "That is, unless you want another one."

She fanned herself. “One is more than enough for me.”

“There’s a club nearby. We can go there and listen to music, and if you want, have another drink later.” And without waiting for a response, Alvise stood up. “Ready?”

“What about the bill?” said Victoria.

“It’s taken care of,” he said.

“But this was an expensive . . .” said Victoria.

“Really, we’re used to paying.” Jackie held her wallet.

Alvise had heard that in America, men their own age rarely paid for their dates’ dinners. He couldn’t expect them to split the bill. Victoria may not realize that two gondoliers could afford such an elaborate meal. He didn’t earn millions like her Hollywood clients. Still, tourism was Italy’s and Venice’s top industry, and that permitted him to enjoy life’s simple pleasures and to live a comfortable existence. He’d let his gallant ways surprise and, hopefully, please her. Maybe she’d like the idea of a young Venetian pampering her.

“Are you ready?” he said.

The club, a retro 1970s discotheque, with a rotating mirror ball spinning its light over the disc-jockey booth and a portable wooden dance floor, looked as badly dressed as the bleached-blond woman who stood at the bar wearing a tight leopard-print dress, and feather earrings. They took a seat at an empty red leather booth. The same short, hefty woman, waddled toward them in high heels, called the men by name and filled their drink order.

Jackie and Ciano left for the dance floor, leaving Victoria and Alvise alone for the first time. Overcome by desire, his heart beat fast. But he didn't want to rush anything, nor frighten her away by making the wrong moves or simply by kissing her. Still, he wanted nothing more.

He raised his glass.

"Here's to your first time in Venice."

"Cheers." She raised her glass to his. "I hope it's not my last."

"I'm sorry you're leaving tomorrow. I would have liked to show you more of my city."

Victoria smiled, sipped her drink and then took his from his hand, and set both glasses on the table. She rested her arm on the booth behind him. In a calm manner she turned to face him, leaned into him and gave way to the touch of his lips on her bare shoulder.

Her perfume streamed through his nostrils, and all his doubts disappeared. He reached his hand toward her and outlined her face with his fingers, tracing its graceful oval form and apple-shaped cheek bones. Her eyes crinkled up in a ticklish, seductive smile. Then she closed them, and he kissed her lips. He felt her hands run through his hair and caress his neck with tender strokes.

He pulled his lips from hers gently, with reluctance, and waited a moment before he spoke. "I wanted to do that the first time I saw you."

She blushed and leaned against him, and twisted the locks of his hair around her fingertips.

He felt inebriated by her touch and his carnal appetite grew, as if his soul were famished. He wanted to go on all night this way—kissing her, caressing her, whispering in her ear.

"Ahem." Jackie cleared her throat. "Sorry, lovebirds." An amused look extended over her face. "I'm going to the bathroom." She grabbed her purse from the back of the booth. "Are you coming?"

Victoria freed herself from Alvise's tender embrace and smoothed her long curls. She slid her handbag's leather strap over her shoulder, then scooted around the cocktail table and stood up. Quick to regain her composure, she disappeared with Jackie behind the door marked SIGNORE.

Watching her, Alvise saw that her nonchalant movements couldn't hide her lightheadedness. He smiled.

A smug grin crept up on Ciano's face. "How's it goin'?"

"You're asking me? How about you? What happened?"

"Nothing. We danced, talked. Did Victoria say anything?"

"No. Can't you tell if she likes you?"

"Nah. She's pretty and all that, but . . . it's like water in the desert—you don't know if it's safe to drink it."

"What are you going to do?"

"The usual...take her for a ride in my gondola."

"Go ahead. I think I'll stick around."

"Tomorrow, I want all the details."

The girls returned to the table. They looked at Alvise and Ciano, as if daring them to step up and announce their plans. Ciano took Jackie by the hand.

"I need fresh air. My gondola isn't far . . . I can show it to you."

"Only if you let me row." Jackie leaned into Ciano.

"Do you row?"

"No. But I can try." With a quick look at Victoria, as if giving her reassurance, Jackie grabbed the rest of her things, and let Ciano lead her toward the exit.

Alone at last with Victoria, Alvise decided to take the next step. He'd never wanted another woman like he wanted her.

"I don't live too far from here." He kept his eyes steady on her face. "If you want, we can go back to my place, have a coffee."

"I think it would be better if we go back to my hotel. If the restaurant is closed we can order room service."

He understood that she didn't feel altogether safe going home with him, and he couldn't blame her. But he also knew that Italy's strict hotel rules only allowed registered guests in their rooms. At this late hour, the doorman wouldn't even let him in the lobby. "I can take you back to your hotel if you want, but they won't let me come up with you."

"I'll ask the concierge. When he sees you're with me, he won't say no. Why would he? I'm one of their guests."

Alvise, captivated by her confidence, understood that she'd have to see for herself. So he agreed, hopeful that she might change her mind, and come home with him. Exiting the club, he rested his arm across her shoulders, feeling comfortable. Their synchronized footsteps clicked through the dark passages, and their hips swayed, and meshed with each forward motion. The flow of their bodies, side by side, increased his desire and frustration. He feared the evening's outcome lay in the doorman's hands. Certain of the hotel management's reaction, he waited outside when she went in.

Soon, Victoria returned, scowling. "I don't see why there's a problem. If I agree, why won't the concierge let you come up?"

"It would take too long to explain all the absurd situations that exist here." With a sad smile, his eyes still fixed on her luscious mouth, he leaned in for one last kiss. He felt her succumb to their bodies' yearnings, neither wanted to let go. Until, finally, he separated his lips from hers. He sighed, and then stepped back. "It's been a fantastic evening, though I would've preferred to end it in a different way. I'd ask you to stay in Venice a little longer, but I'm going out of town tomorrow." His tone sounded apologetic. "Now all I can do is hope that someday we'll meet again." He held her hands in his and kissed them. "Good-bye, Vittoria." He turned away from her sad eyes and let go of her, and walked away.

She watched him cross the bridge. Inside, reason battled desire. She'd never gone home with a man she'd just met or after a first date. She'd never trusted one enough to do so. Changing that habit in a foreign country wasn't wise. She waited until he reached the bottom of the bridge, and then turned her back on him. Straightening her purse strap up and over her shoulder, she went to the hotel lobby door, and waited for the electric eye to trigger the rotating glass. *This is my last night in Venice, and Alvise isn't a maniac.* The thought held her from stepping in. *I'm on vacation. Why not enjoy a little romance?* She stepped back and away from the revolving glass, and rushed to the top of the bridge. "Alvise, wait!"

His drooped shoulders straightened. He turned around and saw her biting her lower lip, and her childlike smile. Drawn in by her charm, he dashed back up the bridge.

"You said your house isn't too far from here, right?"

"Nothing is far in Venice." He wondered how he would keep from sweeping her up in his arms and carrying her home at a run. "Are you sure? I don't want you to do anything you don't want to do."

She looked into his eyes, and twisted a lock of her own hair around her finger. "I haven't been spontaneous in a very long time…especially with a man."

"I wish I had more time to make you feel safer with me. But since I don't . . . if you think it's better not to come home with me, I'll understand. It won't change anything. It'll just mean . . .

"…we'll never see each other again."

He nodded and paused, wanting to be careful with his words. "If you think you want to come with me, tell me what I need to do to make you feel comfortable, and I'll do it."

She stepped close, and caressed his face. Then she brought her lips to his and whispered, "You're already doing it."

Chapter 5

A BRISK WALK later, the lock clicked and the heavy green door gave a guilty squeak as Alvise swung it open.

"It needs oil." He closed the door behind them. "This was my grandparents' home. They left it to me."

"It's charming, and a very nice gift," said Victoria.

"It's mine because I became a gondolier. If I'd chosen another profession the family would have turned it into a boatyard."

"Did that influence your choice not to find a job in your field of study?"

"It played a part." He led her by the hand across the ground-floor entryway to a small window. He opened it, and pointed beyond the wrought iron window grill. "See those plants?"

She stepped closer, and leaned against the windowsill. A brick planter box framed the moonlit courtyard. "The hydrangea and rose bush plants?"

He nodded. "My grandmother grew them from cuttings that came from her mother's garden. She planted the hydrangeas the day my sister was born and the roses the day I was born. She said it was a good omen, and that my sister would grow like the hydrangeas…the colors of her beauty changing with the seasons of life."

"She was very poetic." Victoria continued to look across the courtyard. "Why did she plant rose bushes for you?"

"That's a little embarrassing."

She turned away from the garden, and looked up at him. "Ah, come on. Please?"

He couldn't refuse her smile. "She said that like the long stem roses, I'd grow tall and strong."

"She was right. There's nothing embarrassing about that."

"There's more." He tugged at his collar. "She said, like the roses, I'd always have thorns to protect my heart."

Victoria's smile softened.

Alvise traced his finger around her lips, and then he kissed them lightly, again and then once more. *I hope she was right about the thorns.*

He led her by the hand up the entryway stairs. At the top, he unlocked the double glass doors, pushed them open, and let her enter first. The house, more spacious than it appeared from the outside, was well cared for. "I'm fixing it up, but it still needs work."

"It feels cozy."

"That's my grandmother's touch. Besides refitting the brick pizza oven in the kitchen, replacing the old refrigerator and retiling the bathroom most of the house is the way they left it."

She tilted her head up, and eyed the heavy wood beams that ran across the ceiling.

"It must be a lot more rustic than what you're used to in Los Angeles."

"It looks sturdy."

He laughed. "You're right. The building was built before your country existed, so I guess 'sturdy' is a good word." He turned toward the living room. "Let's go in here."

She followed him in and sunk into the couch. "This feels divine," she said. "We've been traveling at such a pace since we left home that I haven't had much time to relax."

"*Fai come se fosse casa tua.*"

"Make yourself at home? Is that what that means?"

He nodded. "Your father taught you well."

"I do okay. Not great." She sank deeper into the soft couch.

"Do you like opera?"

"I've never listened to it."

"Your father doesn't listen to opera?"

She shook her head.

"Then tonight is more special than I thought."

"Why is that?" She smiled, and nibbled on her lip.

He could sense she liked their exchange. "Because tonight, for the first time, you will hear opera in Venice, and I get to decide which piece that will be." He thumbed through a collection of records in the stereo cabinet. "This one...Puccini's *Tosca.*" He extracted the LP, slid it out of its sleeve, and set the large record on the turntable.

"My parents' old LPs and CDs are mostly 1970s and 80s American music. Carole King, Joni Mitchell, James Taylor, Neil Young...and a few Italian rock albums...musicians whose names I don't remember."

"Hippies?"

"You'd never know it to look at them today...all business."

"These records belonged to my grandparents. They liked opera, Ennio Morricone soundtracks, and of course Frank Sinatra. My grandmother listened to Sinatra while she cooked. She said it made the sauce come out better." He laughed and placed the needle on the rotating turntable. "Understanding isn't as important as feeling. Listen—you'll feel the passion." *E Lucevan le stelle* played. "Would you like wine . . . cognac . . . another *grappa*?"

"No, not another *grappa*...wine would be nice."

He pulled a slim bottle from the credenza. "Recioto...it's sweet, like port wine, but better. It's from Valpolicella, an area not far from Venice and near Verona."

He opened the bottle like an expert sommelier and sniffed the subtle cherry bouquet from the cork, then held the wine goblets up to the light before pouring, to ensure they were spotless. He watched her relax, listen to the romantic music and watch him move around his home. Immersed in the tranquil surroundings, they studied each other's simple gestures and words.

He handed her a glass of wine, almost spilling the purple-red liquid when they locked eyes. "It's excellent," he said. She was reclining on the couch, and looked more enticing and elegant than before. "But, I don't think I'm thirsty."

Her smile sank into seriousness. "Neither am I."

Alvise set the glasses down and pulled Victoria to her feet, feeling the strength of her body next to his. He kissed her and tasted her sweet lips, winning her with tenderness. He left her mouth and let his lips travel down and around the curve of her neck causing her to quiver. He smiled at finding her ticklish spot and continued, sending passionate chills over her soft skin. He caressed the small of her back, rising up to her shoulder blades, and descending once more to her backside, her hips. She let him explore, running her hands along his firm arms, wrapping her own arms around his shoulders and pulling herself closer.

"Come on." He took her by the hand, and led her to the bedroom. The moonlight pierced the window and cast a soft glow throughout the room. "I must have left the shutters open. Do you want me to close them?"

"Can anyone see in?" she said.

"No."

"Then leave them open." She slipped her shoes off and unbuttoned her blouse.

"Can I help?"

"Yes, if I can help you."

With gentle hands they unbuttoned and undressed one another, each discovering the other's vibrant body, never once removing their eyes or hands from each other. Finally, wearing nothing more than their firm anatomy, they slid under the sheets.

"I thought you were beautiful. I never imagined you could be this beautiful." He lay behind her and, with tender caresses, circled the sinuous curves of her waist, hips, and thighs, guiding the palm of his hand over her well-proportioned backside before crossing over to explore the roundness of her breasts. "*Mamma mia,*" he said, breathless. "You could be her . . . you could be *Venere*." He would tell her another time about the art exhibit he had seen as a high school student, how her body reminded him of Diego Velàzquez's *The Toilet of Venus* and what an immense impression the painting, and now she, had left on him. *Another time.*

He felt her vibrate with each caress, and her waves of excitement sent electrical rushes through him. He sought her out and held her close, in constant movement as he kissed her body, wanting the moment never to cease. All his senses were engaged in possessing every inch of her, and after having made love to her and abandoned himself in the pleasure she gave him, he watched her sleep, peaceful, spent. He softly stroked her, listened to her breath, and smelled the sweet scent of her mixed with the light saltiness of their sweat. He couldn't sleep, didn't want to sleep, and instead continued to drink her in, wondering if this was their one chance—fearing he would never see her again.

Chapter 6

BACK IN LOS Angeles, jet lag woke Victoria before dawn, giving her good reason to stay put within the cloud of familiar bedding that covered her own bed. She lay cuddled there, and reminisced about her vacation time spent in Venice, imagining what this Sunday morning would be like if Alvise were there, too. She felt lazy, but got up and pulled on a thick pair of cotton socks, wrapped herself in her Chenille robe, and plodded across the white carpet to the bathroom. She tied her hair back and brushed her teeth, and then followed the rich smell of coffee coming from the kitchen. *How nice to come home to a coffee pot with a timer* she thought.

She poured herself a cup, gathered the mail and her MacBook, and settled into the lounge chair on the balcony. The morning fog drifted over the marina, and blocked the sun's attempts to peek through and warm the yachts and sailboats docked near the apartment complex. She closed her robe tight against the Pacific Ocean air, sipped her coffee, and noticed how the sky, the marina, the boats, the road that curved beyond the black iron fence, the Olympic sized swimming pool below her balcony, her own apartment and her coffee mug, appeared bigger than when she had left. She'd traveled Europe's quaint towns for less than a month, but now her home, its surroundings, and the city of Los Angeles appeared oversized in comparison.

The coffee comforted her, and gave her the boost she needed to sort through the mail pile: the usual monthly bills, three back issues of *Variety* magazine, and store Christmas catalogues from *J. Crew, Anthropologie* and *Marc Jacobs.*

She tossed the snail mail onto the patio table, and flipped open the MacBook. She ran her index finger over the trackpad and tapped the MAIL icon. At the top of her Gmail account inbox sat the name ALVISE MORO. Her eyebrows rose, and a smile lit up her face.

They hadn't spoken since the morning after their night together in Venice, when a sentimental knot had wound so tight in her stomach that she couldn't finish the brioche or cappuccino he'd ordered for her at the corner café. Their arms wrapped around one another, they had left his quiet neighborhood as the early morning sun brightened the autumn sky. They walked in silence to her hotel. There, they had kissed and hugged, again and again, and then some more. The words *arrivederci bella* had fallen from his lips, and his warm touch had left her hand. Somewhat confused by the sad feeling that overcame her when he'd turned and walked away, she had wiped away the tears blurring her eyes. That sadness had accompanied her from Venice to Florence and onto Rome, and then home to Los Angeles.

A long-distance relationship was unrealistic. No matter, her unrealistic heart wanted to hear from her gondolier again. She puffed out her cheeks, and tapped the trackpad again, opening his email.

> **Subject: Mia Bellissima Vittoria**
> **I haven't stopped thinking about you or our night together. How I wish you could have spent more time in Venice. I should have followed you to Florence, or convinced you to stay here. You see, two days is never enough in Venice—and it wasn't enough for you and me.**
> **I'm sad that you are so far away. Will we ever be together again? I don't know, I can only dream. Now all I think about is you and how nice it would be to visit you in America. Would you like that?**
> **I will wait for your reply. If you want, you can call me, and I will write again soon.**
> **Alvise**

Victoria thought she'd gone crazy, opening her heart to a man who lived so far away, but now those feelings turned to bliss. Of all the men in Los Angeles, why hadn't she met one who thrilled her like Alvise did? He was special. She could sense it.

She hurried back into the apartment, and looked at the clock. Twenty minutes to eight. That made it almost five p.m. in Italy. *Would he be home? Was he at work?* She didn't care. She wanted to hear his voice, and she knew he wanted to hear hers, too. She plopped herself down in front of her suitcase, and rummaged through three weeks' worth of worn clothes. There, in the side pocket, she found the slip of paper. She dialed his number.

"Pronto," said a woman.

Her spine shot up straight. "Hello. My name is Victoria. May I speak to Alvise?"

"Cosa? Alvise? Non è a casa." Then, the woman hung up.

Victoria pulled the sound of the rapid dial tone from her ear. *Did I dial the wrong number?* She redialed.

"Pronto." The same woman answered, her voice more irritated.

"Excuse me, but I'm looking for Alvise…."

"Ancora…no Alvise."

"But, he gave me this number."

"Alvise vork…lavoro…trabajo…gondola. . .gonnn-dooo-laaa. Me… mamma."

"Oh . . . you're Alvise's mother. My name is Victoria, from California."

*"Un momento…*Gina." Victoria could hear his mother place the phone in another set of hands while mumbling the words *"Queste donne…francese, spagnole, inglese…mai un'italiana".*

"Hallo?" said a younger woman's voice.

"Hello. I'm Victoria . . . a friend of Alvise's from California."

"Vittoria?"

"Yes."

"I'm Gina, Alvise's sister."

"Oh…nice to meet you…can you please tell him I called?"

"Let me write down your name. He receives many calls…but you're the first from California."

"Oh." Her heart went limp. *The first from California?*

"Does he have your number?"

"Yes."

"Then I'll tell him *Vittoria* from California called."

"Thank you." Victoria hung up. Joy and insecurity played leapfrog with her sentiments. Was she another tourist on his long list? Did that matter? What could she expect from this *relationship*? Could one night of great sex and a sweet email be called a relationship? *For goodness sake, wake up! We live on different continents. It's only a fling.* Common knowledge said distance was the number one killer of relationships. The Surgeon General probably had a warning label for it. So she'd label theirs a *spicy affair.* She'd read the warning signs, and expect nothing more.

She looked at the time once again, and dialed Jackie.

"Hello." Jackie's voice came through the receiver.

"Did I wake you?"

"What time is it?"

"It's almost eight, and you'll never guess who sent me an email."

"Eight o'clock in the morning? How long have you been up?"

"Long enough to read a super romantic email from Alvise... he wants to come to Los Angeles."

"Hold on . . . I need coffee. Let me call you back."

"Come over. The fog is burning off . . . we can sit by the pool, and I'll tell you all about it."

"I've got laundry to do."

"Do it here."

"Are you in love?"

"Hurry over, and I'll tell you."

Victoria couldn't keep still. She dug through her unpacked suitcase and pulled out the blue-and-white-striped shirt Alvise had given her. She threw off her robe and nightgown, slipped on the oversized shirt, and put on the last pair of clean leggings she could find. She stared at herself in the mirror and wondered how many striped shirts he had given away.

Victoria hadn't always made the right choices with men—another reason why she'd thrown her effort into her career. Now, she knew little about this man. How could she let him come and stay at her home? She doubted her ability to reason. Her emotions toiled with her common sense. Her thoughts wanted to surrender and side with her heart. *That's absurd. He's so sweet and gentle. He's* got *to be a good person.*

She'd do the laundry while she waited for Jackie—it would clear her mind. She threw the last few sets of lacy lingerie onto the heap, grabbed the detergent from under the sink, and plucked a handful of quarters from the crystal bowl on the book shelf. Heaving the laundry basket out the front door, she carried the load downstairs to the laundry room. She found all three washing machines empty, and loaded them, set the empty basket and detergent on the shelf, and headed back to the apartment.

Back, at her front door, she heard the phone ring. She rushed in to answer it, stubbed her toe on the bedroom door, tripped, and fell over the open suitcase.

"Ouch! Hello."

"Vittoria?"

She blushed at the sound of his lyrical voice. "Alvise."

"Are you okay?"

"Yeah . . . I hurt my . . . I'm fine. At least, now I am." Reclining on the fluffy bed comforter, she rubbed her throbbing toe.

"I was thinking about calling you…on my way home, and then my sister gave me your message . . . anyway, I finished work early today. It's been raining a lot. There's *acqua alta*, the high tide, and a lot of wind, too, and . . . well, when it rains, we don't work much." He sounded like the weatherman, and his rambling told her that he felt as nervous as she did.

She wrapped herself around her pillow and imagined him peeling off his rain drenched work clothes. "I have a nice, dry striped shirt on if you need one."

"Hey . . . that's not fair. I know how good you look in it. Vittoria, hold on a minute."

She listened to his footsteps cross the floor, and heard the sound of a door close. Then silence, as if waiting for something or someone. "Everything okay?"

"Yeah, just need a little privacy from my family. I'm at my parents' house now—I gave you their number because I don't have a landline at my grandparents' house yet. But soon I'll be living there fulltime."

"What's keeping you?"

"I need to finish a few more repairs. Now, what were you saying about a striped shirt? I'm warning you, I'll be on the next flight to Los Angeles."

"I got your email."

"I thought about writing you every day."

Joy tickled her heart. Still, she questioned how many other tourists he'd said that to. "Are you coming to Los Angeles?"

"Do you want me to?"

"I do."

"Ciano has plans to vacation in the Caribbean. I haven't decided if I'll meet him there, after I see you."

He's chosen to visit me rather than go to the Caribbean with Ciano. "You can stay here. That is, if you want to."

"I'm coming to California...to see you."

"When?"

"The repairs on the house should be finished by the end of November, so I thought December would be a good time."

"Will you be here for Christmas?"

"Yes, unless you'll be out of town."

"I'll be here. But won't your family want you there for Christmas?"

"Probably...we always spend Christmas at our place in the mountains, so my mom won't be pleased. But this year...well...I prefer to spend it in a *warm* place with you."

Victoria thought about the last time she'd brought a man to Christmas dinner. It was the day that Philip, her ex, had opened her eyes and closed her heart. Between the fruitcake and the coffee, when her mother had asked Philip about his upcoming divorce and his intentions with her daughter, he'd complained that too much food had given him a headache. Then he'd left, leaving her behind. That same evening, snug and alone in bed, Victoria's smartphone *pinged.* She'd lifted her iPhone from the nightstand, and saw Philip's response to a text she'd sent him earlier, asking if his headache had passed. *I've got to make it work for the kids*. That's how he put it. Those words glowed on the screen, and crushed her heart. A dam of tears had broken, and kept her in bed for days. Still, as hard as it was for her, she understood. The kids had to be his priority. But that horrible breakup, and two years of mending scars he'd carved into her heart, had made her wiser, and cautious.

"Alvise, I always spend Christmas with my family. They'll love having you, but I need to warn you, they ask a lot of questions."

"They can't be worse than my family."

"And there will be lots to eat. My mom always makes a huge turkey."

"You eat turkey with marmalade, right?"

"Cranberry sauce, not marmalade…don't they have cranberries in Italy?"

"I don't think so. We don't eat meat with marmalade in Italy."

All so sudden, yet it felt so good, so natural. *Caution!*

"Vittoria, I wish you were here with me right now."

She closed her eyes and pictured his strong body entwined with hers. Breathless, she felt her heart sink. Their encounter had been brief, but he had made her feel like no other man had before.

"I like that you call me *Vittoria*…and your accent is so… sensuous."

"Okay, I should say good-bye now, or I'm really getting on the next flight. It'll be a long month until I see you."

"But think about how much fun we'll have when you get here."

"*Mamma mia,* my *bella* Vittoria."

She smiled into the telephone. *Thank goodness we went to Venice. Was that a coincidence? Were we destined to meet?*

Jackie wanted to visit Portofino, but Victoria had insisted on Venice. If she hadn't, she would never have seen him on his gondola. Then, if Chloe hadn't asked her to check on her Murano glass order, they may have never seen each other again.

"Ciao, bella."

"Ciao." Victoria put the phone back on its cradle and wrapped herself in the unmade bed covers. She let out a delightful scream into the pile of pillows, and rolled over and lay there, twisted in the sheets, laughing, smiling. Never before had she felt so enticed by a man. Her skeptical friends would call her insane. But it felt wonderful and she didn't care. Still, she'd remain cautious, but wouldn't let anything or anyone dissuade her from enjoying this adventure.

She jumped up from the bed, peered out the window and saw that the morning fog had lifted. Weekend sunbathers were filling the poolside lounge chairs. She straightened, smoothed and tucked-in her bed linens, and fluffed and stacked the plush down pillows, and then unpacked what she hadn't thrown in the wash. She stored her empty suitcases in the walk-in closet, and turned to pick through a neat stack of bathing suits on the shelf. She chose the floral-print bikini, slipped off her clothes and slipped on the bikini bottoms, and secured the crisscross halter top behind her back and at her neck. The internal security phone rang as she grabbed her tanning cream from the bathroom shelf. She went to the living room wall, and pressed the intercom button, opening the guest parking gate. Then she unlocked the front door and went into the kitchen to prepare their usual poolside drinks.

With two large plastic cups filled with iced tea came a knock at the door. Jackie stepped through the doorway. "I bring gifts." She held up a white paper bag from *The Rose Café and Market.*

"Poppy-seed muffins?" Victoria's eyes widened.

"Yep."

"I missed those while we were away." Victoria turned, opened the freezer door, and grabbed a handful of ice. She added the cubes to the tea, and then took a sip from the cool drink. "Alvise said he'll be here for Christmas. He's coming to stay with me."

"Wait a minute . . . isn't he still too much of a mystery man to let him stay here? And for Christmas?"

"No." She set the glass down. The sticky beverage splashed over her fingers, and formed a puddle on the tile countertop. She turned, grabbed a few paper towels, and wiped her hands and the countertop clean as if the vigorous strokes would also clean the doubt rising in her mind.

"What I mean is. Who really is this guy? You only spent one night together. Maybe he's one of those foreigners looking for an easy way to get to the U.S."

"Thanks for the compliment. Is it so impossible that he likes me and wants to be with me?"

"No, I didn't mean that, and you know it. It's that . . . there are guys who will do anything to be able to stay here."

"You might want to quit while you're ahead."

"I don't mean 'anything' . . . meaning *you* . . ."

"That's not the case, Jackie. Alvise told us how much he loves what he does. And, he can only do it in Venice. So I don't think he's looking for a way to live here in the U.S."

"Don't get me wrong, okay? He's really cute and very sweet, but are you sure he's your type? I mean, isn't being a gondolier like being a limousine driver?"

She looked at her best friend. What she was saying sounded arrogant, but was it the truth? She had been raised to value people based on who they were, not on what they did or how much she thought they made. She shook her head. "I don't know."

"Then let's be realistic. You drive a BMW, you lunch on Rodeo Drive with movie stars who might one day be your clients, and you attend red-carpet events."

"I take notes at those lunches, and I observe red-carpet events from behind the scenes. Chloe is the one who *walks* the carpet."

"Still, with that lifestyle in front of you, how can you hook up with a gondolier?"

"Who said I'm hooking up with him? He's just coming to visit."

"*Just coming to visit* is traveling a few miles in a car, not a few *thousand* in an airplane."

Victoria stood her ground. "He said he wants to spend the holidays in a warm place…with me. Even if I find out that he's taking advantage by staying her so he can visit California, I refuse to rationalize my way out of this. And I like him."

"Liking him is fine. But we're not in grade school anymore."

"So we'll have more good…make that great sex, and then he'll go back to Venice."

"I'd believe that if you hadn't told me, minutes before you first laid eyes on him, that you want more out of life than a career."

"Just because I met a gorgeous Italian man doesn't mean I'm losing my senses. I'm not giving up on my career."

"Remember, I'm on your side." Jackie lifted the *Rose Café and Market* bag off the kitchen counter, and tore into a muffin and offered the other half to Victoria. "Any more talk about that promotion?"

"It's been a while since Chloe mentioned it. Hopefully something shifted forward while we were away."

Chapter 7

ALVISE ROWED UP to the *squero* at San Trovaso to store his gondola for the winter. Luigi, the artisan gondola builder, stood at his work bench molding and shaping a set of eleven-meter mahogany boards to fit the gondola he had been building since midsummer. Alvise watched Luigi set his tools on the sawdust-covered sideboard, pick up a worn sheet of sandpaper off the ground, and continue to ignore him while he went on with his work.

Alvise sculled the gondola Luigi had crafted for his grandfather more than two decades before into position for unloading. Pressured by his longtime family friendship, and accustomed to being ignored by Luigi, he yelled out a sarcastic, "*Buon giorno.*"

The boatyard workers responded with dirty looks and continued their tasks. Their lack of cordiality, well known among the gondoliers, was no surprise to Alvise.

"No need for everyone to run and give me a hand. I can do it myself, thank you," said Alvise, yelling out.

"Ooh . . . *Il Doge* Alvise . . . hurry, get the red carpet," said the boatyard boss. He stepped out from behind a gondola, black paint covered brush in hand, and continued to holler. "What ya waiting for? Empty it…then bring it to the landing. That damn boat is heavy enough—we ain't pulling it out of the water loaded."

"*Proprio, oggi?*" said a boatyard hand. Complaining, the man busied himself with a rag and turpentine in an attempt to clean the black paint from his fingers and fingernails. "You were supposed to come tomorrow."

"There was a last minute change in plans. Still, what difference does it make?" Alvise tied the gondola to the dock and began unloading its contents.

"The difference is that tomorrow's my day off." The boatyard hand hollered over a row of black gondolas that had been pulled from the water and tilted on their sides, their green bottoms exposed like the bellies of beached whales on dry land. "And I woulda saved my ass from pulling that aircraft carrier you call a boat out of the water."

The *squero,* the oldest in the city, didn't have a crane or winch to hoist the boats on dry land. That had to be done by manpower, making it the worker's least loved part of their job. However, Alvise knew how to sweeten their response.

"Yeah, but then you wouldn't have been able to taste the salami and wine I brought." Alvise yelled across the distance. He pulled out a brown paper bag and a bottle from beneath the prow, setting the two packages dockside. Curious head's popped out from the boatyard's many hidden corners.

"That'll only get the boat out of the water," said the boatyard hand. "You're gonna have to put all that stuff in storage by yourself."

Alvise finished unloading the equipment—love seat, foot stools, gold-plated seahorses, leather cushions, floorboards—and made a dozen trips, back and forth, to carry it all to the storeroom. He untied the hollowed-out gondola and rowed in reverse into a perpendicular position across the canal, then backed onto the landing. The men dropped what they were doing and moved forward to give a hand. Standing at the rear of the gondola, they formed two lines—one on each side—and waited for Alvise to disembark. Bombarded by their impatient threats, he hurried and put his oar in the storage room and then rejoined them for the much-hated part of pulling the gondola to dry land.

"Now, men, when I give the order, pull at the same time," commanded Luigi. "Make it smooth, and no jerking. And don't get your feet caught in the rollers. I don't need anyone getting hurt."

The men leaned forward, reaching inside the gondola for a stronghold. At Luigi's command they tugged and pulled her out of the water, and then pushed to hold her steady. With each strenuous heave, they spewed personalized profanities at Alvise, the gondola, and their damned jobs.

"My mamma told me I shoulda stayed in school." The boatyard hand grimaced.

"All you'd have done is take space away from the guy who's got a brain," cracked another.

A roar of laughter broke their concentration.

"Men…stop wasting time." Luigi's forbidding look brought them back to order. "You're *all* lucky to have a job. Now, ready… *oh-issa*."

The men combined their muscle to heave and thrust the gondola out of the water. With strength and delicacy, they tilted the vessel on her side and held her upright until Luigi secured a wooden Y-shaped pole that propped her up.

The boatyard hand, quick to complain but quicker around food, went to the boatyard's tiny kitchen and grabbed a sharp knife. He rinsed a hodgepodge of old drinking glasses and carried them back to the men. He blew the sawdust off a square of cherry wood lying on the ground, and used the makeshift cutting board to slice the salami into thin rounds. They finished their snack and emptied the bottle with little effort, and used their soiled shirts to clean their mouths and wipe their greasy hands, and went back to work.

Alvise ducked out the boatyard's low-rising backdoor, and stepped up into the campo. The December sunshine filled the spaces that separated brick dwellings leaning against other brick dwellings.

"Alvise." Luigi frowned and followed him into the campo.

Alvise turned, and faced the boat builder's stony aspect.

"There's something I've wanted to tell you for a long while now."

"I know…the boat needs a lot of work."

"That…and that you did the right thing."

Alvise stepped forward, and noticed Luigi's usual dismissive expression soften.

"Your father would never tell you to your face, but he's proud of you for keeping up the family trade and, I'm sure as hell, your grandfather would be proud of you, too."

Alvise swallowed the knot rising up from his chest. "I owe a lot of what I know to them. Papà is a good gondolier, like Nonno was. They were both great *regatante*."

"Your father is as strong as your grandfather was, and when he raced, he was hungrier to win."

"He wanted to beat Nonno's record."

"Seeing your father race a gondola was like watching Satan run through hell."

Alvise smiled at the comparison. "He used to tell me that I should spend less time writing, and more time rowing." He looked at the stone pavement beneath his feet, and his smile faded.

"*Ascolta*, I've known your father since we were kids. He was as reckless as his temper was fierce. Trying to convince him of anything was like trying to stop the tide from flooding the Piazza."

Alvise raised his eyebrows to the truth in Luigi's words.

"But even if he never told you, I know he's proud that you got that degree, too. Just never forget that all *this*..." he raised a hand toward the gondolas, the boatyard and the quiet canal alongside the campo "is in *your* blood, too."

Alvise didn't answer, as there was no need. He accepted Luigi's stately embrace, and then crossed the campo accompanied by a small dose of freedom. A few more hours, and he'd be on a plane to her.

Familiar shortcuts took him down the stone walkway abutting the canal, past the hospital and over the Ognissanti Bridge, through the narrow alleyway, and then left onto Calle Lunga San Barnaba. A few steps and a right turn set him across the canal from his new home. He looked up with pride at the weathered stucco façade and the faded green shutters. They would be next on his list of repairs.

Hurrying toward his parents' home, he avoided his usual hangouts. No time to run into friends for a pre-lunch *aperitivo*, his mother had prepared a feast to bid him farewell.

He closed the apartment door behind him and prepared himself for the loud, chaotic conversation and laughter coming from the living room. His family members sat crowded around the oval table that his mother had set with her finest porcelain plates, and Venetian lace linens. He gave each of them a patient smile, a kiss on each cheek, and avoided getting entangled in their idle chatter and stereotypical opinions on the American way of life.

"*Basta* . . . Enough about America." Anna set down a steaming terrine of pasta dripping with meat sauce. "*L'America* is right here, too. No need to go searching when you've got everything you need here at home, and don't go putting ideas in Alvise's head. It's bad enough he'll be away for Christmas. God only knows what they'll feed him over there. Now, *mangia* before it gets cold."

After their meal—hearty enough to hold him over until he returned from overseas—and as soon as his mother started to clear away the *tiramisu* dishes and espresso cups, Alvise excused himself from the table. He showered and finished packing.

Alvise heard his mother's brisk footsteps arriving from the kitchen. Her ample hourglass shape filled the bedroom doorway, and she whimpered into her apron as he closed his suitcase.

"Mamma, I'm not going off to war." He pulled the suitcase from the bed to the floor, and stood across the room, looking at her.

"I have a bad feeling." She moved closer, and rested her head against his chest.

"Please, don't start."

"Watching you leave reminds me of my parents." She dabbed her apron to her eyes. "I'm afraid you're not going to come back either."

He stepped away from her and to the desk, and zippered his passport and airplane ticket into his backpack. The room fell silent, but his mother's voice rang through his head, repeating the story he'd heard time and again. Her words told about a ship headed for Australia, and the captain's rules prohibiting sick passengers aboard, especially small children running high fevers like she was then. He pictured the scene at the port, her parents crying, forced to leave their only child behind, yet certain that, when they'd become sugarcane plantation owners and struck it rich, they'd come back for her. He saw images of grandparents he had only met in a photograph: hope filled emigrants standing on the dock wearing their best clothes and holding the few belongings they could carry in a leather suitcase—their smiles revealing joy and fear and the certainty that they'd find a better life in Australia, or return to Italy with pockets filled with money. He remembered how his heart shivered the first time his mother told him that, days before reaching Australian shores, his grandmother had fallen ill and died onboard the ship. They'd kept her body in a cold locker until the ship docked in Melbourne.

Anna sobbed into a tissue. "All I have of them is the photo Zio Vincenzo took the day they boarded the ship." She blew her nose, tossed the tissue into the wastebasket and pulled a clean one from her apron pocket, and wiped more tears.

Alvise saw her eyes change color, the way they did whenever she cried or thought about never having seen her father again. Now, they appeared even less like the color of his own, and more like the palm leaves from her native Sorrento.

Alvise pulled his suitcase off the floor, and glanced at the ticking brass clock on the nightstand. It was late, and he needed to pick up Victoria's gift before he caught his flight.

"My father was your age when he left, and not much older when he died."

He wouldn't comment. His heart didn't have room for the guilt she was unloading. He looked at the clock again, put the suitcase down, and pushed the backpack strap higher over his shoulder. He took his mother's hands in his. "I'm sorry you never knew your parents. But, as unfair as that is, you had Zio Vincenzo who was as good a father as his brother ever could've been."

"*Sì,* he was a good man. But Zia Flora was spiteful—God bless her soul." Anna raised her hand to her forehead, and then crossed her heart and her shoulders. "She said death brought me to Venice, but being raised by her, in her city, didn't make me Venetian. She was right. Death, like birth, puts us where we belong, even if we don't belong there."

"Then don't be afraid to let me go."

"I don't want more death telling me how to live."

"Geez…I'm not going to disappear or die." He lifted his suitcase by the handle, and stepped away from her.

"This *Vittoria*…she's not our kind. She's…"

"…wonderful." Alvise didn't want to hear what his mother had to say, not about Victoria, or fall prey to her manipulative ploy any longer. He tightened his grip around the suitcase handle. "You don't know Vittoria. And I don't know what my future with her will be, but you won't get in the middle of it."

"Me, in the middle…when have I ever gotten in the middle?"

When have you ever not *gotten in the middle?*

"Don't you look at me that way."

"I've got to go." He held back his anger, headed out into the hall, and avoided challenging his mother any more. He couldn't continue making choices to make her happy.

Chapter 8

THROUGH THE ELEGANT two-story windows, Victoria Greco could see the quiet lobby's marble walls and the vacant security guard's post. Alone, with an assortment of bulky packages occupying her hands, she forced open the heavy glass doors and entered backside first. Tripping, she quickly balanced her weight on her high heels.

Not very graceful, she thought.

She squeezed the colorful shopping bags through the doorway, and then rushed to catch the closing elevator. "No…wait!" She'd been out of the office far too long. Relief calmed her when they slid back open.

"Need help there, Miss Greco?" The guard blocked the doors and stepped out.

"Thank you."

"Tenth floor?"

She nodded.

On the tenth floor, Victoria paused as the World Talent Agency office glass doors slid open. Her heels clicking across the beige tile floor, she entered the luxury office space and walked into the receptionist's lighthearted looks.

"Someone went shopping on her lunch break," said Barbara.

Victoria held up her new purchases and headed toward her desk. "You could've come with me instead of leaving me alone to face tauntingly beautiful Christmas displays in every store window in Beverly Hills."

"What did you buy?"

"A dress to wear to the office Christmas party."

"One outfit…in all those bags?"

"The other things are Christmas gifts Chloe asked me to pick up. And an outfit for tomorrow. Did she call?"

Barbara nodded. "She'll be back by five o'clock. What's tomorrow?"

"My friend is arriving. Do I need to confirm her car pick up?"

"I took care of that. Your friend, the Italian guy you met on vacation?"

"Uh-huh."

"Do we get to meet him?"

"I'm bringing him to the Christmas party."

"Lucky you…you have a date."

"Aren't you bringing the musician?"

Barbara leaned across her desk, and shook her head. "No, I guess he realized I'm nobody around here. Seems he was dating me in hopes he'd get a recording contract."

"I'm sorry…and you're not a *nobody*."

Barbara forced a smile. "No great loss…his music was crap."

Victoria giggled and sauntered down the hallway.

"Oh, I almost forgot. Chloe wants a meeting with you, and asked that you be here when she arrives."

"Where else would I be?"

Victoria entered Chloe Anders' office, and arranged her boss's shopping bags on the counter and next to the brass plaque that read: There's a Special Place in Hell for Women Who Don't Help Other Women. Skirting the wide desk, she looked out the panoramic windows at the Santa Monica Mountains. She smiled the way someone might when greeting an old friend, and wondered when she might have an office with a view of her own.

Outside Chloe's office, she stepped into her gray cubicle and dropped into the matching leather chair. She swiveled toward the widescreen Mac display, and sorted through the *urgent* emails addressed to Chloe Anders: the Beverly Hills Hotel's final food and drinks price list for the office Holiday party; the dermatologist confirming Chloe's next Dermal Oxygen face treatment; Jamie Foxx's attorney reminding Chloe to sign their new contract; and a screenplay submission from an unknown writer with *Perfect for Meryl Streep* in the subject line. Without blinking, Victoria sent the screenplay and its email straight to the trash file. Chloe was kind and tolerant with new talent, but refused unsolicited screenplays. No matter how this writer got Chloe's email address, Victoria had been instructed to never accept them. Efficient and quick, Victoria responded to or filed the others away, and then checked her own inbox.

That's odd. In the last month she'd received one, sometimes two emails a day from Alvise. All sent to her private Gmail account. Why had he sent this one to her office account?

Dolcissima Vittoria,

Sorry for bothering you at the office. There's been a change in plans. My flight scheduled for tomorrow was overbooked. The only seats available were on today's flight or one at the end of December. Of course I chose today. I'm in transit now, on the Delta flight leaving New York for LAX. Sorry I couldn't write sooner...no time...security was a mess...all so last minute. I arrive at 3 p.m.

I'd take a taxi from the airport, but I don't have your address. Send it if you can or, better yet, pick me up.

I can't wait to kiss you!

Alvise

She looked at her watch. It was 2 p.m. "Damn!"

She rocked the chair back and forth, tapping her manicured fingers on the leather armrest, and then sprung to her feet and went back to the panoramic windows. Down below, the afternoon traffic clogged Wilshire Boulevard. Her stomach tightened. If she hurried she might make it to the airport and back before Chloe arrived—but maybe not. She could send a car for him. No, she didn't want that.

She looked down at her nails, and her casual Friday attire. Her weekly manicure and pedicure appointment was for the next morning, too. Her denim jeans, leather heels and silk blouse weren't the outfit she'd planned on, but they'd do. She grabbed her purse, hurried passed her colleagues' offices and Barbara's desk, and reached the front door.

"I have an errand to run."

"What about Chloe?" said Barbara.

"If I'm not back before she arrives, tell her I went to pick up a Christmas gift I forgot."

"Pick up from where?"

Victoria looked at her watch. "Please, just tell her that."

On foot, Victoria exited the Los Angeles International Airport's grimy parking lot stairwell, and hurried down the sidewalk. Ahead, the pedestrian crossing stoplight flipped from green to yellow. With no time to waste, she scurried in her high-heeled boots, stepped off the curb and into the crosswalk. A whistle shrieked and forced her to stop. A uniformed Airport Police officer stood at the opposite end of the crosswalk. He raised the palm of his hand and then pointed at her, and blew his whistle, again. Her face flushed. She rolled her eyes and stepped back up and onto the curb. She straightened her clothes, and raised her hand to shade her face from the sun. Impatient, she checked her watch and then the red-light, and then her watch, again. Nudged to the edge of the curb by travelers and suitcases that crowded her space, she held to the faith that Alvise's plane would be on time, and that she'd get back to the office before Chloe arrived.

Stretch limousines and black town-cars, Hummers and SUVs as big as small European garages glistened in the hot California winter sun and down the airport's five-lane avenue. Traffic separated her from her goal. Panic stirred in her gut. Organized delirium surrounded her and twisted her enthusiasm into turmoil, and then into doubt.

What if it was all a mistake and Jackie was right? Maybe Alvise did just want an easy way to get to America. He wouldn't be the first person in search of a guaranteed green card.

The light went green. Now, part of the thick crowd she let it sweep her across the street and to the front of the arrivals gate. In clear view of the passengers streaming down the hall, Victoria felt her head spin. The crowd around her stifled the stuffy air. She stretched her neck and looked past a wall of strangers, and saw no sign of Alvise. Then, as quick and frenzied as the Delta corridor had been engulfed by the mob, it emptied out.

She turned, raised her gaze and scanned the crowd exiting the glass doors. She noticed the hour on the large wall clock. *Where the heck are you? I'm going to lose my job.* She couldn't wait any longer. She had to get back to the office before Chloe did.

She exited the arrivals room, and stepped back onto the street. She felt blood rush to her face. Why hadn't she sent a car for him? She checked her iPhone. No emails or messages. She double checked the outdoor arrival screen. The Delta plane from New York had landed on time. Had she missed him? Did he take a cab? Of course not, where would he go? Then, a pair of strong hands grasped her waist and spun her around. Alvise took her in his arms. His loving embrace erased her anxiety and insecurities. His soft lips pressed upon hers, and desire bolted through her body. She didn't care that they were in public and surrounded by strangers. She let him kiss her, and didn't pull away until a group of teenage boys yelled *take it to a motel.*

She giggled. "Well, hello."

"*Buon giorno.*" Alvise smiled and ran his fingertips lightly down her spine, resting his hand just above the small of her back. "I thought you had changed your mind and decided to leave me here."

Engrossed in the details of his handsome face, she felt safe and glad she hadn't sent a car to pick him up. "I wouldn't do that. But unfortunately, I need to get back to the office. My boss wants to see me."

"Did the change in my travel plans cause problems for you at work?"

"No. No problems. I'll drop you off at my apartment. It's on the way to my office. There's wine, cheese...in fact my refrigerator has never seen so much food." She looked at her watch. At this hour, she'd be driving against traffic. Everything was working out. She'd make it back before Chloe. "My meeting shouldn't take long."

"I'm so happy to see you, Vittoria."

"Me too, Alvise." She let him kiss her long and sweet, again. When he pulled his lips from hers, she waited for him to wheel his luggage closer and drape his down-jacket on top. "You're not going to need that jacket here." She smiled. Standing next to him felt good, and natural—as if they belonged together. She took his free hand in hers, and led him down the sidewalk.

Passing the loading and unloading curb, she picked up the pace, never leaving his hand. When she took her eyes from his to insure she wouldn't walk into something, she locked eyes with someone else. "No. . .it can't be." The color drained from her face.

"What's wrong?"

She squeezed Alvise's hand, and pulled him to slow down.

"What is it?"

Two parked car lengths away, Victoria saw Howard Woodcock, Chloe's equal at World Talent Agency. Together, they'd climbed up the ranks of success from the mailroom to become Hollywood's top agents. Some said they had the entertainment industry in their back pockets. His salt-and-pepper hair and deep tennis-court tan were his trade mark around town, and often the butt of jokes. Now, he was arm and arm with Chloe—their behavior more than business friendly.

Seeing them shocked Victoria. Not because this confirmed the industry gossip about their affair or because she was surprised to see them together. She knew they had gone to New York to meet with the agency's founding partners. She was shocked because she didn't expect to see them there, at the Los Angeles airport. She'd confirmed the arrangements for Chloe to fly on a client's private jet from New York to the Santa Monica Airport. So what happened?

Her back turned to them. She hoped they hadn't seen her, too. "See the woman with long blonde hair?"

"The lady who looks like a morning talk show host?"

Victoria chuckled through her desperation. "Yeah, she's the one. She's my boss. And the man she's with is another top agent at our agency…who happens to be married."

"Hmm…it looks like you work for a very friendly company. Does anyone know they're…involved?"

"Their affair is an industry secret, which means everyone knows."

"It looks like they're saying goodbye. He's getting in the car."

"Is she getting in the car, too?"

"No. She's talking to the driver of another car. Now she's walking our way."

Victoria's eyes widened and she let go of Alvise's hand. A smile plastered on her face, she slowly turned around. Chloe was close enough for Victoria to see her blue-green eyes, and her usual pleasant expression shift into that poker face—the one Victoria saw whenever Chloe negotiated tough client contracts.

"It looks like that meeting of yours might take place here," said Alvise.

Chapter 9

"VICTORIA?"

Anxiety flushed Victoria's face at the sound of her name. *Shit!* The fear that crept under her skin froze her to where she stood. Her lower lip trembled, and she faced her boss.

"Howard was right. You didn't come to pick me up." Chloe gave Alvise a quick once over and a smile, and then extended her hand to him. "I'm Chloe Anders. Nice to meet you..."

He took her hand, and shook it. "Alvise Moro."

"You were on my flight from New York." Chloe dropped his hand. "I saw you walk through Business to Economy."

"Alvise is the person I met on vacation. That's why I'm here... and not in the office. His flight got changed..." Victoria's voice quivered, barely audible above the traffic.

"It's okay. I was beginning to think you were too perfect to be true." Chloe placed her hand on Victoria's shoulder.

"Can I drive you back to the office?"

"No need. The driver is waiting. You two go catch up...have a good weekend. We'll have that meeting another time."

"Anything I need to prepare for?" Victoria's face lit up. Her anxiety slowed to a whisper.

"No. You're all set." Chloe turned on her tan pumps, and walked away.

They watched her climb into the back seat of the town car, and be whisked into the thick Friday afternoon traffic. Alvise wheeled his suitcase along the sidewalk with one hand, and took Victoria's hand in the other. "What does she mean by *all set*?"

"I wish I knew."

The night was warm and dry in Marina Del Rey. The Santa Ana desert winds cleared the horizon of its usual brown haze, and swirled thin clouds high in the golden sky. From the balcony, they watched the sun set. Victoria sipped her wine, and leaned her head back against Alvise's broad chest.

"How can anyone prefer four changing seasons over this?" said Alvise. "Who needs a white Christmas in the Dolomites?"

"Is that where your family's mountain home is?"

He nodded. "It's a small place, outside of Cortina. The mountains there are spectacular."

"A getaway to the snow sounds nice." *Still, I prefer Southern California's practical, reliable weather.* Reliability supported her search for perfection. She'd been raised around routine and hard work, and saw how they glued her household and family together. That logic comforted her, and helped her move up in her professional life, too. Good at overlooking flaws in others, she rarely allowed room to make her own mistakes.

"It must be nice living in a place where you don't have to dress in heavy layers."

"I assumed it was warm year-round in Italy, too…until I saw the down-coat you brought with you." Her eyes on the red and purple sky, she let him take her wine glass and place it on the balcony table, next to the cheese and fruit. She felt his strong hands run across her shoulders and down her bare arms. His touch was different now. Not like the cautious manner that had caressed her in Venice. Now, his hands and fingertips lingered at her neck. He seemed more confident. She felt him lift her curls, and kiss her earlobe. It tickled, and she squirmed and giggled until she could feel the heat from his breath on her neck. She inhaled the dry marina breeze. Losing herself to his gentleness, she cracked open the door to her heart.

In the morning, Victoria slipped from her bed. She stood on the tuft carpet, and watched Alvise sleep. His handsome tanned face sunk deep into the soft pillow, a light snore puffing from his lips. She liked him, and was concerned about liking him too much.

Gentle, smart and handsome his traits were on the list of requirements she thought she needed to fall in love—right down to the freckles on his shoulders. But the profile of the man she'd choose as her partner, and marry someday, had other strict requirements, too.

Raised in comfort, she had chosen a career that exposed her to the rich and famous. The man she'd marry would have to be a successful business man to complement her own desired success. Together they would buy a luxurious home in Malibu or in Beverly Hills, perhaps in the Pacific Palisades. She'd allow that man to be, at times, egotistical, but never cruel. She might even accept a man who was less handsome and sometimes boring if he had an important business title and paycheck. Secretly, she'd imagined herself walking down the aisle to take the arm of an important producer or director. But now, as if waking her from a silly, selfish dream, Alvise challenged those requirements. That superficial image of the perfect man began to fade. Doubt rolled through her head, and warned her heart. Her image of her life at thirty began to change.

Showered, she pulled on a two piece bathing suit, a pair of denim shorts and a loose cropped tee. She left the bathroom and noticed the bed was empty. Outside her bedroom, she stopped in the hall when she saw Alvise moving about her kitchen. He looked as comfortable and commanding there as he did on his gondola. Her soul smiled, and she stood, unnoticed, and observed him.

He grabbed a Whole Foods bag from the refrigerator and extracted an assortment of roast turkey and avocado, and vegan sandwiches, and a container of grilled vegetables. He opened the Williams-Sonoma wicker picnic basket she had left on the counter the night before, and paused as if studying its content. He took the wine duffle from the basket and stuffed it with a bottle of white, and then placed the food into matching Tupperware containers.

Delighted at his ease in the kitchen, she watched him finger over and count the porcelain plates, wine glasses, and silverware and cloth napkins. She stepped into the kitchen and behind him, and wrapped her arms around his waist. The oven clock read eleven o'clock, and the sun was shining through the kitchen window. "Good morning."

"*Buon giorno.*" He turned, gave her face a leisurely once over and kissed her cheek. "Black, milk, with sugar?"

"A dash of milk, please."

"*Macchiato.*" He grabbed the milk container from the refrigerator, spotted her mocha with white, put the container back, and handed her the warm mug. He pulled her close and kissed the top of her head. "I'll be ready in an instant, and then we're on our way."

Thirty minutes away from home, the sunroof open, Victoria drove her white BMW north on the Pacific Coast Highway. She pulled off the busy coastal road and onto a quiet street, and into the semi-deserted beach parking lot. "Welcome to Paradise Cove," she said. *Thank goodness it's not crowded.*

Red, pink and purple bougainvillea plants climbed the rocky hillside and palm trees dropped their shade and dry leaves on the sand. The ocean was ink blue.

"How cold is the water?" Alvise looked out the car window.

"Cold enough that I won't be going in."

"Hmm…we'll see about that."

"I'm not getting out of the car until you understand that I don't like swimming in cold water."

He brought her hand to his lips and kissed it.

"Promise you won't throw me in."

"Okay, I promise. But I'm going in…now." He grabbed the picnic basket from the back seat, and rushed across the warm sand like an excited child. Near the shore, he set down the basket, tore off his t-shirt and sprinted into the surf.

She studied his uninhibited, honest manner, and smiled. No one, other than her father, made her smile the way Alvise could.

Slipping off her sandals, she crossed the warm sand behind him, and pulled the beach blanket from the wicker basket. The blanket spread out on the sand, she spread tanning lotion over her skin. She watched Alvise swim and dive like a dolphin at play. He was a breath of fresh air in a town overrun with self-conscious, self-centered men. She could see he didn't care if he impressed those around him. She could see that he lived without pretense. She liked that.

She met him at the water's edge with a dry towel, and hung it around his wet back. "Cold?"

"A little." He laughed, and then grabbed her, pulling her under the towel with him.

"No." She shrieked and laughed, breaking away from his cold torso and tender hold. "You promised you wouldn't..." She ran back to the blanket.

"I never promised I wouldn't hug you." He yelled out, catching up to her.

Victoria smiled up at him, the sun and breeze drying her damp skin. She lay down on the warm blanket and gestured for Alvise to join her.

His torso warmer, now, he pulled her close. There was tenderness in the way his mouth touched hers. His gentle kisses flavored with sea salt. She responded, desire leading her heart to a place she wasn't sure she was prepared to go.

His lips paused, and moved to her cheek. He pulled her hand to his chest and rolled onto his back, and softly sang. "*Io non ti conosco, io non so chi sei...sono nata ieri...*"

"I know that song."

He stopped singing, and raised his eyebrows. "You're familiar with Mina's songs?"

"I am with that one. My father used to listen to it."

"Do you know what the words mean?"

She shook her head. "No, but I recognize the tune."

Unguarded, his eyes sparked. He cupped her hand in both of his. "It goes something like this…*I don't know you, I don't know who you are, I was born yesterday in your thoughts, and yet today we're together… even if for only one day…you know I won't ask you, how long you'll stay, if my life lasts one day, I know I will have lived it...even just one day, but I will have stopped it together with you.*"

Tears shone in her eyes. She studied his sincere expression, and felt a lump rising in her throat. Surprised by her sentimental state, she moved closer to him and listened to the surf pounding against the shore. Unrecognizable emotions ran through her. She squeezed the hand of the dream lying beside her. She hadn't expected the intensity that came when they'd first met or the balance his honest ways helped her find since his arrival. She would have to give those feelings, and where they were taking her, some thought. That would wait until later. For now, she'd nap in the glorious winter sun, and relish in the comfort and pleasure his presence brought.

The sound of squawking seagulls diminished into the distance, and the ocean mist sprayed its salt their way. Falling asleep, she felt Alvise drop her hand and jump to his feet. She propped herself up on her elbows, and watched him race toward the ocean. *Another swim* she thought. He ran along the surf, zigzagged on the wet sand, and then stopped. Then he ran and zigzagged, again.

His back to the ocean, he extended his arms and bent his knees, stomping the wet sand and moving about as if performing a Maori war dance.

She looked around. The few people on the sand didn't seem to notice him. She pulled herself to her feet. *What is he doing?* Embarrassed, she questioned his silly ways. She hesitated, and then stepped off the blanket and closer to the water's edge. She sighed at his gestures. They weren't silly after all. A gray kitten was romping near the water.

Alvise stopped the kitten with one hand, and then swept it up and off the wet sand. He walked back to Victoria, the corners of his mouth turned up, and the ball of gray fur resting in his hands.

"Hey…little one. Where did he…she come from?"

Alvise sat down on the blanket, and turned the kitten stomach side up. "*He* is probably a stray cat. Didn't you see him race by?"

She shook her head, and sat down on the blanket next to Alvise. She took the kitten from his hands, and caressed it again, and again. The kitten purred and ran its rough tongue across her chin. She giggled and held it closer. "Do you like cats?"

"I do."

"When I was little, my dad brought one home. *She* was white with a black spot on her head. I named her Princess. But we couldn't keep her. My mom found out she's allergic to cat dander."

"When I was about six years old, I tried to teach the neighborhood cat to swim."

"Cats can't swim."

"Actually they can, for a little while."

"I'm afraid to ask how you discovered that." Holding the kitten to her chest, she dropped her gaze to Alvise's long strong legs. She imagined them shorter with scraped knees and wearing children's tennis shoes, and scurrying across cobblestone streets, chasing a cat.

"I was with Ciano. We were fishing from the side of a small canal and *Caigo,* the neighborhood cat, came by."

"*Caigo*?"

"It means fog in Venetian. *Caigo* was about the same color as this kitten." He petted the kitten's soft fur. "We weren't catching any fish, so Ciano got the brilliant idea to teach Caigo to swim."

"No."

"Being just kids, we thought cats were like dogs. So I picked up Caigo and put him in the water. When he swam back, we honestly thought we were teaching him to swim."

"You're lucky that didn't turn out bad."

"It didn't end there."

Victora pursed her lips, and held the kitten closer.

"Ciano picked up Caigo, again, and gently…really, it was gently…put him back into the canal."

That's awful she thought, but tried not to laugh. The image of Alvise and Ciano as innocent little boys trying to teach a cat how to swim made her smile.

"I'll never forget the blank stare on Ciano's face or the cold sweat that came over me when Caigo went under."

"You drowned the cat?" She stopped smiling.

"I jumped in after him. Fortunately, the tide was low, and I got to him in time."

"Thank goodness." Victoria let out a deep sigh, and hugged the kitten.

"I was a little less fortunate."

"Did *you* almost drown?"

"No. Ciano helped me and the cat out of the canal, but I was covered in sludge up to my thighs."

"Mud sludge or disgusting sludge?"

"The disgusting kind."

Victoria shuddered. Her chin leaning on the kitten, she squeezed her eyes shut, and refused the image of a little boy's short legs covered in mud, seaweed and sewage.

"My mom wouldn't let me in the house. She stripped me down to my underwear, pulled me back into the campo, and washed me off in the public fountain."

"Did you tell her about the cat?"

"I told her I was reeling in a big fish, and I fell in the canal. She knew I was lying. There are no big fish in the small canals."

"Did you get in trouble?"

"She put me in *castigo*…detention…for what seemed like an eternity."

"She grounded you?"

He nodded. "Caigo avoided us after that." He rubbed the kitten's belly, and let it nibble at his long fingers.

"If I were Caigo, I'd avoid you, too."

"There you are!" A woman dressed in a t-shirt, yoga pants and a white apron came striding up from the shore, kicking sand behind her with every step.

"Pardon me?" Victoria looked up at the woman.

"You've got my kitten. I'm the owner of the restaurant." She smiled and gestured past the pier, toward the beachfront café. "I was afraid he'd gotten too close to the water."

"He did get close." Alvise took the kitten from Victoria, and stood up. "*Ciao*, little *Caigo*."

Victoria watched Alvise stroke the kitten's fur, turn it around, and look straight into the cat's gray eyes. She'd never met a gentler man. "We had fun taking care of him." The corners of her eyes crinkled.

"I can spot cat lovers a mile away. If he wasn't the last one left from the litter, I'd let you two take him home. Stop by the restaurant, and have a drink on me." The woman took the kitten from Alvise's hands and tucked it in her front apron pocket. Holding her hand there, she hurried back across the sand.

"Why not have that drink right here." Victoria opened the wicker picnic basket, and pulled out two wine glasses. Alvise lifted the wine from the chest, and Victoria arranged the sandwiches on a plate. He uncorked the chilled bottle, and then poured the wheat colored liquid.

"Here's to childhood stupidity…." He sat back down, and raised his glass to hers.

"…and innocence."

He sipped the wine. "This is good."

"It's a California wine, from Napa Valley."

"Did you do anything as a kid that you aren't very proud of?"

She felt him scrutinize her face. She studied him take a bite off a turkey and avocado sandwich, and thought about the time she stole a greeting card from a Hallmark store. She sipped the fruity vintage, and wiggled her toes in the warm sand. "When I was twelve, I heisted a greeting card."

"And you did jail time for that." Alvise chuckled.

"I felt bad about it. I still do."

"Then why did you steal it? I'm sure it wasn't because you couldn't afford it."

"I was at a stationary shop, looking at cards for a friend's birthday. I didn't find one I liked, and when I left the shop I was still holding onto one of the cards."

"So technically you didn't steal it. You just forgot to put it back."

"I suppose."

"Then why didn't you take it back?"

"I wanted to. I was about two stores away when I realized I was still holding it. But I was with a girl whom I was hoping might be my friend. *She* was the girl in school who was the first to get a nose ring, never wore pastel colors and wore black nail polish. My mom wouldn't let me wear black nail polish until I graduated from college. God forbid I got a nose ring."

"I dated a girl like that in high school."

"You did?" She sat up straight. She hadn't thought about him with other women. Now she couldn't help but wonder if she fit in with his taste for the unconventional. A touch of jealousy tingled inside.

"She's a marine biologist now. And last time I saw her she was dressed in pink."

"Now you're making fun of me."

"No...it's true...well except for the pink dress part."

"So you're attracted to girls with a rough edge." Silly insecurities popped up. She remembered how she'd felt through high school. The girl inside remembered she'd once been considered a geek.

"I'm attracted to you, and there's nothing rough about what I see."

Victoria blushed. His straightforward ways made her feel sexy and safe. "I didn't take the greeting card back, because she would've seen I was a geek."

"*Sfigata*..you? Never."

"If *sfigata* means geek in Italian, then I was *sfigata*...with braces on my teeth and eyeglasses. I was quite a vision of beauty in my school uniform."

"Where did the eyeglasses go?"

"Laser eye surgery."

"Nah...I don't believe you spent one day of your life as a geek. You're too beautiful."

She leaned in and kissed him. Her eyes glistened, and she nudged him with her shoulder.

"That makes you an accidental thief and me a *would be* assassin." He placed his wine glass and sandwich down, and pulled her close.

"Tell me more about the girl in high school." *Was it serious?* she wondered.

"We lasted through college. Then she went to Portugal to get her Master's. I decided that being a gondolier was what I wanted most. She didn't approve. She wanted me to follow her, and find a teaching job at the university there. I thought about it for a while. But it wasn't what I wanted. I guess I didn't love her enough. Our relationship ended when she met the guy who is now her husband. They live in Lisbon. I think they have two kids."

Victoria raised her eyebrows. *Wow, two kids and a career.*

"It would be nice to have kids. Eleven is a good number."

Her mouth fell open. An Italian family with lots of kids was a stereotype, wasn't it? *He can't be serious.*

"I'd have my very own soccer team…you need eleven players." He laughed. "I could be their coach."

She laughed and sighed. *Thank God you weren't serious.*

"What about you? Do you want children?"

She'd never given children much thought. They belonged in the lives of women who drove SUVs, shopped at Target and posted every step of their infants' lives on social media networks. None of her friends, male or female, married or single, had kids. Like her, their goals and lives revolved around blossoming careers. There simply was no time for children, and she doubted she'd be good at raising them. "Having kids and a career can't be easy."

"You wouldn't be the first woman or man to do it."

"Sure…my mom did it. But she had help. I mean…kids are great. My ex had twins. But as hard as I tried, we couldn't relate to each other."

"He was divorced?"

"Separated, getting a divorce…when we met."

"Maybe that's why you had a tough time with his kids. I'm sure divorce is hard on kids."

"It was. That's why he went back to his wife. They decided to make it work."

"Ouch. That must have hurt."

"It did for a while…until I found out he was having affairs with other women while he was promising to divorce his wife to be with me."

"He sounds like a saint. Where did you meet him?"

"At an industry event. He's an Entertainment attorney. But being a jerk is what he does best."

Alvise chuckled.

"He made the promises, I fell for the lines." She thought about the promises. They'd travel the world, live in a million dollar home in Malibu, and throw lavish celebrity parties. "Unfortunately, it took me about two years to see the jerk part."

"Well, you saw it." Alvise brushed a curl from her forehead. "Anyone else…important since then?"

Hmmm. Where should I put you? Isn't it too soon to put you on the important list? Alvise was kinder, more handsome, and made her laugh more than Philip had. She felt prettier and happier in his company, too. Shouldn't that qualify him as important to her? Shouldn't that encourage her heart to continue to open the door she had closed tight against Philip? "Important? No."

Maybe not until now.

Chapter 10

EACH MORNING, BEFORE leaving Alvise's arms for the office, Victoria encouraged him to spend his day poolside, bike riding to Santa Monica or joining a soccer game on Venice Beach. Each evening when she returned home, she opened her apartment door to a warm embrace and flavors of his world. A soft kiss on the lips and a glass of Prosecco placed in her hand, she kicked off her heels and changed from her work clothes—the sound of soft opera and kitchen utensils clanging against pots and pans she'd never used. The delicious scent of simmering tomato sauce and crushed fresh basil or porcini mushroom risotto or his special egg and bacon *pasta alla carbonara*—a candlelit table set for two.

Since Alvise had arrived, she let her heart lean in closer to his. She worked eight instead of ten hour days, and waited for Chloe to call that meeting. What was it that her boss had hinted to when they'd unexpectedly met at the airport? The week went by without Chloe mentioning their meeting again. Then on Friday, all Chloe said was *be patient. An announcement will be made soon.* Was she hinting about a new Junior Agent position? Might it be Victoria's turn to be promoted? If not Victoria, who? If so, when would the announcement be made? She couldn't ask. It wasn't her place. She could only wait, and hope.

Saturday night, at precisely six forty-five p.m., Victoria pulled her sporty German import off of Sunset Boulevard and drove up the Beverly Hills Hotel's palm tree lined driveway. She took one final look in the rearview mirror. Lipstick—perfect. Hair—perfect. Straightening a Tiffany pearl necklace over her strapless neckline, she turned to Alvise. Sitting in the passenger seat and dressed in a black Brioni jacket and gray pants, he looked sexy and handsome. "Ready?"

He nodded.

A preppy looking valet swung open the car door. "Good evening. How long will you be?"

"We're here for the World Talent Agency Holiday party." She left the motor running, stepped onto the driveway, smoothed her bubble skirt and, taking Alvise's hand, walked toward the pink hotel's red-carpeted entrance.

Nervous, she glanced over each shoulder as if looking for support—and spotted Chloe's car parked out front between a Porsche and a Ferrari. No doubt about it, that was hers—after all, she had suggested the cranberry color. Chloe's first choice had been too traditional, and Victoria had convinced her that in sunny Southern California, as striking as the Tesla luxury electric car was, it needed to turn heads. She still thought it had been a good choice.

They stepped onto the Polo Lounge outdoor terrace. Twinkling lights twisted through tree branches and lush greenery. Victoria gave the space a slow once over. Silver and white floral arrangements and floating candles sat in the center of each round white-linen clothed table. A tall, fat Christmas tree, decorated in white-only, shimmered alongside a glass-topped table holding a silver Hanukkah menorah, five of its nine candles burning—symbols which acknowledged the agency's Christian and Jewish employees. Around the perimeter of the terrace, the outdoor heaters glowed. They warmed the winter evening, and had been placed, as she had requested, far enough out of sight not to ruin the elegant atmosphere. She took a second look around the festive space, and sighed at the celestial feel. It looked beautiful. The way Chloe had demanded—exactly how she had planned.

Victoria saw that Chloe, chatting with Howard Woodcock and his wife Emilie, had spotted them. Chloe crossed the terrace and greeted Victoria with an affectionate hug. Her familiar scent, mandarin orange and oriental spice, filled the air. Wearing a black tuxedo inspired dress—a diamond pendant gracing her modest cleavage—Chloe radiated power, and shook Alvise's hand. "Everything looks marvelous, Victoria. I especially like how they arranged the white orchids on the buffet tables. They cost a fortune. So, after the party, let's make sure they get delivered to the office."

"I've already made those arrangements with the florist."

"You did all this?" Alvise smiled.

"She's my star!" said Chloe.

Proud of her accomplishment, Victoria had never felt this insecure around Chloe. *Will I be ordering flowers my entire life?* She hoped Chloe couldn't see her heart pounding beneath her taffeta dress.

"You are the most handsome couple at this party." Chloe stopped a white-jacketed waiter, took two glasses of champagne from his silver tray, and handed them to Victoria and Alvise. She took another for herself. "Get something to eat…and then make sure you mingle. Agency parties are work, too. Now have fun." Chloe turned on her velvet heels and crossed the terrace. Victoria watched her command a waiter to remove used Champagne glasses cluttering the buffet table, and then join Howard, his wife, and the agency's partners and their companions at the center table.

Victoria and Alvise lined up to be served from one of four white-clothed buffet tables. Silver trays held fresh shrimp canapés, chicken salad and bacon in puffed pastry, fig and blue cheese popovers, and caviar garnished tidbits. The salad table sported large glass bowls. One filled with quinoa, kale and avocado, another with red cabbage and cranberries, and another with orange orzo, cubed zucchini and feta cheese. Another table, lined with silver chafing dishes, served up Kosher Hanukkah recipes: braised short ribs, crispy potato latkes, and baked salmon with herbs. The elaborate banquet, chased down with an appropriate amount of chilled Champagne, ended with the dessert table. There, tiered dessert plates of chocolate raspberry macarons and eggnog tarts crowned the end of a laborious yet prosperous year for the agency, and its employees.

"This is the fanciest party I've ever attended." Alvise placed his plate and glass of Champagne on the clothed table, and helped Victoria with hers. He pulled out the heavy iron patio chair and scooted it under her, and then took his place at the table, next to her.

His manner charmed Victoria, and seemed to do the same to her colleagues. He looked dashing, and her sense of them being a couple was more acute now. Proud to show him off, she noticed the glances and smiles thrown his way by the other women in the room and at their table. All appeared to be quite captivated by his good looks, too. The attention paid to him didn't make her jealous. She could see he only had eyes for her.

"You're a gondola?" asked Barbara, the office receptionist. Sitting next to Victoria, she batted her perfectly made-up eyelids.

"I'm a gondolier. My boat is a gondola."

"It's all the same to me. Are all the gondolas"—Barbara snickered—"oops . . . I mean *gondoliers* as cute as you?"

"My mom doesn't think so."

The ladies at the table laughed.

"But yes. I've got a few good-looking colleagues."

"Then I might visit." Amber, Howard Woodcock's executive assistant, raised her long manicured fingers, calling for another glass of Champagne from a passing waiter. "You can introduce me to one of those rugged, seafaring guys."

"Hey, princess, you better slow down there with the bubbly." Amber's date put a plate of short ribs and potato latke on the table in front of her. Then, sitting down across the round table from Alvise, he attempted to draw in his gut. "So you're a gondolier from Venice. I was there once, with my ex-wife...before we got married. Not my favorite place in the world . . . or maybe that's because I was with my ex-wife." He got a boisterous laugh from the others. "I do remember spending a fortune on the hotel. Always do when I travel—nothing but the best for the ladies in my life."

He winked at his date. "Don't remember the name, but it was right next to one of those gondola stations. You know which one I mean, Arturo…the *best* hotel in Venice."

"His name is Alvise, not Arturo." Amber pushed her plate of meat and potatoes aside, and lifted her Champagne glass to her glossy lips.

"Whatever…my ex-wife wanted to take a ride, but I didn't like the way those suntanned and tattooed boat paddlers were eyeing her. You know what I mean Arturo. My ex didn't seem to mind. Hell, I should've known right then that we were doomed. I could've saved a lot of money on legal fees."

Victoria found it insulting and gratuitous the way this man talked about his personal life, and the way he belittled gondoliers to mere 'boat paddlers'.

"I can see how some gondoliers might be a little intimidating," said Alvise. "But I can assure you that over the centuries those 'boat paddlers' have learned to bite their tongues before offending others. And if they were paying attention to your ex-wife that just means you've *always* had good taste in woman."

"Oh, isn't he divine?" said Amber.

"Yes, princess, you're living proof that I have good taste in women," said her date.

"Is it true that Venice is sinking?" Passing by, Emilie Woodcock stopped at their table. Dressed in a navy blue sequin dress, she seemed quite unaware that within her question might be an analogy for her own lifted face.

"Hello, Emilie." Victoria stood up and walked over to greet her. "Alvise, this is Emilie Woodcock, Howard's wife."

Alvise stood. "I haven't formally met Mr. Woodcock. But Victoria has mentioned his name. It's very nice to meet you, *Signora* Emilie."

"Would you like to join us, Emilie?" said Amber.

"No, dear…but thank you. I'll be on my way in a moment. I overheard your conversation and thought I'd ask about Venice sinking…I love that city so."

"Some say it's sinking…it's certainly settling," said Alvise. "Though I think the tide problem has more to do with the sea level rising. Venetians have always had to adapt to the sea." He paused, and reached for his Champagne. "One of the first things we learn as children is that the tide goes up and the tide goes down, every six hours. Only now, we have excessive high tide more often. At times the tide is so high, it's impossible to pass under some of the lower bridges by boat or by gondola. The more often and the higher the tides rise the more damage it causes to the city."

"Well, my dear Alvise, then maybe you can help me with something else I've never understood." Emilie adjusted the diamond bracelets around her thin wrist. "Was the seawater brought in before or after the city was built?"

"They built Venice in the lagoon *because of* the seawater," he said. "It's built on marshland, and the water protected the first inhabitants from invaders."

"So the water was already there . . . before the city was built."

"Yes, without question."

"Thank you. I love it when I'm right and Howard is wrong," said Emilie. "It was nice to meet you, Alvise."

"*Il piacere è stato mio*. . .it was my pleasure."

Emilie turned to Victoria, and whispered. "He's a charming fellow."

Victoria smiled, and watched Emilie move on to greet the Junior Agents at the next table. Refined and calm, referred to as the First Lady of Hollywood, Emilie worked the room. Table after table, she shook hands, and greeted the Agents seated at the tables which encircled the table of power. Victoria had been instructed to arrange the seating according to employee status. Rank was measured by how close they were to the table in the center of the patio. Victoria watched Emilie take her seat, and wondered if next Christmas she might be seated closer to the most powerful.

"Hey, Arturo . . . You could give us rowing lessons, couldn't you? It can't be that hard," said Amber's date.

Victoria's brows snapped together. "Alvise . . . his name is Alvise."

Alvise sat back down, and placed a comforting hand on Victoria's. "I'd be happy too . . . the next time you're in Venice. It should be amusing . . . for everyone."

Victoria held Alvise's hand, and observed the macho banter among the men and the quiet infatuation from the women. Alvise's indifference to it all made him even more appealing. Before her colleagues had met Alvise, she saw how they had struggled to put a label on him. Like Jackie had, most referred to his job as that of a limousine driver. Yet the reactions she witnessed, now, told her they'd begun to wonder if there might be more to this man, and his trade.

"Hello, Howard." Victoria looked up from the table. "We were just having a lovely conversation with Emilie.

"She told me. She loves it when I'm wrong."

Alvise stood, again, and extended his hand. "Alvise Moro. It's very nice to meet you."

Howard looked up into Alvise's eyes, and shook his hand. "Well this is a first. I've never met a gondolier."

"Would you like to join us?" Alvise pointed to an empty chair.

"Please, you sit down." Howard remained standing, and sunk his hands in his tailored pants pockets. "Tell me, how many gondolas do you have?"

Alvise sat down, again, and looked up at Howard. "I have one gondola, sir. Each gondolier has one…unless they also have a deluxe gondola. But there aren't many of those. They're only used for weddings or when dignitaries come to town."

"But you can have more than one license, right?"

"No. The licenses are issued and governed by the city…so only one license per gondolier."

"How many rides can you make in a day?"

"That depends on the season…we work more in the summer months, a lot less during the low season in the winter months."

"Well, how much does a gondola ride cost?"

"The present city tariff is 80 euros for 30 minutes."

Howard knitted his brow. He glanced over at Victoria, and then back at Alvise. The others at the table listened as if trying to understand a foreign language.

Interested, yet irritated by Howard's questions, Victoria listened, too. Howard seemed to be calculating Alvise's net worth.

It seemed as if he was asking himself: *Is this gondolier a pauper, and if so, why is she with him?* She watched Alvise. His comfort level with himself and his ability to shrug off, and at the same time comprehend, the reasoning for these intrusive questions demonstrated to her that he didn't need or want to impress anyone. He was who he was, and he was proud of it. She admired his dignity, and felt the door to her heart crack open a little more.

"Well…you're good looking enough to be in the industry. Can you act?"

"No sir. I can't act."

"Still, we might be able to use a gondolier with your looks. Tell you what. Next time our talent makes a film over there, we'll contact you. We like to shoot in Venice, even if it's expensive. Nine times out of ten, movies filmed there are box office hits."

"Howard." Chloe stepped up to the table. "I need to talk to you." Without waiting for a reply, Chloe whisked her colleague and longtime lover away from the assistants' table.

Victoria whispered in Alvise's ear. "I think we need to set up a question-and-answer session at our next party."

"They're only trying to understand a reality they know nothing about."

"Still, Howard's questions were far too intrusive."

"I'm used to getting asked those questions…especially from American tourists. I've found that once they realize I make a comfortable living being a gondolier, they back off."

"I've never asked you about that…about your income."

"I'll tell you about that. But right now, I'm still hungry."

"While you go to the buffet, I'm going to the ladies room."

"Can I bring you something?"

"No, I'm good."

Victoria left the terrace, crossed the dark carpeted Polo Lounge, and exited the bar known to host Hollywood's most famous stars and deal makers. She headed for the main lobby, and smiled at two slightly inebriated colleagues dressed in dark suits, walking in her direction.

"Hey, Victoria." The one wearing all black held up his hand, inviting her to meet his high-five. "Nice gig you organized."

She met his hand with hers. "Thank you."

"Yeah...great party...great Champagne." The other colleague held up his glass.

"The band should start playing in a bit, too," she said.

"Save me a dance," said the one in all black.

"Sure, I don't think my date will mind."

"I'll dance with your date!" said the other.

"I am *not* sharing him with *anyone*." She laughed, and continued across the vast lobby. Beyond the sweeping staircase and massive chandelier, she followed a brass arrow that indicated *Business Center - Restrooms*. Down the pink and green banana leaf wallpapered hallway, she placed her hand on the Ladies Room door knob, and heard voices coming from a nearby sitting area sheltered behind a tall planter box. When she heard Chloe's voice, and her name, Victoria dropped her hand from the door knob and inched closer to the conversation. Hidden by the tall planter and plants, she heard Howard's voice, too. She stood there, and listened.

"She'll come with me," said Chloe.

"So you've told her you're leaving...that we're leaving?" said Howard.

"Not yet. You haven't told *your* assistant, have you?"

"No. She can't be trusted with a secret like this. I've only told the agents we're taking with us, and swore them to secrecy."

"They better not talk."

"If they want to continue working in this town, they'll keep their mouths shut."

"I negotiated a Junior Agent deal for Victoria. God knows I should have promoted her ages ago. The new partners reneged at first, and then finally agreed."

"Kudos to you, and to her. I wouldn't take on a Junior agent without a portfolio."

"She's smart, and useful. Had this deal not come up, I would have promoted her anyway."

"I don't know. You're taking a risk. She can stay at World Talent. Let them promote her."

"Without me there, she'll never make agent. They won't keep her as an assistant once I'm gone either. She's too loyal to me. She'll jump at the chance to make Junior Agent and come with us."

"That's not my concern. We're about to become *bigger* than any major players in the industry."

"Then we're set for the 26th, the day after Christmas?"

"First thing in the morning, we show up at the new agency and messenger our resignation notices to World Talent. Simultaneously, we'll inform our clients that we're bringing them with us. The industry won't know what hit it."

"Now I just need to get Meryl to come with us. You know how loyal she is to World."

"She's a top client. So that could be a deal changer."

"Don't worry. I'll convince her."

Victoria's heart skipped. She couldn't believe what she'd heard. She left the planter box, and rushed into the Ladies Room. She steadied herself against the marble lined wall, and then sat in front of the neon lit mirror.

Joy rose from her stomach to her face. Tears of happiness wet her eyes. All along she knew Chloe was on her side. Now, her boss had knocked down road blocks to her career—because she was smart and useful. Her only option was to keep this a secret. Chloe would tell her when the time was right. After all, it was only until after Christmas. She'd continue in the role of her Executive Assistant for a few more days.

Excitement shot through her veins. She grabbed a tissue from the mirrored box, and blotted her happy tears. Her boss's know-how, thirst for power and profit had rewarded her years of dedication and hard work. She understood the competitiveness of the industry, the need to stay on top and keep this secret in order to hang onto lucrative clients. That's what attracted her to the Entertainment industry. That made her think she'd find a shining future at World Talent Agency. Now her career would bloom in this new agency.

Her elbows propped on the powder room table, she rested her chin on her clasped hands, and looked in the mirror. *If I were in Chloe's position, I'd do the same thing.*

The Ladies Room door swung open. Victoria looked up and in the mirror, and saw Chloe step inside. Victoria's face blanched, and she felt her excitement block in her throat.

"Hey, there," said Chloe. "Wait for me. I'll just be a minute."

"Okay." Victoria surveyed her boss in the mirror, snapped open her bejeweled clutch, and pulled out a tube of lipstick. She wouldn't say a word about what she'd overheard. The water closet door closed behind Chloe, and Victoria turned back to her own reflection. She swiped a line of burgundy color gloss over her lips, popped the lipstick back into her bag, and then cleaned smudges of mascara from under her eyes. At the sound of water flushing and the door lock clicking, she smiled, and she sat up straight.

Chloe strode over the marble floor to the wash basin. Washing her hands, she looked at Victoria in the mirror. "Enjoying the party?"

"Very much." Victoria stood on her heels, towering her boss by a few inches.

"You look happy. Something happen that I'm not aware of?"

"No...not really...I'm just pleased the party is going so well."

"I know you, Victoria. What's up?" Chloe smiled at her, and dried her hands on a cloth towel.

Victoria pursed her lips.

"How long have you been in here?"

"Long enough to freshen my lipstick."

"Any chance you overheard me talking with Howard?" Chloe's mouth set in a hard line.

Victoria looked at the marble floor, and nodded. "I swear I won't say anything to anyone."

"How much did you hear?"

Victoria looked around, and assured they were alone. She sighed, and kept her voice soft, "I know about the day after Christmas, and me getting promoted to Junior Agent."

"That promotion will only happen if you keep your mouth shut." Chloe tossed the damp towel through a hole in the marble countertop.

"You can trust me."

"Not a word to anyone, not even your neighbor's dog or cat or goldfish. Understand?"

"Not anyone. I'm so excited. I swear the words are locked in my mouth. Except for thank you! I really appreciate you going to bat for me. You won't be sorry."

"This move will be good for everyone involved…as long as you keep what you heard a secret. If this gets out, we're ruined."

"I've never betrayed you or the agency."

"Now would not be a good time to start."

Chapter 11

THEY LEFT THE office Holiday party behind and, when Alvise had buckled-up, Victoria pressed her foot to the floor, and sped the car down the Beverly Hills Hotel drive way onto Sunset Boulevard. Zipping through the light, night traffic, she thought about the conversation with Chloe. She'd finally have an office of her own, maybe with a view, and an assistant as dependable as she had been, and still was, to Chloe. No longer would she stand in the wings during awards season, she'd walk red carpets behind famous clients she'd call *hers*. She'd read scripts from well-known writers, and then decide whether to pass on them or pass them along to top box-office earning producers, directors and actors. The news, her promotion, she daydreamed about her future. Elation percolated through her pores, and she drove the car toward Pacific Coast Highway, and then turned onto Ocean Avenue.

"Pull over," said Alvise.

His voice jerked her out of her daydream. "Why?"

"You can park there."

"The curb is red."

"It's almost midnight. No one's going to notice."

"The Santa Monica police always notice."

"Then your surprise will have to wait."

"What surprise?"

"The one I want to surprise you with."

"That's not fair." *What if I get a ticket?*

"All is fair in love…"

Did he say love? Victoria swerved the car to the right and parked at the curb. "Okay, mystery man, now what?"

"What's up? You've hardly said a word since we left the party."

Victoria shrugged her shoulders, and shook her head.

"Is it that bad?"

Out the car window, the Santa Monica pier lights shimmered on the breaking Pacific Ocean waves. Days away from becoming a Junior Agent, she could see the headlines in Variety and the Hollywood Reporter: *Earthquake in Hollywood - New Talent Agency Shakes Industry*. She tapped her fingers on the steering wheel, and pried her mind away from that thought. No wonder Alvise could tell something was up. They'd grown close, and could read each other like lovers do. He'd chew the inside of his cheek, the same way she chewed her lip or tapped her fingers whenever she was nervous or thinking deeply. She trusted him, and longed to tell him the good news. Instead, she'd be professional and honest. She'd keep her promise to Chloe, and protect her career. A few more days—she'd tell him after Christmas, and the moment she set foot in her new office. "Things couldn't be better."

"Then let's go. Bring your scarf." Alvise opened the car door, and stepped onto the curb.

"Go where?"

"Do you trust me?"

She did. She trusted him like no other. She buttoned up her evening coat and draped her silk scarf around her neck. The December night felt crisp. Alvise wrapped her in his powerful embrace and led her down the sidewalk to the pier. Greeted by the whirling merry-go-round's melody and the Ferris wheel's bright neon lights, he stopped.

"Choose, the merry-go-round or the Ferris wheel?" he said.

"You want to go on one of the rides?"

"Take your pick."

Victoria was fascinated by his wonderful, childish way. She tilted her head to watch the big spinning wheel light up the sky. "I've never been on the Ferris wheel."

"Never…and you call yourself a Southern Californian? Okay…we're going on the Ferris wheel."

"It looks higher from here than it does from the street."

"Are you scared?"

"Just don't make it rock."

"And I thought you were a woman who wasn't afraid of anything."

"I'm not going up there if you..."

"Trust me." He took her hand in his. "Come on, before they close."

Victoria did her best to keep up with Alvise, and hurry across the pier's wood planks without twisting her ankle, or scuffing her holiday heels. She kept her eye on the giant yellow-neon wheel in the distance, watching it come to a lazy halt and then, unhurriedly, spin again. One by one, the wheel emptied its filled passenger cars onto solid ground. She felt Alvise anchor his arm around her, almost lifting and carrying her down the pier—and she felt safe. When the last car had been vacated the operator stepped from the control booth, and turned his back on them.

"Sir," said Alvise, at last within earshot. "Can we take a ride?"

The old man waved a crooked finger back at them, signaling *no*.

"But sir, please," said Alvise.

The man, once again, turned his curved back on them, limped toward the control booth, and padlocked the door.

"*Maledetto*...damn it."

Victoria loosened her scarf, caught her breath. "We'll come back another time."

She felt Alvise's arm drop from her waist, and watched him march straight to the operator. His exaggerated hand gestures and pleas surprised her, and got more dramatic with every shake of the operator's head. She heard Alvise speak rapid Spanish, as if he had spoken it his entire life. The old man looked back at him, continued to shake his head, waved his broom and walked further away. She stood back and watched, while Alvise stayed on the man's heels, and spoke either the right, or the wrong word. The man stopped within inches of Alvise, leaned on the broom handle and said something she couldn't decipher. She watched Alvise place a tip in the operator's free hand and a smile brighten the man's sun beaten face. When he dropped the bills in his soiled shirt pocket, she joined Alvise, again. The operator let them through, latched the safety chain across their bright yellow passenger car, limped back to the control booth, and then lifted them up into the night sky.

The city lights and coastline glittered below, and the brisk ocean air nipped at her face. The sound of waves crashing below got louder and faded away, and then got louder and faded away, again, as the Ferris wheel rotated on its journey.

"Come closer." Alvise opened his jacket to her.

Victoria snuggled next to him, "Did you know that we're sitting in a gondola?"

"Really?"

"Uh-huh . . . in English, these buckets are called 'gondolas.'"

"Then the gondola is more important than I thought." He leaned his head over the side and let out a quick, loud whistle.

The Ferris wheel slowed down.

"What are you doing?" she said.

"I asked him to give us a minute."

"You asked him to stop the Ferris wheel...with us way up here?"

He let out a sincere chuckle. "Don't worry."

"He better not leave us here."

"I doubt he will." Alvise looked over the side.

"What?"

He pulled her closer. "Let's enjoy this beautiful view."

"I can't look down. It makes me dizzy."

"Then look out, along the coast."

She leaned against his extended arm and took a long, deep breath, and the scent of saltwater filled her nostrils. The cold ocean breeze rustled through her hair, and the gondola swayed and rocked as gentle as a baby's cradle. She rested her head on his shoulder, and looked up at the stars. "It's quiet up here...peaceful."

"What do those lights remind you of?"

"Twinkling stars."

"No, those…over there."

She shifted her weight, and popped her head up, "On the hillside?"

"*Sì.*"

Christmas lights. "A billion white blinking Christmas lights."

"It's the right season. But do they remind you of anything else?"

"Is my surprise a guessing game?"

"Maybe."

"Then give me a clue."

"No clues."

"I told you what they remind me of, so it's your turn."

"The surprise is yours, but you have to give me a better description than Christmas lights."

"That's the literature grad in you…isn't it?"

"I suppose. Come on."

She tightened her scarf against the midnight breeze, and then leaned back on his shoulder to contemplate a better comparison. She enjoyed this game, and his playfulness. They soothed her, and lightened the desire to tell him about her encounter with Chloe. She closed her eyes to the gentle kiss he placed on her forehead, and thought a moment longer, and then opened her eyes, again. "I got it. They remind me of the tiny white rhinestones on a velvet evening coat my mother had when I was little. She looked beautiful in it, and wore it on every special occasion. I remember her saying wearing it made her feel like Lady Diana."

"That's a winning analogy." Alvise reached into his jacket, and handed her a small box. "I hope you like your surprise."

The lights along the coast dimmed in comparison to the excitement she saw in his eyes. She hesitated before opening it, filling her lungs with the fresh ocean air while cradling the elegant leather box in her hands. One thought ran through her mind. *Was it a ring?* Her heart fluttered and her breathing seemed to stop.

Between Venice and Los Angeles, they'd physically spent ten days together. That brief time had done much to make her feel secure, and fall fast for him. Though she wouldn't concern herself yet about what tomorrow would bring, she now considered Alvise in terms of *more than a vacation affair*. What they had, now, made it easy for her to admit: She loved being with him.

"What is it?"

"Open it."

Her hands trembled as she lifted the box's leather lid and read BUCCELLATI engraved in gold on blue satin. Set in velvet sat the same ruby-and-diamond ring she had admired and tried on in Venice.

"I can't believe you chose this ring for me." Her mind reeled back to that morning in Venice when, for fun, she and Jackie had entered an exclusive jewelry store near Piazza San Marco.

"If you don't like it, I can take it back."

"No. I love it. When I was in Venice, a kind salesman in a jewelry store near St. Mark's Square humored Jackie and I by pulling this very ring from the store window. He let me try it on. I'm sure he knew I had no intention of buying anything in his shop."

"That's my uncle's shop. It had to be him. His is the only store in Venice that sells Buccellati. I wanted to get you something really nice, so he said I can pay for it over time."

"Your uncle? That's a crazy, wonderful coincidence." Her eyes widened and she squeezed him so tight she didn't notice the gondola swaying.

"Venice is small…but…yeah, it is a coincidence. Here, let me do that." He took the ring from the box, slipped it on her finger, and sealed it with a tender kiss.

She extended her hand, and admired the sparkling stones. "This is an extravagantly beautiful Christmas present, Alvise. Thank you. I'm sorry I don't have yours here."

"*Amore*, this isn't your Christmas present."

"Then, what is it?" Her voice quivered, and her heart dropped.

He took her hands in his. "Think about it. I chose to work as a gondolier instead of a profession using my degree, and you chose to visit Venice over Portofino. If we hadn't made those choices we would never have met. Now, I discover that you tried this ring on at my uncle's store before I picked it out for you. I think the universe is telling us we belong together."

"What are you saying?"

"With this ring, I'm asking you to come back to Venice with me."

She studied his sincere eyes, and felt as if her lungs had shut down. "You mean to visit…take another vacation, right?"

"I'm proposing to you."

She brought her hands to her mouth, and swallowed hard. How could she say yes…or no? How could she move to Venice?

How could she not tell him about her promotion? How could this happen within days of her starting her dream job?

"It's all fast and sudden, and I understand it's a surprise. But I love you, Vittoria. I know that. And I want you in my life, forever. I want to marry you."

Tears pooled in her eyes, and she listened. *No. This can't be happening. Not now.*

"I'm not a rich man, but I can guarantee that I'm a hard worker, and that you'll always have a sturdy house to call home, a warm bed with me in it, and lots of great food...and wine...on the table."

Acknowledgement crossed her face. She saw the title *Junior Talent Agent* on a business card after her name, and the company car and the perks that went with that earned promotion. She saw the luxurious beachfront home she always thought she and her imagined lawyer or producer or film director husband would buy. She heard doubts about a Hollywood marriage rolling through her head, and the arguments that would surely go on when that husband came home late at night or called to tell her he had another business dinner. Instead with Alvise, she saw comfortable and secure, yet simpler, surroundings filled with love and honesty. A solid, if more modest, home life like the one her mother and father had built around her. And she saw the door slam shut on her cherished career.

"Will you, Vittoria? Will you marry me?"

She exhaled and looked back at the glistening ruby-and-diamond ring . . . the twinkling lights along the Pacific coast . . . and the man she was falling in love with. She'd never felt so sure about a man, and so unsure about the rest of her life. "It's been an overwhelming night…for so many reasons. I wish I could explain, but I can't…not now, anyway."

"It's too soon, right? I was reckless…I should've waited."

"I'm flattered and charmed…the ring is beautiful…you're more than wonderful. But I just don't know?" *What about my family…my friends…my promotion.* "Would you move here?"

"I would do anything for you…but what kind of job am I qualified to do here?"

"You could teach."

He shook his head. "I have a degree, but no experience teaching. No university here would hire me, certainly not for a decent wage."

"There are gondolas here, too. I've seen them in the marina around my apartment, and in Newport Beach. You could do what you love here. "

He held her hands in his, and then kissed them. "Rowing a gondola in a beautiful California Marina or bay is wonderful, but it isn't the same as being a gondolier in Venice."

But you're asking me to leave everything.

"I hope my reasons don't sound selfish…they're not meant to be. It's just that I don't know how to do anything else."

She sighed. "It's not simple for me either."

"Of course not." He caressed her cheek. "When life got tough or decisions needed to be made, my grandfather used to say, *Quando si chiude una porta, si apre un portone.*"

"When a door closes a bigger door opens?"

He nodded. "Won't you help me open the bigger door?"

Chapter 12

ON CHRISTMAS DAY, Victoria parked her car on the wide coral tree lined street where, as a child, she had learned to ride a bicycle. She took Alvise's hand, and they walked past the three-car garage and up the brick path to the Greco Family's stylish Brentwood home. Purple and magenta bougainvillea blazed across freshly painted white stucco walls. The properly trimmed lawn looked as if it had never been violated by a stray dog or a fallen leaf. They paced themselves past the shaded planter box of hydrangeas, and then up steps that put them at the front door. Shadows moved behind the double-doors' beveled glass, and muffled laughter came from the other side of the bay window.

"You didn't tell me you lived in a mansion." Alvise eyed the tall portico.

"It's more of a house than a mansion."

"My house is a house. In Venice this would be called a palace."

"Mom told Dad what she wanted, and though his construction company builds hotels, he had them build this. I think it's a bit pretentious."

"I don't think so."

"I'd prefer a home where you didn't need an intercom to talk to each other." Victoria gave him a nervous smile, and then gave his lips a light kiss. She straightened his collar, and then adjusted the hem of her wide leg jumpsuit over her strappy heels. She turned the brass door handle, but it was locked. She pressed the doorbell, and they waited.

A woman wearing an apron and practical shoes greeted them. "Merry Christmas." Her Eastern European accent slight. She stepped aside, and they entered the huge foyer, and the smell of furniture polish and fresh cut flowers. A crystal chandelier hung in the gentle curve of a sweeping staircase, and spilled light onto white enamel walls. Shiny black and white marble, set like a chess-board, spread beneath their feet and ended on the opposite side of the house, where a wall of French doors opened onto a rose garden and a built-in swimming pool.

Victoria hugged the woman, and kissed her round face. "Olga, *this* is Alvise."

He held a wood wine box embossed BERTANI in one hand, and shook Olga's hand with the other.

"Olga is the one who keeps us in line, and this monster of a house spotless."

Victoria noticed his eyebrows rise, and hoped he didn't feel uncomfortable. She wondered if she should have told him about the house or that as far back as she could remember her parents had had a housekeeper. She'd grown up in a privileged household—but she considered Olga part of the family. Out of all the housekeepers that had come and gone, Olga was her favorite, and she had endured her mother's perfectionism the longest.

She watched Olga's eyes shift from Alvise's face to his leather loafers, and then back again. Relieved, she sighed when Olga smiled kindly at Alvise and took the wine from his hands. Victoria hooked her left hand on Alvise's arm.

Olga set the wine down on the Biedermeier hall table, and next to a vase filled with white hydrangeas. "Your mother should be down in a moment, and your father is in the family room with the others." Her eyes smiled, and then shifted to Victoria's right hand and the ruby ring on her finger. Her eyebrows rose. "Please join the others. I need to check on the caterers." Olga left the foyer, and headed for the kitchen.

Victoria tightened her hand around Alvise's arm. Walking toward the chatter of voices, they crossed the long foyer past her parents' collection of modern art. Watching Alvise study a 3 ft. x 3 ft. painting of haphazardly stacked books, she paused next to him.

"This is nice. I like the colors." Alvise stepped back, and observed the painting.

"My mom bought it a long time ago from a gallery, somewhere in the mid-west, before the artist became well known."

"I'm sure I saw something similar to this at the Venice Biennale."

"Could be. The artist's paintings hang in the lobby of One World Trade Center, too."

"Wow." He swallowed hard. "Then this must be worth a fortune."

She shrugged her shoulders, and led him down the hall.

Each day spent with Alvise nudged her heart closer to surrender. But the excitement of soon becoming a Junior Agent commanded the notion of moving to Venice to the corner of the attic. Now, holding his arm with one hand, they entered the family room. Plush and white, the wall-to-wall carpet complemented the French doors and deepened the tone of the pearl gray walls, and velvet overstuffed sofa and side chairs. Her nerves bubbled beneath the surface. She waved to her father with her free hand. Too kind, too educated, the chances of him rejecting Alvise were slim. Still, her palms moistened and her hands shook. She wanted them to like each other. Wearing the Ralph Lauren shirt and khaki slacks she'd bought him for his birthday, wisps of gray highlighting his dark curly hair, her father smiled back, and her heart sank a little. She rarely kept secrets from her father. Now, she was hiding two.

She thought about their Saturday morning ritual, and how he would sit across the booth from her at their favorite coffee shop in Beverly Hills. She always ordered blueberry pancakes and he, Eggs Benedict. He'd drink his coffee black, and she'd splash the stack with maple syrup, and tell him about her job, her dilemmas and decisions. He'd listen, and never interrupt. It didn't matter if he agreed with her choices. He supported her. Since Alvise had arrived in town, they hadn't had a Saturday morning together. There hadn't been time. Though she missed those moments together, for now it was better they hadn't met. How could she not talk to him about her promotion or explain that the ruby ring on her right hand was meant to be worn on her left? One more day, and she would officially hold the Junior Agent title. Then she could tell the world that years of ordering flowers and taking notes had finally paid off. Still, only a few weeks remained until Alvise returned to Venice. *What will my life look like, now, without him?*

Standing at the long white enamel bar, her father lifted his beer from the black marble counter. He headed toward them, leaving her Aunt Iris and Uncle Bob laughing at what was probably one of his silly jokes.

"Merry Christmas, Dad."

"Merry Christmas, honey." He leaned down, and kissed her on the cheek.

"Dad, *this* is Alvise."

"*Buon Natale, Signor Greco.*" Alvise extended his hand.

"*Buon Natale a te*, Alvise. Please, call me Michael." Michael met Alvise's hand, and shook it.

"Thank you, sir…Michael."

"Welcome to our home."

"It's very nice to be here."

"I'm sure Victoria told you my family was originally from Italy…Calabria."

"She did. It's a beautiful region…especially the seaside."

"I haven't been since I was a young man. Victoria's mother and I traveled through Italy…riding trains and carrying backpacks. We loved Venice. But our budget then didn't allow for a gondola ride. I'd like to return and do that someday."

"I'd be honored to take you as my guests."

"We'd like that. Now, what can I get you to drink?"

"A beer sounds good." Alvise pointed to the bottle of Blue Mountain in Michael's hand.

"Champagne for me." Victoria smiled at her dad, and then reached up and gave him a kiss on the cheek. "Thank you."

"For what?" said Michael.

"Just…thank you." *Could I move a continent and an ocean away?*

Michael's smile faded. He looked at Victoria and then at Alvise, and then at Victoria, once again. He gave her a kiss on the forehead. "I'll have the bartender send the waiter over with your drinks."

"Okay…but where's mom?" Victoria watched her father head back to the bar.

"I'll go check."

"Merry Christmas." A chorus of greetings came from her relatives.

Victoria leaned over and kissed her grandmother's powdered cheek. "Alvise, I'd like to introduce you to my Grandmother… Eunice."

Eunice, the family matriarch, dressed in a jacquard jacket and skirt, an emerald green scarf tied around her lavender-white hair, put her gin and tonic down on the side table, and stood up from the sofa.

"*Signora* Eunice, no need to stand up." Alvise extended his hand.

"Young man, when you get to be my age and you *can* still stand, you do so whenever possible." Her accent was British. She took his hand and held it, and looked through pastel colored eye-glasses. "Handsome, and has a good handshake. You can read a person's character by how they shake hands."

Victoria smiled, triumphant at her grandmother's approval of Alvise.

"Then you must have a fine character...Signora Eunice." Alvise placed his free hand on top of hers.

"Oh my...he's charming, too." She gave his face another hard look, and held onto his hand until she was seated, again.

Victoria adjusted a silk throw pillow behind her grandmother's back, and then turned to the other relatives standing nearby. "Aunt Iris and Uncle Bob, this is Alvise. Aunt Iris is my mother's sister.

"Welcome." Aunt Iris stood behind the sofa, and swirled her pomegranate martini.

"Good to have you here." Uncle Bob held a beer bottle in one hand, and shook Alvise's hand with the other.

"It's nice to be here, and to meet you all."

"And this is Eddie...the best cousin a girl could ask for." Victoria stepped around the white stone coffee table, and opened her arms to her cousin.

Eddie slipped his hands out of the pockets of his corduroy slacks, and adjusted his horn-rimmed eyeglasses. "We're more like brother and sister, than cousins." He wrapped her in a bear hug.

Eddie, older than Victoria, was there during the dark days that followed her breakup with Philip. After she'd cried her eyes red on his shoulder, he said, *No man dumb enough to leave you is worth one tear let alone a thousand.* That's when he pulled her out of bed, tossed her a pair of jeans and a sweatshirt from her closet, and sat her on the back of his Harley-Davidson. The wind in her hair, they shot up Pacific Coast Highway. At a dive café on the beach, she drank beer and he drank water, and they devoured a bucket of steamed clams and mussels. Watching the sunset over the ocean, he handed her a rock as big as a baseball, and a pen. *Write his name on it,* he had said. So she did, and then she stood, and hurled that rock, and metaphorically Philip, as hard as she could out of her life, and into the ocean. A silly, symbolic gesture, it helped her move on. Eddie's opinion of Alvise mattered. "Where's the girlfriend?" said Victoria.

"Apparently, with some Silicon Valley guy."

Victoria frowned and squeezed Eddie tight. "I'm sorry."

"I never liked the girl," said Eunice. "She was too involved with herself to be involved with anyone else."

"If only I had your intuition, Grandmother," said Eddie.

The waiter approached Victoria. "Miss, here's your Champagne…and for you sir, a Cold Mountain beer." He turned to Eddie.

"I think the beer is for Alvise," said Eddie.

"You take it. I can wait for another one."

"Thanks, but I'm not drinking."

"At all?" said Victoria.

"The project I'm working on hit a few glitches. I've got to go in tomorrow."

"Eddie works for NASA, at the Jet Propulsion Lab in Pasadena." Victoria turned to Alvise.

Alvise's eyes widened. He lifted the beer bottle from the waiter's silver tray. "Are you an engineer?"

"I'm an astrophysicist."

"He inherited his brains from his mother," said Uncle Bob. "While I'm running supermarkets, she's teaching physics at the University."

Aunt Iris drank her martini slowly.

"I did better in the Humanities," said Alvise.

"Some brains are better suited for classical studies," said Eunice.

"And then there are those, like Mom, who excel in both science and humanities." Victoria raised her glass, and sampled the chilled sparkling wine.

"God decided to give our family big egos and a shrink to keep them tame," said Eunice.

Alvise chuckled. "Shrink? Is that slang for Psychiatrist?"

Victoria smiled at that, and watched him from across the coffee table. "It is. And we use it so flippantly here to refer to my mom that I've never stopped to think how silly it might sound."

Eunice lifted her glass from the side table, and finished off her drink. "Don't let these titles and degrees fool you, Alvise. We're simply another stressed out family of over achievers."

Alvise listened, and raised the beer bottle to his lips.

"Alvise has a degree in Italian Literature." Victoria moved from her cousin's side, and back to Alvise's arm.

"But you're a gondolier," said Eddie.

"I chose to continue my family's tradition."

"It must be nice…working outside in the fresh air," said Eddie.

"It's one of the benefits."

"I've been to Rome…on a work assignment…but never to Venice. Victoria tells me the word *beautiful* doesn't do it justice," said Eddie.

"It doesn't…not in any language," said Alvise.

"I must have been fifteen when I went to Venice on holiday with my mother. It was before the Germans occupied it," said Eunice. "I got my first kiss there."

"You never told me that." Victoria's eyes lit up, and the nervousness that had accompanied her into the room, somewhat, subsided.

"She never told me either." Aunt Iris stepped closer, and sat opposite of Eunice, on the sofa.

"Out of respect for your grandfather and your father, I never mentioned my first kiss."

"Who was the man who kissed you?" Aunt Iris emptied her martini glass.

"He was a strapping young Italian, a few years older than me. Black hair slicked back, and a fine wool suit. I can still remember the fresh smell of the fabric. It was the last good wool I'd smell for some years to follow."

Victoria sat on the arm of the sofa, next to her grandmother, and listened.

"You see, in the early 40s in England, new fabric was hard to come by, and the British wore their older clothing with pride… as a way of supporting the war effort. But this young Italian man's suit smelled new. I wish I could remember his name. He said his father was a Count, and he kissed me in the courtyard that bared the family name. It wasn't far from our hotel…The Bauer."

"Corte Barozzi is near The Bauer Hotel. It's named for a palace that once stood there. It was owned by a noble family," said Alvise.

"Barozzi…you're right, dear Alvise. That was his last name… Or so he said."

"Grandmother, a Venetian Count. That's incredible. Did you ever see him again?" Discovering another link that tied her family to Venice made Victoria's grin widen.

"The war started and ended, and then I met and married your grandfather. But that first kiss left me with fond memories of that romantic city." Her ash colored eyes sparkled. "Now, Victoria, will you please go to the bar, and ask the bartender to make a Hendricks gin and tonic the way they were intended to be drunk. The one the waiter brought me had too much tonic. And tell him to give it a solid twist of lime."

Victoria turned to Alvise. "Would you like another beer?"

"No, I'm fine." He took a swig from the brown bottle.

"Another one, Mother? It's not even four o'clock," said Aunt Iris.

"Iris, my bladder may not hold water like it used to, but I can sure as hell hold my liquor."

Laughter shot through the room. Alvise rushed his hand to his mouth, and blocked the beer from spewing out.

"Get your aunt another martini, too." Eunice winked.

Aunt Iris lifted her eyes to the ceiling and tossed her hands up in the air.

Victoria left her wine glass on the side table, and went to the bar. She leaned on a bar stool, and waited for the bartender to prepare the drinks. She watched Alvise get on well with her family. Laughing, he finished off a pleasant conversation with Eddie, and then moved to the silver-framed photographs on the Grand piano. He tilted his head at one of a young, rounder image of her wearing a white dress and veil, kneeling and holding a rosary, as if praying. Then he picked up another, taken a few years later, of her with her mother and father, standing on the wharf in San Francisco. She observed him set down the frame, and browse over a dozen or so still testimonies of her childhood. He bent forward and, without picking up the large frame from the center of the others, studied the wedding portrait of her parents. His shoulders rose and he exhaled deeply, and nodded to no one but himself.

She couldn't keep him waiting much longer for her answer.

Entering the room with Michael, Rose Greco slipped a smooth lock of gray behind one ear and, with eyes that revealed she had once been even more beautiful, she scanned the large salon full of guests. She wore a silk blouse and a pair of matching palazzo pants. Satin ballerina shoes covered her feet, and a large solitaire diamond hung around her neck. She paused, greeted and kissed her guests, laughed, paid and accepted compliments, and made her way toward Alvise.

"*Benvenuto*," she said. "Alvise…is it? That's a charming name."

"*Grazie, Signora Greco.* It's a traditional Venetian name."

"Merry Christmas, Mom." Victoria crossed the room from the bar. She handed her aunt the cranberry martini, and then gently placed the gin and tonic in her grandmother's gracious hands. She retrieved her glass of Champagne from the side table, and joined her parents and Alvise. Standing by the piano, she kissed Rose's rouged cheek. Embraced by her mother's jasmine and may-rose scent, her thoughts skated back to her childhood, and those nights when Rose would sit by her bedside and read to her out loud.

Night after night, little Victoria would pull *The Napping House* from her wooden bookshelf, and insist her mother read the rhyme about a grandmother and her precious things piling up on top of each other, and falling asleep on an old bed. The book's delightful, blue illustrations never failed to call up sweet dreams. Now, looking at her mother, those precious memories touched a soft spot. *I have so much to say goodbye to, if I were to say yes.* "You look and smell beautiful, Mom."

"So do you, sweetheart." Rose touched Victoria's cheek, gave her an approving once over, and then eyed the wine glass in her right hand. "Are you driving?"

"Let her enjoy a glass of wine," said Michael.

"Then eat something." Rose raised her hand at the waiter carrying the appetizer tray. "One should never drink on an empty stomach."

"Whatever you say, Mom." Victoria rolled her eyes up to the crystal chandelier and the light it splashed across the ceiling. She sipped her wine.

"Thank you for including me." Alvise nodded to Rose, and then lifted a spinach and cheese popover from the waiter's tray.

"Victoria's friends are always welcome in our home."

"I understand that you speak Italian," said Alvise.

"Only what I learned from my husband. But I do love Italy. The Amalfi Coast in particular. The saltiest sea I've swum in… and those Sorrento lemons. *Sono deliziosi.*"

"Speaking of friends…" Michael grinned and went to the foyer.

"Jackie." Victoria's face lit up.

Wearing an oversized sweater and velvet skinny jeans, Jackie hugged Michael and entered the room. The plush carpet silenced her ankle-boots' chunky heels. "Hey, everyone…Merry Christmas." She hugged Victoria and Alvise, and then turned to Rose.

"Hi, Rose. My mother sent a plate of homemade chocolate brownies. I left it with Olga." Jackie kissed Rose on the cheek.

"Thank *you* and your dear mother. You're staying for dinner, right?" said Rose.

"Another time? I promised my mother I wouldn't be too long."

"There's plenty to eat, if you change your mind." Rose set her elegant stride toward the bar. Her force and movement commanded the air around her, as if dispersing it in the room. She gave the barman orders to pour the guests more drinks, and told the waiters to keep the appetizers coming.

"It's great to see you Alvise." The corners of Jackie's blue eyes crinkled.

"It's good to see you, too."

"How's Ciano?"

"He's in the Caribbean…so I guess he's fine."

"Lucky guy…tell him I said hello when you next see him." Then Jackie turned to Victoria. "Thanks for the invite."

"Hey Jackie…it's been a while."

"Eddie?" Jackie's jaw dropped open.

"How are you?" Eddie gave Jackie a lopsided grin, and pushed a lock of thick hair off his forehead.

"I'm great…wow…you look…*good*."

"Thanks. You're as pretty as I remember." Eddie sunk his hands deep into his pants pockets.

"Last time I saw you, you were..."

"Overweight..." Eddie nodded.

"I wasn't going to say that."

"It's okay...I get that reaction a lot. Actually, it makes all those grueling hours at CrossFit classes worth it."

"I've wanted to try CrossFit."

"What's CrossFit?" said Alvise.

"It's an intense, total body workout." said Victoria. "I'll stick with yoga."

"I go to a gym downtown...on Hill Street. It's close to my condo," said Eddie.

"Hill Street is close my office," said Jackie.

"Come by. I'll introduce you to my trainer."

Jackie pursed her lips.

"Or maybe not?" His smile faded.

"No...I mean...yes. I'd like that."

"Are you on Facebook, Instagram...Twitter?"

"All the above," said Jackie.

"I'll be in touch." The expression in Eddie's eyes said he would. "Can I get you something to drink?"

"Sparkling water would be great."

"What about you, Vittoria?" Alvise put his hand on Eddie's shoulder.

"Thank you, but I'm good."

Jackie tilted her head. Her eyes glued to Eddie's backside as he and Alvise walked to the bar. "Wow...your nerdy cousin is *hot*."

"The girlfriend is gone, too." Victoria watched the men walk away, and twisted her ring around her finger.

Jackie looked down, and at Victoria's right hand. "Is that the ring we saw in Venice?"

Victoria bit her lip.

Jackie's eyes lifted to Victoria's. Her mouth dropped open, again.

"It's just a ring."

"A damn expensive one."

"Would you like an appetizer?" The waiter held out a tray of cheese and bacon stuffed mushrooms.

Jackie pressed her lips together, and shook her head.

"Nothing for me either. Thank you." Afraid to admit to anyone, including herself, that she was falling in love, Victoria listened to the screaming in her head instead: *Are you nuts? You can't move to Venice. You have too much to lose.* Yet she wanted to confide in Jackie, and tell her about the honest sentiments that had tied ribbons around her heart. The soft, loving feelings she'd never felt before. The ones that told her Alvise was one of a kind—and she'd be stupid to let him go.

"Well? Is there something you need to tell me?"

Victoria shook her head, and felt her purse vibrate. She reached inside and pulled out her iPhone. "It's work. I've got to take this."

"On Christmas Day?"

"Stuff is happening." Victoria hurried across the family room and crossed the corridor to the study, and closed the door. "Merry Christmas, Chloe."

"Same to you, dear," said Chloe. "Forgive me for bothering you today…so many last minute details to take care of before we go to press tomorrow."

"No problem." *I can't wait.*

"I'm calling because, as I feared, Meryl refuses to leave World Talent and come with us."

"Oh, dear."

"Our new partners are *not* happy. We've been in negotiations for days. But now we've found common ground."

"Great. Anything I can do before tomorrow?

"Yes…understand that one of the things we need to do is take a step back. I'm bringing you along as my Executive Assistant."

"What?" Victoria fell back, leaning against the antique desk.

"Meryl not coming with us decreases the value of our portfolio. I can no longer quantify bringing you along as Junior Agent when you have no portfolio of your own."

"But you said…"

"Be patient."

Patient? You said I should have been promoted a long time ago—that I would have been if we had stayed at World Talent. I heard you tell Howard that at the office Christmas party.

"In a year or so we'll talk about that promotion."

Talk about it…in a year or so?

"My hands are tied."

Damn it, Chloe! I trusted you. What about that plaque in your office? The one that says: There's a special place in Hell for women who don't help other women. *How can you preach that and then go back on your promise to me?"*

"We make a good team. I'll continue to nurture you and teach you. You've come a long way under my supervision. No one did that for me."

Victoria listened, and watched the daydream of her office with a view and her walking red carpets fade away.

"Be in the office tomorrow at eight o'clock sharp. You'll see. This is going to be grand."

Victoria set her smartphone on the desk, and fell into her father's leather arm chair. *Now what? What incentive do I have to go into the office tomorrow?* She understood Chloe had to protect the new agency's best interest. But now, their work relationship, she didn't trust her anymore. *I'll spend the next year or so like I've spent the last four—ordering flowers, arranging parties and making travel arrangements. With Chloe gone to the new agency, the top brass at World Talent Agency won't keep me there either.* She was stuck.

Her heart raced, and her breathing quickened. She tapped her index finger on the desk. "Merry Christmas to me," she said. She gathered her wits and grappled for a strategy, and came up with nothing. She pulled herself out of the chair, and dragged herself back to the family room. Standing at the entrance, she locked eyes with Alvise. He smiled, and seemed to know something wasn't right. She explored his face. Sweet emotion stirred inside, and she listened to her heart. Drowning out the noise, it wasn't screaming 'he's the one'. No, it was quiet, and determined to make her listen. Love whispered and dimmed her disappointment, and then freed the feelings she'd been denying. Flexible in her career, she knew there was no negotiating with the heart. Either it was love or it wasn't.

She glanced around the room. Everyone was there, except Olga. "Would you ask Olga to come in here?" she said to the waiter. When he moved away, Victoria felt her heart flutter faster. Pressing a hand against her chest, she took another deep breath to calm her nerves. "Mom, Dad... everyone..."

"Did something happen?" whispered Alvise.

"It opened."

Alvise looked puzzled, and shook his head.

The murmur in the room quieted, and the attention turned to her. Standing near the piano, she reached for Alvise's hand, and felt her own shake. Her heart pounded beneath her jersey jump-suit. She surveyed the room and the people she loved, and cleared her throat. "It's so special to be here with all of you today. You are the most important people in my life, and I thank you for the warm welcome you've shown Alvise. Christmas is my favorite day of the year…" Her eyes glistened. "So there is no better moment than today to..." She let go of Alvise's hand, and removed the ruby ring from her right hand, and handed it to him. She saw his shoulders slump, and sadness turn his face sallow. She placed her hand on his arm, and noticed Olga entering the family room, and looking her way. Victoria turned to her parents. "Mom…Dad… not long ago, someone special told me that when a door closes a bigger door opens. A few minutes ago, an important door closed on me. It's a hard pill to swallow, but now I see that I wasn't meant to walk through that passage. Instead, a bigger, brighter door, *un portone* as they say in Italian, is waiting for me to walk through it." She turned to Alvise. He was smiling, now. "I want to walk through that door with you," she whispered, and then held out her left hand. "Forgive me for taking so long to see the open door."

His eyes lit up and filled with compassion. He slipped the ring on her left hand, lifted her in his arms, and kissed her softly.

Her feet back on the ground, she caught her balance, and said "I guess you've figured it out. We're getting married!" Then she blurted out, "And after the holidays, I'm returning to Venice with him." She held up her left hand, and received a communal gasp.

Glass shattered against the marble floor, and Rose brought her hands to her mouth. Victoria's smile vanished, and she watched her father's tanned face go pale.

"Bartender, stir up a round of strong cocktails." Eunice ordered from the sofa.

"Congratulations." Eddie's mouth turned up in a half-smile. He patted Alvise on the back, and then hugged Victoria. "Little cousin, I hope you know what you're doing."

So do I. She thought.

Jackie pulled Victoria aside. "What the…?"

"Trust me. This is a good thing."

"You said you're going to Venice with him. But you're coming back, right? Alvise is going to move here?"

Victoria shook her head.

"What about your job…your promotion?"

"Chloe is leaving World Talent Agency."

"And you're not going with her?"

"I can't continue to be her assistant or anyone else's for...who knows how many more years."

"Then find another job."

"You know it's not that easy…and it's not what I want. Not now. This career change…this dead end…whatever we want to call it, has freed me up. It's let me see how much I want to be with him."

"You hardly know each other."

"It feels like I've known him forever." Victoria turned her eyes to the opposite side of the room, and smiled back at Alvise. "He makes me happy."

Jackie stood there, silent.

Victoria sighed, and frowned at Jackie's sad expression. Since they'd met in Junior High School, a week hadn't gone by without them doing something together. "This won't change our friendship."

"But it won't be the same."

"It's more than doing stuff together."

"Then we'll have to hang onto the *more* part of it." Tears wet Jackie's eyes, and turned them a deeper shade of blue.

"Let them be happy tears." Victoria wiped a tear from her own cheek.

Jackie laughed, her lower lip quivered. "I better be your maid of honor."

"Then you're with me on this?"

"I won't wear taffeta or chiffon."

Eunice arrived from the sofa and, with Aunt Iris and Uncle Bob, gathered around the young couple. Smiles replaced their surprised faces. Victoria showed them her ring, beamed at their best wishes and saw her parents drifting toward her. Olga stood behind them. She smiled at Victoria, and brought the corner of her apron to her face, and wiped her tears.

"Will you excuse us?" Rose shifted the room's attention to her. "Victoria, would you and Alvise please join your father and me in the kitchen?" Without waiting for a reply, Rose left the family room.

"Dad?" The nerves that had left her earlier returned.

"We're asking for a minute, Victoria." Michael followed his wife.

Alvise nodded, and took Victoria's hand in his.

Olga followed them to the kitchen, and ushered the waiters out the back door, and then closed it behind her.

Without speaking, Rose motioned for Alvise and Victoria to sit at the kitchen table. Michael poured his wife red wine, and took his place at the head of the table, next to her. Holding Victoria's hand, Alvise avoided Michael's stern stare, and watched the steam rising from the pots on the stove. He felt his stomach growl at the delightful aromas that crisscrossed through the shiny kitchen. From where he sat he eyed a baking dish of mashed potatoes, bubbling and forming a crisp brown crust in the oven. He glanced away from the oven, and recognized the same controlling look he often saw on his mother's face, only now it was swept across Rose's.

Rose didn't touch her drink, but instead slid the wine glass back. Sitting as rigid as the kitchen chair, she folded her hands on the table as if conducting a therapy session. "Victoria is a bright, attractive woman, and I understand why you've fallen in love with her..."

Victoria leaned her head in her hands.

Michael furrowed his bushy brows. "Alvise, forgive our directness...but what can you, a gondolier, offer our daughter?"

"Dad, not you, too?"

"It's important for us to know."

Alvise's caring eyes turned serious. He stood. "Mr. and Mrs. Greco, I understand your concern. I wish I could comfort you by saying that my salary equals that of a millionaire. But it doesn't. However, I am proud of my trade, of who I am and of where I come from. I have my own home, and a good job."

"Dad, tourism is a good trade in Venice."

Alvise stepped behind Victoria. He faced her parents and placed his hands on her shoulders. "I guarantee that Vittoria will never want for anything."

"I'm sure, that in Venice, your job is quite a good one," said Rose "but my daughter has never *wanted* for anything."

"Mom…Dad…you taught me to go after what I want. I'm doing just that. A life with Alvise is what I want. I love him, and he loves me."

Rose stood. "Do you realize how much you'll be giving up if you move to Venice?"

"How about how much she's going to gain." Eunice entered the kitchen, and crossing the room, she turned to Victoria and Alvise. "When I told my parents I was leaving London to marry an American soldier, they told me I was ruining my life, and theirs. And when I told them he was a Catholic, they threatened to disinherit me. All he had was a patch of land in California's Central Valley, and a roadside vegetable stand. My parents were hard working, well to do, city people. And even after the war had taken most of their wealth, they didn't think their daughter should marry a manual labor type. But we were in love, and we didn't listen to them. I left England, and moved into a one bedroom flat in the driest, dustiest town I'd ever seen. And then we proved my parents wrong. We turned that fruit stand into a supermarket, and then we opened a second one. Now, it's the largest chain of supermarkets on the Pacific Coast. Michael, I never told you or Rose, but when you asked her to marry you, her father didn't sleep for months. Every evening after work, I'd hand him his Bourbon on the rocks, and he'd hand me a rant about how all you were good at was driving a nail into a four by four. After arguing and reminding him a gazillion times about how my parents treated us, his gripping lessened, but until the day he died, it never stopped. Now, I'm not going to lie. I was scared to my wit's end for my daughter." She turned to Rose. "Michael didn't have a penny to his name. But look at you two now. Look at what love and hard work has built for all of us. But what's more important than all the stuff we've accumulated is that you've raised an incredible daughter. Trust in the good job you've done as parents. Let her live life the way *she* sees fit."

Alvise watched Rose blink back tears, and then take Victoria's hands in hers. Victoria's eyes swam with tears as she stood, and hugged her mother.

Alvise turned to Eunice. "Thank you."

Eunice's jaw tightened. "Don't make me regret what I said."

Rose released her daughter from her embrace. "Your leaving after the holidays means the wedding will be in Venice. I've always dreamed about planning your wedding…"

"We haven't discussed it yet, but if we hold the wedding here, my parents may not come." Alvise looked into Rose's moist eyes.

"But the caterers, the flowers…the cake…"

"I'm sure they have all that in Venice." Michael put his hands on Rose's shoulders.

"And your dress!"

"What better place to find the perfect wedding gown than in Italy?" Victoria gave her mother a half-smile.

"Without me?"

"Then come to Italy…we'll shop for it there, together," said Victoria.

Rose shook her head. "It will be hard enough to reorganize my patients' appointments for the wedding. I can't dishevel their therapy sessions twice."

"What century do you two live in?" Eunice scolded. "We all have smartphones…and iPads. We can FaceTime shop for the dress together."

Victoria's eyes smiled, again, and she hugged her grandmother.

Alvise didn't want to hurt or disappoint her family, especially not her mother and father. But life had handed him Victoria. He wanted them to be happy for her, happy for them.

Chapter 13

Surprised to find the Los Angeles International airport overcrowded in mid-January, Alvise noticed the organized pandemonium switch Victoria's expression from enthusiasm to turmoil. He, too, felt suffocated by the impatient mob, but kept calm. He followed Victoria to the Alitalia gate. Boarding passes and passports in hand, he joined her at the end of a long line of passengers flying to Venice.

Excited English and impatient Italian conversations hummed through the waiting area, the Italians unaware that, outside of Italy, lines form from the back. Alvise understood most Italians found standing in line an unnecessary option, and too constraining for their spirited way of life, but noted Victoria's concern at the mayhem his fellow citizens caused.

Victoria nodded toward three young Italian men sporting sunglasses and wearing sweaters tied around their necks. "Where are *they* going?"

Alvise watched the group ignore and walk ahead of the hundred or so passengers standing in line in front of him—the same sly, rude behavior he often witnessed in Venice while at the post office or in a doctor's office, or while doing business at a bank teller window. But now, his compatriots' rude behavior there, in Los Angeles, was too offensive to observe without comment.

"Gli italiani, ovunque vadano, si fanno riconoscere." Alvise called out.

Two of the men slowed their pace, while the third one stopped and looked back. *"Farti i cazzi tuoi, no?"*

Startled by the angry exchange, Victoria turned to Alvise. "What did you say?"

"Italians make themselves known wherever they go."

"What did he say?"

"He told me to mind my own business…but with more colorful words." Alvise watched the group proceed to the front and ignore the astonished comments coming from the passengers standing in line.

The airline clerk smiled at the men, and extended her hand requesting their boarding passes.

Victoria stepped out of line and tilted her head. "Maybe they're in First Class."

"They're not in first class." Alvise discerned the clerk's calm manner, how she paged through the boarding passes, one by one, and then handed them back to the men. She smiled and with a firm gesture directed them to the back of the line. "You see? There's a bit of poetic rebellion in every Italian."

"So not standing in line is acceptable…that's normal behavior in Italy?"

He grimaced and nodded. He saw the apprehension and the frustration in her eyes.

"It's not considered rude?"

"Sure it is. But when most people behave that way, you start to say…*va bene cosi*…leave it as it is. If you don't, you'll find yourself arguing with them all day long. Few people want to do that, and fewer hold the conviction needed to change things."

"How can you ignore a situation you find unacceptable?"

"Sometimes you don't and other times you decide it's not that important."

Victoria scowled, and watched the sly Italians pass them by and join the end of the line.

"Our chaotic behavior stems from years of instability in the country. We've mastered getting by because, as a whole, we fear what life would be like if things changed as much as we fear being left behind."

The frustration in her eyes, now, looked more like preoccupation. "That's a contradiction."

"Contradiction is exactly what holds my country back. But as quick moving and service oriented as America is…no place is perfect."

They stood opposite each other, the polite, disciplined American woman who followed the rules and the *leave it as it is* Italian man who felt forced to close an eye to his country's disputable ways.

Had he said too much? In his eyes, the time spent in Los Angeles had evidenced the cultural differences between his country and the United States. But how much of that could he explain to her without scaring her away? Living in the *Bel Paese* was certainly different than vacationing there.

He put his hand on her waist, and pulled her near. "You're giving up so much." He kissed her hair, and inhaled the fresh bergamot scent in the perfume he had given her for Christmas. "I promise to do whatever it takes to make you happy."

She smiled and she leaned into him as the boarding gate line moved forward, taking them into the waiting Boeing Jet.

They settled into their places and belted themselves in. The jet sped down the runway, swooped up into the clear sky, and circled back over the Pacific Ocean. He watched Victoria view the coastline she had flown over a multitude of times, no doubt she felt proud to be a part of it. He wondered if this time, when she looked out over the arid landscape, if she had accepted that Los Angeles would no longer be her home. He was taking her away from everything she had ever known, and she knew little about where they were headed. He noticed her try to hide her tears, and keep her head turned away from him, toward the window. Without saying a word, he touched her cheek and wiped away a tear.

"I'll be fine," she said.

"And I'll be right here beside you, forever." His words were sincere, comforting . . . but it wouldn't be easy.

Alvise knew they faced difficulties ahead. He had telephoned his family as soon as they had gotten engaged. His mother made it clear she would be their next hurdle. Convinced that no woman was good enough for her son, Anna didn't hide her aversion to Victoria. But, to protect Victoria, Alvise kept this knowledge to himself. How could his mother not change her mind once she met Victoria? How could she not love this special woman?

At the Venice Marco Polo airport, they loaded their luggage, and Victoria's few boxed personal belongings onto the water taxi. Standing beneath the motorboat's canopy they headed home under the winter sky. The afternoon fog wrapped the lagoon in its gray cloak, and the mist that prickled at their faces felt more like rain. The biting, misty air was too much for Victoria's California winter coat, and her shivering body told him she'd never felt such bone-penetrating cold.

"Makes you wonder how it can be so sunny in Los Angeles." Alvise spoke over the engine noise.

"What happened to sunny Italy?" Victoria stepped behind him, shielding herself from the cutting wind. "Is it always like this?"

"No . . . except in the winter."

"Very funny."

He wasn't kidding. "If you're too cold we can sit inside."

"Not yet. I want to see the lagoon."

They traveled through the vast wetlands, at first speeding through wide, open waterways and then slowing through the narrower channels bordered by sea grass and marshland. The fore of the motor boat sliced the placid water, sending ripples folding onto the shore and frightening a nesting white heron into flight. Nearby, a group of mallards swam for cover beneath an isolated wood shack built upon stilts.

Venice's bell towers and brick buildings grew clearer in the fog, and soon the water taxi left them in front of Alvise's home. Welcomed by the warm cast-iron heater, they hooked their soggy coats on the entryway coatrack. The smell of fresh paint and pine-scented household cleaning products filled the air.

"It looks smaller than I remember," she said.

He shrugged his shoulders, and watched her gaze around the entryway.

"Did you do all the painting and cleaning?"

"The painting, but my mom must have cleaned up. I had asked her to come by and turn up the heat. I'll get these." He motioned to their luggage. "Go on up . . . it should be warmer upstairs."

One by one, Alvise carried the heavy boxes and suitcases up the steep stairs and stacked them in the hall. He turned up the thermostat, and then led Victoria to get reacquainted with her new home. They entered the familiar master bedroom and she placed her beauty case on the antique bed bench. The double bed, made up with pressed sheets and a matching down comforter had only one pillow centered at the head. Alvise saw Victoria bite her lip, and he struggled to overlook his mother's intentional slight. He followed Victoria into the adjacent bathroom where one set of towels sat warming on the heated rack. When he entered the guest room in search of another pillow, he found it bare and cold.

"Do you have extra pillows and towels?" she said.

"They should be in the armoire in the bedroom." *Why didn't my mom put them out.* He scratched his head, and grimaced. "Are you hungry?"

"I'm famished."

They entered the kitchen to find fresh salad soaking in the sink, a tepid pot of vegetable soup on the stove, and one place setting on the table. This not-so-subtle sign troubled Alvise. He knew his mother. Anna had known, of course, that her son was bringing his future wife home with him. *Why does she have to make things so difficult?* He reached into the cupboard and pulled out another set of dishes.

"At least now I know where everything is," she said.

The light-hearted comment chased the tension from the room, and he wrapped his arms around the woman who had given him one more reason to love her, and covered her neck with kisses.

In the morning Alvise rose to prepare Victoria breakfast without waking her. He hurried down to the corner *panificio* and picked up fresh-baked brioches to serve with coffee, and returned without her knowing he was ever gone. She didn't awake until he set the breakfast tray on the nightstand.

"Good morning." He kissed her lips with tender strokes, and brushed her thick mass of curls from her face.

"You're spoiling me."

"Get used to it . . . because this is only the beginning." He kidnapped her with his touch, and watched her linger under the warm, soft blanket and indulge her senses in the aroma of fresh coffee.

She stretched and twisted like a waking cat, sat up and leaned back against the antique headboard.

He handed her the warm cup of *caffé latte.* "Did you sleep well?"

"Uh-huh. What time is it?"

"Eleven."

"Is it that late? It must be jet lag. Or maybe it's you. You do have a way of relaxing a girl." She sipped the coffee.

"Then I guess I need to help you wake up."

He took the mug from her hands, slipped off his sweat pants, dropping them on the floor, and then slipped back under the covers. He tickled her, and she laughed out loud. "I want to make you do that more often."

"Do what?" She giggled.

"Laugh. You have a fantastic laugh." Outlining her face with soft kisses, he continued the trail behind her ears and down her neck, until goose bumps covered her flesh. He paused to savor her full breasts and protruding nipples, peeking out from behind the lace of her nightgown. After caressing her thighs with one hand, he moved the other to the small of her back, cradling it with his strong forearm. He was gentle as he placed her beneath him. The heat of his body covered her, and she succumbed to his touch. Not content to be only the receiver in their lovemaking, she wiggled out from under him.

"Lie on your back."

He complied, and she draped herself on top of him, her thighs around his hips. He smiled, and she pulled her nightgown up over her head, and tossed it to the foot of the bed. She took his hands in hers, inviting them to trace her breasts, her waist, her round hips. His manhood responded. He watched her hips. Back and forth, back and forth, they swayed, again and again. He sunk his head back into the pillow, closed his eyes, and smelled her sweet skin. He felt her draw near. Her warm breasts brushed his chest, her lips explored his neck. Synchronized in movement, he listened to her soft breath, and searched for her lips with his. Lost in their lovemaking, they ignored the sound of the doorbell.

Brrring.

Whoever it was would go away.

Brrring.

Keys jingled in the door lock. A shrill whistle halted their passion.

"Damn." He opened his eyes, and let go of her warm, supple body.

Victoria pulled the covers up under her chin. "Who is it?"

"*Porca vacca.*" He hopped out of bed and pulled on his sweatpants, again. "It's my father . . . that's his whistle."

Her eyes were glued to the bedroom door. "He has keys? Is he coming in here?" She sat up, binding the bedcovers to her body with one arm, she stretched out the other to grab her nightgown from the foot of the bed.

"Yes . . . I mean no, at least I hope not. He does have a key to the house though…I'm sorry…this is not how I planned our first morning here." He gave her an apologetic look. "I'll go deal with him."

He entered the kitchen. "Papà, what are you doing here?"

"Mamma sent me over . . . She said the water heater wasn't working and was afraid the house would be cold when you got up."

"It's fine . . . the water heater is working perfectly. Couldn't you have called first?"

"I told her to call. That woman . . . sends me all the way over here for nothing," said Bruno. "Well, where is she?"

Victoria appeared in the doorway wearing an old U.C.L.A. sweatshirt and leggings, unable to hide her embarrassment. "Good morning."

"Papà, this is Vittoria."

"*Buon giorno,* Vittoria . . . good morning." Bruno's voice was deep, firm, yet kind.

"It's nice to meet you." She extended her hand.

Bruno looked at her outstretched hand and paused before conceding, "*Benvenuta in Italia* . . . welcome to Italy." He shook her hand as if afraid it would break. "You must learn Italian. I speak some English . . . but mostly for my work. Alvise, he is good at languages. He can teach you."

"I hope I learn to speak Italian very soon," she said.

"Strange…you don't look American."

What do Americans look like? "My father's family was from Calabria. And my mother's family was from England. But we were all born in California."

"Ah, then you're *Calabrese.*"

"Yes…but mostly American."

"My wife is from the south, too."

"Alvise told me we have that in common."

"You do, if you're as hard-headed as the goats her grandfather raised."

Alvise smiled at Victoria, and then looked at his father. "Victoria is smart, not hard-headed."

"We'll talk about that after you've been married awhile." Bruno chuckled. "Your mother is expecting you for dinner. You know what time, so don't be late. *Arriverderci,* Vittoria."

"It was nice to meet you."

"*Ci vediamo,* Papà." Alvise escorted his father out the front door and bolted it shut, and then ran back upstairs.

Victoria waited for him in the hall. "For some reason I imagined your father to be short and round, with thinner, less gray hair. He's just the opposite."

"I hadn't noticed." Alvise tickled her, making her laugh. "I love that laugh almost as much as I love you. And I have more important things to be concerned about than my dad's appearance." He took her in his arms and carried her back to bed. "Where were we?"

Chapter 14

SITTING ON THE bathroom counter, he watched her color her lips with a small brush and looked at her as though he wanted to kiss her. "You'd better bring your gloves and scarf. The forecast is for snow."

She tossed a bewildered reflection at him through the mirror. "It snows in Italy?"

"It does here in the north."

"Great." She stepped back from the mirror. "Is this alright?"

Out of all the outfits lying discarded on the bed she chose a pair of tailored black wool trousers and a matching cashmere twin set.

"Should I wear my pearls? Or are they too much? I could wear my earrings. Or just the necklace?"

"Relax, *vita,* you look great." He stepped behind her and kissed the back of her neck.

"You're not helping." She nudged him to hook the necklace. "I want to make the right impression."

"So be you." He hooked the necklace, and turned his attention to her shoes. "Are those heels warm enough?"

"They go with this outfit."

"Okay then . . . we don't want to be late. Dinner is at eight. And no matter how you look, what my mother will remember is if you were on time."

They stepped into the biting night air. The ground, littered with streamers and small bits of paper, warned them that masquerading mobs gathered in the campo ahead.

"*Carnevale* is early this year." Alvise led her through the lesser-known alleyways to avoid the crowds, though, now and again, they got drenched in a cloud of colored confetti.

The sweet sound of Vivaldi's *Allegro Primavera* rose up at them as they descended the mountainous Academia Bridge. A street string quartet playing Venice's most respected composer's music stood at the entrance to the Benedetto Marcello conservatory, and nodded toward a violin case that cried for compensation.

A display of *Carnevale* costumes floated through Campo San Stefano while hiding their occupants beneath layers of tulle, velvet, and brocade. Papier-mâché masks hand-painted gold, silver, or white, and bejeweled with faux pearls or stones, shielded the identity of a group of women who balanced their towering wigs with enough grace to make Marie Antoinette envious. Their brocade gowns, coordinated in color and style, had fitted bustiers that exposed the tops of their suffocated breasts to the piercing cold night air. The outfits, so tight, surely hindered the maidens' breath, yet all appeared willing to ignore their discomfort in exchange for the attention of the cloaked, masked admirers lurking around.

"Shouldn't we bring a bottle of wine?" Victoria tightened her scarf around her neck, against the cold.

"My Dad has plenty of wine."

She sunk her calfskin gloved hands deep into her coat pockets. "What about dessert?"

"My mom always makes my favorite *tiramisu,*" he said. "You're cold...aren't you?"

"A little."

His arm around her shoulders, he pulled her closer. "It's not necessary to bring anything."

"I can't arrive empty handed. Not the first time I'm meeting your family."

Alvise checked his watch, and kissed her cold rosy cheek. "Okay. We can pick up *frittelle*, and let you warm up, too."

"What's *frittelle*?"

"My other favorite Venetian pastry." He pulled her in another direction.

Forced-air heating and the sound of steam pressing espresso into ceramic cups floated through the Rosa Salva *pasticceria.* A group of women, sporting enough gold and fur to open a boutique, occupied the long marble counter. With their backs turned on Victoria, they sipped their orange *aperitivi* as their costumed children warmed up with hot chocolate thick as mud, and ignored her polite attempts at stepping close enough to order.

"You can't be shy." Alvise reassured her with his smile, and then hollered their order over the women's heads.

Victoria moved away from the crowded counter, pulled off her gloves, and loosened her scarf against the stifling heat. Crumpled used napkins littered the base of the stainless steel bar and the gray marble floor she stood on. She noticed the drab walls, and remembered they'd had breakfast there the morning after their first night together. But the pastry shop that had seemed quaint and unique that morning months ago, now appeared small and outdated. She opened her coat collar against the hot air blasting overhead, and considered waiting outside. Uncertain which was more uncomfortable, the bitter cold or the overheated pastry shop, she ran her hand down her coat, undid the buttons, one by one, and watched the salesgirl serve up the *frittelle.*

Careful not to squeeze the weighty morsels between the pastry prongs, the young woman plucked meatball size rounds of fried dough covered with sugar, raisins and pine nuts one at a time from the serving dish, and placed the delicacies in neat rows on a cardboard tray. Then, setting the tray on a stack of wrapping paper, she folded the top sheet to cover the sweets, and finished the package by tying it with a white ribbon that doubled as a handle.

Snowflakes fell, replacing the *Carnevale* confetti, and dusted their coats when they stepped back out into the cold alleyway. The joy in watching the city turn white couldn't overcome Victoria's displeasure with her ruined designer shoes and the numbness that had returned in her toes. She hid her discomfort—he had warned her about the shoes.

Their footsteps echoed, and they said nothing. Victoria pulled up her coat collar, and surveyed the paths she had walked months before. The quaint backstreets that had enchanted her while on vacation, now, struck her as being bleak and gloomy. The window sills that had dripped with vibrant colored geraniums and petunias in the autumn sat lifeless and shuttered, the way an abandoned neighborhood might. Coarse salt scattered across the pavement crunched beneath her shoes, and she hooked her arm through Alvise's against the black ice, and climbed the Ponte de le Bande Bridge. Before descending the other side, she looked down at the still canal, and the tarp covered boats docked and destined to be forgotten until spring. She wouldn't tell Alvise that, somehow, his city felt as dark and dreary as its residents' winter clothes. Nor would she tell him that the cold and damp made her miss sunny Southern California.

The street lamp cast an amethyst light over the snow-canopied ground, and the church bells struck eight as they reached Campo Santa Maria Formosa.

"I'm sure they're already at the table." Alvise pushed open a heavy, centuries-old door.

Victoria stepped into the shadows of the dim entryway, and checked her watch. *But, we're right on time.*

Unlike the blasting heat in the pastry shop, little by little the apartment building warmed her limbs. Each step up the stairway brought them deeper into the pleasant aroma of Anna Moro's cooking. She exhaled a deep breath. *This won't be so bad* she thought. On the fourth-floor, and stepping in front of the apartment entrance, she spied a small masked figure hiding behind the potted plants on the third floor landing.

"*Chi è?* Who is this scary person?" Alvise stepped behind Victoria and stooped down like a coward.

"*Sono io,* Susanna." His niece jumped out at them. The pretty, costumed princess's eyes beamed and laughed at her uncle, and she swirled and danced as if the entire world were admiring the lace slip and satin gown her *nonna* had made. Her tiny, pink painted fingertips held on tight to the rhinestone tiara slipping from her brown French braid, and she curtsied for her admirers. "And I'm not scary . . . I'm a *principessa*."

"You're the *più bella principessa* I've ever seen." Victoria tried to use a few simple words in Italian. "The prettiest princess," she repeated. She stepped aside to free Alvise from her protection. It warmed her heart to see him play with his niece, and to see how much Susanna adored him, too.

"You talk funny." Susanna eyed her with interest. Turning her affection toward the wrapped pastry, "What's in there?"

"*Frittelle,*" said Alvise. "Can we come in now?"

"Only if you give them to me."

"Take them to your *nonna*." He pushed the front door further open.

"Nonna. They brought *frittelle* . . . can I eat one?" Susanna skipped down the hall with the pastry package banging against her leg.

"*Cosa?*" said Anna. "I work hard to make *tiramisu* for you." She whisked the package into the kitchen, and pretending to whisper, but speaking loud enough for everyone to hear. "My *tiramisu* better than *frittelle*."

"Your mother speaks English?"

"She studied English in school, and is a fan of American movies. She understands a lot, but speaks a little less."

Anna's soft, lined face lit up when Alvise entered the room, and her sparkling eyes filled with tears. "Alvise . . . *figlio mio*. . .my son . . . my masterpiece . . . you're home. Tell me I not create the most *bellissimo* gondolier in Venice." She greeted him with arms wide open. He gave her a warm embrace and spun her around, causing her to laugh like a schoolgirl. "Look at me," she went on, trying to regain her balance. "*Maria Vergine* . . . poor child. You skin and bones. You miss my cooking."

Victoria thought Anna was beautiful, with a cool, bourgeois air about her. She noticed that, though Alvise kept his arms around his mother, he didn't bother to answer her. Still, she liked the warmth and affection he shared with his mother. His kind, playful manner pleased her. She could see they had a close relationship.

"Mamma, this is Vittoria."

"*Ciao*, Vittoria." Anna forced a smile. She held onto her son as if high tide had flooded her house and he was her only pair of rubber boots. "Call me Anna . . . *però* . . . but," she corrected herself. "I never called *my* . . . *suocera* . . . ?" She looked at Alvise.

"Mother-in-law."

"*Sì*, mudder-n-low, I call her '*signora*' . . . until the day she die."

Victoria hesitated and washed down what little moisture lined her mouth. "It's nice to meet you . . ." She choked back her unexpected fear. Her hands twisted and turned on themselves, until she caught Alvise smiling back at her and continued, ". . . Anna. Thank you for inviting us to dinner."

"*Grazie*?" Anna peered at Victoria. "What you mean? Alvise need no invitation. *Presto*, go now. Put down your coats." Then, she looked at Victoria from head to toe, and shook her head. "No, no, no. Shoes . . . off. . .put on slippers . . . there, under furnace."

"That's kind of you, but I'm already warming up."

"I work all day waxing floors, and those *stiletti* . . . heels. *Maria Vergine* . . . what shoes do to floors." Her strict tone made it clear. She left no room for debate. "Now go...go to table." She returned to her private refuge in the kitchen.

Did I say something wrong? Victoria thought.

Alvise touched her arm. "You don't have to change your shoes. . .unless you want to."

"Your mother sounded pretty. . .."

"She's fine. Come and meet my sister."

"*Ciao*. Welcome home, little brother." Gina reached out and gave him a hug. "I heard Mamma sent Papà over this morning for an unexpected visit."

Alvise shrugged. "Vittoria, this is my sister Gina and her husband, Alberto, Susanna's mother and father. You'll be glad to know that they both speak English."

"We've spoken on the phone." Victoria's smile brightened. She extended her hand and shook Gina's before turning to Alberto. Unlike Alvise's father, he looked at ease shaking a woman's hand. "It's nice to meet you both. Your daughter is precious."

"*Grazie* . . . I mean, thank you." Gina's kind tone didn't cover her gaze. She studied Victoria from head to toe and back again.

Alvise hoped it was curiosity he saw on his sister's face. When he broke the news of the engagement, Gina had said to him that "No one would leave their country unless they were running away."

"Vittoria . . . sit here . . . next to me." Bruno grinned, smacked a welcome kiss on both of her cheeks, then turned to the others and barked out orders. "Alberto, move down two places. Alvise, you sit next to Vittoria."

Alberto didn't say a word. Nothing but a gracious, tobacco-tinted smile showed on his face. He moved his thin frame from his usual seat—a place that he had occupied since he'd married into the family. Today he would indulge his father-in-law, but Alvise could see his brother-in-law didn't like it.

"No, Papà," said Alvise. "They don't have to move. We can sit over there."

"No . . . I want you and Vittoria to sit right here."

Surprised and disturbed, Alvise took his seat according to his father's wishes. His father was treating him like a grown man, an equal, and no longer like the youngest in the family. Even more—he took his father's gesture as an acknowledgment to Victoria, to welcome her and show his acceptance. Gina and his brother-in-law, on the other hand, hadn't welcomed her as warmly as he had hoped they would. Perhaps his father's quick approval of Victoria made Gina and Alberto jealous? He looked across the table at Alberto, hoping to make conversation. Instead, his brother-in-law's dark eyes were glued to his cellphone.

Anna walked in with a heavy metal pot filled with steaming fish soup, and didn't comment on the new seating arrangement.

But Alvise saw his mother's eyes narrow when she noticed Victoria seated next to Bruno, her high-heeled shoes still on.

"Alberto, *il cellulare*." Anna kept her eyes on him while he darkened the cellphone screen, and set it on the table. Then, preparing to serve she said, "Susanna—pass plates for me. *Attenzione*, it's hot."

"It smells wonderful." Victoria folded her hands on her lap.

"*La migliore zuppa* . . . best soup in world," said Anna. "*Mangia* . . . eat. It gets cold."

"We're waiting for you, Mamma," said Alvise.

"Me? I don't eat fish soup. Now go, *mangia* . . . It gets cold."

"Since when, Mamma?" Gina rolled her eyes up to her mother, and lifted her soup spoon.

"Since I'm tired of eating and cooking. Good, isn't it?" Anna winked at Susanna.

"Papà," said Alvise, "we're planning to have the wedding in September . . . I'm hoping that two of the men will take us from the church to the restaurant in one of the deluxe gondolas."

"They're already talking about it." Bruno paused, and slurped his soup. "We'll have gondolas for all the guests to ride in."

All of our guests? Thought Victoria. "That'll be wonderful."

Gina tore into a bread roll. "We only had one gondola at our wedding."

"Because you're not a gondolier," said Bruno.

"And that's because I'm a woman."

Bruno pointed his wide index finger at his daughter. "*Attenzione*. . .watch yourself young lady."

Victoria put her spoon down. "Aren't there any female gondoliers?"

Alvise coughed and came close to choking on his soup. He knew that his father would never be ready for the world as Victoria knew it. Many Venetians lived as if in a history book, respecting and holding on tight to the past, fearful of losing themselves to the future. If change came slow in Italy, it came slower in Venice, making it difficult for women to enter the small, reserved world of the gondoliers. He understood that Victoria's question wasn't meant to be polemic. It came from a woman born in a society where, if she wanted to, she could do anything a man did.

However, Alvise knew what most of the elder gondoliers—his father, in particular—thought about women joining their trade, and he wasn't in complete agreement with them. He calmed his cough with a sip of red table wine. "A few have tried, but only one woman has passed the test."

"So there is a female gondolier in Venice?"

Alvise nodded. "Her name is Ivana."

"Women don't belong in the *traghetto.*" Bruno slurped up the last bit of soup straight from his bowl, and blotted what remained with a crust of bread.

"I used to go to the traghetto when I bring you lunch," said Anna. "Now that you eat out or come home to eat, I never set foot near your work station."

"That's *precisamente* . . . precisely . . . the way it's always been, and the way it should stay," said Bruno. "I think about what my grandfather, your *Bisnonno*...a man who fought in and survived two World Wars. What would he say about us letting women into the profession?" Bruno couldn't hide his emotion or his pride. "There wasn't a lot of work for gondoliers in wartime, so when my grandfather wasn't in combat, or lucky enough to find rich folks to row around town, he was working the land on the outer islands of the lagoon."

Victoria put down her spoon and folded her napkin on her lap. Alvise watched her listen the way an interested student pays attention to a teacher.

"There were no motorboats back then," continued Bruno. "Every morning before dawn, he rowed for hours, back and forth to the Rialto market with fresh vegetables, so he could provide for his family. There was no time to go to school, but that doesn't mean he was stupid, and he sure wasn't naïve. It was hard work then, and it's hard work now, with no room for the weak." Bruno raised his wineglass to his lips, emptied it, and turned to Alvise. "He was a man of another era, who knew better. This is a man's job and you, as a fourth generation gondolier, need to protect that."

Alvise was sympathetic—his father's mentality was stuck in another time. Bruno believed all a woman needed was to stay home, tend to the house and family. He deemed other activities unnecessary. Yet Alvise understood that, for the gondoliers, times had changed and that he and his colleagues had to adapt. They all agreed that letting females into the trade strayed from historical tradition, and made for organizational problems.

"For hundreds of years gondoliers worked for the noble families of Venice and often, as partners in crime with their *padroni*, they kept their secrets," said Alvise. "They protected the well-being of the families. So, it's always been an exclusive men's club of sorts." Alvise directed his explanation at Victoria. He liked how her eyes lit up with such interest, as if asking him to continue. "As far back as the 1700s, Carlo Goldoni, the famous Venetian playwright, wrote about Bettina, a female gondolier in *The Venetian Gondolier.* It's not by chance that he described her with astonishment: 'What extravagance, what situation, what amazement'," recited Alvise. "And this woman was only a fiction—a character who dared disguise herself as a gondolier to spy on her mischievous fiancé, a gondolier named Buleghin."

"That's just nonsense from a story-teller," said Bruno.

A historically important story-teller thought Alvise, and not waiting for his father to continue, he did, "Over the centuries gondoliers have been loved or hated, envied or insulted. Up until World War II their privileged status of serving the upper class often triggered criticism from their fellow Venetians. Yet no Venetian will deny that we're part of our city's tapestry. Those social differences don't exist anymore, and so we're no longer criticized for that. Instead we're criticized for being a closed group, and for not wanting to change with the times. But sooner or later we'll have to adapt. There will be more women gondoliers."

"*Mah*...women gondoliers." Shouted Bruno. "Thank God I only have a few years left to work. It's the ruin of the gondoliers."

"It's not our ruin," said Alvise, "not if the women are good with the boat, and work the way they're expected to."

"And what about the *casotto*?" said Bruno. "If more women become gondoliers, how you gonna solve that problem?"

"What's the *casotto*?" said Victoria.

Anna, Gina, and Alberto watched in silence, united by their discomfort, annoyed that Victoria had been included in a conversation that had always excluded them.

"It's a small enclosed space in each traghetto. We use it to dress and store our things, like a locker room," said Alvise. "If the number of women gondoliers grows, it'll be hard to accommodate them. They'd need their own space, and that's not easy to come by in Venice."

"Women don't belong in the *traghetto.*" Bruno shouted louder.

"Papà, the rules don't prohibit women—they can't. If a woman is good enough to pass the exams and the jury doesn't eliminate her, nothing can stop her from becoming a substitute. Ivana is proof of that."

"And that's good?" said Bruno.

"Good, only after she, or they…"

"They? You keep saying they…what do you want…a team?"

"No, Papà." Alvise smiled.

"You wanna woman rowing next to you?" Bruno looked at his son as if he'd gone mad.

"If she's capable, and respects our trade and our city, then I'll have no problem with it. It'll be okay, Papà…it has to be."

Anna cleared the first-course dishes away and swept back and forth from the tiny kitchen, each time carrying another gastronomic delight to the family table. The simple wine and hearty meal warmed them, and put everyone at ease.

Young Susanna announced she was finished and stepped down from her chair. She walked over to Victoria, taking her hand and scooting onto her lap. The little girl, enchanted by the strand of pearls around Victoria's neck, caressed them with her small, curious hands, and glowed when Victoria let her try them on.

"Fancy." Anna took the necklace off her granddaughter's neck, and fastened it around her own. "A gift from Alvise?"

"No, Mamma."

Anna cast a look of doubt at Victoria. "Another man?"

"No," said Victoria, her brows knitted. "They were my grandmother's. She gave them to me when I graduated from college."

Anna slipped the necklace off and lifted it toward the dining room light, and then gave it back to Victoria. "Beautiful."

"Alvise told us you worked in Hollywood." Gina shot Victoria an inquisitive look. "Is that true?"

"Of course it's true," said Alvise.

"It's hard to believe she would quit such a glamorous job," said Gina.

"I had a very good reason." Victoria smiled at Alvise. "But I hope to find work here."

"The cleaning lady who usually works at our Bed and Breakfast is recovering from surgery. Do you do windows?" said Gina.

"That's not my best skill…but thank you for offering," said Victoria.

Alvise ignored his sister's judgmental look, and noticed how Victoria sat confident, and played with Susanna's soft braid. "You speak English, and with your work experience…you'll find something suitable." When he looked at her, she left Susanna's braid for his hand, and gave it a reassuring squeeze.

Alberto broke the tension in the room by talking about the latest building restoration contract he had won. He gave credit to Gina, and admitted that he would never have become an architect if she hadn't pushed him. Anna stood in the background, listening, observing, and eyeing her family. Pleasing her family with her culinary abilities, she served Bruno a second serving of *branzino*—sea bass, but, once again, maintained her distance. Her sudden silence made Alvise nervous. Did she feel crowded out by the new female presence?

Then with conviction, and as if her ego needed a dose of attention, Anna made an announcement. In rapid Italian, leaving it up to Alvise to translate for his bride-to-be, she described what she wanted to wear to the wedding. *A classy white dress and an enormous white hat, like the American women wear on television*—were her exact words. Circling her hands around her head, she depicted her hat, and posed as if being photographed by paparazzi.

Alvise remained silent until Victoria whispered, "Did your mother say she's wants to wear white to our wedding?"

He nodded.

"But only the bride wears white—isn't it the same in Italy?"

He nodded, again, and then raised his eyebrows at his sister, pleading her to speak up. But he received a smirk instead. His mouth dropped open in disbelief when he saw her mouth form the silent words: *one gondola at my wedding.* To him it didn't matter if his mother wanted to dress up like a television star—as long as she didn't wear white. How could his mother be so rude? How could his sister act so infantile?

"Mamma . . ."

"Sì amore? Pensa quanto bello quando arriviamo all'altare insieme."

Alvise knew his mother speaking Italian was no accident—she wanted to exclude her future daughter-in-law from the conversation.

Victoria leaned toward Alvise, her eyebrow raised. "The mother walks the groom down the aisle?"

She comprehended Italian better than Alvise thought. "Yes."

"That's a thoughtful gesture, Anna. That would be lovely." Victoria smiled at Anna.

Anna studied Victoria, and didn't answer.

Bruno emptied another glass of wine in one swig. He wiped a cloth napkin across his lips, and then let it drop on the table. "Even I know no one but the bride wears white."

Alvise shot a surprised look at his father and, out of the corner of his eye, saw the color rise in his mother's face.

"I mother of *sposo*, and I wear what I want."

"Any color but white," said Bruno.

"Anna." Victoria sat up straight, her hands politely crossed on the table. "Alvise and I are very happy to get married in Venice. It's the most romantic city on earth, and having the wedding here makes it easier for your family members to participate. Of course my parents will be here. But since all this happened so fast, I didn't have much time to shop for a wedding dress before leaving Los Angeles. My mother is very disappointed that she can't shop for the dress with me, as am I. I'm sure you would agree that it's an important moment that every mother and daughter want to share. But since she can't be here, I'd be honored if you…and Gina…would come with me to look for my wedding dress. I'm sure the salesladies can help you find your outfits, too."

Anna's face softened.

Victoria turned to Gina. "And we'd love it if Susanna would be our flower girl."

"Sì, Mamma…Papà…please…please." Susanna jumped from Victoria's lap.

Alvise sat back and smiled. He looked around the table at the men grinning to themselves. The woman he loved had disarmed his mother and sister like no one from outside the family ever had. For that, he fell further in love with her.

Gina looked across the table at Victoria, and then at Alvise. She laid a hand on her husband's arm. "Thank you. We would like that."

"We would." Alberto smiled at his daughter.

"We go to my friend…she has *un negozio per le spose…*" said Anna.

"Bridal shop?" said Victoria.

"*Sì…*I take you there."

Victoria's eyes widened. "Perfect…absolutely perfect…and this…" she sunk her fork into the creamy dessert on her plate "…is the best Tiramisu I've ever tasted. May I have the recipe?"

"I don't use recipe," said Anna.

"Could you teach me to make it?"

"*Forse…un giorno.*" Anna hovered over her dinner guests, waiting for their dessert plates to be emptied.

Victoria turned to Alvise. "What does *forse* mean?"

"It means *maybe.*" Gina looked sideways at her mother.

"*Maybe,*" repeated Anna.

"Maybe is good," said Victoria.

"Mamma, *maybe* you could write the recipe down for Victoria," said Alvise.

Anna clattered all the dessert plates but Alvise's into a stack. She let her son finish his more abundant portion, and carried the tiramisu smeared dishes into the kitchen.

Alvise wiped his fork across his plate and took the last bite of the creamy coffee and chocolate dessert. He'd settle for his mother's half-hearted attempt at accepting Victoria—for now. He left his empty plate and the table for the nearby credenza, and pulled a bottle of brandy from the shelf. Offering it to the others he satisfied the takers by pouring the amber liquid into three snifters. When his father and Victoria had taken theirs from his hand, he sat down, once again, and sipped the pungent, smooth liquid. He watched Victoria laughing, conversing with his father. It was obvious to him that her charm and intelligence had captured Bruno, too. He savored the amber liquid and thought: *Maybe this won't be so hard, after all.*

Chapter 15

In late March, the gondoliers' tourist season had begun to pick up speed. Alvise entered the Molo gondola station's invisible confines and glanced over the boats lined up and resting in the algae-shrouded low tide. His gondola swayed safely in the *cavana*—boat slip—where he had left it the night before.

"*Buon giorno*, Papà. How's it going?" Out of habit and respect, Alvise greeted his father first, before acknowledging the other gondoliers who, hoisting up a rust-colored awning in preparation for the sunny day that lay ahead went about their business.

Bruno fit his gondolier's hat snug over the red bandana that encircled his head. He didn't look at Alvise, but instead continued to scan the Piazza for customers. "*Tutto in ordine* . . . Everything's in order." He pulled an envelope from his pocket. "This arrived with the traghetto mail. It's got your name on it."

Alvise glanced down at the envelope. No name. No return address. He read the postal stamp. Stockholm. His mind sat blank. Then . . . there was one person he'd met from there. *Why would she write, now, after so many years?*

They hadn't spoken since that night when they'd gone back to her apartment with Ciano and her friend. The same night when too many beers and a heavy dose of loneliness had turned their encounter to *a one-night-stand*, and then been archived in his mind to the forgotten file.

He had no time to read a letter from a woman he'd forgotten. He had to prepare his boat. He dropped the letter in his bag, hopped into the gondola, and set the bag on the prow steps. He wiped the sea salt from the boat's surface, set out the seats and cushions and looked up to see his father trying to convince a young couple to take a ride. Business was slower than usual. His turn wouldn't be up for a while. *I could have stayed under the covers with Vittoria longer.*

Sitting near the prow, he thought about the many occasions when, as a child, he'd taken the gondola out, accompanied by his father or his grandfather: *Grip the post with everything you've got, and draw the gondola close to the landing,* his father would say. *Extend your forearm to the clients when they board and exit the gondola.* He could still hear his father's voice yelling out, *row without tugging. No rough movements.* And *always watch out for the other boats.* He remembered his grandfather's words, too. *You can only say you know how to master a gondola when, while rowing, you're able to place a full glass of wine aboard and not spill a drop.*

Alvise looked up at his father hurrying down the dock toward his own boat, now. A family with three skipping children followed behind him. Alvise gave the happy family a quick once over and, based on their mullet haircuts and Velcro strapped sandals, knew they were German. Soon, his turn would be up. He reached into his bag and pulled out his mariner's jacket—with it came the envelope falling to the floor.

He'd received other letters from girls he'd met at work, often addressed to the *traghetto*, most with a photograph of them riding in his gondola. But after so many years, a letter from Stockholm... from...*What was her name?* That surprised him. He hesitated for a moment, and hoped the letter wasn't announcing an upcoming vacation of hers to Venice. He tore open the envelope, unfolded the letter. She, too, had sent a photograph. From the photo, a small child with a kind face, waved, smiled and was seated on a merry-go-round. He read the brief letter:

Dear Alvise,

I'm Magda. We met in Venice. I was with my friend Zinnia.

"That was her name...*Zinnia*," he said to himself, then and continued reading.

Since then she has a son, Thor. He is your son, too. He is four years old. I thought you should know.

Magda

Alvise fell back on the gondola steps. Disbelief bolted through his limbs. In one hand he held the photo, in the other, the letter. His heart raced, his head spun. *How is it possible . . . ?* Why hadn't Zinnia told him about this child before? Why did she have Madga write? And why had they waited until now to write? Was this a joke? How could this boy be his son? He studied the photograph, pulling it closer to his face. The boy's eyes were ice blue like he remembered his mothers to be, but their shape...his smile.

Alvise felt nothing, heard nothing, saw nothing. Memories came to him, muffled, as if belonging to another. They obliterated everything around him.

One evening five years earlier, their appointment had been for eight o'clock in Campo San Bartolomeo. As usual, he had arrived a few minutes early. He still smoked then, a habit he'd set aside since he'd met Victoria. But then, leaning against the iron railing at the base of the Carlo Goldoni statue he drew smoke from a cigarette, and waited until he heard Ciano's loud laugh coming from the direction of the Rialto Bridge. Ciano's chest puffed out like a peacock, he remembered him escorting the two tall, blond Swedes in his direction.

He remembered Zinnia's staring, ice blue eyes, and how, when he went to shake her hand, she asked him his zodiac sign and turned the palm of his hand up, and then studied the lines. He remembered the expression on Ciano's face, too. His friend clearly agreed that she was a bit strange.

Then, on their walk to the pizzeria, Zinnia had bored him with talk about astrology and horoscopes, while he concentrated on the effects of the evening breeze swishing through her skirt, pressing her transparent blouse against her breasts. After pizza, too many rounds of beer, and a marijuana cigarette shared by Ciano and the girls, they went to the girls' rented apartment, and then broke off into separate bedrooms.

His last memory of Zinnia was of her sprawled out on the sheets, beside him. He'd tried not to make a sound when he got up from bed, and got dressed. It was clear that she had wanted nothing more than to make her stay in Venice more interesting. Still, his good manners and chivalrous side had written his work station's address on a slip of paper, and left it on the dresser. That done, she must have known they'd never see each other again.

How could a woman whose last name or birthday or favorite color he didn't know give him a son?

He hadn't heard Ciano yelling out his name. "Alvise…*Cristo Santo*…are you deaf? I got an appointment for my tuxedo fitting this afternoon. You gonna come with me?"

Ciano's question came at him like a fist to his stomach. Victoria had begun organizing the wedding. The invitations had been ordered—the date set for September. This could ruin everything. Was this boy his? Yes or no, how could he tell her, now, that he might have a son? He loved her so much, too much. He didn't want to hurt her. But if this was true…if another woman had given him a son . . . would she accept that? Could he accept that? Victoria was the only woman he wanted to have children with. Would she leave him, return to Los Angeles? That thought terrified him more than the others. And, what would his mother do if she found out? He shoved the letter and photo back in his bag, and looked up to see Ciano standing above him.

"Hey man, everything okay? You're whiter than a corpse," said Ciano.

"I got a bad headache."

"So you gonna come with me?"

He found it hard to concentrate. "No."

"Whatever." Ciano walked back toward the *traghetto.* "It's your wedding."

Fear stole Alvise's breath. It felt as if a steel blade tore at his ribs, slicing his heart to pieces. All they had together, all their plans for the future began to crumble like his city's weather-beaten walls. He couldn't let this letter...this news...stand in the way of marrying the woman he dreamt about, even while she lie sleeping next to him. He could continue to live without the boy in his life. But how could he live without Victoria?

If four years could go by without him knowing about this boy, then this could wait, too. If the moment ever came, he would explain everything to Victoria, and convince her that Zinnia had meant nothing to him. For now, he'd keep this beautiful boy a secret. He wouldn't, he couldn't tell anyone he might have a son—above all, not his mother.

He pulled the letter and photo from his bag, again, glanced down at the smiling boy's sweet image and, wrestling with the guilt battling his conscience, tore them both into pieces, and tossed his secret in the water.

Chapter 16

SPRING AND LONGER fresh dew-kissed days came to Venice and, with only five months until their September wedding, Victoria found lots to do. Her life had become an untested routine, and she didn't mind.

She pulled herself from Alvise's loving arms, rose from bed and dressed before he did. She prepared coffee and breakfast while he showered and shaved and, reading out-loud, fumbled the Italian language while attempting to comprehend the local newspaper. They left the apartment together. Riding the vaporetto down the Grand Canal, they chattered about unfinished wedding plans, and her ideas about remodeling the kitchen, installing a dishwasher. He assured her that he, too, preferred the kitchen cabinets stripped of their dingy white paint, but they'd need to wait and see about a dishwasher. With her in charge, the wedding would be perfect, too. At the San Marco stop they shared a quick kiss before he stepped off, and she continued across the sea-basin to the Arsenale, where she had enrolled in the Italian Language for Foreigners School.

After her morning class, resume in hand, she walked the long Calle XXII Marzo—Venice's equivalent of New York City's 5th Avenue or Beverly Hills' Rodeo Drive. Louis Vuitton, Cartier, Prada, Gucci, Tod's—shop by shop she put on a pleasant smile, and stepped inside the posh designer boutiques. One by one, a snooty salesperson informed her that it didn't matter that she had once organized costume fittings for movie stars at their stores in Beverly Hills or that she was fluent in English. They wanted someone who spoke Chinese or Korean. If she could do that, they might consider her application.

Rejected, and standing on the wide alleyway, she looked at her engagement ring, the same ring she had tried on, months before, in Alvise's Uncle's shop. He was her last choice, and now her last option. Though she had wanted to find a job based on her own merit, disappointment and desperation took her the short distance to his jewelry store. She rang the security bell, and entered the space that was so familiar to her.

Except for eyes that smiled like a warm embrace, Zio Fausto was ordinary looking. He wore custom-made suits cut to hide his roundness, and lifts tucked inside his dress shoes to make him appear taller. "Vittoria. What a nice surprise." He smacked a kiss on each side of her face. "What brings you here?"

"I was wondering…I didn't want to ask…but, I'm not used to having so much time on my hands. And I'm getting better at speaking Italian…I thought that, if you needed anyone…"

Fausto smiled beneath his bushy mustache. "I was waiting for you to ask."

"Really!" *Why didn't you say something?*

"I could use a good salesperson who speaks English."

"That's great." *Everyone I've spoken to wants someone who speaks Mandarin.*

"Americans are my best customers. When do you want to start?"

"Just like that?" *I have a job!*

"I trust my nephew's opinion. If he wants to marry you, that means you're a good person. That's all I need to know."

Victoria threw her arms around Zio Fausto's wide neck. "I won't disappoint you."

"We open at 9 a.m. See you next week."

She felt as if she were walking on air. She headed toward the vaporetto stop, and paused at every canal she crossed to see if Alvise was passing by. When she stopped at the top of a bridge she spotted him. Alone, he was rowing his gondola down the small canal, toward her. She shot her hand into the air and waved. He smiled back, and she thought what a handsome fiancé she had. She scampered down the bridge steps and under the portico, and waited for him to stop his boat canal side. *You were right, Alvise. All I needed was time to get to know the city, and let the city get to know me.*

"*Amore mio*," he said. "This is my lucky afternoon."

She saw something in his smile, the same look she'd seen in those last few weeks—whenever she caught him alone or in deep thought. "Is everything okay?"

"You're getting better and better at reading me." His right foot on the bow, he touched his left foot to the marble slab she was standing on, held the oar firm in the nook of the forcola, and steadied the boat. "There *is* something I've wanted to tell you for a while now. But the time never seems right, and this certainly isn't the place to talk." He raised his eyebrows at the water traffic on his left and at the crowd moving through the portico.

Whatever it is, it can't be more exciting than my new job. "Okay, but let me tell you something first. I just left Zio Fausto's jewelry store." Her smile was as bright as the yellow stucco walls reflecting in the canal. "He hired me. I start next week."

Her joy flashed in his eyes, too, and covered the concern she had seen moments before. "That's fantastic."

She felt his eyes caressing her face, the way they had the first time they'd met. "Now, are you sure you don't want to tell me what's on your mind?"

He lowered his voice. "It's something that happened a long time ago."

She placed her hand on the nearby marble column, and leaned closer. She smiled and listened, prepared for whatever was troubling him.

"Long before I met you..."

"*Alvise spostati,*" called out a raspy voice.

Their eyes broke away from each other and turned down the canal toward a gondolier rowing in their direction.

"You're in my way." The gondolier pressed a cigarette between his lips. "I gotta drop off these folks."

"*Amore*, I'm sorry. I'm in his spot. I've got to go."

She bent forward and touched his mouth with a soft kiss.

"We'll talk about it tonight." He stepped back, both feet on the bow, now. He tightened his hand around the oar and gently pushed off the marble column with his foot, moving the gondola forward.

On the vaporetto, she traveled back down the Grand Canal toward her home, and tested her language skills on the locals. A secure *buon giorno* or *permesso* came from her lips as she squeezed her way through the crowded water bus. Anyone who didn't catch her American accent might think she was a local, and had been using public transportation her entire life. At the Ca'Rezzonico waterbus stop, she gradually inched her way forward, and followed the crowd past the embarcadero, and into the commotion that filled Venice's *calle* at midday. Like a car surpassing slower vehicles on a highway, she broke from the masses and hastened her step down the shaded alleyway, until she reached the *campo* and the local bakery.

The baker's wife who, engaged in cleaning the already spotless glass counter, set aside the cotton cloth and wiped her hands on her white apron, and then greeted her with a bleak smile. "*Signorina Vittoria*, you are late today. I don't have much left."

Victoria gave a quick glance at the empty wicker bread bins: one long baguette. "*Nessun problema*, I'll take the baguette."

The baker's wife pressed the hard crust between metal prongs and slid the baguette into a paper bag which left a third of the loaf exposed. "And this raisin pound cake? I baked it this morning," she said, intent on selling the last of her daily creations.

She nodded. *Alvise will love that with his morning coffee.*

Bread and pound cake in hand, Victoria crossed the campo, came to the final bridge on her way home, and made one more stop at Dario's boat—a flotilla of fruits and vegetables anchored in the narrow canal.

"*Buon giorno, Signorina Vittoria.* I have special *fragole*...strawberries... for you today. You won't find a better price for such quality. Here, taste one." He placed a dark red berry in her hand.

She bit into the fruit, and let the morsel quench her palate. It was both juicy and sweet. *Dario knows his produce* she thought.

"I'll take a basket."

"*Bene*...they ... are *fa-vo-lo-se* ... fabulous. What else? Zucchini ... you like zucchini, Signorina Vittoria. I brought them in this morning from Saint Erasmo Island."

Her face reddened and she let out a nervous chuckle. Soon after she had arrived in Venice, and before she had taken her first language class, she hated to go grocery shopping without Alvise. She felt humiliated to have to point to the produce and then hold up her fingers to communicate the quantity. Dario must have noticed her face brighten whenever she saw zucchini—one of the few vegetables pronounced the same way in both English and Italian. *How silly* she thought. *There's no need to be so self-conscious and hard on myself. Dario, merely thinks I like zucchini.*

"They are so fresh. Don't cook them. Slice them very, very thin . . . add salt, pepper, olive oil and lemon." Dario drew his fingertips to his lips, and gave them a light kiss. "Voilà, you have excellence."

"That sounds wonderful. I'll take a few zucchini flowers, too."

"*Sì*...zucchini flowers...perfect for risotto *or* simply dust them with flour and lightly fry them in extra-virgin olive oil." He wagged a finger at her. "You know, Signorina Vittoria, only extra-virgin." He looked around, as if ready to commit an illegal act, reached under a crate of tomatoes and pulled out a bottle filled with the green liquid. "Here…it's pressed from the olives in my sister's father-in-law's orchards in Puglia. But don't tell anyone. I sell it only to my special customers—a special price for you, Signorina Vittoria."

"Thank you, Dario. But, I haven't finished the bottle I bought from you last week."

With the same secretive movements he placed the precious bottle back under the crate. "Oh yes . . . yes . . . good." He cast his wide smile, "You see how special I treat you? I forget. What else, Signorina Vittoria?"

"*Basta così*…that's all for today."

Victoria watched him tally the receipt in longhand, double-check his addition, and step off the boat to hand her the bag of goods, and collect his earnings. "Enjoy your day, Signorina Vittoria. And remember, you are a special customer."

Toting her groceries through the sun-splashed Dorsoduro district, Victoria approached a small trattoria at the foot of the bridge. A young woman sat alone at an outdoor table. Her short tousled red hair glistened in the sunlight. She wore a red and white striped sweater, and black pants.

Ivana.

Victoria watched her fill a drinking glass with sparkling water and then chew a bread stick like a beaver gnawing wood. Their eyes met.

Victoria smiled, and walked up to the table. "Ciao. You must be Ivana."

The young woman stopped chewing, and dusted bread crumbs off her pants. "You're the American…Alvise's girlfriend."

I'm his fiancé. "My name is Victoria. How do you know who I am?"

"Venice is small. Everybody learns about everyone else's business…even if they don't want to."

Alvise told me about you, too.

"And we gondoliers are always outside. We pretty much see everything that goes on."

"It's nice to meet Venice's first female gondolier."

"First and *only*…it's nice to meet you, too." Ivana leaned back in her chair, and made room for the waiter to set a small carafe of white wine on the table. A second waiter placed a steaming plate of pasta with fresh mussels in front of her and a mixed seafood salad on the paper placemat next to her.

"I'll let you get to your lunch. *Buon appetito.*"

"My friend Cinzia is in the bathroom. Why don't you join us?"

That would be nice. "Thank you, but I'm expecting Alvise's mother at home in a bit."

"Ooh, no…Anna." Ivana shook her head. She grabbed the carafe of wine and filled two small glasses. "Then you need a glass of wine."

Victoria chuckled, and then checked her watch. "Well…I suppose I have time for a glass of wine." She dropped her grocery bags in an empty chair, and sat down in another. "You know Anna?"

"Everyone knows…"

"…everybody in Venice." Victoria laughed. She picked up her glass of wine. "Here's to becoming more like everyone."

Wearing cropped black hair, and a tailored jacket and skirt, a tall thin woman walked up to the table. "*Buon giorno.*"

"Cinzia, this is Vittoria."

"Ah…Alvise's girlfriend." Cinzia pulled the empty chair away from the table, and sat in front of the seafood salad. "It's nice to finally meet you."

"I told you everyone knows everyone here." Ivana laughed.

Victoria raised her eyebrows, and smiled. "It's nice to meet you, too."

"*Come ti trovi a Venezia?*" said Cinzia.

A line appeared between Victoria's brows. "How did I *find* myself in Venice? I came with Alvise."

Cinzia laughed, and shook her head. "No…"

A loud chortle rose from Ivana's chest. "Not how did you get here. *Come ti trovi a Venezia* means…how do you like being in Venice."

"Doesn't the verb *trovare* mean *to find*?" Victoria's face flushed.

"Well, yes. It means that, too." Cinzia picked up her fork, and pierced a chunk of steamed octopus.

Victoria frowned into her wine glass. *Damn it! Learning Italian is harder than I thought.*

Ivana held a long blackish shell between her finger tips, and using her other hand, extracted the coral colored flesh with a fork. She dropped the sautéed morsel on the pasta, and tossed the empty shell in a bowl filled with the others. She licked the light tomato sauce from her fingers, and then wiped them with a paper napkin. "So how *do* you like Venice?"

"It's beautiful!" *When it's not frustrating.* When she was on vacation in Venice, she'd experienced public office and store hours being different there than in the States. A system that seemed to suit the employees more than customer or client needs. Now, no longer on vacation, the charm of the slower Italian pace, an average of three hour midday breaks, and the *there's always tomorrow* mentality began to tire and wear thin. She wouldn't tell them how, days before, she'd gone to the Post Office and found one service window open, and a line of people streaming out the door and into the campo. She'd also refrain from complaining or telling them how she hadn't waited in line. That, instead, she'd returned the next morning and was welcomed by a locked Post Office door, and a notice taped to the glass window with the words: *Incontro con i Sindacati*—Labor Union Meeting - Post Office closed until *domani*—tomorrow.

So how did she like Venice? Silly, petty things that weren't life changing bothered her, now. Second-hand smoke irked her. She knew Europeans smoked, a lot, and it seemed often without regard to those around them. That, too, while on vacation hadn't bothered her. Then, she'd found smoking *very European chic.* However, now, when she struggled to hide her irritation and, for fear of being perceived as *the bossy American*, she'd move out of the smoke's way, and bit her tongue.

She put her wine glass back down on the table. *Maybe I can share my frustrations. Maybe they have some of the same.* But she wouldn't ask them, nor take the chance they'd find her as irritating as she'd begun to find herself. "What can I say…Venice is simply wonderful." She lifted a packet of bread sticks from a stainless-steel cylinder and tore open the plastic wrap. She extracted a thin stick, and snapped it in half. "Where do you work, Cinzia?"

"In a bank."

Victoria nodded. "That's a nice job." She stopped herself from vocalizing another petty frustration—bank hours in Italy.

"I bank online." Ivana rolled her eyes from Cinzia to Victoria, and then shoved a fork wrapped in spaghetti noodles into her mouth. "You know...banker's hours."

Whew...so it's not just me.

"Where do you prefer living, Venice or Los Angeles?" said Cinzia.

Take Alvise out of the picture and, no doubt, I'd say Los Angeles. "I hate to compare the two."

"Cinzia and I have both been to the States. She had a university internship there, and I've gone on vacation, twice. We know about cities that don't sleep...big business, grabbing fast food on the run, twenty-four hour service and all that...which is great. Still, in Italy, and especially in Venice, most stores, trattorias, and shops are family-run small businesses. Here, a nice break for lunch, sharing a table, food and drink is the fabric Italian culture is cut from." Ivana wiped a chunk of bread across her plate, and popped it in her mouth.

"Having seen the differences, does the pace here ever frustrate you?" said Victoria.

"What frustrates *me* is that I'm the first female to be accepted in a trade that's been around for centuries."

"That makes you a pioneer," said Cinzia.

"Or a red rag in front of a bull," said Ivana.

"Bull meaning?" said Victoria.

"Some of the gondoliers…certainly not all of them, like to throw subtle insults my way, or ignore me. At times, it can be lonely."

I understand lonely, thought Victoria.

"But I worked hard to break that barrier. So I deal with it. Still, I wouldn't mind working with other women."

"What brought you to become a gondolier," said Victoria.

"My mom…she likes to row. She taught me how when I was a kid."

"Then you don't come from a family of gondoliers?"

Ivana shook her head. "No…I come from a family of passionate rowers. At first I hated it. It didn't matter what the weather was like…rain, fog, freezing cold…my mom would force me to get on the boat after school, and row with her. But when I finally mastered the physical movement and the skill needed to command the boat, I fell in love with it. There's something peaceful in the rhythm… in the sound…the oar touching and sculling the water, it's home."

"And it's a sport you're good at," said Cinzia. "She's won more than a few regattas."

"Women compete in regattas, too?"

"They do and have, on and off, for centuries," said Ivana.

Victoria noticed the dry cracked skin on Ivana's fingertips. "At least now anyone can become a gondolier."

"Yes and no. There are rowing exams, and a jury decides which applicants are good enough to attend the gondolier training school." Ivana filled half of her glass with wine, and then topped it off with sparkling water. "Even if there's a woman on the jury now, other women have tried and failed. Honestly, they just weren't up to the task."

Cinzia pushed back her empty plate, and wiped the napkin across her mouth. "Have you tried rowing?"

Victoria didn't see herself as the rowing type, and shuddered at the idea of trying and failing. She'd watched Alvise maneuver his gondola through the tight canals, and wider waterways with ease. But, for her, holding a heavy oar steady in an open oarlock and keeping it from slipping into the water, and possibly her after it, would be difficult to accomplish. "No. But it looks fun."

"The ladies at the rowing club give lessons," said Cinzia. "That's where I learned. You should give it a try."

"Oh, I don't know that I'd..."

"These women are interested in preserving Venetian traditions and rowing as a sport." Ivana looked at Victoria's manicured nails and designer jacket.

Then rowing is definitely not for me. "My sport was a weekend yoga class in Los Angeles."

Ivana raised her eyebrows.

"What?" said Cinzia. "That means she's agile."

Ivana pushed her plate back, too. "These women are serious *athletes*. They compete in and win regattas."

Victoria felt a buzz of excitement. Conversing with women her age harnessed the loneliness that had weighed on her since she'd arrived in Venice. She was thankful for their company. Ivana and Cinzia were the only women in Venice, who weren't related to Alvise, who had taken the time to talk to her.

"Is it true that you worked with movie stars?" said Cinzia.

"I worked for a talent agency. But I just got a new job here. I'll be working at Alvise's uncle's jewelry store."

"You gave up a career in Hollywood to sell jewelry in Venice?" Cinzia plucked a cube of celery from her plate.

Victori grinned. "Blame it on love." *And on the fact that things didn't work out the way I'd planned.*

"Then you're lucky family hires family here. Still, I'd never give up my job for a man." Cinzia turned to Ivana. "Would you?"

Ouch! Victoria understood Cinzia's comment. Before meeting Alvise she'd have questioned anyone who'd have done the same. Still, it hurt to be harshly judged by a woman she'd just met.

Ivana's smile slipped. She looked across the table at Victoria. "I might…for the right man."

Really? thought Victoria.

"You've worked so hard to get where you are," said Cinzia

Haven't we all. I never thought I'd leave my job for a man, either. Not to mention life as I knew it. Victoria sighed and sat back, extending an arm across the back of the chair holding her groceries.

Ivana shrugged the topic off, and grabbed her satchel from the back of her chair, and pulled it to her lap. She reached inside it, and pulled out a packet of tobacco and a stack of rolling papers. "Do you smoke?"

Victoria studied the smoking paraphernalia, and shook her head.

"Will it bother you if I do?"

Victoria forced a smile. "No, it won't. But thank you for asking."

Ivana laid a thin sheet of paper on the placemat in front of her, and sprinkled it with fine cut tobacco leaves. A delicate scent of tea filled the air. She licked the thin paper, folded it over, twisting the ends, and sealed the tobacco inside, and then lifted the cigarette to her lips, and lit it.

Cinzia emptied her glass of sparkling water, and stood. "I've got to get back to work."

Victoria checked her watch. "I need to go, too." Anna would be waiting. She stood and set some euro coins on the table. "For the wine."

"Think about the rowing lessons." Cinzia smiled at Victoria, and then turned to Ivana "see you later." Cinzia left the trattoria, and hurried toward the campo. Ivana remained seated. Enjoying her cigarette, her look said: *Rowing lessons? We'll see.*

Was Cinzia's encouragement to learn how to row polite conversation filler? Victoria was torn by the thought. She wasn't keen on learning to row, but she did like the idea of seeing these women again. She lifted the grocery bags from the chair. "*Arrivederci*, Ivana."

"Yeah. See you around."

Victoria reached the courtyard. Pushing hard on the heavy green door she opened it, stepped inside, and let her eyes adjust to the light. The thick walls and shutters barred the warm midday air and kept the entryway cool, but musty. The sound of footsteps came from the floor above. Alvise was at work, so those footsteps could only mean one thing—Anna had let herself in. At the top of the worn marble stairs, she took a deep breath and opened the glass double doors, and entered the heart of their home. She stepped into the kitchen surrounded by the smell of brewed coffee, chocolate and Anna's sweet honeysuckle perfume.

"This kitchen was fine before." Anna stood at the kitchen table, dividing egg whites from their yolks. "You make it look old…it was better white."

Victoria had stripped the cabinets of their dingy white paint and varnished the wood. *I think the contrast better suits the terracotta tone on the walls.* She set the groceries on the counter, and noticed an extra house key. It was Anna's. "You're early." She looked at the wall clock.

"Five minutes."

Victoria filled a small blue vase with water and the yellow zucchini flowers.

Anna set the egg shells down, and eyed the grocery bags. She wiped her hands on her apron, and then reached in and pulled out the wrapped pound cake. "*Una torta?*"

"Yes, a pound cake. Would you like a slice, with coffee?" said Victoria. "I could put on a pot."

"Now? I'm here to make tiramisu."

Victoria plastered a smile on her face. *Of course…I just thought you might like a piece.* "I'm ready."

Anna picked up the bowl of egg whites. Chocolate shavings, spilt coffee, a packet of petit Oro Saiwa biscotti, and empty egg shells crowded the kitchen table. "Put on that apron." Anna pointed to a pressed square of cloth draped over a kitchen chair.

Victoria tied the floral-print apron around her waist, and washed her hands in the kitchen sink. She felt them shake, and watched Anna whisk the bowl of sugar and egg-whites.

"Take biscotti...dip one by one in coffee...not too much, because they break. Lay them flat at bottom of cake dish."

Victoria lifted a cookie from its package and set it in the plate filled with black coffee. The delicate wafer soaked up the coffee like a sponge, and turned to mush. *Shit!*

"Not too long." Anna scolded. "They break..." Anna handed her the bowl and eggbeater. "Here—*mescola bene*...mix. I do biscotti."

Victoria wrapped her delicate fingers around the wire whisk, and whipped her wrist as fast as she could. She had never beaten egg whites before, not by hand or with an electric mixer. *I can do this,* she thought. However, the faster she beat the foamy substance the more it turned into a slimy mess.

"No." Anna yelled. "They must grow, not sink." She grabbed the bowl from Victoria's hands, and whisked the egg whites hard and fast, mounting them into fluffy foam. "Like this...better you watch."

Great! Now Anna knows I'm not much of a cook. Victoria stepped back and watched Anna add the egg yolks to the whites, fold the soft mascarpone into the mixture and then gently blend the ingredients.

"Take the pieces of chocolate...add them...here in the bowl."

Victoria followed directions and then, like an obedient sous-chef, moved out of the way to observe Anna work like a master

Pastry Chef. Anna moistened a few more cookies with black coffee and added them to the first layer.

"I can help with that." Victoria stepped forward.

Anna answered with silence, and spooned and spread the rich chocolate-chip mascarpone blend over the dipped cookies. She repeated the same layering technique, again and again, letting the creamy mixture seep into every nook and cranny until the cake dish could hold no more.

Feeling useless, Victoria stood at the table and watched, as Anna continued topping off her sweet masterpiece with a thick layer of chocolate shavings. "*Ecco.*" She wiped her hands on her apron, evidently quite pleased with herself. "Put the *tiramisu* in the refrigerator. Leave it for two, three hours before you eat it."

"Thank you." *Next time, maybe you'll let me make it.*

"Now, you clean. I go to home." Anna left her apron for her purse, and grabbed the house key off the counter.

Victoria eyed the key in her hand. "Anna, now that I'm living here…now that this is my home, too…there's really no need for you to have a house key."

Anna's eyes narrowed. She pulled out a business card from her purse, and set it on the counter. "Tomorrow…four o'clock we have appointment at my friend's bridal shop. See you there." She dropped the house key in her purse, and swept out of the kitchen and down the stairs. The heavy front door slammed shut behind her.

Chapter 17

VICTORIA STOOD BENEATH the storefront awning, and studied the white taffeta, lace, pearls and ribbons that embellished the wedding dresses in the window. Did she want a ball gown or a mermaid style? Should it be stark white or ivory? Each of these dresses had some lace. Maybe she wanted silk? Or was satin more traditional and well suited for a romantic wedding in Venice? She had to choose the most important dress she'd ever wear, and had no idea what she wanted. She missed Jackie, and her mom. She smoothed her skirt and adjusted her blouse, and then pushed the heavy glass door open. She stepped inside. Greeted by piped-in classical music, she crossed the parquet floor in her five-inch heels.

A woman dressed in black, her short hair dyed platinum, stood behind the counter. She looked up from a computer screen. *"Posso aiutarla?"*

*"Buon giorno. Mi chiamo Vittoria...*I have an appointment."

"Sì, Vittoria...l'americana...the American? You are Anna's daughter-in-law, yes?"

Victoria nodded. *Future daughter-in-law.*

"Anna and Gina are inside. They're looking at dresses for themselves."

Already? "Did they ask for a certain color?"

"Anna asked for white." The saleswoman smiled.

Victoria's eyes widened. *She agreed she wouldn't wear white.*

"Don't worry. I said no, and brought her a few very nice mother-of-the-groom dresses. Soon you can see for yourself. But first, tell me...how do you see your wedding day?"

"Well, we're getting married here, in Venice, so I imagine it to be very romantic...in a historical setting, but I'd like to give it a contemporary flair."

"Something like...Juliet Capulet meets the red carpet?"

"Exactly...do you have something like that?"

"We do. The designers we carry are very talented. I think you'll look wonderful in any of the creations I have in mind. Now, follow the hallway past the gowns until you reach the sitting room. Anna is trying on dresses in the room on the left. I'll be right there with your dresses."

Victoria's hands jittered, and her heart fluttered. She wondered if all brides-to-be felt this nervous before trying on wedding dresses. She followed the saleswoman's directions and passed the gowns, and entered the sitting room. A gigantic gold-gilded mirror leaned against the wall and reflected a sprawling Murano glass chandelier, and an empty satin loveseat. Center stage, a rectangular pedestal made of lacquered wood sat on an Oriental carpet. She took a deep breath, and knocked on the dressing room's closed door.

"*Avanti.*" Anna's voice rang out.

Victoria entered the small room.

Anna faced her image in the mirror. She wore a knee length satin and lace dress with a bolero jacket—the color of olive oil.

"*Bellissimo*, Anna. I thought I might have Jackie wear a shade of green." *Or maybe tan? I haven't decided which.* "That dress and the color would be perfect for you."

"It's not white...." Anna winked. "But maybe I like it."

"Well you look lovely in it. And the color complements your eyes."

"I need to hear what Gina says. Where is she?"

"Here we are." Hand in hand, Gina and Susanna entered the dressing room. "We were looking at flower girl dresses."

"See anything you like?" Victoria turned to Susanna.

"I saw a lot of them." Susanna held her mother's hand, and twisted her hips, making her circle skirt shift and spin. "Wow… *Nonna. Sei bellissima.*"

"It's a beautiful dress on you, Mamma," said Gina.

Anna turned and looked sideways. She studied herself in the mirror.

The saleswoman peeked into the dressing room, one hand on a rack of hanging taffeta, silk chiffon and beadwork she'd rolled into the sitting room. "Okay ladies. Let's give the bride a chance to look at her options, too. Then we'll find the right dresses for you. *Vittoria*, come with me. I'm putting you in the Brides' dressing room."

"I come, too," said Anna.

"Anna," said the saleswoman "did you decide on that dress?"

"Maybe."

"Did you see anything else you'd like to try on?"

"No. I like this best…so far."

"Then while you're deciding, why don't you change and then wait out here in the sitting room. Gina and Susanna, you can take a seat, too. *Andiamo, Vittoria.*"

Victoria entered the large Bride's dressing room, and pulled out her iPad. "You have Wi-Fi, right? I can't get a connection." *I need to FaceTime my mom.*

"We've been having problems with our internet service. The phone company said it would be resolved by now. Try inserting the password, BelleSpose." The saleswoman pulled an ivory, dropped-waist with sweetheart neckline gown from the rack, and held it up. "Do you want to try this one first?"

Victoria punched in the password, and waited. *Damn it!* "There's no internet access. I can't try anything on without my mother at least being here…electronically."

"Why don't you slip into this dress? I'll button you up, and then I'll try getting the connection for you."

I promised her. "She's waiting for my call." Victoria's eyes flashed.

"I understand that this is important. Trust me a little."

I should've waited. I didn't have to leave Los Angeles so quickly. My mom was right. We're not going to be able to do this together. "I can't do this without my mom."

"Your mother-in-law and sister-in-law are here."

Victoria looked at the saleswoman, pressed her lips together and thought: *My mother-in-law is more interested in her own dress.*

The saleswoman's eyes sparked behind her eyeglasses. "I've known Anna for many years. She comes across harsh, but she's a good person. She's having a tough time letting go of what she loves. All mothers do when their children get married."

So you can imagine how my mother feels about me being here…without her.

"And mothers of sons…well they're different. One day, if you have a son, you'll understand."

Who said anything about me being a mother…let alone having a son? Geez…I haven't picked out my wedding dress yet, and you're talking about my children. That's so…so…not me.

The saleswoman gently laid the dress over a satin upholstered side chair. "I'll give you some time. Call me if you need help."

Victoria sat on the small sofa. Her lashes fluttered, and she pounded the password into her iPad, again and again, and then once more. No network. No 4G or 3G. No nothing. Her eyes welled up. Tears fell onto her cheeks, and into her hands. She felt alone.

Stupid, she told herself. If she had waited, she could have shared this with the people who loved her. She pictured her mother's face and Jackie's smile, and then heard her Grandmother Eunice's voice in her head. *Fight when it matters…and keep a stiff upper lip.* She thought of Alvise, and how sweetly he had kissed her that morning. She pictured him working on his gondola, surrounded by a city she struggled to call home but, day by day, had begun to appreciate. She had him, she reminded herself. In time, the rest would come. Wouldn't it? She chased away the tears, and pulled herself up from the sofa. She slipped off her heels, and got undressed.

Standing in her bra and panties, she lifted the gown from the side chair, and slowly stepped into it. One eye on the mirror, the other on her iPad, she cringed at the way she looked. The taffeta skirt and the puffy sleeves should've been retired in the 1980s. No. Not if it were the last wedding dress in Italy. She wouldn't let anyone see her in this one. She moved to the rack. Pink organza…what was the saleswoman thinking? Next to that hung a simple white satin sheath…pretty, but more like Marilyn Monroe than Juliet. A strapless gown cut from fabric that looked like ready-made store curtains would never do either. One by one, she passed over the others. At the end of the rack, she perked up in front of the last two gowns. She let the gown with the 80s sleeves fall from her shoulders to the floor. She stepped out of the pile of meringue, and into one of the last two gowns. Strapless, white silk covered a nude satin slip. A matching sash accentuated the bust line and waist, and was intended to be tied at the back. Delicate white silk flowers dripped off the bustier and down the flowing skirt like falling blossoms in a spring breeze. More whimsical than she had imagined herself in, she fell for the gown's exquisite detail and fit. She looked down at her iPad, and sighed—still, no connection. Holding the strapless bodice to her breasts with one hand, she stepped back into her heels and opened the dressing room door with the other.

The saleswoman smiled, and rushed forward. She zipped and hooked the gown's bodice, and tied the sash. "I knew you'd like this one. It's from Reem Acra's latest collection. We're the only store in Veneto to carry her collection."

Victoria moved, and the fabric rustled softly as she lifted the gown's skirt. She stepped up and onto the pedestal, and studied her reflection. She approved of what she saw and how she felt in the gown. "What do you think?"

"Sei più bella di una principessa." Susanna touched the dress's train.

"I feel prettier than a princess." Victoria smiled. "Anna…?"

"*Bellissimo*…the *sottoveste*…

"The slip?" confirmed Victoria.

Anna nodded. "The color…what would you call that… *persichino*?"

The saleswoman lifted the dress tag from the back of the dress. "*Sì*, Anna. It says Renaissance peach…perfect for a wedding in Venice."

Victoria swirled the silk skirt, and turned sideways. Looking at her reflection in the mirror, she studied the fitted bodice and the gown's train spilling over the pedestal. "I like it…very much. But there's another one on the rack that I want to try on."

"Only one?" asked the saleswoman.

Victoria nodded. "The white silk chiffon with the beaded bust and cap sleeves."

"That's another favorite of mine from this year's collection." The saleswoman approved.

I wish I could show my mother.

"Wow!" Gina entered the sitting room. "That's gorgeous."

"Do you really like it?"

"I do." Gina tossed her purse on the sofa. "But before I forget, I just heard from Alvise…he said he's been trying to call you, and that you're not answering your phone."

How could I get his calls when there's no….wait? Victoria turned from her own reflection to Gina's. "How did you hear from him?"

Gina shrugged. "I was outside, looking at the flower girls' dresses in the store window when he called. Why?"

Victoria pulled the pile of silk fabric up and held it in a ball above her knees. She hopped off the pedestal and rushed as fast as her heels would permit back into the Bride's dressing room. She grabbed her iPad, and whisked back out into the sitting room, and into the hall.

Anna rose from the sofa. "*Maria Vergine…sei matta*? Are you crazy…what you doing?"

"Wait." The saleswoman yelled.

Victoria pulled the shop door open and stepped onto the canal side stone pavement. Careful not to let the fabric touch the ground, she held the pile of silk with one hand, and flipped open her iPad cover with the other. Still, no connection. She turned to her left and a boat docked canal side. To her right sat a bridge. Holding the dress up, revealing her long legs and high heels, she rushed past amused stares and whistles. At the top of the bridge, she heard her iPad ping. Connection! She flipped it open, again. She selected Mom on her FaceTime address book, and heard it ring.

"Mom!" Victoria looked at her iPad screen.

"Hi Honey, we've been waiting. Jackie and your Grandmother are here, too."

Victoria caught her breath. "Sorry…I'm here now…but I've got to hurry. Can you see me…the dress?"

"I see your head and water. Are you outside?"

"I am." Victoria stretched her arms out in front of her. "Can you see the dress now?"

"Only just a little," said Rose.

"Is that pink?" said Jackie. "You're not wearing pink."

"No…it's not pink. It's beige under white."

"I see tiny flowers," said Eunice. "I like flowers."

Victoria looked around. A small crowd of tourists had formed and were snapping her photo. She rushed up to a Chinese man and held out her iPad. "Please, sir?"

He nodded, and smiled back.

"Thank you." She tried to hand him her iPad, again.

The man stepped beside her, held up his selfie-stick, and then clicked a photo of the two of them.

"No, not a selfie!" She stepped away, and looked behind her. *Shit!* Gina, Susanna, Anna and the saleswoman were at the foot of the bridge, and coming her way.

"Victoria, hold that damn thing still. I'm getting dizzy," said Rose.

"Looks like you're in a big crowd," said Eunice. "They must like your dress."

"Or they hate it," said Jackie.

"You know you guys are not helping matters. I wanted to share this with you. But there's no WiFi connection in the Bridal Shop, so I ran out of the store, and now I'm standing on a bridge."

"You went A.W.O.L. on a Bridal shop? Now I'm really sorry I'm not there." Jackie laughed.

"Uh-oh…I hope there's no law against running out of a store while wearing unpaid merchandise. If so, you're going to have to come bail me out." Victoria stood facing the saleswoman. She swallowed hard. Anna and Gina frowned, and Susanna giggled.

"Give that to me." The saleswoman held out her hand.

"You want me to undress in public?"

"The iPad…give me the iPad."

She handed the iPad to the saleswoman.

The saleswoman looked at the screen. "*Buon giorno*, I am the owner of the bridal shop."

"Hello." Rose answered. "My daughter can be…unpredictable at times."

"I see that. This is a most unusual practice. I could press charges."

"I don't think that will be necessary…she didn't steal the dress," said Eunice.

"No. She looks beautiful in it. Since I am an old friend of Anna's, and we are already outside, I'll make an exception…but just one time. There is another dress, *inside*, that she wants to try on. You will see that one in a photo. Agreed?"

"Yes…and we thank you," said Rose.

The saleswoman turned the iPad around and showed Victoria walking to the other side of the bridge, and stopping at the thick marble balustrade.

Victoria turned and faced the saleswoman and the iPad, and let the silk skirt fall and flow to her feet. She smiled and felt beautiful. Outside, she could see that the dress would be a good choice. It was as romantic as the city that surrounded her. She turned her back to the iPad, and looking over her shoulder gave her audience time to judge the back, too.

"Okay." The saleswoman turned the iPad around and, escorting Victoria down the bridge steps, she spoke into it. "I'll let you quickly talk to your daughter. I must get the dress back in the shop."

"Thank you," said Rose.

Victoria joined Anna and Gina waiting at the foot of the bridge, and took the iPad from the saleswoman. "Mom, real quick...say hello to Alvise's mother and sister. They're here with me." She turned the iPad toward them.

"Anna hello...Gina...oh and little Susanna is there, too. We're very anxious for the wedding and to meet all of you," said Rose.

Anna, with the same wariness she had first greeted Victoria, studied Rose, Eunice and Jackie on the iPad screen. "We are happy to meet you, too."

Gina smiled. "We'd love to host any family members or guests who want to stay in our Bed & Breakfast. We have six rooms."

"That's very kind of you Gina," said Rose.

"*Signore.*" The saleswoman yelled from down the walkway.

"We must go...*arriverderci.*" Anna smiled into the iPad, and then took Susanna by the hand.

"I'll hold the rooms," said Gina.

"Thank you," said Rose.

Victoria turned the iPad around. "I have to go, too. But I need to know what you think about the dress I'm wearing?"

"As long as you say it's not pink, I think it's beautiful," said Jackie. "Have you decided what color I'm wearing yet?"

"I'm leaning toward sage or pistachio...but if I choose this dress, maybe toffee or cappuccino would go better...I'll let you know."

"If you're happy with it, so am I," said Eunice.

"It's gorgeous, and it's gorgeous on you," said Rose. "Now, go along…the saleswoman has been kind enough. Send us a photo of the other one. We'll talk soon about what color you want me to wear, too. I love you."

"We all love you," said Eunice.

"I miss you…" Then, the FaceTime line went dead before Victoria could add, *more than I thought I could.*

Chapter 18

THE CLOCK TICKING, and the wedding mere months away, they spent an afternoon together ordering his tuxedo, the right flowers for their wedding and *bomboniere* gifts for their wedding guests. Then Alvise surprised Victoria with a stroll under the stars. They traveled the uncongested streets, and reached the top of the Academia Bridge. He held her hand, paused and inhaled the cool night air and the vision of the Santa Maria Della Salute Cathedral rising in the distance. Like halos crowning sanctified heads, light encircled the monumental church domes and reflected upon the Grand Canal. Stroked by dusk, the water wore the guise of indigo ink. He leaned against the thick wood railing, pulled her close and took a memorizing look at his city, and then at her. *This can't wait any longer. She has a right to know.*

Resting his chin on her head, he held her tight. Her touch and the splendor that had surrounded him his entire lifetime, beauty he'd become accustomed to but would never take for granted, swelled the nagging uncertainty inside of him. He had assured himself that things would get better once she started working, and they had. She was finding her place in Venice, outside of being his fiancé. Now, it should be easier for her to understand his predicament, and then accept the he might have a son. He took another lingering look at the Grand Canal, and then, his arm draped around her shoulders, led her down the steep bridge, and into Campo Santo Stefano.

Past rows of café tables teemed with patrons dining al fresco, and further down the campo, two musicians sat on stools and played soft sensual music. Alvise led her toward the music. Toned, male and female physiques twisted, turned and quick stepped to the Milonga beat, and Tangoed under the stars.

"Want to give it a try?" he said.

Her mouth dropped open. "Are you sure?"

"Why not?"

"Can we just walk up and join them?"

"There's one way to find out." He squeezed her hand, and they stepped closer to the dance floor.

"*Buona sera.* I am Alejandro, the instructor." Dressed in black slacks and a fitted white cotton shirt, his wide smile greeted them.

"Good evening. We'd like to take a tango lesson," said Victoria.

"Will this be your first?"

"*Sì,*" said Alvise.

"Would you like to begin now?"

They nodded.

"Follow me." Alejandro led them across the stone pavement, to the far side of the make shift dance floor. "This is the beginners' area. We work here. We don't want to intrude on the advanced dancers' space." He tilted his head, and looked at them from head to toe. "Now, the first thing you must learn is posture. I show you." Alejandro raised his arm to the height of his shoulders. He bent his left elbow, and held his left hand up in the air. He wrapped his right arm in front of him as if holding an invisible partner. "The man holds the woman like this." He looked at Alvise. He turned side to side, at the waist. "You try."

Alvise followed his directions. His hands in the air, he twisted his torso from side to side, too. "I look like a fool, right?"

"Maybe a little." Victoria giggled.

"No, he is good, continue like that." Alejandro smiled at Victoria. "Now, the woman must keep her body relaxed. Don't push your chest out. Keep everything in a vertical line." He touched the small of Victoria's back, making her stand taller. "Yes, like this… good. Now, Alvise come here. Embrace each other, softly. Feet together, firm on the ground…turn your torsos, only your torsos… side to side. Repeat…smoothly…side to side. Practice this…I'll be back." Toe to heel, Alejandro stepped away.

Dancing, without moving their feet, Alvise held Victoria in his arms. They twisted their fit torsos to the sweet guitar and bandoneon sounds coming from the two musicians. He studied her face, and felt the urge to kiss her.

"Thank you for this. I know you don't like dancing very much."

All I want is to make you happy.

"*Molto bene.*" Alejandro placed a hand on Alvise's shoulder. "This exercise helps relax the body. Now, I show you the walk. Usually we walk heel to toe, but in Tango we must be light on our feet. You must walk toe first. So walk, toe to heel, toe to heel, stepping with your foot, diagonally crossing your legs. Like this… follow me." Alejandro walked forward, and looked back. "Very good…fast learners…now continue…walk…walk…walk. I'll be back."

Alvise walked to the tango beat.

Victoria joined him, and walked by his side.

He continued walking, placing his right foot in front of his left, again and again. He raised his eyebrows at the couples on their left and at the watching crowd. He stopped walking, and took her hand. "*Amore*, a while back, I received a letter from a person…"

"Who still write letters?"

"It was sent to the traghetto. I guess that's the only way this person could contact me."

"Who is this person?"

"Someone I knew before I met you…"

"Alvise…Vittoria…" Alejandro called from the opposite side of the stone dance floor. "Now, use the same steps, and walk backwards."

Their eyes turned across the campo. Alvise took her hand. They moved backwards, and to the beat.

"Toe to heel…toe to heel…and don't stop." Alejandro yelled. "You must practice…exaggerate the movements. It will make them natural. And…*attenzione*…the other dancers…"

"Hey, watch it." A young man grumbled.

Alvise pulled Victoria to him, and then to the side.

"You keep getting in our way." The man whisked his partner by.

"Vittoria…Alvise you must concentrate." Alejandro scolded.

"*Amore*, we'll talk about the letter…after the lesson." Alvise could see the concerned look on Victoria's face had nothing to do with their dance lesson.

Alejandro approached them. "Remember, the leg movement originates in the torso. Let your body move. Don't hold it back." He looked at his watch. "Enough torso movement for this evening…I show you breathing before we end your lesson. It is very important to dancing. Alvise, stand straight, body weight on the balls of your feet, arms up."

"Like this?" Alvise raised his arms, once again.

"Yes, that is good. Victoria, you do the same. Now breathe deep…deeper…very nice. Now let all the air out. Now, inhale… and step backwards…and now to the side. Repeat the steps together."

Alvise wrapped his arm around her waist, and let the music lead them.

"Good…practice this at home. Remember, we begin each class with these exercises. They will help you master the dance steps. *Arrivederci*." Alejandro stepped away, and held his hand out to a woman dressed in a tight black dress. As if born together on a dance floor, they swept across the campo, stepping to the beat.

Minutes later, Alvise led Victoria through their neighborhood. She hummed the sensual tune they'd left in the campo, and he listened. At home, he followed her up the entryway stairs.

"You look stunning tonight."

"In jeans and a top?" She laughed, and walked down the hall to their bedroom.

I've got to tell her.

"...the Tango lesson was wonderful, even if I felt completely uncoordinated." She smiled, and stopped to let him unzip the back of her top.

"About that letter..." He opened the armoire, and hung up his jacket.

She slipped off her top, and stepped out of her jeans.

He unbuttoned his shirtsleeves. "I don't want to keep anything from you."

"What's to keep?"

He slung the Oxford shirt over the back of the chair, and then sat down and pulled off his jeans. "It was from a friend of a girl I met about five years ago. They're Swedish."

Victoria slipped a silk nightgown over her head. "Who's the girl...the one you met?"

"Her name is Zinnia. I haven't spoken to her since...I'd forgotten all about her."

"Then you couldn't have spent much time together."

"One evening, that's all. I was with Ciano. He had met Magda...the friend who wrote the letter. He wanted to go out with her, so I went along for pizza..."

"Anything else...besides pizza?"

Alvise nodded. He sat on the corner of the bed, shirtless and wearing boxer shorts—his feet and knees spread apart formed a 'V'.

Victoria stood in front of him, between his knees, and like a sculptress molding clay, caressed the back of his neck. "Of course I don't like the idea of you with another woman. But that was long before we met. We both know we weren't each other's first. But why would her friend write you?""

He sighed. "There was a photo of a little boy with the letter."

Victoria looked down at him, her eyes narrowed.

"His name is Thor." His eyes traced the curves of her face, and then dropped to her bare feet. He swallowed. "She says I'm his father."

"What?" She stepped back.

"I find it hard to believe, too."

"No. If it were true, she…the boy's mother…would have told you years ago. It makes no sense that her *friend* would write you now."

"She said she thought I should know."

"You're talking as if you're convinced that this child is yours? Why? Where's the proof?"

"The photo…the similarities are strong."

"Your proof is a photo? No…I'm sorry. You can't buy this story…not just like that."

"What else can I do?"

"Get a paternity test, to start. Did you contact this *friend*?"

"No."

"Show me the photo." Victoria paced the bedside oriental runner.

"I don't have it. I got rid of it."

"Why would you do that?"

Fear and shock. Alvise stood, and faced her.

"How long have you known?"

"A while."

"And you're only telling me now?"

"I was afraid you'd leave." He went around to the chest of drawers, and pulled a slip of paper from the top drawer. He held it out. "This morning, I received a second letter at work."

Victoria took the paper from his hand. She unfolded the printed letter, and read it out loud:

Alvise,

Zinnia would be mad if she knew I write. She told me not to. She was very sick. There was nothing more the doctors could do. We had a beautiful funeral for her.

Victoria stopped reading and stared at the page. "Oh my goodness. This is terrible."

Alvise nodded. "Go on."

Victoria sighed deeply and sat on the bed, and then continued reading out loud.

The boy will stay with me. Zinnia had no one else.
Magda

Alvise watched her face go pale, and the letter drop from her hand to the bed. He sat next to her, as she fell back on the soft covers. "I need you with me on this." He took her hand and fell back on the bed, next to her, and looked up at the corniced ceiling.

She rose from the bed. Her back to him, she removed her hoop earrings, and set them on the chest of drawers.

Alvise stood, and turned her to face him. "Like you said. We don't know if I'm his father."

Standing in the bedroom doorway, Victoria turned around. "I need time to digest this."

Alvise rushed to her side. "None of this changes us or how I feel about you." *Please don't let it change how you feel about me.*

Victoria looked up at him, her eyes wet with tears. "When you write Magda, tell her that *we* want a paternity test."

He shook his head. "She didn't leave an address or email... nothing."

"That makes even less sense."

"Maybe all she wants is to let me know the boy exists."

"Then why wait until now to tell you?" Victoria threw her hands in the air, and walked away.

"Where are you going?" He followed her out of the room.

"It doesn't matter that he's in Sweden. We need to confirm whether this boy is or isn't your son. Do you have Zinnia's or Magda's last name." She entered the study, sat down at the antique desk, and opened her MacBook.

Alvise filled the doorway. "I barely remembered their first names."

"Great. Then a web search won't work." She tapped her fingers on the desk. "Jackie's a juvenile court attorney. She'll know about paternity tests and such."

"I'll contact an attorney, here, in the morning."

Victoria looked up at Alvise. "I need a second, okay?" She waited for him to leave the room, and then turned back to the MacBook. She typed Jackie's email address, and then *you won't believe this*, in the subject line. She gave details about Zinnia and Thor and Magda. She asked for her friend's advice, and then added: *Please don't tell my family. I'll do that when the time is right. I await your thoughts.* She hit the send tab, sat back and then Googled paternity test. She clicked DNA paternity testing Wikipedia, and her iPhone rang. *Jackie.*

"You got my email."

"What the heck…? Is this a joke?"

"I wish it were."

"Shit. What are you going to do?"

"Get a paternity test. How easy is that?"

"It's hard to say how things work there, but here you need to go to a qualified lab or it won't be accepted in court…if you need to go to court. And, since the boy's mother is dead, you'll need his guardian's approval. Is that this…Magda?"

"I guess so. She said he's living with her. But we have no way to contact her or the boy."

"Well, if you do find a way to get hold of her, get her to consent to a paternity test…better if she does it in writing in front of witnesses."

"What if we can't get hold of her?"

"Well, you either ignore the situation, or go to court. Do you know the boy's last name?"

"No."

"That's makes it pretty difficult. I'm sorry. I wish I could be more helpful…but you're dealing with hearsay, and Swedish and Italian law. Get an attorney there to counsel you."

"We are…in the morning."

Chapter 19

THE SUN BLAZED, the air turned humid, and June arrived with no further news from Sweden. Madga's silence blocked Alvise from requesting a paternity test, and the boy remained a stranger in and out of their lives. Together, Victoria and Alvise decided not to tell their parents about Thor. *No need, until we're certain he's your son.* With time rushing them closer to their September wedding date, Victoria sent the boy and the situation to the back of her mind, and mailed their wedding announcements out.

Three months until the wedding, and two months since Victoria had taken a job at Uncle Fausto's jewelry store, everyday life rushed time along. Still, she missed her old job and colleagues. She wondered what the new agency offices looked like, and: *Who replaced me as Chloe's executive assistant?* When she'd read the Vanity Fair online article about her former boss, their famous clients, and Chloe's and Howard's successful Hollywood industry shake up, she imagined being part of that, too. June was summer blockbuster premiere season—a time when, almost nightly, red carpets were laid out for movie stars to walk on along Hollywood Boulevard or in Westwood Village. Nostalgia pulled her back to those celebrations and the excitement felt when she was a Hollywood insider. Instead now, she was an outsider who sold stunning jewelry to rich tourists, and felt she could do more. *That's normal,* she would tell herself. After all, she hadn't gone to university to be a salesgirl. On the other hand, she had to admit, she welcomed the lack of pressure at work. No long afterhours, no fretting over work matters at home.

Fausto treated Victoria like family, and called her *sveglia*—smart, alert. Pleased with her work ethic, he trusted her to handle the most finicky customers with little interference on his part.

On the contrary, Debora, the shop's other saleswoman, and someone Alvise had known since grade school, clearly had no intention of playing runner up to Victoria or becoming her friend. Wise to her reputation for being very popular around town, Alvise had warned Victoria that she was known as someone who didn't mind her own business. Victoria wasn't concerned. She'd kept Alvise's secret, and had nothing else to hide.

Her workday routine marched on. She'd learned that the late spring season brought well-to-do tourists into the store, each searching for the perfect luxury keepsake to take home. That afternoon, she showed a silver-haired Swiss couple a Blackamoor brooch. The exquisite piece, carved from onyx with turban and bust set in yellow gold, sapphires, emeralds, rubies and diamonds, was one of the shop's more expensive items. She followed Fausto's training advice, and informed the couple that the inspiration for Blackamoor jewelry came from Shakespeare's Othello.

"I'm a great fan of Shakespeare, and the opera." The woman lifted her square chin up, and let Victoria pin the brooch to her jacket. She adjusted the countertop mirror, and studied her dignified reflection for a long while.

"The sapphires make your eyes shine even more," said Victoria.

The woman tucked a wave of silver hair behind her ear, and moved closer to her reflection. "Do they, darling?" She spoke to her husband, never taking her eyes from the mirror.

Victoria watched pride soften the gentleman's face. He scrutinized his wife and the precious pin, and then nodded in agreement. The woman glanced at her husband, and nodded back. Satisfaction lifted the corners of Victoria's lips: *Sold* she thought.

"Such a beautiful piece." Debora stepped behind the woman. She looked over the customer's shoulder, and into the mirror. "Some say it might actually have been inspired by an African slave, not an African General."

"A slave?" The woman turned from the mirror to her husband, and then to Debora, whose grin made it clear she enjoyed the turmoil she had caused.

The husband's thin pale skin had turned pink. "Well…now that you mention it…one might think it was a slave."

"I could never…" The woman turned back to the mirror.

Time and again, and up to that moment, Victoria had heard Debora describe the classic Venetian brooch as Shakespeare's Othello, and without making a sale. It was Victoria who, on her first day at work, had said the pin reminded her more of an African slave. Fausto and Debora had instructed her to never present it as such, and assured her that the original had been designed to represent the Moor of Venice. Now, Debora chose to use Victoria's words to jeopardize her sale.

"A glass of wine, while you think about it?" said Fausto.

"That would be lovely." The woman's complexion flushed with indecision.

"Do you have Prosecco?" said the gentleman. "We're quite fond of Prosecco."

"Yes, we do. Debora!" Fausto tilted his head toward the back room.

"Me?"

"Bring the chilled bottle and the proper glasses."

Victoria, raging inside, appeared as cool as the spring day. She waited, and watched Debora storm out of the room. Still standing behind the counter, she caught Fausto confidently smiling in her direction. She took a quiet, deep breath, and said "The truth is, Madam, that no one really knows where the jeweler's inspiration came from. So, its meaning is quite subjective. What matters is who's wearing it." She had pulled the couple's attention back to her. "Sir, what did you think when you first saw the piece?"

"I was convinced it was the Moor of Venice."

"As was I convinced." The woman's expression was like that of a child yearning to believe a fairy-tale. "That's why we came into your store."

Victoria nodded. "Then that's who this exquisite brooch represents. It would be the same if you were viewing a painting. Art...beautiful objects...conjure up different sentiments in different people. What matters is how you feel when looking at a painting or wearing a stunning piece of jewelry. And, I've never seen this brooch look more stunning than it does now, on you."

"I do love it, dear." The woman glanced at her husband. "And I did, honestly, think it was the Moor of Venice. Otherwise, I'd have never put it on."

"Then it's yours. No need to take it off." The man pulled his wallet from his jacket.

"Thank you, darling," said the woman. "I'm going to wear it the entire time we're in Venice. And I can't wait to dazzle the ladies at the club with it."

Triumphant, Victoria took the credit card from the man's hand. She avoided making eye contact with Debora who had returned to the showroom with a scowl, and the Prosecco. Fausto filled the wine glasses, and then raised his to their good health. Victoria fit the empty brooch box in its draw-string sack, and slipped the sack into a royal-blue shopping bag. She waited until the couple had emptied their glasses and, escorting them to the door, placed the bag's silk cord between the woman's fingers, and thanked them both with a solid handshake.

Back at the sales counter, Victoria folded the felt showroom pad, slipped it into a drawer, and then wiped the glass countertop clean. Fausto stood opposite her, punching numbers into a calculator. He repeated the gesture twice, and then turned the calculator for her to read. The hefty sales commission amount filled the gray screen. She released a broad smile, and silently rejoiced at the jaundiced look frozen on Debora's face.

"See you tomorrow, Fausto." Ending her shift, Victoria grabbed her purse from the backroom. "Goodbye, Debora." She ignored her colleague's silence, and exited the store.

Walking toward the Rialto, she stopped for a quick look at the Fratelli Rossetti shoe store's new window display. Bright-yellow leather walking shoes and matching bag sat center stage. *They would look great with shorts or jeans…but no time for shopping right now.* She'd come back after pay-day, and add the sunny color, which dressed about every shop window in Venice, to her wardrobe.

She tilted her head to study the stylish spring collection, and saw Ivana's reflection in the window. She stood behind her. Speechless, her eyes glued to Ivana's reflection, Victoria didn't move. Somehow, seeing Ivana there made her nervous.

"Hey…it's been a while." Ivana tapped Victoria's shoulder.

Victoria turned. "This is a surprise to see you here." She glanced around. "Are you working nearby?"

"I'm substituting for a colleague at the Carbon traghetto… near Rialto."

Victoria took a step back, widening the distance between them. "I'm on my way to meet Alvise."

Ivana narrowed the distance between them. "I heard about the boy."

Victoria's mouth dropped open.

"Ciano told me."

Of course Alvise would confide in Ciano. But why would Ciano tell you?

"You see…we've been…well we're dating."

The corners of Victoria's mouth turned up. *Why does everyone in town know my business, and I know nothing about anyone else's?*

"We're keeping our relationship private, for now."

I'd like to keep my private life private, too. "I like that idea…of you two together."

"Me, too. Listen Vittoria…I've been meaning to get in touch."

Ivana seemed sincere. Even if she was being polite, Victoria liked the idea of her wanting to get in touch.

Ivana stepped out of the way of other window shoppers. "Can we go someplace where we can talk?"

"Alvise is waiting." Victoria glanced at her wristwatch.

"It won't take long."

She followed Ivana across the campo and up the San Salvador Church's steep marble steps. Ivana pulled the heavy wood door open, and let her enter the cool, quiet cathedral first. Victoria touched her fingertips to the holy water, sending quiet ripples to the baptismal basin's marble rim. She crossed herself, and let the dab of water linger on her forehead. She slid into the first pew from the entrance and waited as Ivana did the same.

"I guess I need to be careful what I say in here." Ivana smiled, and her voice echoed up to the cupola.

"We better whisper." Victoria spoke, as if in prayer.

"Please don't take what I have to say as meddling."

Victoria looked embarrassed. *What could she possibly have to say?*

The wooden pew creaked under Ivana's weight. "Don't ruin what you and Alvise have together."

What else has Ciano told you? "What are you talking about?" Victoria's voice ricocheted back from every altar, and dome. She looked up as if watching the sound of her own invisible voice, and met the critical eye of a young nun who had appeared as if from out of nowhere. The nun's quiet steps paused at their pew and, holding her index finger to her lips, she reminded them that they sat in a holy place.

"Ciano says that Alvise is afraid things might change between you two, because of the boy."

Victoria felt vulnerable, but saw the sincerity in Ivana's eyes. *If the boy is his, how can things not change?*

Ivana pulled a worn photo from her wallet, and handed it to Victoria. "This is my mother. We have the same red hair, but besides that…"

Why are you showing me this photo? Puzzled, Victoria observed the photo, and then Ivana's face. "She's very pretty. You got her freckles, too."

Ivana took the photo back. "She died when I was six years old." She held the photo between her calloused fingers, and studied it.

Compassion crossed Victoria's face, and her shoulders slumped.

"My mother who raised me isn't my real mother."

Victoria sighed, and glanced up at the statue of the Virgin Mary—her arms opened to the world. "I'm so sorry."

"I'm not telling you this for pity. I'm telling you because I know how frightened and alone that little boy feels right now. He probably thinks he's responsible for his mother's death. For a long time, I did."

"I don't mean the boy any harm." Victoria looked around the sacred grounds, and hoped God didn't think she was a terrible person. "We've tried to contact him." *This situation isn't the same as yours. Is it?*

"I don't mean to insinuate anything…you and Alvise aren't even married yet, and you have to deal with a boy neither of you know. My mother, the one who raised me, knew what she was in for when she married my dad."

"You must think I'm awful for not…well, jumping for joy." *Honestly, I don't recognize myself anymore.*

"I think you're an awesomely strong and courageous woman. Otherwise how could you have left everything for a place you knew nothing about? The world tells us it's okay to sacrifice for and follow our career—that it's acceptable. But few women, today, take that same chance on love."

It's not for the faint hearted. Victoria raised her eyebrows. "When things get tough, I tell myself that this was meant to be...that destiny had me fall in love with a wonderful man, and decided to put me here in Venice." *And then dropped me into this predicament.*

"Destiny?" Ivana shook her head. "Nah. I believe life hands each of us our share of shit, and then sits back and lets us decide if we want to sink or swim in it."

Victoria glanced at her wrist watch. She stood, and hugged Ivana. Turning to the altar, she made the sign of the cross. *God, I miss this. Friendship feels good.*

When she had first met Ivana, Victoria thought she was obstinate and rough around the edges. Now she realized she had been wrong. There was more to her, and she liked what she saw. Side by side, they exited the sacred church, and then, standing in the nearby campo, exchanged numbers on their cellphones.

"You've got a rowing lesson waiting," said Ivana.

I could give it a try. Victoria shrugged her shoulders and smiled. Waving goodbye, she rushed toward Campo Santa Maria Formosa, and Alvise.

Chapter 20

VICTORIA AND ALVISE found the ground floor door ajar. They stepped into the eerie silence of his parents' apartment building, and shut the heavy door behind them. The light was dim, the air was musty, and the cooler temperature inside the large entryway felt more like early spring than summer. One behind the other, they climbed the steep flights of stairs. It seemed to Victoria, that with each visit to Anna's, the marble steps up to the top floor multiplied. When they reached the third-floor stairwell, Victoria stopped and caught her breath. "Did you know that Ivana and Ciano are dating?" she said.

"No. That son of a..." Alvise laughed. "Who told you that?"

"She did. I just ran into her."

"Then that's why he's always at her traghetto."

"They make a nice couple. And she knows about Thor." She kept her voice low, and followed Alvise up the last flight of stairs.

Alvise didn't answer.

"What if word gets around...gets to your parents?"

"I think we can trust her...them."

At the top, Victoria straightened her skirt, fluffed her hair, and felt the nervous tension that choked her spirit whenever she visited Anna. "Did your mother say what she wanted to talk to us about?"

He shook his head.

Victoria inhaled another deep breath, and then exhaled a fraction of her anxiety. Alvise kissed her cheek, and then raised his fist to the ironclad door, and knocked.

Gina opened it, her smile more tense than usual. "Ciao."

"What no clients at the B&B today?" Alvise kissed his sister's cheek.

Gina didn't smile. "Mamma called me over."

"Yeah, she called me, too. Any idea why?"

"She didn't tell you?" said Gina.

Alvise shook his head, and they entered the apartment. Victoria hooked her purse on the coatrack, and Alvise crossed the hall and walked into the living room. Susanna sat on the terrazzo floor brushing the long purple mane of a plastic miniature pony.

"Hey, what's up?" he said, and then his eyes widened. A tow-head child, dressed in jeans, a plaid shirt and slip-on Vans tennis shoes, trotted a similar orange pony in and out of a pink plastic castle, and played next to her.

"Ciao, Zio." Susanna flashed a sweet smile, and continued to comb her pony's mane.

Alvise stared long and hard at the boy. The little boy halted his pony's trot. He tilted his head, smiled up at Alvise and then at Victoria.

"His name is Thor," said Susanna.

Victoria stood opposite Alvise, and felt her heart jump to her throat. She looked at the boy, and then at Alvise, and then back at the boy. Disbelief swelled in her veins, and her hands trembled. She searched the boy's face for some resemblance to Alvise.

"Who are you?" The boy resumed racing his pony around the castle.

Alvise glanced at Victoria, incredulous at the situation. His voice came out in a whisper. "I'm Alvise, and this is Vittoria."

Thor studied him. "Are you my daddy? My mommy said my daddy is Italian, and Aunt Magda said he lives in Venice, and drives a boat."

Speechless, Alvise's face went blank, his eyes left Victoria's, and went to Gina, sitting on the couch. The suddenness of the boy's comment seemed to take them all by surprise.

"He's Zio Alvise." Susanna braided her pony's mane. "You can call him Zio, too."

Thor eyed Alvise as if deciding, and then shook his head. "You want to play?" He held up a third miniature blue pony with a long yellow mane.

Alvise stepped forward, and then slowly sat down cross-legged on the terrazzo floor. He took the pony from Thor's tiny hand, and talked into the toy's blue face. "My name is Alvise. So why don't you call me Alvise?"

"We can call him Alvise," said Thor to his toy pony.

The children laughed. Stunned, Alvise chased their ponies with his. Their cheer confused Victoria's heart. She bit her lip, and then forced a smile on her face.

Anna stood at the living room entrance. "Alvise…Vittoria, come I make coffee."

Alvise left the toy horse and the children to play. He stood up, and took Victoria by the hand.

"What is going on?" whispered Victoria.

"We're about to find out," said Alvise.

They followed Anna into the kitchen, and watched her fill the aluminum six-cup moka pot with tap water, and spoon black ground coffee into its funnel. Anna lit the gas burner, and placed the tightly closed coffee maker on top. "*Allora…*well? How do you think I feel?"

"I can explain," said Alvise.

Anna placed her hands on her hips. "First, you listen. A few hours ago a woman rings the bell. She says she's looking for gondolier named Alvise Moro."

"How did she find the house?" said Alvise.

"She says she asks people, and a gondolier says the Moro family live here. So I open the door, and find her and this beautiful boy standing outside my door. Her name is…"

Magda thought Victoria.

"Magna...Maga…*no lo so!* She says the boy is your son…*my grandson.*" Anna raised her hands to the ceiling, and then, as if in pain, pulled them to her chest. "And, *Santa Maria Vergine*, the mother is…" keeping her left hand on her heart, she made the sign of the cross with her right hand "…*morta*…dead."

"She never said she was bringing the boy to Venice." Victoria turned to Alvise. *Or did she?*

"You know about the boy?" said Anna.

Victoria brought her hand to her mouth, and nodded.

"Magda wrote, twice, a while back. But I had no way of contacting her," said Alvise.

"Is he your son?" said Anna.

Alvise threw his hands up in the air. "I don't know."

"You don't tell me I have a grandson?"

He may not be your grandson, thought Victoria.

"Where is she? Where's Magda." said Alvise.

"She took her things to a hotel." Gina stepped into the kitchen. "I offered her a room at the Bed & Breakfast, but she'd already made reservations elsewhere."

"Her things?" said Victoria.

"She left Thor's things here." Gina's jaw tightened.

He's staying here? Victoria shot a puzzled look at Alvise, and then at Anna.

Anna pulled a round Tupperware holder from the pantry. "He's my grandson. While he's in Venice, I want him here." She filled a plate with homemade 'S' shaped egg cookies. "Now, Vittoria…get the fruit juice from the cupboard."

"Anna, we need to be sure. We need to question this whole thing." Victoria went to the cupboard.

Alvise turned a silent, grave look toward his mother. "Mamma, it's too early to jump to conclusions. I'm going to ask for a paternity test."

Silence fell upon the kitchen, but Anna's glare underscored her acceptance that this boy was her grandson. "What will a test prove? That this child has no mother *or* father? Do you want to deprive him of having even one parent?"

That's not fair. Alvise and the boy deserve to know the truth. Victoria lifted a bottle of apricot nectar from the shelf, when a knock came to the front door.

"*Vado io,*" said Gina, exiting the kitchen. The children, and their laughter, followed her to open the door.

A high pitched woman's voice, calling out in an unrecognizable language, entered the apartment, and caused Thor to walk down the hall, not run. The children giggled, nudging one another until they took their places in front of the pony castle, once again. Magda, dressed as if she had stepped off the pages of a 1970s beatnik magazine, followed the children to the living room. She stopped when Alvise and Victoria entered the room, too.

Holding the plate of biscotti in one hand and the apricot nectar bottle in the other, Victoria noted the woman's Nordic good looks. The odd combination of one blue eye and one brown made Victoria take a second, longer look. The woman's powerful features made Victoria feel less pretty. She nodded at Magda, and then set the refreshments on the table.

"Hallo, Alvise." Magda's eyes widened.

"Hello, Magda." He reached for Victoria's hand, and brought her to his side. "Vittoria, my fiancé, and I are very sorry to hear about Zinnia."

"I'm certain you're *surprised,* as well." Magda glanced at Victoria, and then across the room at Thor.

"We'll talk about how surprised later," said Alvise.

"*Caffè*?" Without waiting for a reply Anna clutched the hot espresso pot's handle through a frayed kitchen glove and poured the bubbling, tar-colored liquid for her guests.

"Thank you." Magda reached for the ceramic demitasse.

"Sit, Maga," said Anna.

"Mag—da." The Swedish guest corrected Anna.

"*Sì, va bene*…Alvise…Vittoria you sit there, next to Gina."

Victoria sat and stirred her coffee, and scrutinized Magda. *How could this woman show up unannounced? What does she want?*

Magda stared back at Victoria, and then looked at Alvise.

"I left a message for Bruno at work . . . *prima*." Impatience written on Anna's face, she sat down. "I called the traghetto *before*."

"We don't need to wait." Alvise drank the small dose of espresso in one quick gulp.

"We need a discussion as family—*è una situazione molto seria* . . ."

"A very serious situation." Gina interpreted between sips of coffee.

Anna stumbled between the two languages. Her frustration bellowed to the surface.

Victoria's eyes darted from Anna to Alvise, and back.

"Mamma…Alvise, I think it *would be* better if we waited for Papà to arrive," said Gina.

"Don't you interfere." Anna's voice startled the children's attention away from their toys.

Humiliation painted Gina's cheeks. She hid her embarrassment behind a long sip of coffee.

Anna stood and walked over to the young boy. "*Questo bambino* . . . this little boy . . . this *bellissimo* child is . . . *mio nipote* . . . my grandson." Tears drowned under her voice.

Alvise stood. "Gina, would you please take the children out... to play?"

"I'd be happy to." Gina jumped up from her chair. "Come Thor...Susanna. We'll be in the campo. We'll wait for Papà there." The children scurried through the front door, and Gina followed, closing it behind them.

Alvise turned to Magda. "I imagine this period has been difficult. Still, your visit is unexpected...almost as surprising as finding out after four years that I, apparently, have a son."

"Did you look at him?" Anna protested. "He is you...with blonder hair and blue eyes."

"Mamma, as I said before, it is only fair, and intelligent, that all doubt be cleared from everyone's mind."

"Magda, you understand that we need proof that Alvise is Thor's father," said Victoria.

"Anna is right. There *is* a very strong resemblance." Magda placed her demitasse cup on the table. "And Zinnia told me, before he was born, that she got pregnant on our trip to Italy...and that Alvise is his father."

Honestly, I don't see the resemblance. Victoria squared her shoulders and pinned her spine against the rigid dining room chair. She wasn't about to concede her fiancé. She stopped her hands from shaking, and placed her empty coffee cup on the table beside her.

"A paternity test will prove if I am," said Alvise.

A flurry of questions flashed through Victoria's mind, but only two came to her lips. "Madga, if Zinnia was so sure Alvise was her son's father, why didn't she tell him she was expecting his child? Or contact him when the boy was born?"

"She never told me why. She loved Thor very much. Maybe she was afraid she would lose her son, if the boy's father knew he existed."

"Thor is my grandson. *Le nonne*...grandmothers...know these things. And nothing stands in the way of family." Anna insisted.

Alvise held his head in his hands. "Magda, if Zinnia hadn't died, would I have ever known about Thor?"

"What difference does that make now?" Magda brushed back a strand of hair.

"From what I understand, Zinnia asked you to be his guardian, so it makes a difference." He stood and went to the nearby console. "As his guardian, you need to authorize a DNA test. We'll get that done, while you and Thor are in Venice." Alvise took a sheet of paper and a ballpoint pen from a drawer. He scribbled out an agreement, like Jackie and his attorney had suggested, and then handed the paper and pen to her. "Please, sign it. It's the only way we can be sure."

Disappointment pulled Magda's face into a frown. "The boy needs his father." She took the pen, and scrawled her signature and the date at the bottom of the page.

His mother didn't seem to think so, thought Victoria.

Alvise took the pen and document back.

"Life changes," said Magda.

"Zinnia's decisions have certainly changed mine," said Alvise.

"She never wanted anything from you," said Magda.

"Maybe not. But, if Thor is my son, I had the right to know long before now."

The lock on the front door clicked. Gina's voice and the children's laughter entered the apartment first, and Bruno's deep laugh followed.

"The boy will stay here. This is his home." Anna moved around the coffee table, and gathered the empty coffee cups and saucers onto a tray.

Stay here? Home? He's just here to visit, thought Victoria.

Bruno entered the living room, behind the children. He nodded at Magda, and then at Alvise and Victoria. He flashed an irritated look at his wife. "Gina filled me in...but what the hell are you doing?"

"I'm protecting our family." Anna lifted the tray of coffee stained cups and saucers from the table, and set it on the credenza.

Bruno stepped into the core of the room, and turned to Magda. "Young lady, I'm warning you. You better not try and fool a Moro."

"No sir. I'm not." Magda twisted the handkerchief hem on her skirt around her long fingers. "But the truth is...the reason we came to Venice is because...I'm pregnant."

Except for the children quietly playing in the corner, the room fell silent.

Magda looked up at the ceiling, her eyes were wet. "Izak, my boyfriend, won't take the boy in. We can't afford two children. If he stays with me, my boyfriend won't."

Victoria's mouth fell open. Her face mirrored the shock on Alvise's. *Is she saying, the boy stays with us or...what?* Victoria pulled herself up from the chair, and went to the window. Outside, the setting sun washed the sky pink and purple.

"I love Thor, like he was my own. But I love my baby and my partner, too." Magda laid her hand on her stomach.

"Didn't his mother leave anything…financially?" said Bruno.

Magda shook her head. "Very little…I used most of it to come here." She picked up her coffee cup. "We traveled here by ferry boat and then by train…to save money."

Victoria watched Magda grip the demitasse. *They traveled all the way from Sweden by train? That doesn't sound right. Wouldn't it have been cheaper to fly?*

"Papà, it's not about money." Alvise stood behind Victoria, at the window.

"When you have a family, money is always a problem." Bruno threw his hands up to the ceiling.

Victoria turned her back on the window, and stepped around Alvise. "Magda, we don't know if he's Alvise's son."

"Say what you will, he is the very picture of Alvise." Magda moved her hand out to Thor who, smiling a grand smile skipped to her, and settled onto her lap.

Victoria took another long, hard look at the boy. She thought about what Ivana had told her about children being the ones to suffer most. *How could this innocent child be put in the middle of such turmoil?* Still, she didn't trust Magda. She listened to her gut, and then sat quiet and listened to the others.

Bruno walked across the Persian rug, and settled into the overstuffed arm chair. He leaned forward, resting his elbows on his knees, and clasped his calloused hands together. "Young lady." Bruno called to Magda. "I understand the predicament you're in, and what you're trying to do for the boy. But I need to speak with my family now. Give us a moment alone." Bruno gestured at Magda, asking her to leave the room.

Magda gently set Thor down and then stood up, her eyes lowered to the terrazzo floor and away from Bruno. Without a word, she took Thor and Susanna with her to the kitchen.

The kitchen door closed, and Bruno continued. "Alvise, if you take this boy in…you need to consider everything."

Alvise nodded, his eyes widened.

"Nonno's will, too." Anna brushed a piece of lint from her housedress and finger-combed waves of brown hair away from her face.

"What's his will got to do with this? I inherited his house, when I became a gondolier," said Alvise.

"Actually, you're its custodian," said Bruno.

A serious look covered Alvise's face. "I understand that."

Well I don't, thought Victoria.

Bruno looked at Alvise. "Your grandfather's decision to leave you the house already caused one family feud, and now this. Son, Victoria needs to know."

What do I need to know?

Alvise sighed, and turned to Victoria. "Not long after my grandmother died and before my grandfather fell ill, my grandfather wrote his will…a handwritten letter with instructions for the house in Dorsoduro."

"Anna, get the letter." Bruno pointed to the wooden console.

Anna crossed to the console and found a thin envelope at the bottom of a stack of papers. She pulled out the will, and held it out to her husband.

Bruno took the will from Anna's fingers. "He wrote that since all his children owned homes in Venice already, his home would go to his eldest grandson."

Victoria listened.

"He doesn't name Alvise in the letter. It just says the eldest grandson." Bruno handed Victoria the single-page letter, and softened his tone. "There were two conditions. One, his eldest grandson had to become a gondolier. And two, the house would then be passed onto his eldest grandson's eldest son, who in turn would acquire the house once *he* became a gondolier, too."

Anna stepped forward. "No mention of a wife, or other children."

Troubled by the letter in her hand, Victoria shifted her gaze from the rudimentary writing on the page to the framed watercolor of Alvise's grandfather staring back at her from the living room wall. She found it difficult to control an unexpected surge of insecurity. Did that mean if Thor was Alvise's son, and something happened to Alvise, she would be out on the street? She went back to the window, and looked at the scattered chimneys rising from the adjacent rooftops.

"My father loved that house and he worked hard to get it," said Bruno. "He lived most of his life there, and he wanted it to remain the home of a gondolier. Nothing would make him sell it. That is the reason why the family stopped feuding over it, and agreed to let Alvise have it. Because he's the one left who can continue the trade. The same will happen for *his* son."

Bewildered, Victoria stood looking out the window. The powerful news left her wondering whether his grandfather's wishes were a blessing or a curse. "What if, one day, we have a child?"

"It states eldest great-grandson." Bruno's face was serious as stone—as serious as the legacy he had revealed.

Victoria turned and faced the room, her eyes filled with concern and disbelief.

The expression on Alvise's face confirmed that he too felt locked in. "I'm sorry…this is all unexpected…and unwanted."

"Unwanted or not, you need to decide what you're going to do about the boy," said Bruno.

Victoria stepped closer to Alvise. "Do you remember what you said, the night you asked me to marry you?"

Alvise swallowed.

"Why didn't you mention that the roof you promised I'd always have over my head would never be ours?"

"But it is my home, and it will always be your home, too."

"If the DNA test proves that Thor is your son, then your home is his. Right now, I'm nothing more than your fiancé. Who am I to keep him from living there?"

"You're my future wife…my family…that's who you are."

Victoria paced the oriental carpet. "Even then…it's crazy… it's unimaginable. How can Magda leave this boy here? Isn't that abandonment? Is it even legal?"

"There's always the chance that he *is* my son." Alvise sunk his hands deep into his pants pockets.

Victoria stood still, now. Her mouth dropped open, she looked at Alvise. "Then you're saying you want him to come home with us?"

"*Cosa*?" said Anna. "He stay here."

"Anna…this is their decision." Bruno rubbed his forehead.

"But Vittoria works."

Alvise kept his eyes glued to Victoria's. "Mamma, we'll need your help, too."

"Like a baby sitter?" Anna frowned.

"If that's what you want to call it," said Alvise. "But Vittoria and I will decide how to organize our lives." Alvise took Victoria's elbow, and led her aside. "I'm sorry. But could you respect me if I turned my back on this child?"

"You know…I was coming around to accepting you having a son…that charming child…for Christ's sake he has no one, and he was born before I met you. But the house thing, too…"

"I wasn't keeping anything from you…I took it for granted that we'd grow old and gray there together…and then we'd leave it to *our* child."

She moved closer. So close she could kiss him, but she didn't. She looked into his sad eyes. Her voice became a harsh whisper. "When it matters, you don't tell me the whole truth."

"Vittoria…amore mio, I just want to protect you."

"I don't need protection. I need the truth." *And a paternity test.*

Chapter 21

THAT NIGHT, THOR rested his head on Alvise's soft curls, as he carried him on his shoulders. Victoria clattered the boy's suitcase over the stone pavement, and the improvised family walked the dim path to their home. Within steps of a deserted low-lying bridge, the flash of a gondola's iron *ferro* caught Victoria's eye. Gliding forward, the steel ornament filled the narrow space between the bridge and a stone palace.

"Did you know that Alvise has a gondola a lot like that one?" Victoria looked up at Thor, and forced an uncomfortable smile.

Thor's head popped up, and he looked toward the passing gondola.

"Do you like boats?" said Alvise.

"I like trucks," said Thor.

"Boats are Venice's cars *and* trucks," said Alvise.

Thor's eyes widened. He tilted his head. "Can they carry cows? Our truck carries cows."

Alvise chuckled. "I haven't seen a cow on a boat here, but centuries ago horses were kept near St. Mark's square. And my grandfather told me that the circus brought elephants into town once, too. They surely would have had to bring them in by boat."

Victoria watched Thor study the gondola's prow, its elegant swirls and flowers carved into its black enamel surface, as it slid further under the bridge. His eyes darted here and there. He seemed to be gathering the details of his surroundings—much like she had done during the few months she had lived in Venice.

Down the walkway, segments of soft yellow flowed from the streetlamps and onto their empty stone path. Victoria looked up at the dwelling she had no more than started to call home. Now, feeling somewhat like a guest, she entered the courtyard, and unlocked the front door. She let out a deep, nervous breath and, jostling the suitcase from the ground floor up the steep marble stairs, she followed Alvise and Thor inside.

In the guest bedroom, Victoria opened the suitcase. Beneath neatly folded t-shirts and jeans, she found a pair of Spiderman pajamas, a matching tooth brush tucked in a side pocket, and a brown *Bukowski* stuffed teddy bear.

"Felix!" Thor squealed with delight. He grabbed the soft stuffed toy, and held it to his chest. "Mr. Alvise?" His smile faded.

"You don't have to call me Mister."

"Yes, I do. My mommy said I have to call older people Mr. or Ms., except for Aunt Magda."

"Your mother taught you well, but it's fine if you call us by name." Victoria felt her heart bend a little. His polite manner showed that—no matter what she thought of the situation—he had received good care and direction back in Sweden.

Alvise sat Thor and the bear on his lap, and helped the boy out of his clothes. He slipped off his tennis shoes and jeans, and then unbuttoned his shirt.

"Mr. Alvise, am I going to live here now?" Thor looked around the room.

Victoria's jaw tightened and she struggled with the sinking feeling empathy tossed her way. She took a long look at Thor, and then at the bedroom—at the drab walls, the old wooden bed and the simple curtains.

Alvise pulled the Spiderman pajama top over Thor's head. "Would you like that?"

The boy nodded, and stepped into the pajama bottoms. He squeezed his stuffed bear, and laid his head on the white bed pillow.

"Not so fast." Alvise pulled the boy up and back into his arms. "Teeth need brushing before you go to bed." He tickled Thor, making him giggle and drop the stuffed toy. Toothbrush in hand, Alvise carried the boy toward the bathroom.

Victoria gathered the teddy bear from the floor, and watched them leave the room. Alvise continued to astonish her. It wasn't his composure or his ability to comfort the boy that surprised her—she knew how effortless it was for him to put others at ease. It was his ability to trust and therefore love—that's what had drawn her to him. Love and kindness came easy to Alvise. She held the soft toy in her hands and studied its crooked smile and bowtie. *If the DNA test is positive, will I accept Thor as part of my life, too?*

She set the toy back on the bed, and opened the armoire. Its door hinges cried for oil as she reached for a blanket. She spread the tartan plaid across the single bed, straightened and then pulled back the bed covers. The pillow fluffed up, she sat the teddy bear snug on the fresh sheets, and glanced up as they reentered the room, laughing.

Alvise plopped Thor on the bed. "Let Vittoria see your clean teeth."

Thor sunk into the bed pillow and stretched his lips, and grinned. "I beat him."

"They're blindingly white." She winked.

"We had a 'who can better brush their teeth' contest…he won," said Alvise.

"That means I'm the only one here with teeth that need to be brushed." She moved to the bed. "Goodnight, Thor."

Thor jumped to his feet, standing on the bed. He tossed his arms around Victoria's neck. "*God natt*, Ms.Vittoria."

His reaction rattled her. She smelled tooth paste, and felt flannel pajamas and fine hair against her cheek. With his little arms around her, her insecurities bubbled over. She knew little…no, she knew nothing…about children. Yet this boy's spontaneous affection felt genuine. Her heart wept for the boy, and she wiped away a silent tear. How could she refuse him? She had heard it said that being a parent comes natural. Was that why Alvise seemed to slip right into his role? *Was* he Thor's father? Even so, Thor wasn't hers. Or was he, now? Life hadn't prepared her for this.

She pulled back and cupped Thor's chin in her hands. She left a kiss on his cheek, and then went for the guest room door.

"Wait for me, please." Alvise stopped her from leaving the room.

She stood in the doorway, her back to the room, and wiped away more silent tears. "It's been a long day. I'm going to take a shower, and get ready for bed."

"Make sure you brush your teeth." Thor plopped back down on the bed. He pulled Felix the bear and the covers up under his chin.

"I will." Walking down the hall, she smiled to herself.

"I'll give you some time." Alvise called out, and then sat down on the side of the bed.

A tap against the bathroom door, Alvise gently opened it, and entered the bathroom. He leaned against the tiled wall. "Thank you."

Wrapped in a towel, she leaned forward, and swung her wet hair in front of her eyes. She crunched styling mousse into the long locks, and then threw her head back. Standing up straight, her wet curls framed her tense eyes. "Thank you for what?"

"For thinking about what is best for Thor." He stepped deeper into the bathroom, and watched her put more space between them.

"Right now, I need time to let it sink in." She stepped past him, and stopped in front of the mirror. She looked up at their reflection. "I'm still unsure. I don't like the fact that his mother decided not to tell you about her son and, though she is no longer alive, now has inched her way into our lives." Her words ricocheted off the shiny bathroom walls, leaving no room for a reply.

"What kind of person was Zinnia? Was she some…bohemian butterfly?" Her arms flailed in the air. "Someone who thought nothing of using you…or another man…to father her child…not caring about how her decision might affect the boy's father, not to mention her son?" She hated her harsh tone and wished she could stop, but she couldn't. She leaned back against the bathroom wall. Her sudden silence made them lock eyes. "You spent time with her. So tell me, what pushes a woman to let years go by without telling a father he has a child? I don't get it. Call me judgmental, call me old-fashioned. I don't understand. If she hadn't died, none of this would have happened. Frankly, I don't know what's worse."

"I don't know anything more about her than you do. *Amore*, you have every right to be unsure…and upset. But what other choices do we have?"

"None." *Still, you can't expect me to smile and say everything is fine.*

Alvise sat down on the side of the tub, and put his head in his hands. "Whether Thor is my own blood or not, the doubt about his mother's actions will never go away."

"Then what happens if he's not your son?"

His eyes told her he didn't know. "I've asked a lot from you, and until this evening, you've never complained."

She raised her eyebrows.

"Well…you've hardly complained." He smiled.

"It's not just about Thor. He's a sweet child." She stood a moment in silence, and then took a tissue off the shelf. *If you only knew the part of me I'm good at hiding from the world. It's stupid and it's insecure, and it's afraid to fail.* "I don't know how to be a mother."

"What? You think I know how to be a father?" He stood and pulled her to his chest, and wrapped her in his arms. "We're in this together."

She drank in the comfort of his words and his arms, and let them subdue her anxiety. Then she backed out of his embrace, turned to the mirror, and dabbed cream on her face.

"Remember, there isn't a soul in the universe that could dim the love I feel for you." He stepped closer and slipped her robe down one shoulder, and kissed the curve of her neck. "I love you, Vittoria."

Was this boy's presence dimming her love for Alvise? She ran her fingers over the back of his hand. The words *I love you, too,* stayed behind her lips.

Chapter 22

IT WAS EARLY July. Tourists packed Venice's waterbuses, canals and alleyways, and geraniums cascaded from kitchen window boxes and apartment terraces. Dressed in a striped shirt and dark pants, Alvise entered the sun filled kitchen, and kissed Victoria on the cheek. "I'm off."

"No breakfast?" *Again.*

"No time. We've got a big group this morning—eight gondolas, and I can't be late."

Victoria glanced in Thor's direction, and set her empty coffee cup on a pile of dirty dinner dishes. *I thought we were going to do this together?* Then she leaned back and against the marble counter. Her arms crossed, she pursed her lips.

Alvise pulled her close, and whispered. "I know you've got a lot on your shoulders. But this time of year is my busiest season. It's when I make the bulk of my income, which will help carry us through the slower winter months. I can't be *here* when I need to be *there*."

"You do remember that I'm working now, too? And I can't be here, there, and taking care of Thor and…" she turned to the kitchen sink "taking care of this house, too."

"Dirty dishes in the sink are not a problem."

"Not if you're not the one washing them."

"Things will slow down at work, again. This is just for a few months."

A few months? She raised her eyebrows.

He scratched his shaven face. "You could ask my mom to help a little more."

"I didn't move to Venice to have a relationship with your mother."

He checked his wristwatch. "Okay, you're right. So, trust me. It's just because of the high season. I'm sorry…really I am…we'll talk about it this evening." He gave her cheek another kiss, left one on Thor's forehead, too, and then rushed out of the house.

Thor sat at the kitchen table staring at a bowl of granola. Victoria turned back to the kitchen sink, and scowled at the soaking dishes. *How can a kitchen not have a dishwasher?*

"I don't like this cereal," said Thor.

"It's granola. You like granola." She doused the dirty dishes with more liquid soap, opened the hot water, and watched the suds rise like a fluffy cloud.

"This isn't the granola my mom used to give me."

"It's the granola you've eaten here before."

"It doesn't have raisins."

"Granola is granola."

"It has the wrong nuts."

For Heaven's sake! Victoria turned off the hot water, and turned her back on the sink. "Which nuts are the right nuts?"

"They're white."

"Almonds?"

"I'm allergic to these nuts." He shoved the breakfast bowl aside. Milk sloshed over the rim, and spread across the table, and then dripped onto the floor.

"Look what you've done…" Victoria grabbed a damp sponge from the sudsy water. She wiped the milk from the table and the bowl, and then set the cereal back in front of him. "Eat the cereal. Your Aunt Magda said you weren't allergic to anything." She stooped down, and cleaned the spilt milk off the floor, too.

"I'm allergic."

"You're four…you don't even know what allergic means."

"I'm almost five. And allergic means your face gets big and red and you die."

"Listen young man, you are not allergic to anything…and there are starving children…" Victoria stood and stopped herself, incredulous how much she sounded like her mother. *Geez…just eat the damn granola.*

"I want toast and juice."

Victoria looked at the wall clock, and sighed. She slid a slice of toast in the toaster oven, and opened the refrigerator. "Orange, apricot or pear?"

"Apple."

"We don't have apple juice."

"In Sweden I drink apple."

"You're not in Sweden."

"Apple."

"Pear, then." She pulled the carton from the refrigerator, and poured some into a glass.

"You're not my aunt or my mom. You can't make me drink it."

"You're right…I'm not." *And I'm as sorry as you are that you're stuck with me. But that's the way it is.* "But if we want to get this right, you're going to have to work with me here."

Thor climbed down from his chair, and stood in front of the open refrigerator door. He grabbed a can of Coca-Cola from the side shelf.

"Absolutely, not." Victoria latched onto the soda can and placed it back in the refrigerator, and out of his reach. "What did I just say?"

"My toast!" Thor pointed to the smoke spilling from the portable oven.

"Shit!" Victoria rushed to the toaster oven, and flung open the chrome door. Smoke rose to the ceiling. She unplugged the small appliance, grabbed the charred bread with an oven mitt, and tossed the toast in the sudsy water. She threw open the kitchen window, and heard the key in the front door. "Damn it."

Anna held a warm homemade fruit tart, and entered the kitchen. She sniffed the air.

"It's nothing," said Victoria.

"We burned toast," said Thor.

Anna rolled her eyes at Victoria. "Good thing I bring breakfast. Hurry…you can eat it on the way to school. You like apple tarts, right?"

Thor nodded.

Victoria's mouth dropped open. *How did you know he likes apples?* She turned her back on Anna, tucked in Thor's shirttails, and then zipped up his short pants. "Nonna will pick you up from summer school, and I'll meet you at Nonna's a little later than usual today."

"Later?" said Anna.

"I'm meeting some friends after work."

Anna frowned.

"What if you forget to pick me up?" said Thor.

"I won't forget." Victoria hurled a confused expression at the boy.

Thor scowled and crossed his arms across his chest. "Yesterday you did."

"I didn't forget...I was a little late."

"Twenty minutes." Anna knitted her brow.

"Nonna says you need a new watch because you're always late."

Always, Anna? Victoria kneeled down in front of Thor and ran her fingers like a comb through his disobedient blond wisps. "Even if I am a little late, you're not in danger...you're with Nonna." Victoria checked her wristwatch. It was late for her, too. "I'll be there, and we'll go for gelato."

"Meet us in the campo." Anna led Thor down the stairs. "It's better when he plays there, instead of inside."

Word had gotten back to Victoria that, under a watchful eye, Anna encouraged the admiration some had for the attempt Victoria was making to care for a boy who may not even be her stepson. However, Anna didn't silence her own criticism. Instead, she denounced her future daughter-in-law over hot meals with family and friends, and gossiped with the neighborhood shop-keepers and their customers—telling anyone who would listen that the *Americana* was a bad cook and the poor boy only ate what she cooked for him. Quicker than if Mercury had been the messenger, the back-fence talk traveled from campo to campo and through Venice's alleyways.

That afternoon, toting a gym bag over her shoulder, Victoria gathered her nerves and headed for the rowing club. *You can do it.* She told herself. *Rowing will be like riding a bike…it might be difficult to learn at first. But once you got it, you'll never forget…maybe.* Work, Thor, housecleaning, dealing with Anna, and far fewer romantic nights with Alvise had become her life. The routine stretched out in front of her and made her lonely. She wanted to feel good about herself, and do something she had done little of since moving to Venice—spend time with interesting women, and make friends. Finally, she accepted Ivana's invitation to join her, and a group of women, for an afternoon of rowing.

Victoria pressed her weight into the heavy wrought iron gate, and entered the rowing club yard. "*C'è nessuno?*" she called out. "Anyone here? Ivana?" She crossed the concrete pavement, and walked past paddles and oars, and primary colored canoes stacked bottoms up. A thick red tarp hung from a concrete beam, like curtains from a rod. She pulled back a corner of the heavy vinyl barrier, and stepped inside. A bulky wood table, littered with hand carved wood oarlocks and dusty rowing books, filled the center of the room. Red, white, green and blue regatta banners with gold tassel borders were organized by color, and pinned to the rowing club's brick walls. The scent of coffee and the hum of chatter and splashes of laughter exited an open door, and floated across the covered water basin. She followed a narrow brick path that skirted the indoor dock, and entered the rowing club's kitchen.

"Vittoria!" Ivana set her espresso cup on the tile counter, and then raised and opened her arms. "Welcome."

"Buon giorno." Victoria hugged Ivana.

"You remember Cinzia." Ivana turned to her friend with the short black hair.

"Yes, we met when you were having lunch with Ivana in Campo San Barnaba."

Ciniza nodded. "It's nice to see you here."

"And these are a few of the other club members…Marisa, Giuseppina, Isabella and my mom, Paola."

One by one, Victoria shook their hands. She studied their healthy lineaments—faces that had been kissed by the wind, the cold, the heat and the sun. Dressed in the club's blue sweatpants and cotton t-shirts, each wore a bandana or a sweatband around their head.

"Are you ready for your lesson?" Paola, Ivana's mother, had sun-bleached hair and a captivating smile.

"I was until I saw all those winning regatta banners. Now I'm a little nervous."

"No need to be nervous. We all had a first day of rowing," said Paola.

"We're here to help you," said Ivana.

"Do you have rowing clothes in there?" Giuseppina's eyes were big and green, and they looked at Victoria's gym bag.

"I do."

"You can change in the bathroom." Marisa pointed her calloused index finger toward the hall.

"You want coffee, first?" Isabella set her empty espresso cup in the shallow marble sink.

"No, thank you. I brought a bottle of water with me." Victoria's eyes lowered to Isabella's bare feet, and their decorative daisy pedicure.

"I row barefoot." Isabella smiled.

"Last week her toes were painted with roses." Marisa rolled her eyes. "I've never had a pedicure…let alone a flowery one."

"It's my little fetish." Isabella wiggled her toes.

"Okay, ladies. Let's get the *batea da fresco* ready. Victoria, we'll wait for you in the boat," said Paola.

"Which boat is the *batea da fresco?"* said Victoria.

"*La grande barca rossa,"* said Ivana.

"The big red boat?"

"*Sì,"* said Ivana. "Leave your stuff here. Just close the door tight behind you."

In the bathroom, Victoria stepped from her work clothes and into yoga pants and a t-shirt. She wrapped a windbreaker around her hips, pulled her hair up in a ponytail, and then pushed her feet into canvas tennis shoes. A deep breath to shoo the butterflies from her stomach, she grabbed her water bottle and a face towel from the gym bag, exited the club house bathroom and kitchen, and joined the others. Standing on a metal walkway suspended above the dark green water, her heart thumped. "We're all going in the same boat?"

"It's a hearty row to the lagoon." Paola stood aft, and grasped an oar in one hand.

"I thought we were staying on the small canals?" Victoria popped the top on the water bottle, and then took a swig.

"If you get tired, we'll pick up the slack." Ivana stood with the others in the hull of the boat.

"Come on…get in," said Cinzia.

Victoria took a another deep breath, set one foot on the top edge of the side of the boat, and felt her weight tip the boat below her. Pausing for a moment, she waited for the boat to balance, and then gently placed her other foot on the bottom boards and entered the shallow hull.

"You passed the first test." Giuseppina laughed. "Not everyone knows how to step into a row boat without falling in the water."

"I've had practice getting in and out of my fiancé's gondola," said Victoria.

"Now I get it." Isabella smiled. "You're the *Americana* Alvise is engaged to…nice guy, and handsome, too."

Victoria smiled, and steadied her shaking hands.

"Listen up, Victoria," said Ivana. "My mom is rowing aft, and I'm taking the prow. The others are rowing center. You stand in the middle, between Cinzia and Marisa. It's your first time out, so we tied your oar to the oarlock. It won't slip out. But as you've seen around town, with the *voga alla veneta* style of rowing, the oars rest on the *forcola*—they're not locked in."

Victoria moved to the center of the boat, and lifted the oar with both hands.

"Good," said Cinzia. "Now position yourself further away from the forcola, and closer to the end of the oar. Shoulders forward. Place your right foot forward, left foot back, both slightly turned out. Keep your right knee in line with the forcola. Knees bent."

"Like this?" said Victoria.

"Bring your left foot forward…"

Victoria slid her left foot over the red floor boards, closer to her right foot.

"Good…it's important that you keep your feet in that position. Now hold the oar firm with both hands, keep them waist high. Roll your wrists forward, and hold the *pala*…the flat part of the paddle…horizontal to the water. Then, when you push the oar forward, roll your wrists up, as if you were revving a motorcycle engine, that way the oar will enter the water in a vertical position. Keep your arms a little wider than your shoulders, and push your weight onto your right leg."

"Like a lunge?" said Victoria.

"That's right." Cinzia led her through the steps, again. "Now, for the return…roll your wrists back to their original flat position, turning the flat part of the oar back into a horizontal position and parallel to the water…smoothly…without friction…good."

Like a school girl on the first day of class, Victoria fixed her attention on Cinzia's directions.

"Now, that movement straightens your body, shifting your weight to your back leg. That's pretty much it."

"You make it sound easy." Victoria wiped her brow with her t-shirt sleeve.

"With practice it'll come natural, and you'll find your rhythm," said Marisa.

"*Pronte donne*?" Paola yelled from atop the aft.

"*Voga via*." Ivana yelled back from the front of the boat.

The oars hit the water, and the boat slid forward.

Her knees bent, Victoria dipped the oar in the green seawater. She lunged forward, and then back, forward and then back, again. She tried to keep rhythm with the other women. The oar, heavier than she'd expected, splashed and pulled against the current, and then slipped from her hands. "Shit!"

"Pick it up." Cinzia yelled from behind her.

Victoria felt her hands and her knees shake. She stooped down, grasped the oar, and lifted the flat end out of the water, and away from the moving oars. Her feet back in position, she watched the other oars thrust forward when the women pulled back, and then turn dip and slice the water. *Flatten, turn, dip and slice. Flatten, turn, dip and slice* she recited to herself.

"Give it another try," yelled Paola.

Victoria did. Determined, she controlled the oar, and lunge by lunge, she pushed and pulled, and felt clumsy.

"Don't look at the oar," said Cinzia. "Keep your eyes forward."

Victoria looked away from her oar, and ahead. They'd left Venice's small canals behind, and were heading to open water. In the distance, she spotted the island of Murano, and the glassmaking island's brick chimneys rising from terracotta rooftops. Sweat dripped down her face, and she recited the rowing movements over and again, and in her head. When a speeding motorboat left waves and wakes in the big red boat's path, Victoria followed her rowing companions' lead, and Paola's command. She lowered her oar deeper into the water, and then pushed and pulled, rowing harder, faster.

The wakes and waves flattened, and San Michele, Venice's island cemetery, lay to their right. A brick wall encased the island, and protected the quiet shrine from the sea. A cluster of tall cypress trees stood watch at one end, and a gondola stripped of all its adornments came in their direction. On board, two gondoliers dressed in black, purple sashes tied around their waists, nodded as they rowed by. No doubt, they'd carried someone through the Venetian lagoon to their final resting place.

"We need to make a pick up." Paola shouted from the back of the boat. "Bepi's waiting on his boat."

"Who's Bepi?" said Victoria.

"He's an old fisherman from Burano Island. We get our fish from him. Paola serves his catch at her osteria, too," said Marisa.

"He says his fishing spots are the best in the lagoon, and only he knows where they are," said Cinzia.

"Name me a fisherman who doesn't say that." Marisa laughed.

"I can't. But there's no better seafood than Bepi's catch," said Cinzia.

The women continued to move the big red boat forward, never breaking their rhythm. Paola used her oar like a rudder, and veered the boat toward Murano. Victoria held her oar, tight, and friction seeded blisters on the palms of her hands, between her thumbs and index fingers. She kept the pain to herself, and continued rowing. By the time they entered Murano Island's main canal, her arm muscles burned more than her hands. She'd caught on to the basics of rowing. She found her rhythm, and something told her she was making new friends.

"You like *seppie*, Vittoria?" Marisa yelled over her shoulder.

"Are they the black-ink cuttlefish?" Victoria tasted sea salt on her dry lips.

"*Sì*," said Cinzia.

"Then I like them." Victoria sliced at the sea with her oar, and with more confidence.

A loud whistle came from the back of the boat. "In front of the *Museo del Vetro*." Paola shot her hand in the air, and indicated a beige-stucco palace.

Docked in front of the Murano Glass Museum, fishing pole in one hand and a cigarette clutched between his lips, a tired looking man sat on an old kitchen chair in a small wooden boat.

The women slowed their rhythm and their boat, and sided up to Bepi's *cofano*. Oars up and out of the water, the women dismantled their rowing order. Some sat on the rim of the boat, while others stretched their backs and legs. Victoria popped open her water bottle and drank, and then splashed what water was left on her hot, blistered palms.

Paola stood aft, and looked down at Bepi's catch. She studied the fresh fish, and then called out, "Vittoria, *vieni qua*...come here."

Victoria caught her breath and wiped her hands, and then her forehead with her towel. She kept her balance on the rocking boat, and stepped around Cinzia and the other rowers. At the back of the boat, she smiled at the fisherman, and then up at Paola.

"Help me choose," said Paola.

"You want me to choose the fish for your osteria?"

"No." Paola chuckled. "Today we're buying fish for us. We're going to heat up the grill when we get back to the rowing club. What do you like?"

"I'm not sure I can…."

"You like fish, yes?"

"Very much."

"Then go ahead…tell Bepi what you want."

Victoria leaned over the rim of their boat, and looked into Bepi's. A plastic bucket filled with clear seawater held silvery scaled fish shimmering in the sun. "They're still alive."

"*Pescate mezz'ora fa*," said Bepi.

"You caught them a half an hour ago?" *I've never bought fish that was still moving.*

The old fisherman crushed his cigarette into a glass ashtray, and then reached into the bucket, and grabbed a large wiggling fish by the gills. "*Branzino*."

"Seabass?" Victoria looked up at Paola.

Paola nodded. "You like seabass?"

"I do."

"Give us two," said Paola.

Bepi tossed two wiggling fish into a sack of ice, and handed the sack up to Paola.

Victoria peered into the next bucket. Snake like creatures twisted and tangled around one another. "Eel?"

"*Sì*," said Paola. "*Anguille*, in Italian. Very good grilled."

"I've never eaten them."

"*Anche le anguille, Bepi*," said Paola.

Bepi handed the bucket of eels to Victoria.

The whole bucket? Victoria took the bucket from Bepi, and held the squirming creatures at an arm's length.

Paolo laughed. "They won't hurt you. The bucket makes it easier to transport them." Paola reached down, took the bucket from Victoria, and secured it next to her feet. "What else?"

Victoria pointed to a smaller bucket. Stained with black ink, it held cuttlefish. "*Le seppie*."

"Good choice. Marisa makes delicious black ink risotto," said Paola. "You're staying for dinner, right?"

Victoria checked her watch. *I wish I could.* "Thank you, but I have to be somewhere."

Paola shrugged, and then turned to Bepi. While she haggled with him over the price of fish, Victoria sat on the edge of the boat and let the sea breeze cool her perspiring body. In the distance, the Murano Cathedral bells rang. Victoria checked her watch, again. Five-thirty p.m. She went for her Smartphone, and then remembered that she'd left it in her purse. "Ivana, do you have a cellphone I can use? I left mine at the rowing club."

"We don't bring them with us when we train," said Ivana. "Is something wrong?"

"I wanted to tell Anna I'm going to be a little late. I didn't plan on being out this long."

"When we get back to the club, ask her to keep Thor for dinner, so you can join us."

"I would love to. But I promised Thor we'd go for gelato."

"Get gelato another time."

Victoria was tempted. She tried to remember the last time she'd felt this welcomed by a group of women—and had this much fun. "I can't. And I'm sorry, but I need to get back as soon as possible."

"That means we'll have to row faster, and harder. Are you up for that?"

"I think so." Victoria took her towel to her palms.

"Of course you're up for it. You did good." Cinzia nudged her back.

"Mamma, it's time to head back." Ivana shouted back to Paola, and then grabbed her oar. *Bepi* stashed the cash Paola handed him in his front pocket, and then lit another cigarette. Paola tucked the bags of fresh fish out of the evening sun, and the women returned to their rowing formation. Victoria took her place, too, and cringed from the pain when her blistered hands grasped the oar, again.

Smartphone in hand, Victoria rushed through the tight alleyway, and telephoned Anna for the fourth time—still, no answer. She exited the *Calle del Paradiso*, and climbed the bridge. Passing under a crooked triangular Gothic arch—which appeared as if it had been cemented there to hold up or to be held up by its two adjacent buildings—Victoria hurried down the other side of the bridge. Over another and down the walkway, she stood at the entrance to the campo. She scanned the wide stone neighborhood meeting place for Thor. A flurry of children wearing t-shirts and shorts whizzed their tricycles and bicycles in circles, and a soccer team of young boys kicked a ball on an imaginary field, and into an invisible net. Elderly men puffing tobacco pipes or cigarettes sat on a bench while their gray-haired ladies sat opposite them fanning themselves in the shade. Their animated hands, nods and faces, said they were, no doubt, exchanging local gossip. Victoria walked deeper into the campo, and searched the unfamiliar faces of children running after a ball. She watched the ball bounce to the far corner of the campo and stop at the Moro's condominium entrance. The door was closed. *They must be here, somewhere.* She held her hand above her eyes, shielding them from the sun, and browsed the campo, once again. There, beneath the green awnings of the open-air produce stand, Anna loaded paper sacks of fresh fruit and vegetables into a canvas bag with the care one might give to glass. Victoria marched toward her. "Anna, sorry I'm late. I've been calling your cell number. Didn't you hear the phone?"

"*Arrivederci,*" said Anna, speaking to the green grocer. She clenched the canvas bag and her handbag with one hand, and searched the handbag for her cellphone with the other. "I thought I had it with me."

"Where's Thor?"

"He's over there." Still searching her purse, she didn't look up.

Victoria eyed a group of children chasing one another. "Where? I don't see him." She felt a shattering sense of panic.

Anna shifted the bags from one hand to the other, and looked up and about. "I told him to go play with the other boys over there." She pointed toward a group of boys playing near the marble water well.

"Well he's not there."

"*Maria Vergine.*" Anna's free hand shook, and went to her throat. "Where did he go?"

"If you don't know..."

Victoria ran from child to child, bench to bench and from corner to every corner of the campo. "Have you seen Thor...a little blond boy with blue eyes...*l'avete visto...un bambino biondo con occhi celesti...si chiama Thor.*" She asked all who could hear her. Heads shook, and panic clogged her chest. She took a broken breath, and then another, and ran back to the middle of the campo, to Anna.

Alarm lined Anna's face. "What if the gypsies took him? What will I tell Alvise?"

The color drained from Victoria's face. "Were there gypsies in the campo?"

"Not that I saw."

Victoria's hands grabbed Anna's shoulders. "Listen, this is no time for guessing. Did he say anything...?" *Or did you say anything that would upset him?*

"No." Anna looked at the squares of stone pavement beneath her feet.

Victoria didn't believe her. "Go home, and wait there."

"But..."

"Just go."

Victoria rushed out of the campo, and tripped over the bridges she had crossed minutes before. She rushed under the arch and down the tight alleyway yelling Thor's name into every restaurant and store along the way. She stopped every passerby she crossed, asking if they'd seen a small boy walking alone. At last, she reached the end of the long alley, and turned the corner. She crossed her fingers that her hunch was right.

Steps from the blue and white awning, relief replaced the fear in her heart, and stopped her hands from shaking. Thor sat on the step of La Boutique del Gelato, licking chocolate ice cream and whipped cream from a cone. She stepped up to the small boutique's open window, and nodded to the girl behind the counter. She pulled a napkin from the counter and stooped down in front of Thor, and wiped the chocolate from his face. "Don't you ever do that again." She cleaned his cheek.

He looked up at her. His eyes, bluer than the sky above them, gave way to his defiance. Yet she saw sadness there, too. A wistful spirit she had never noted in him before.

"Why did you run away?"

"I pushed a boy."

"Why did you push him?"

"He wouldn't let me play in the campo."

"Did you tell Nonna that?"

"She told me to tell him it's not his campo."

"Did you?"

"Yeah, but he told me *go away, baccalà*, so I pushed him."

"Do you know what *baccalà* is?"

"It's that ugly fish that comes from Sweden, right?"

"No, it comes from Norway."

"I don't come from Norway, so I'm not a *baccalà*."

Victoria tried not to smile, and held her laughter. "Next time this boy calls you that, instead of pushing him, just tell him he needs a geography lesson."

She pulled him off the step and up into her arms. She held him close, squeezed him to her chest, and felt his sweet breath and sticky fingers on her neck. "You're a good boy," she whispered in his ear. "But don't ever run away like that again. I was afraid I'd lost you."

"I'm not lost. I'm at our gelateria."

That night, after receiving Magda's most recent letter and a photograph of her and her boyfriend on their farm in Sweden, Thor skipped his favorite television cartoon, and went to his room. Victoria stood at the sink and watched his sad little body walk out of the kitchen. She looked up at the clock, and wiped beads of sweat from her forehead. Alvise wouldn't be home from work for another hour. She rubbed the back of her head, assessing what she should do next. She'd finish washing the dishes—let Thor be for a while.

When she entered his room, she saw him sitting cross-legged on the bed. His blond head drooped over photographs of his mother scattered across the duvet. She cleared a space on the bedspread, and sat next to him. Her hands on her lap, she ran her eyes across the photographs of Zinnia posing in front of a windmill or the Eiffel Tower or the Roman Colosseum. Asking his permission, and waiting for his nod, she picked up the one half hidden under his bare chubby foot. She studied Zinnia and Magda arm in arm, posing. They wore trendy dresses and sandals, and Piazza San Marco stood behind them. She took a deep breath, and wondered if the photo might have been taken by Alvise.

"You look a lot like your mommy," said Victoria, at a loss for more profound words.

Thor dropped back against the bed pillow and pulled his stuffed bear closer. "When moms die, do they ever come back?"

"Moms are always with us…even when they're gone, even when we can't see them."

"How do you know if you can't see them?" He squeezed the bear tighter.

"We don't have to see them, we feel them…here." Victoria took his hand in hers, and laid them on his heart.

"I've never seen your mom…is she dead, too?"

"No…she's in California." Victoria smiled.

"Maybe my mom is in California with your mom."

She watched his eyes widen and brighten. "No Thor. She's not in California."

"Then she's in heaven, right?"

"I think so."

"A boy at school said I don't have a real mother and no one knows if I have a father, so I'm going to *inferno*. Where's *inferno*?"

Victoria smiled, and tried not to laugh. "It's a place I guarantee you will never see. And don't listen to that silly boy. You're surrounded by people who love you."

"Like ghosts? He said my mom was a ghost, now."

Victoria rolled her eyes, and shook her head. "That boy is something else…there are no ghosts. But I believe good angels watch over us."

"That's what I said. I told him my mom was an angel…like the ones with big wings on the churches?"

"You're right…similar to those. Do you have a favorite one?"

His mouth twisted and he pursed his lips. "My favorite angels are on the big church in the Piazza...the ones with gold wings."

"Saint Mark's Basilica...those are pretty special angels."

"Do you think my mom has gold wings?"

She nodded and, for the first time, reconsidered the kind of person Zinnia may have been. *Anyone who raised a sweet child like you deserves gold wings.* She picked the scattered photographs up like a precious deck of playing cards, and made a neat stack. She pulled the cookie tin that held his precious things up off the floor, and set the photographs between his crayons, a palm-sized book in Swedish, and a toy Ferrari. The toy car covered a photo of him in Zinnia's arms, and a small oil painting of a field of yellow flowers beneath a bright blue sky. She lifted the painting and the photo with its frame from the tin, and held them up to the light.

"This is a pretty painting."

"They're the flowers around our farm. Mommy said painting them was on her list."

"Her list?"

"Things to do before she got too sick."

Her bucket list. Victoria sighed. "I think we should frame it. Don't you?"

Thor nodded.

"And this photo would look better here." She placed the frame on the nightstand.

He studied the photo, and nodded. "Mommy said I cried a lot when I was a baby."

"Babies do that."

"Is that why she got sick and died?"

She watched him for a moment, and remembered Ivana's comments about her own sense of guilt when her mother had died. "No," she said, placing her hand on his.

"Then why did she?"

She let out a sigh. "Life can be hard to explain."

"Can you try?" His lip quivered.

She swallowed, and searched for a reasonable excuse. "I suppose because she already did what she was meant to do here on earth. She had you."

"Did she have me so I could be with you?"

His comment surprised her, and wet her eyes with tears. She wrapped her arms around him, and hugged him long and sincere. *Maybe she did.* How could she tell this sweet child that it was complicated? She folded the bed sheet, and tucked him in. She gave him another squeeze and a kiss, and switched the table lamp on and the overhead room light off. "*Buona notte,* Thor."

"*Buona notte, Mamma Vittoria.*"

Her heart dropped. His comment stole her breath. Her intentions had never been to replace Zinnia.

Victoria poured a glass of Valpolicella, and took the wine to the study. She opened the terrace door, and heard rain falling on the hot terrace floor. Steam hovered above the terracotta tiles, and the humid summer night felt stifling. She flipped on the ceiling fan, and opened her MacBook. She slid her index finger across the Trackpad, and opened the email account she held with Alvise. Scrolling down the inbox list, she skipped the phone and gas bills, and paused at the email they'd been waiting for. The subject line read *test di paternità*. She clicked it open, and struggled to decipher the letter from their attorney, written in Italian. Frustrated, she drank the wine.

The antique wall clock's brass pendulum swung. Its gears shifted and sprung the minute hand to number six: Nine-thirty p.m. Alvise would be home soon. But it was twelve-thirty in the afternoon in Los Angeles. Jackie would be at lunch.

Victoria turned back to the MacBook, and typed an iMessage: Hey, can you talk?

Seconds later she received a reply: Yeah, FaceTime me.

Relieved, Victoria scooted closer to the screen, selected Jackie Cellphone from her FaceTime contacts.

The call rang. Jackie's smiling face appeared on the screen. Victoria saw that she was adjusting her earphones. "Hey…I miss you."

Victoria smiled. "I miss you, too. Are you at lunch?"

"I'm at Manuel's."

"No…El Tepeyac in Boyle Heights?" Victoria's shoulders dropped. "I haven't been there since my college days. Did you order a burrito?"

"Yep…waiting for a mini chicken Hollenbeck."

"With rice and beans?"

"Of course." Jackie laughed. "It sounds like you miss Mexican food, too."

"You have no idea how much."

"Besides all that pasta you must be eating…how are things?"

"Thor called me Mamma earlier tonight."

"Wow. How do you feel about that?"

"Confused…honored…a little scared."

"At work, I sit on the other side of the desk from parents and children in similar situations, and it's never simple. I admire your stamina. I don't know what I'd do in your place."

"You'd react the same way."

Jackie shook her head. "I don't see myself as a mom."

"Neither do I…but here I am. We were wrong about women with children. Taking care of a child is tough, and exhausting. Thor sees and imitates everything we do. I don't even say *shit* in front of him anymore."

"Well that sucks. Is there anything good being a mom?"

Victoria thought a moment, and then smiled. "Evenings are nice. After his bath, he cuddles up next to me on the couch, and I read to him. You know what his favorite book is?"

"I don't know…The Lord of the Rings?"

"He's not even five yet. I can't read him that."

"You'd think I'd know that. You see…I'd be a crap mom."

"It's The Napping House."

"You found The Napping House in Italy?"

"I ordered it online. This makes him a second generation to love the book…we're making it a classic."

"Thor is lucky to have you. You know that, don't you?"

"He lost his mom. I don't know how lucky he is."

"Good point. Any news about the paternity test?"

"I'll know more as soon as Alvise reads the email in our inbox from our attorney. It's in Italian legalese, which I can't understand."

"Things run slow there."

"And we might need authorization from the Swedish courts."

"You got Magda to sign the paternity test consent, right?"

"She signed it when she was here."

"Still, it would've been much easier if this had been done before the boy's mother had died."

"Probably less expensive, too…we're paying a fortune in attorney fees."

"Sorry, that's how I make *my* living, too."

"I hope this attorney is as competent as you are."

"Do your parents know about Thor yet?"

"No."

"Why not?"

"I'm waiting until we have the paternity test results. There's no need to involve them…yet." Victoria watched the computer screen. Jackie looked up and away from the screen, and then moved out of Victoria's sight. A hand blurred the image, and then swooshed back revealing bubbling cheese melted over refried beans, a round of rice and a folded flour tortilla bulging with shredded chicken, onions and tomatoes—fresh guacamole slabbed on the side. "Oh my God…my mouth is watering at your lunch."

Jackie turned the iPad screen back, showing her face, again. "I wish you were here to share it with me."

"So do I." Victoria frowned. "I'll let you eat your lunch while it's hot."

"Wait…before we hang up. Did you see the photos of the bridesmaid dresses I sent?"

"I did. Sorry. So much is going on."

"You still want me to order one, right?"

Victoria took a deep breath.

"Victoria?"

"Of course I want you to."

"Are you sure? Because if you're not..."

"I like the strapless one. Was it sage or pistachio?"

"Pistachio."

"You'll look great in it. Send me a fabric swatch so I can match the sash on Susanna's flower girl dress to yours." *Only two months until the wedding.*

"I miss you."

"Same here...enjoy your burrito."

The FaceTime screen went still. Victoria swiveled the desk chair toward the open terrace door. She watched and listened to the rain fall, and raised the wine glass to her lips. She sipped some more and then, startled by Alvise standing behind her, she jumped, spilling her drink. "Shit!" Red wine seeped into her cotton top and denim shorts. She grabbed a tissue from the shelf, and wiped her clothes. "I didn't hear you come in."

"I'm sorry. I didn't want to make any noise and wake Thor." He moved closer.

She handed the glass to him. "Great...all I need is more laundry to do." She stormed out of the study, and down the hall. In the bathroom, she undressed, and threw on a terry-cloth robe.

"I said I was sorry. I didn't mean to startle you." Alvise stood in the hall.

"We got an email from the attorney. You might want to look at it." She carried the soiled clothes to the kitchen. "And will you please get the extra house key from your mother? She walks in, whenever she wants." *Don't people ring doorbells in Italy?*

"Hey...what's wrong?" Alvise followed her.

"It's been a long day." She went to the pantry and pulled the salt canister from the shelf, and then stepped to the refrigerator for a bottle of club soda. She poured a thick layer of salt on each stain, and then wet the spots with club soda. She shoved the soiled clothes aside, and let the concoction she'd read about online set in.

"It's been a long day for both of us."

"Exactly...you're working longer hours." *And more of my day is spent taking care of Thor.*

"This time of year I usually finish after midnight? Instead, I've been coming home early...to be with you."

"Well, thank you. I appreciate that. And forgive me if I get lonely. A four year old's company has its limits." She added more club soda to the salt and watched the stains bubble and turn to shades of pink. Leaning on the kitchen counter, she closed her eyes. If only she loved Alvise less, she would return to Los Angeles. Instead, each day that passed added more pieces to the puzzle that held her there. Was this the price she had to pay for true love? Or was it the price she was paying for her impulsive decision to leave Los Angeles? Was she the strong woman Ivana saw in her? Could she stick with their engagement, and walk down the beautiful Venetian church aisle? She shifted her gaze to Alvise. "He called me Mamma tonight."

Alvise's shoulders dropped. He pulled her to him, and kissed the top of her head.

Back in the study, Alvise sat at the desk and in front of the open MacBook, and read.

"Well?" Victoria stood by the open terrace door, chewing her thumbnail.

"Thor's birth certificate doesn't name a father, and Magda was never appointed Thor's legal guardian."

"What? But she signed the paternity test consent as if she were."

He took a deep breath, and rubbed his eyes. "We need permission from the Swedish court to test Thor's DNA. We need their consent."

"You mean he's an orphan of the State?"

He nodded.

"I wondered why Magda brought him here by train, and not by plane."

"Sì. No custom controls on trains in Europe."

"Should he be here in Italy…I mean…living with us?"

"The attorney said that when we ask the Swedish courts for a paternity test, he'll explain the situation, and then I can simultaneously ask for temporary custody."

"You?"

"*Me*. We're not married yet."

Victoria lifted a brow. *We got bulldozed by those women, didn't we?*

Chapter 23

Victoria and Thor crossed the canal to the densely populated quarters of Sacca Fisola. The mariner jolted and banged the waterbus against the landing, while children and parents pushed and crowded around the boat's steel railing, positioning themselves to be the first to step off and follow the long path toward the public swimming pool.

Mothers' warnings and children's laughter burst through the locker room while t-shirts, jeans, socks and shoes came off and swimsuits, caps and terrycloth robes were pulled on. Victoria scooted Thor toward his place in line and with a peck on his cheek left him for the noisy observation deck. The muggy air made her curly-hair tighten and her crisp cotton blouse weep. She took her place among the crowd and smiled at a few familiar faces. Some returned her gesture, but most shot cold, dubious looks her way. Still, no one invited her to join their group. The forced smiles and once-over glances read like disapproval. She leaned her elbows on her knees and her face in her hands, and wondered why. *I've always made friends easily. So why is it so difficult to do that with some women here?* She stared down at the pool and sighed. She missed Jackie.

She pulled out her iPhone from her purse, and wrote Jackie a text:

Missing you.
Magda isn't Thor's legal guardian.
Should get the DNA test, soon.
The process is taking longer than expected.
Still, he's an angel.
Let's talk soon.
Hugs, Me.

The poolside shower splashed against the pale blue mosaic tile and the children's laughter echoed to the rafters, grabbing her attention. One by one, the small students stepped in and out of the foot wash, tossed their terrycloth robes on the bench and then gathered at the call of their instructor's whistle. Victoria sat up straight, lifted her chin, and looked for Thor over the heads of the other people sitting on the bleachers. At the end of the grandstands she saw Ivana standing and waving—her red hair glistened beneath the aquatic center's lighting.

"*Vittoria… vieni qua…*come sit here." The children's laughter and splashing couldn't drown out Ivana's husky voice.

Victoria smiled and waved back, and quickly gathered her things. It had gotten easy for her to communicate with Ivana. She was more open than the others. She felt the unfriendly women's glare on her back, and ignored them. Ivana didn't sit her athletic form down until Victoria had whisked past the stone faced group, and slid onto the bench beside her.

"*Ciao bella.*" The two spoke in unison, and swapped double-cheek kisses.

"What are you doing here?" said Victoria.

"I brought my nephew. He's in the older kids' class." She pointed at the deep end of the Olympic size pool. "Where have you been hiding? I haven't seen you since the rowing lesson." Her banter rang out like a familiar song.

"At work…at home…running Thor around. There's not much time for anything else." She scanned the children's pool and spotted Thor making waves behind a yellow kickboard.

"Life must be different with children." Ivana's face was cheerier than usual. "Do you want one of your own?"

"Maybe…one day." Victoria liked Ivana's honesty.

"So then you're taking precautions, now?"

"Yes. I'm on the pill." Victoria smiled at her friend's straightforwardness.

"I'd like to have children, too." Ivana let a smile cross her lips.

"How are things working out with Ciano?"

Ivana sighed. "Great. We're talking about moving in together."

Victoria's eyes widened. "I thought you were just a casual thing."

"It started that way. Now we've decided to go exclusive." Ivana's face glowed with excitement.

"Wow." *I never saw Ciano as the settling down type.*

"He's a pretty remarkable guy. We love being a couple."

Then you found the real thing.

Ivana smiled. "Only thing…my parents want us to get married. But we don't think that's important."

Victoria was surprised, and pleased, to find such a nonconformist woman in Italy.

"We've decided to find an apartment, and move in. But how are things with you…and with Thor?"

"He's...*un tesoro*—a treasure." Victoria tried for the right accent. She paused and stood, bringing Ivana to her feet, too. They watched Thor take a poolside leap into the deep end.

"*Bravo* Thor." They hollered when he hit the water. Their cheers bounced off the domed ceiling and brought disagreeable sneers from the same testy group of women. Victoria didn't care. She wanted Thor to hear her. She looked over her shoulder, and then turned her back on the snooty group, but not before noticing that their animosity was also directed at Ivana.

"Why are these women so unfriendly?" Victoria sat back down on the bleachers.

Ivana sat down next to her. "They're jealous."

"Of what?"

"We both nabbed a gondolier, and I am one."

"And?"

"In Venice, a gondolier is a good catch…and they're often much better looking than say…doctors or lawyers." Ivana smiled.

"They talk to you."

"I'm Venetian. I know too much about each one of them." Ivana winked.

"Great." Victoria laughed. "Unless I learn the dirt on these women, I can give up trying to make friends."

Ivana squeezed Victoria's arm. "You've already made one."

They sat in silence. Victoria watched Thor dog-paddle to the side, clear his wet bangs away from his eyes and climb the pool ladder. He kept his head down, slapped his bare feet to the cement pavement, and ran back in line. She hoped she hadn't embarrassed him. Then, before hitting the water a second time he looked up at the grandstands, flashed a precious smile and waved back at his adoring fan.

"Have you talked about him living here, permanently?" Ivana kept her eyes on Thor.

"We're still waiting for consent to get a paternity test."

"What if he's not Alvise's son…then what?"

Victoria watched Thor holding tight to his paddleboard, once again, and kicking hard, moving himself to the shallow end of the pool. "I have no idea."

"How could his aunt leave such an angel?" said Ivana.

"It's hard not to criticize her. But I suppose you do that when you have your own child to think about."

Victoria resented Zinnia for having hidden her son's existence from Alvise for years, and condemned Magda for dropping the boy off when he became an inconvenience. But though she considered their actions selfish, she also envied their reckless ways. Now, the mother in a prefabricated family, she wished her ego would let Anna do more. Too often, she begrudged her stepmom role.

"When will you hear from the court?" said Ivana.

Victoria shrugged, and shook her head.

"Before your wedding?"

"I hope so. In the meantime, we're planning Thor's fifth birthday."

"A party?"

Victoria nodded. "The same day as the Redeemer celebration. In Italian it's called *il Redentore*, right?"

"Correct. You must join us. We're having a family dinner at my parents' osteria at the Rialto. My mother is making *i bigoli in salsa*—the thick spaghetti like pasta." Ivana elongated her fingers as if pulling taffy "served with onions and anchovies."

"Alvise loves that. Do I understand correctly that the Redentore celebration commemorates the end of a plague?"

"Yes, and it's the Venetians' most important celebration of the year. Since the 16th century, every year on the third weekend of July, we honor the end of the plague that killed more than 50,000 Venetians. Back then, that was a third of the city's population, today it would be its historical center's entire population. The plague hit so hard that the Venetian Senate prayed for divine intervention, promising to build a cathedral if the city was saved. Then, in 1577, after Venice was freed from the plague, the Senate commissioned the Venetian Republic's greatest architect, Andrea Palladio, to build the Redentore Church. They had it built where it stands today, on the Giudecca Island."

"I thought celebrating the 4th of July in America was an old tradition."

"And like your tradition that calls for turkey on Thanksgiving, on the night of the Redentore it's our tradition to serve *i bigoli*. You must come. Alvise's parents should be there, too."

"Can I bring a birthday cake for Thor?"

"*Sì*," said Ivana. "We'll make a big party. And after dinner we'll take our gondolas to watch the fireworks. I can guarantee that you've never seen anything as beautiful as fireworks over the San Marco basin."

Chapter 24

BY THE END of July, Victoria, Alvise and Thor found their daily routine, and Victoria balanced her time between learning how to cook, bake and not burn toast, ringing up precious jewelry sales at the boutique, and waiting for the court's authorization to get Thor's and Alvise's DNA tested.

"The annual Jewelry Trade Show at Lago Maggiore brings top sellers from around the globe." Zio Fausto sat in the jewelry store's back office, and spoke to Victoria and Debora. "Vittoria, I'm making you my assistant manager, and I'm sending you to the fair as our chief buyer. You've proven that you have elegant taste, knowledge of what customers want, and how much they're willing to pay. You'll represent our store."

Victoria's eyes sparkled. "Fausto…thank you for the promotion, and for your trust."

"Debora you'll go, too, and you will *assist* Vittoria. You will not make any purchases…is that clear?"

"Assist?" Debora wore her pompous air.

"Yes, and you will do as Vittoria requests. I'll man the store. But if there are any doubts or problems, you call me."

"When is the fair, and where is Lago Maggiore?" said Victoria.

"Some assistant manager…she doesn't even know when or where the fair is." Debora rolled her eyes, and crossed her arms.

"Lago Maggiore is north of Milano. You leave Sunday afternoon, after the Redentore holiday. The fair starts early that Monday. Your train tickets and hotel reservations have been arranged. I'll give you a file on what products I'm looking for. I've set up an appointment with the Damiani people. I want you to pay particular attention to their brand."

"May I suggest we up our supply of engagement rings, diamond solitaire pendants and earrings?" said Victoria. "Traditional is making a comeback." Victoria appreciated fine jewelry—pieces that would last generations.

"See what I mean?" Uncle Fausto stood, and looked at Debora. "Engagement rings are at the top of my list. High quality solitaire diamond rings. Now back to work." He left the small office space for the showroom.

Victoria moved her gaze to a small shopping bag dangling from Debora's fingertips.

"I'm off to deliver the gold cuff bracelet I sold this morning." Debora smirked.

"Fausto must be happy about that sale," said Victoria.

"The sale could've been yours."

"How is that?"

"The man, who bought it *from me*, said he was your customer."

"My customer?" Victoria's stomach tightened. "I don't remember showing the bracelet to anyone lately."

"Well...you can imagine how sorry I am that you weren't here when he came back, and *I* had to make the sale."

Victoria stepped around Debora. "Congratulations on the sale."

"Disappointed that I made it?"

I have no desire to compete with you, Debora. "You were doing your job." *And I'm trying to do mine. Why can't we do that together? Maybe we could even get along.*

Debora threw her nose up in the air. Her heels clicked across the marble floor, and her sleek ponytail swung in rhythm with her hips.

Victoria watched her colleague exit the shop, and wondered how difficult it might be to be her boss.

The summer days were hot and golden, and their life together moved ahead. Over the last six months Victoria had gained control over their lives—somewhat less over the situation. The bond she had created with Thor was genuine. But that morning, with its cloudless sky, she felt out of control of her future, and of her nerves. The Swedish court's consent for a DNA test had arrived, and their lab appointment was scheduled for ten o'clock.

Victoria pulled the bedcovers up around her shoulders, and then lay there, half asleep, looking at Alvise through sleepy eyes. She did as he said and stayed in bed, while he rose and dressed, and woke up Thor, and then prepared breakfast. She moseyed in her cotton slippers across the marble floor and joined Thor, sitting at the kitchen table. Alvise had set it with their mixed-matched table ware and a fresh bouquet of miniature roses. She watched him move through the kitchen like a sous chef competing for a title, and listened to him whistle a rendition of *New York, New York*. He turned off the flame beneath the espresso pot and silenced the bubbling mocha. Then he moved down the sideboard, squeezed pink juice from a halved grapefruit with one hand, grabbed a pot-holder with the other and pulled crisp honey-wheat brioche from the hot oven.

"Tea or coffee?" said Alvise.

"Tea, thank you," she said.

"Apple juice and coffee for me," said Thor.

"Apple juice for you, not coffee," said Victoria.

"Nonna lets me drink it." Thor dug his spoon into a bowl of milk covered granola.

Alvise dropped a tea bag into a pot of hot water, and met Victoria's irritated stare. "I'll talk to her about it."

"Thank you." She returned his slow kiss and let him lay the cloth napkin across her silk nightgown. "Aren't we lucky to have such great service, Thor?"

"We take care of each other," said Alvise.

"Is that why we're going to the doctor?" Thor's short legs and little feet dangled and swung from the kitchen chair, and he drank his apple juice.

Alvise tousled Thor's hair, and stooped down beside his chair, looking him in the eye. "We're going to take a routine test to see if we have the same blood type."

"You mean like on television…when there's a big accident and they rush the people to the hospital yelling *we're losing him… we're losing him,* and then they find someone else's blood to save him?"

"Kind of…but where did you see that?" said Victoria.

"On Grey's Anatomy…with Nonna."

"Coffee *and* violent television programs?" She tore the flakey pastry apart and watched Alvise fill her cup with hot tea.

"Grey's Anatomy isn't violent," said Alvise.

"He's only four." She spooned honey from a jar into her cup.

"You keep saying I'm four. I'm almost five." Thor wrapped his pudgy hands and fingers around the juice glass, and drank. He set the glass back on the wooden table, and wiped his pajama sleeve across his mouth.

"Use your napkin." Victoria lifted his napkin from the table.

Alvise chuckled, and Victoria tried not to. *Don't laugh* she mouthed at Alvise, and wiped Thor's mouth, again, with a cloth napkin.

"They kiss each other a lot." The corners of Thor's eyes crinkled as he giggled.

"Who?" Victoria placed the napkin on Thor's lap.

"The doctors on T.V." Thor chewed his breakfast roll.

"Your mother needs a *not to do* list to use…especially while I'm away at the jewelry show." Victoria shot a frustrated look at Alvise.

"I said I'll talk to her." Alvise scratched the back of his head and looked sideways at Victoria. "You go ahead and get dressed. I'll get Thor ready."

Victoria carried her tea down the hall, leaned against the guestroom door, and envisioned a proper young boy's bedroom. She tilted her head and eyed the walls she could paint calm, protective sky-blue, and the window and glass-paned door she might ask her neighbor, the seamstress, to fit with matching gingham curtains. The eastward facing room got the brightest early morning sunshine, and would make a cozy, warm play space on cold winter days. She sipped her tea, and saw the old drab guestroom decorated and stenciled with airplanes and boats. She sighed at the laughter, coming from the bathroom, and bit her lower lip. *We'll know the truth soon enough.*

She'd begun to care deeply for Thor—that she couldn't deny. A sense of responsibility and compassion, and love for Alvise, let that happen. She played her part with grace and vigor, and to the best of her abilities. Still, she silently struggled with the resentment that came and went, whenever she missed being a normal engaged couple without children. Uncertain as to which DNA results she'd prefer, she kept those thoughts quiet. Speaking them out loud would sound selfish and immature. *If I'd known about Thor sooner, would I have left everything behind and said yes to marrying Alvise?*

"It's getting late." Alvise yelled from down the hall.

The image of the redecorated guestroom erased from her thoughts, Victoria crossed the hall to the master bedroom. She set her cup and saucer on the bureau, pulled on a cotton shift dress, and stepped into a pair of black ballerinas.

Victoria grinned as Alvise guided them through the shaded *calle* and sun filled *campi* with the care a maiden gives fresh eggs in a basket. They walked through doors he opened, and sat on chairs he pulled out and drank water he fetched. She could see he couldn't relax either.

"The results will take about a week." Their case counselor ran a silver ballpoint pen across a pile of documents.

Alvise sat across the glass desk. "I thought they said it would take a few days."

"That's correct." The counselor nodded his shiny head and didn't look up from the pile of documents. "But our laboratory runs DNA tests three times."

"We'll wait." Alvise turned to Victoria, sitting next to him. Thor sat on her lap, and in her arms.

She pressed her index finger to the cotton bandage on the boy's arm, and read the counselor's framed diploma nailed to the gray-white walls. It read University of Padova. "When we receive the results, will there be any doubt?"

"No. The tests we run are considered final, and accepted in International Courts of Law." The counselor clicked his pen and placed their file atop the file holder labeled *test di paternità*. He pushed his tall frame up from the leather desk chair and shook Alvise's hand. "I'll contact you when the results are ready."

They exited the lab office and reached Campo San Polo before Alvise broke the silence. "I think this deserves pizza for lunch."

"Yeah." Thor ran across the stone pavement, and toward a pizzeria that sat at the far end of the campo.

Keeping an eye on Thor, Victoria stopped in the shade of an old magnificent tree, beneath broad limbs that stretched above them.

"What is it?" said Alvise.

She swallowed hard, and lowered her eyes to the square of dirt framing the foot of the tree. "I'm fearful of the truth."

He took her hands in his. "So am I."

She stepped from his reach and turned her back on him, and studied the San Polo Church's worn brick façade. "We didn't plan on being a family…especially not before our wedding."

"Maybe this was meant to be."

"We haven't had much time for *us*."

"We'll find time."

She rolled her eyes across the wide campo, and watched Thor running, chasing a small red cat. "What if the test results come between us?"

"*Amore.*" He pulled her close, and held her tight. "Nothing could ever come between us."

In his arms, she kept an eye on Thor. Now, he sat at the foot of a white marble well, petting the kitten. *No* she thought *not if Thor isn't your son. As much as I care for Thor, can I commit to being his mother, forever*? She wouldn't say it. Nor would she remind Alvise that motherhood wasn't the role she had come to Venice to play.

Chapter 25

THE GRAND CANAL bustled with activity. It was the third Saturday in July, and Venice prepared to celebrate *Il Redentore*—as it had done every year since the 16th century when, at last, the plague had loosened its grip around the city. Makeshift tables and chairs were assembled in modest boats dressed up in colorful festoons. Homemade *pasta e fagioli,* and sardines marinated in onions, pine nuts and raisins, stuffed plates and hungry stomachs. Bottles of wine floated in melting ice and ensured glasses would be filled until well after the midnight fireworks spectacle ended.

Mainland Venetians, forced like exiles to leave Venice's historical center for a more practical way of living and more affordable housing, returned to celebrate with old friends. The countryside residents walked shoulder to sweaty shoulder alongside tourists who crowded the tight walkways, while impatient residents screamed out *permesso...permesso,* granting them startled looks, but clearing the stone-paved pathway for them to zigzag ahead of the mob.

Victoria closed the store as the hot summer sun began to set and blaze against San Marco Basilica's gold mosaic lunettes. She rolled the boutique's metal security gate to the ground, and locked it. Standing outside the gate, the crowd forced her back against the gritty iron grill, smudging dusty snakelike patterns onto her clothes. Body heat steamed through the narrow *calle,* and mingled with cheap perfume and the sour odor of backpack carrying tourists who apparently had skipped a shower or two. The smells attacked her senses, and cautioned her from forcing her way into the crowd. She lingered on the doorstep and waited for the pungent smell to go away. She raised her hand to her nose and blocked the offensive odors. She took small, short breaths of her own sweet scent, and when a handsome couple stopped to admire the jewels in the boutique window, she stepped into the human wave. Eyes tilted up, her senses searching for fresher air, she inched forward. Soon, the packed *calle* emptied onto St. Mark's square. She caught a whiff of salty sea air. Tired and hot, she wiped her brow and moved through the thinning crowd, sending pigeons flying here and there. At the far end of the piazza, she paused under shaded archways, and then turned down a quiet route and toward the bakery.

She scooped up the coins and dropped the change in her purse, and slid the heavy pastry box with the *torta millefoglie* from the glass counter. One last glance at the display case filled with colorful fruit tarts, bite-sized chocolate spheres, buttery biscotti, and flakey twisted pastry stuffed with baker's cream, and she was carrying Thor's chocolate-chip *crema pasticcera* birthday cake out the door.

Down the strait alleyway, she moved, step after step, in the same direction as the swelling crowd. Large and small groups of people joined the flow as she crossed the wide campo. At the Academia Bridge, the mob stalled and tightened around itself as abruptly as the throbbing, pressing pain in her feet. She took a deep breath and followed the rush up the wood plank stairs. She stepped out of the never-ending tide of people at the top of the bridge and, holding the pastry box in one hand, grabbed onto the railing with the other. She bent gently forward. Below her, an incessant movement of boats zipped under the bridge and down the Grand Canal toward St. Mark's basin. She looked around at the growing crowd of people and boats, and grew more excited about the evening ahead.

"*Mamma Vittoria.*"

Victoria dropped her hand from the railing, and turned to see Thor smiling, running her way, and Anna trailing up the bridge behind him.

She smiled back and wrapped her arm around him. "Hey birthday boy…how was the beach?"

"Fun." He hugged her skirt and turned his head sideways. "What's in the box?"

She dropped her arm from him, and pulled the box high over his head. "It's a surprise for you."

"Can I see it?"

"You can, after dinner." Victoria looked up as Anna stepped behind him, and returned her critical eye.

Anna dropped her hands to Thor's shoulders. "I left ironed shirts for Alvise, in the *armadio*…closet."

"You don't have to do that, or deliver them," said Victoria. *I asked Alvise to get the spare key from her.*

"He needs clean uniforms."

"I have a woman who helps me out."

"I save you money."

"Anna, I appreciate your help. Without you, we'd have to depend on a baby-sitter. But either you ask before you enter our home or…"

"It's the Moro family home. Remember, you're keeping it for Thor."

It may never be mine, but it's my home now, too. "If you can't respect our privacy, then I must insist that you return the extra house key."

"I only want to help." Anna's eyes teared up.

"And you are, tremendously." Victoria swallowed, and lowered her gaze to the parade of boats cutting white water under the bridge. "It's just that Alvise and I…and Thor… need our own private space."

"Family is everything to me." Anna blotted a tissue to her eyes.

"I respect *that.* So could *you try* to respect *our* privacy?"

"He's my son, and this is my grandson."

Victoria sighed, and then turned to Thor. "Shall we go home?"

"May I go to Nonna's?"

"Is that okay with you, Anna?" said Victoria.

"Of course it is. We meet for dinner at the osteria."

Victoria watched Anna take Thor's hand and descend the steps she had climbed moments before. She waved at Thor waving back at her, and then turned and pushed through the crowd.

Weaving in and out of people who stood in her way, she descended the opposite side of the bridge.

She pulled a plastic water bottle from her purse, and quenched her thirst. She walked along the sun-drenched canal that faced their home. A whistle called her to circle back, and she stopped.

"Madam, are you looking for a gondola…or a gondolier?" Alvise stood on the back of his boat, rowing in her same direction.

"I have a lovely gondola." She flirted. "And the most handsome gondolier in Venice comes with it." She looked straight into Alvise's eyes and saw love reflect back in his smile.

Alvise smirked, and shook his head. She knew he was uncomfortable being referred to as the *most* anything, let alone the most handsome. She waited, and he stopped the gondola canal side and jumped from the stern into the hull. He grabbed the embankment with one hand and placed the cake box in the boat with the other and, extending his hand once again, he led her down the marble steps.

She avoided the slippery moss on the lowest slab, and set her red-ballerina clad foot on the gondola's black rim, balanced her weight, stepped in, and touched a gentle kiss to his lips. Settling onto the loveseat, she propped her feet up.

She watched Alvise place one foot in front of the other, and walk the boat's narrow rim, and grab the *remo* with his right hand and set it on the curve of the *forcola.* He wrapped his left hand around the oar, too, and commanded the gondola forward. She looked to the side, and studied the swift strokes rippling across the water and his reflection moving in well-choreographed steps on the canal. Back and forth, back and forth he shifted his weight atop the stern, advancing the gondola, taking them home.

Victoria used the time without Thor to nap, and then lay in the bath, conscious that the cool water and a leg massage from Alvise would ready her for the long night ahead. Wearing a silk robe, her washed hair blown dry, she stood in front of the bedroom mirror, blended dabs of make-up to her cleansed face, traced her eyes and selected the right lipstick from a large make-up case, and prepared for Thor's party.

She heard a tap against the bedroom door before it opened. Alvise was standing there, his cellphone in hand.

"The lab just called," he said.

Her heart jumped. "On Saturday?"

"The counselor said he thought we should know as soon as possible."

"Well?"

"Why don't you sit down?"

"I don't want to sit down."

His face read like a tragicomedy, and his nerves caused him to chew on the inside of his mouth. "It's negative…the DNA test is negative."

"Negative meaning…?"

"Thor is not my son." He sat down on the bed.

It was as if she had a rope tied to the pit of her stomach and the knot had been loosened. Numbed by what he had said, and by what she might hear next, she crossed her arms and stood straight, not covering her shock. For a long moment she stood, silent. Then her shoulders dropped and a surge of relief came over her. Finally, she knew the truth. From the start, she had questioned the way they came to know Thor. She'd thought it strange that Zinnia had never contacted Alvise, and that Magda had seemed too eager to do so, and then too eager to rid herself of the boy. Definitely, they had been duped.

"I had my doubts in the beginning...but then...now he's part of our lives. I wasn't prepared for this. We can't tell anyone," said Alvise.

"But it's the truth." She moved to the bed, and sat next to him.

He fell back, lying across the width of the bed. "We have to act as if we still don't know." He massaged his forehead. "Today is Thor's birthday."

"Of course we can't tell anyone tonight, but I'm leaving for the jewelry show tomorrow."

"Damn it." He took a deep breath, and rubbed his eyes.

"It's my job, and Uncle Fausto is depending on me."

"I'm not asking you not to go." He stood, pulled her to her feet, and wrapped her in his arms. "Now that we know for certain, the court could force us to send him back to Sweden."

"Alvise, we can't just keep him." She leaned against him, her hands steady. Now what? What would become of Thor?

"He doesn't have anyone else."

"He's got a real father, somewhere. Aren't we obligated to find him?"

"Are you saying that, because you don't want him to stay?"

She moved from his embrace. "That's not fair. For months, I've been a mother to Thor." For Thor's sake she would have liked a different DNA result, but for her own sake—she wasn't sure.

"You have been...I'm sorry. I just don't understand how this could happen...how could Zinnia...or how could Magda do this to me...to us...or to Thor?"

"Evidently, you were the only man in Zinnia's life Magda knew how to contact." Victoria turned, facing him.

He took her hands in his. "I'll speak to the attorney, and ask him what's next."

She saw her make-up had smeared on his striped work shirt. She grimaced at the mess on his shirt, and at the mess they were in. "You better change. Your white polo shirt is clean."

"Think about what you want, too."

She turned to the bedroom mirror. Her make-up needed to be touched up. *I will. But not now...it's late.*

He stood behind her, and unbuttoned and then slipped the stained shirt from his muscular torso, and tossed it on the floor. She knew he'd wear the polo shirt to dinner, and his striped gondolier's shirt on board. He'd never take his gondola out—least of all the night of Il Redentore—unless he was dressed in uniform.

Opening the armoire, she saw that, once again, Anna had done more than iron a few shirts. Her jewelry box had been pushed to the back, and her lingerie rearranged on the shelf. Alvise's well-ironed t-shirts, underwear and socks occupied another drawer, now, too. She didn't say a word. She'd been clear with Anna. She'd no longer stand for her intruding on their privacy. She rearranged the clothes the way she chose to have them, and slid her jewelry case to the spot where it belonged. She'd speak to Anna, again, and get her house key. Now, more than before, she could consider this home hers, too.

She moved to the side of the armoire where she hung her dresses and, one by one, skimmed her fingers across them. She passed the floral print shift, and stopped when she touched the soft emerald green silk. The side slit and draped back sheath was a favorite of hers, and she hadn't put the dress on since she left Los Angeles. She pulled it from its hanger, slipped it over her head and down around her hips, and adjusted the soft neckline. A quick nod in the mirror, and she went back to the jewelry box. She lifted the lid from the top tier where she stored her semi-precious items, and plucked a pair of gold hoop earrings from the mélange of bangles and trinkets. She slipped the posts through the pierced holes in her ears, latched a matching cuff bracelet across her wrist, and stepped into a savvy pair of heels.

Chapter 26

NIGHTFALL LAYERED THE sky orange and purple, and Alvise dipped and pulled the oar in the canal like a loving hand caressing bath water. Victoria closed her eyes to the sensual rhythm, and longed for it to soothe her nerves. Somehow, the more she pushed her troubles away, the more she obsessed about their situation, and the evening that lay ahead. She had met people she didn't like in the past, but she had never felt such deep disfavor for anyone—not until Zinnia and Magda entered their life.

"*Oe*," yelled Alvise. The call rose from his chest and boomed against the sea soaked walls, and warned other boats he was approaching a blind corner.

Startled, Victoria opened her eyes to the sound she usually found charming and, for a moment, she disliked that, too. The gondola swayed onto the busy Grand Canal, and Victoria pushed herself upright against the leather seat cushions. On either side of the canal, open windows boasted translucent Rezzonico glass-chandeliers—their light flickering upon elaborate frescoed ceilings. In the distance, the Rialto Bridge spanned the canal. Low arches stuffed with Murano glass showrooms, jewelry stores and lace shops illuminated the massive footbridge much like side-stones enhancing a solitaire diamond-ring, and commanded her attention.

"The city is especially beautiful tonight," said Alvise. "But not quite as beautiful as you."

Victoria looked about, and then smiled over her shoulder without turning around.

"Thank you," he said.

"For what?"

"For how you tackle what's been put in our way."

Sometimes I wish I could make it go away. She shook her head. "Life does keep getting more complicated and difficult."

"So be it."

"It's not that easy…not for me."

"It's not a row down the canal for me, either." He smiled down at her.

"I'm serious, Alvise."

"So am I."

"You want to adopt him, don't you?"

"It would be the next logical step."

She moved from the loveseat to a black enamel side chair. She looked up at him. "Do I have to remind you that we're not even married yet, and that I'm still trying to adapt to living here?"

"Why are you the only one who doesn't see how incredible you are? You've found a job, you're caring for Thor, learning a new language, making new friends and planning a wedding. That's adapting. What more do you expect from yourself?"

"I might ask you, what more do *you* expect from me?"

Alvise stopped rowing, letting the current slowly take the gondola forward. Holding the oar in his right hand, he stooped down on the back of the boat. "Nothing, but please listen to me. We may have been born on opposite sides of the globe. We may have so called *friends* betting we won't stay together and others who don't believe love like ours even exists. But *we* know that we're meant to be together. What we've got, what we feel for one another, doesn't happen to everyone. I knew the first time I saw you, in that breath when the whole world vanished except for you and me, that you were the one."

Tears clouded her eyes. *Will that be enough in a year, in ten years or in twenty…if Thor doesn't stay with us? Or will you blame loving me for not being able to raise him like your son?*

He stood up, and took control of the boat back from the current. "This isn't about Thor. Is it?"

"It's about the circumstances and our choices."

"I understand the circumstances, and I chose you. *Amore mio*, you must believe that nothing can change my choice or how much I love you. There's only one person who can keep me from you, and that's you."

She blinked the tears from her eyes. *Choosing you was easy for me, too.* The changes she'd made and struggled with to be with him, were hers. If she succeeded that would be incredible, but if she failed, she'd only have herself to pick back up. What if adopting Thor turned out to be a mistake? Who would pick him up?

Alvise looked straight ahead. To their right, a *vaporetto* finished loading passengers from the embarcadero. He steered the gondola away from the water bus, toward the opposite side of the canal. The waterbus's engine rumbled and, as if alone on the crowded canal, the captain pulled away from the dock quicker than Alvise's arms could row.

"Move back to the love seat," he commanded.

Victoria watched the bow of the heavy metal boat heading toward her. She followed his command, and looked back, over her shoulder. She saw Alvise lift the oar off the forcola and plunge it deep in the water. He lunged forward and sculled rapid strokes, churning miniature whirlpools to the surface. His powerful arms worked against the tide and cleared the waterbus by mere centimeters, keeping them from harm's way. He steadied one hand on the oar and threw the other into irate gestures. A flurry of words in Venetian dialect followed, and needed no translation. The waterbus's horn wailed. Victoria looked back at the steel boat, and saw the captain smirk and subtly flip his middle finger at Alvise. The filled-to-capacity vessel squeezed so close that swells rocked the gondola from side to side, and splashed and sprayed seawater over Victoria and her dress.

"*Maledetto.*" Alvise yelled at the captain.

Astonished and dismayed, Victoria shook the beads of salt water from her dress.

"Are you okay?"

"I'm fine. Are you?"

Alvise nodded through his anger, and steered the gondola the short distance to the *cavana* at the foot of the bridge.

A gondolier stood at the dock, giving Alvise verbal moral support and adding his own colorful insults toward *vaporetto* drivers in general. Then, as if the incident was a daily occurrence, he smiled and tipped his straw hat at Victoria and, extending his forearm, helped her off the gondola.

Wiping the last drops of seawater from her skirt, Victoria walked up the bottom steps of the Rialto Bridge, and waited for Alvise to secure his boat. She scrutinized the steep climb laid out in front of her, and then eyed the bridge's rippling reflection in the canal below. Standing there, she felt ordinary. Her troubles, now, seemed trifle in comparison to what Venice had been, was and would be. Centuries of Venetian wealth, commerce and hard work had created this masterpiece. *Millions of people had walked across this bridge, traveled this canal* she thought. They had come and gone, and she, too, was simply passing through. The longevity of the bridge and its city proved that her life was no more than a note in time and, somehow, Venice's resistance, its hidden fragility, mirrored her own insecurities. She felt the city looking back at her—the way a wise old woman might look at a foolish young girl. Venice's permanence and importance seemed to warn her that insecurity and fear of failure were pointless, wasteful emotions. Holding on to these sentiments made her mundane, trivial, and doing so wouldn't change her predicament.

She leaned against the bridge's warm marble balustrade, and looked as far down the darkening canal as the setting sun would allow. She wondered if others appreciated Venice's beauty and fragility as deeply as she had come to or if, like a raging fever, the city infected some while avoiding others. She sighed at the grandeur and at the resilience that surrounded her, and she promised herself she'd try to be more like Venice.

Light spilled from the *osteria* windows, forming luminous squares on the dark alleyway floor, and the sound of clattering plates and laughter grew louder. Steps from the entrance, Victoria pulled back on Alvise's hand and, standing in the shadows, saw through the lace curtains that they were the last to arrive.

Inside, Bruno, Ciano and the other men, seated at the checkered linen draped table, laughed and joked. Anna, Thor and the ladies sat at the opposite end. Two empty seats remained, one at each end of the table. Victoria saw the empty chair next to Ivana who, sitting next to Thor, looked pretty in a pink and white striped shirt. She took a deep breath, and fought the understanding that she had no choice but to put on a smile, and pretend nothing had changed.

Ivana's parents, followed by waiters and waitresses in black mid-calf length aprons, carried seafood appetizer platters, bread baskets and wine carafes, back and forth. Anna stood, holding a knife in her hand, and reached to the center of the table. She sliced strips of white polenta from the round cutting board, and slapped them on plates of black-ink braised cuttlefish. She placed one in front of Thor and then another in front of Ivana. She held Paola, Ivana's mother, back, as if giving her pointers on how to improve each delicacy they served. Turning back to Thor, she turned up the palms of her hands and moved her wrists as if pushing him along—the word *mangia* formed on her lips. Thor responded with a disgusted look, turned away from the seafood, and set the plates in the empty place next to him. He said something to the waitress, and shook his head at the seafood risotto dish, too.

"We can't stand out here all night," said Alvise.

Victoria pulled back on his arm and kept him from stepping closer to the door. "Not a word about the DNA test results."

"We agreed on that."

She sighed and nodded her head. *Who organizes a seating arrangement as if we're at a junior high school dance? Honestly, women and children at one end of the table, and men at the other?* She adjusted her dress neckline, and stood firm inside her designer heels.

"*Vita*, you look gorgeous." He raised her hand to his lips, and kissed it.

They entered the tiny establishment and heads turned. The ruckus around their table fell silent until Bruno and Ciano yelled out their seating assignments, and a few spicy reprimands for being late.

Victoria felt the critical yet friendly eyes of the women canvas her head to toe, and then back again. She clenched Alvise's hand, stood tall, and leaned on his white lie. They were late because *he had left work later than expected.* She glanced up to see Thor jump down from his seat and throw a warm hug around their legs. His gesture cuddled, and then crushed her heart, but made her giggle, too, and sway on her heels. She brushed back his bangs, and sent him to the kitchen with his birthday cake, and instructions to have it stored in a cool place.

"I'm sorry we're late." Victoria noticed Anna's disapproving expression. She sat down when Alvise pulled out her chair, and turned her cheek up to him as he bent down to kiss it. She watched him give a kind hello to his mother and Ivana, and then join the men at the opposite end of the table.

"I love your dress." Ivana leaned in and exchanged a double-cheek kiss.

"How are you?" The look on Victoria's face said *thank you.* She leaned back in her chair, and made room for the waitress to clear away the dirty plates in front of her, and put down a fresh plate of seafood appetizers. She noted that another waitress had set a plate of sliced mozzarella, tomatoes and fresh basil in front of Ivana.

"Great," said Ivana. "We found an appartment."

"When do you move in?"

"Ciano was waiting for you and Alvise to arrive to make the announcement." Ivana eyes twinkled. "Mamma…Papà." Ivana nodded at her parents, and called them away from serving the other patrons. When Ivana's mother Paola, and her father were standing behind her, she looked down the table. "*Amore.* Whenever you want to…"

Ciano stood. He filled the glasses around him with wine, and then filled his own and held it in his hand. He winked at Ivana, and then, like a boxer preparing to enter the ring, twisted his neck and straightened his broad shoulders. His eyes twitched and blinked, and exposed his nervousness. "What I'm going to tell you…well, I won't be surprised if you are. Shit! I never thought I'd see the day I'd find my match. But I have. Ivana and I bought an apartment in Castello." Ciano paused, and the guests applauded. "We move in as soon as the sale closes."

"Another good man…ruined." Bruno raised his glass to Ciano, and winked. "Ivana, you know I don't like women being gondoliers…but you're okay. You're still a woman…and a gondolier…but you're okay. At least you're keeping the gondolier trade in the family. Congratulations."

"Congratulations." Victoria smiled at Ivana.

"There's more." Ivana's lips turned up in a pixyish smile.

"Did you decide to get married?" Paola grabbed Ivana's father's hand, and smiled.

"No, Mamma."

Ciano left his seat, and went to Ivana. He set his wine glass on the table and a kiss on her cheek. Standing behind her, and next to her parents, he gently laid his hands on her shoulders. "One more thing I thought I'd never say..." His usual devilish smile turned tender. "*La mia vecia*…my old gal… is going to make me a father."

The noise level in the osteria went silent, and then exploded with cheers, and bounced off the wood beamed ceiling. Paola hugged her daughter, and tears of joy filled their eyes. Ivana's father filled glasses, again. They were raised, and wine was sipped and swallowed. Chairs scooted across the terracotta floor and out from under the table. The guests moved about, hugging and kissing and congratulating the expectant couple.

The happy news exposed Victoria's nerves. She felt empty, and watched sadness wash away the surprise on Alvise's face. He hugged Ciano, patted him on the back, and then met her own concerned eyes. She searched deep for that inner peace and the promise she had made herself and left at the Rialto Bridge. She shifted in her chair, and waited as the excitement quieted, and the guests took their places at the table, again.

"You both look so happy." Victoria turned to Ivana, sitting next to her again.

"It's a girl…our little Silvia." Ivana's face glowed with happiness.

"That's a beautiful name."

"It means forest. My little forest moved today. It was like being tickled on the inside."

Victoria listened and gave her attention to Ivana, and felt her nerves calm, somewhat. "Was that the first time?"

"Yes."

"What about your job?"

"The baby is due in the off season. I'll stay home for a few months, before going back to work."

"What about now? Isn't it heavy work for you?"

"Not yet. When it gets too tiring, I'll take maternity leave. It's not a problem. My job will be there when I decide to go back."

"That's great. It's not the same in the States. How far along are you?"

"I'm due right before Christmas."

With a smile, Victoria's attention shifted to Thor. He held a bowl of meat lasagna in his chubby hands, and led a line of waiters and waitresses carrying plates of pink shells stuffed with spider crab from the kitchen. He went to his seat. His sweet smile grabbed Victoria's tender spot, and threw her thoughts back to the DNA results.

Standing there, Thor looked up at Anna, then at Victoria, and then back at Anna, again. He smiled and marched the plate of lasagna around the table. Handing the dish up to Victoria, he scampered onto her lap.

Victoria smelled his clean shampooed hair, and felt her hands shake around his small waist. When would they make *their* announcement, and reveal the truth?

Thor plunged his fork deep into the thick meat sauce, cheese and pasta. "*Mamma Vittoria* makes the best lasagna."

"Mamma Vittoria?" Ivana smiled.

Victoria's heart dropped.

Thor continued to stuff his mouth with lasagna, and nestled deeper into Victoria's lap. He gave her a sense of comfort, and sadness. She looked down the table at Alvise, once again. His smile had disappeared, too.

"Vittoria, you want children of your own, right?" Anna looked at Victoria and then at Ivana. Running a sliced lemon across her fingertips, cleansing the fish smell from her hands.

"Am I your children…Mamma Vittoria?" Thor bit into a forkful of lasagna.

Victoria felt her face flush. She didn't answer Anna or Thor. She couldn't. Instead, she kissed the top of his head.

"Any news on the test results?" Ivana leaned in, and whispered.

Victoria shook her head, and removed a spot of red sauce from Thor's face with a napkin.

"*Two* children are hard work," said Anna.

"Please, Anna. I'm not prepared to think about that now. I'm still planning our wedding." Victoria's nervousness crept back and showed through her laugh.

Ivana leaned forward and looked at Anna. "Two would be easy if all children were as sweet as Thor."

Anna lifted the wine carafe and filled her glass halfway, and then filled Victoria's, too. "Of course he's sweet…like father like son."

But he's not Alvise's son thought Victoria.

"*Finito.*" Thor handed his empty lasagna dish to the waitress. He scooted off Victoria's lap, and skipped down the table to Alvise.

Victoria glanced down at the plate the waitress had set in front of her. Pink and white spider-crabmeat filled a coral shell. She squeezed a lemon slice over the seafood, and looked down the table. She watched Alvise pull Thor up in his arms, and onto his lap. She poked a fork into the crabmeat, and brought a succulent morsel to her mouth. The crab pulp tasted fresh and sweet. But her nerves had stolen her appetite.

"I adore how well Thor and Alvise get along." Ivana cut into the moist mozzarella cheese and red tomato slices on her plate.

Victoria kept her eyes on Alvise. She noted his naturalness, his untrained fatherly spontaneity, and his protective hands holding Thor's. He raised a filled glass and Thor lifted another filled with water, and they sent a private toast her way.

Victoria raised her glass to them, too, and then put it down without drinking from it. Twisting a long curl around her finger, she nibbled on her bottom lip. It would be foolish to deny that she cared for the boy. But she would not and could not further attach herself to him. The thought of letting him go had become painful, now, and the possibility too high. Her continuing doubts about falling into a ready-made family were strong. Could she stand in Alvise's way? She loved him so. Could she refuse to adopt Thor? To watch them together, now, see the sadness behind Alvise's smiling eyes—the misery of the truth filled her soul. How much longer would they be a family? She took a deep breath and blinked away the moisture stinging her eyes, and then dried them with a napkin.

When she said yes to Alvise's marriage proposal, she knew her life would change. She took a chance, and crossed the portal. Over and again, the entryway had remained closed until she found a way to pry it open. Now, she couldn't decipher if the path was opened or closed. Decisions would have to be made. But she wouldn't think about that now. Not on Thor's birthday.

"Hey, are you okay?" said Ivana.

"I'm just feeling a little sentimental…about your announcement."

Ivana gave Victoria's hand a squeeze.

Food continued to flood out from the kitchen. The table guests served themselves grilled *scampi* from large platters, peeled the langoustines' transparent skins back with their fingers and ate the sweet meat, and washed it down with glass after glass of the house wine. Victoria took a small portion and passed the plate onto Ivana.

"No thanks. I've become a vegetarian...with the pregnancy. I'm thinking about continuing after the baby is born…but Ciano says there's nothing wrong with meat and fish." Ivana wiped a forkful of mozzarella and tomatoes across the abundant olive oil, and then slid the refreshing combination into her mouth.

"Oh *Maria Vergine*…bambini can't eat only *insalata*…children need meat to grow. *Specialmente*, children growing in a womb." Anna looked at Ivana, and then at Victoria.

Neither answered her.

The waiters and waitresses swept away the last *bigoli in salsa* pasta plates. When Victoria saw Paola returning from the kitchen carrying Thor's birthday cake, she stood and went to his side. Seated on Alvise's lap, his eyes lit up and mirrored the five blue candles flickering on the *millefoglie* cake. The guests' attention turned to the small boy and his cake, and they sang, *Tanti Auguri a Te*...Happy Birthday to You, in Italian.

"Make a wish, Thor." Victoria smiled.

Thor looked over his shoulder and up at Victoria, and then at Alvise. He frowned at the cake and studied the candles. He plucked a chocolate chip from the fluffy custard cream, and popped it in his mouth.

"What's your wish?" said Alvise.

The boy turned his back on the cake, and curled up his legs. He tucked himself in Alvise's arms, his eyes cast to the floor. "I wish my mommy was here."

Victoria's heart sank, and the table fell silent. She swallowed her tears.

"That's a fine wish." Alvise hugged Thor with one arm, and reached his free hand out, squeezing Victoria's. "Your mother is here, in spirit."

"Are you and Mamma Vittoria going to become spirits?"

Alvise pulled Thor to his broad chest. "No. Not anytime soon."

Taking a deep breath, Victoria grappled with the truth, and struggled to stay in control. The boy's reaction stirred her compassion. His fear of abandonment and unrestricted love clutched her heart. How could this child be so loved and yet so alone in the world?

Bruno sighed, and stood. He lifted the boy from Alvise's lap and into his strong arms. "What do ya say, young man? Can your Nonno help you blow out your candles?"

Thor wrapped his arms around Bruno's wide neck and clung to him. He nodded.

Victoria wiped her eyes with her free hand, and then pulled Alvise to his feet with the other. She linked her arm in his.

Ciano stood behind them now, too. One hand on Alvise's shoulder and the other on Bruno's—a loud whistle shrieked from his lips, quieting the osteria and calling for everyone to stand, and join them. All eyes smiled at Thor, and the crowd belted out *Tanti Auguri*, again. Thor's eyes twinkled with delight, and then the chorus of friends and family and strangers fell silent.

"*Pronto?*" said Bruno.

"*Sì!*" he said.

"*Uno, due, tre...*"

Together, they blew out the five melted down candles.

The heat and humidity that had hovered above the city in the early evening had moved elsewhere, and left them with a balmy summer night. Walking beside Ivana and Anna, Victoria held Thor's hand and hurried on her heels down the dark alleyway. They followed Ciano, Alvise and Bruno, and the others to the gondolas. Canal side, they rushed to board the boats. It was close to eleven thirty p.m.—the Redentore fireworks display would begin, soon.

Victoria sat on the love seat, and caressed Thor's fine hair—his head lying on her lap—his eyes ready to close for the night. The warm breeze on her skin, she drank in the scene.

Ahead, the Grand Canal sat as still as a mirror. No *vaporetti*, no row boats, and no motor boats roaring, splashing or making waves. No noise, except for the sound of the gondoliers' oars slicing the dark water, and their gondolas disturbing the reflection of grand palaces. No one spoke. For a rare, magical moment, the heart of the city was theirs.

The Rialto Bridge and the Grand Canal at their backs, the gondolas glided down deserted narrow waterways squeezed in by towering brick palace walls.

Boom!

Thor jumped. He sat up on his knees, and rubbed sleep from his eyes.

Victoria's attention jolted up to the crevice of exposed sky. "Look." She pointed up.

Fountains of red, white and green fire flashed above them, and lit the sky.

Alvise laughed out loud and swore beneath his breath, and raced his gondola forward.

Boom!

Gold and silver light shot across the sky, and then burst and fell to the earth like weeping willow branches.

Thor snuggled closer to Victoria.

"Are you afraid?"

"The boom is in my heart."

"It feels that way, doesn't it?" Victoria smiled and placed her hand on his heart.

Boom!

Thor jumped, again, and giggled.

Victoria pointed up, at the amethyst and blue sky.

The gondoliers rowed faster and faster, laughing, racing and cursing at each other, until their strong bodies jettisoned their gondolas under and past the Ponte della Paglia, and out into the center of the St. Mark's basin.

Victoria's eyes shimmered at the spectacle. From the gondola, she looked back at St. Mark's Square. Tens of thousands of spectators cheered the display of light from the crowded Piazza and waterfront stone pavement. Thousands of others celebrated on docked boats. Aperol Spritz or Prosecco filled plastic drinking glasses in hand, all heads tilted up. A sea of admirers oohed and awed. For thirty minutes, clouds of fire flashed in the sky—their light darkened cathedral towers and domes into silhouettes, and transformed the sea basin into a glossy sheet of changing color.

Victoria felt a hand touch her shoulder, and she looked up at Alvise. On the back of the gondola, he held his oar in the other hand, and kept his boat in place. Kneeling, he smiled down at her and then at Thor—the boy's eyes glued to the sky. In Alvise's serious, loving smile, she could see his question, too. The fear of losing Thor, painted across his face.

Chapter 27

ALVISE WANTING TO adopt Thor and Victoria's indecision to do the same had moved sorrow into her life and brought doubt with it. Together they barged into her heart, massaged the insecurity that had accompanied her since Thor had arrived in Venice, and shoved prenuptial bliss aside. Then, as if being big bullies wasn't bad enough, sorrow and doubt pulled out a double-edged sword and took a deadly stab at moral reason. *Why should I feel pressured to commit to being a mother to a child that isn't mine or his? Does my resistance, my doubt make me a bad person? Isn't giving up everything to commit to a man enough?* The Jewelry Trade Show on Lago Maggiore would give Victoria the excuse she needed to get away from Venice—and decide what she wanted.

The Trade Show welcome cocktail continued at the Regina Palace Hotel, on Lago Maggiore's mainland. Knowing Debora could do no harm to Fausto's shop by lingering-on at a cocktail party, Victoria buttoned her jacket against the cool evening air rising from the lake, and stepped off the ferryboat, and onto the dock on Isola dei Pescatori—the tiny island named for its fisherman.

The busy tourist season on Lake Maggiore had arrived, but at that hour of the evening the small island retreat emptied out, leaving the peaceful getaway to those who chose to stay in one of its few quaint hotels. Looking across the dock she met the curious stares of a group of locals. As if protecting precious goods, they tightened their circle around a gray-haired couple who, elegantly clothed, wore matching corsage and boutonniere. Still, the well-dressed group occupied most of the small dock, forcing Victoria to weave through them. Walking toward solid ground, she overheard chatter about an elaborate luncheon, and how fortunate they were not to miss the last ferry of the day and be taken back to the mainland. She, too, felt relieved to have spared the expense of a private water taxi.

Once past the group, Victoria turned and watched the filled ferryboat pull away from the dock. Alone, she filled her lungs with the fresh lake air, and walked the short distance from the pier. Careful not to dirty her shoes on the damp tree-lined gravel path that circled the island's perimeter, she followed the ferryboat captain's easy directions to the hotel.

The lakeside villa, converted to a hotel in the late 1800s, was once the private home of a well-to-do family, and displayed the great pride taken in its preservation. The iron-gate entrance was defined by raised brick columns camouflaged in manicured ivy, and jasmine veiled walls that perfumed the air. Its brick-red stucco façade shot up two floors from an ample graveled garden, and a fireplace glowed behind a glass enclosed veranda where couples dined by candlelight, sipped wine and held hands across linen covered tables.

Her heart missed Alvise.

She stepped off the cobblestone alleyway, out of the evening chill, and into the warm understated lobby. A narrow staircase led to the floors above, and a distinguished gentleman toiled behind the reception desk.

"*Benvenuta.*" A salt-and-pepper haired concierge smiled.

"*Grazie.* My company's travel agent made the reservations… under the name of Victoria Greco."

"I'll need identification…your *carta d'Identità* will be fine. " He busied himself with the reservation book.

"I don't have one." Victoria pulled a leather wallet from deep inside her purse, opened it. She flipped through the plastic inserts, one by one, and then rummaged through her purse.

"A passport will be fine." He didn't look up.

"I didn't think I'd need it."

"I can't check you in without a valid document." He looked at her over gold-rimmed bifocals.

Victoria pulled a leather wallet from deep inside her purse, opened it, and fingered through it, passing over credit cards she hadn't used since she'd left Los Angeles, and stopped at her California driver's license. "Will this do?" She handed it to him. "It's valid."

He glanced at the driver's license and then back at her. "You live in Marina Del Rey…California?"

"I used to…I live in Venice…Italy, now."

"If you live in Italy then I can only accept an Italian document." He put the driver's license on the marble reception desk.

"I'm here for the Jewelry Trade Show...on business. Could you make an exception?"

"Madam, in Italy exceptions are *always* possible."

"Oh, of course..." She pulled a five euro bill from the wallet.

He frowned and shook his head.

"No?"

"No."

She showed him a ten euro bill. *That's almost twelve dollars,* she thought.

"Marina Del Rey is lovely." He took both bills and put them in his pocket. "I was there last winter." He returned to the hotel log, and penned in her identity.

"I hope you liked it," she said, disturbed that this world traveling concierge had relieved her of more than fifteen dollars.

"It was nice for a vacation, but *casa è sempre casa*…home is always home." He turned the registry, and handed her a pen.

Home she thought signing her name. *Where is mine, really?* She clicked the push button closing the pen, and set it in the gutter of the registry.

"You have the room with the best view of the lake. Are you expecting someone? I see the reservations are for two."

"No…I mean . . . Well, my colleague will arrive later. But I thought we had separate rooms. Whatever you have available will be fine."

"But madam, this is one of our best rooms."

"I understand…but. . .I'd like my own room." Exhaustion pulled at her patience. "If it's at all possible to have a second room for my colleague, please . . ."

"I'll see what I can do. I don't expect we'll have any cancellations. Between the trade show and the wedding here tomorrow, we're booked."

"A wedding...in the middle of the week?"

"Yes. Most of the guests are already settled. A bottle of chilled complimentary Prosecco is in your room, and you have a telephone message." He handed her a small, sealed note and softened his tone. "Would you care for a light dinner before you retire for the night? Shall I reserve a table for two in our dining room?"

"No . . . thank you. I prefer to go to the room." She looked at the envelope in her hand. She peeled open the sealed note and read the short handwritten message printed on the hotel's stationery: *I called and texted your cell. No answer. I spoke to the attorney about Thor today. We have a chance. Love, Alvise.* She took a deep breath, and slipped the note back in its envelope.

She tossed her purse and jacket on the wrought-iron bed, opened the French doors, and stepped out onto the small balcony. Crisp air blew down from the mountains and across the lake, stinging her weary eyes. The lapping sound of the water below couldn't soothe her aching head.

She focused on Isola Bella in the distance, but tears filled her eyes and blurred the view, turning the island into a kaleidoscopic of light under the black sky. Her heart grieved. If she said no to the adoption, would she lose Alvise?

She left the balcony for the pristine tiled bathroom, reached for the antique bathtub knobs marked *hot* and *cold* and commanded them to release a flow of warm water. She took a packet of rose-scented bath salts from the counter and dissolved them under the slow jet. Returning to the bedroom, she closed the French doors and undressed, slipped on the hotel robe, opened the Prosecco, and poured a full glass. Sipping it, she reclined on the soft bed and waited for the tub to fill. The weight of the day lay heavily on her. Alone, and tired of holding back the frustration, she broke down and sobbed so hard she struggled to breathe. She shed all the tears she had, and then a few more, until she was exhausted.

A second full chalice of chilled Prosecco in hand she returned to the bathroom, let the cotton robe fall from her shoulders to the floor and immerged herself in the warm tub of water. The Prosecco softened her despair as its effect weighed heavy on her head. The delicate floral perfume evaporated off the tub water and filled the room. Her tired body relaxed, and her indecision about what she should do next relaxed with it.

The more Prosecco she sipped the more sorrow and doubt sliced apart moral reason. She held the empty wine glass over the rim of the tub and dipped her head back as if christening her selfish thoughts. She splashed upright in the tub, and let the warm water drain from her hair. Stepping from the bath, wrapping a towel around her head and the hotel robe around her body, she stopped the room from spinning by leaning on the bathroom counter.

One hand against the wall for balance, she shuffled her damp bare feet across the parquet floor, and returned to the bedroom. The ramifications of the DNA test, and the words *we have a chance* on Alvise's phone message, hammered her thoughts as she refilled her glass. They pushed her to drain her glass, again, and then grab her smartphone.

She dropped onto the bed and dialed her mother. The phone rang and rang, and then rang some more, and then disconnected.

She redialed the number. Rose's line rang, again, until a woman's recorded voice rolled off something in Italian about the phone number being unreachable, out of the area or out of service.

"Damn cellphone service!"

She scrolled up her phone list, and stopped at Chloe Anders. Her former boss' name and photo stared back at her. They hadn't spoken since the day after Christmas, when Victoria had called the new talent agency, and told her she could no longer be her Executive Assistant.

Victoria sunk deeper into the pillows, and thought about her old office, the view Chloe's office had of the Santa Monica mountains, and the famous clients that had been part of her everyday work life—Bradley Cooper, Jennifer Lawrence, Amanda Seyfried, Miley Cyrus. She missed the fast pace of Hollywood, the elaborate luncheons she'd organized and, at times, attended. The premieres, the red carpets, and the awards season shows.

She took a deep breath, chewed her bottom lip, and punched out a text:

> Ciao, Chloe!
> Hope you are well, and having great success at the new Talent Agency.
> I'm working in fine jewelry, now.
> It's not Hollywood…but I'm learning new things.
> In Italy, life is…

Victoria stopped texting. She couldn't finish the sentence. How should she describe her life in Italy? Complicated. Frustrating.

Unexpected. The love she had for Alvise hadn't changed, but their life had. When Thor arrived, the fairytale come true took a detour to reality.

She backspaced over and erased the last line of the text message, and added:

I miss you, and the glamour.
Victoria

Then, she hit SEND.

Smartphone in hand, she scrolled to Alvise's name. She studied the photo of him on his gondola. The one she had snapped on her first day of vacation in Venice—the moment they'd first laid eyes on each other. *How many people capture such a moment in time?* Mere months ago, now, that day seemed like a lifetime away.

She tapped the keys, again:

Ciao, Alvise.
All good at the lake. It's beautiful.
Going to sleep now. Early day tomorrow.
Phone connection comes and goes, so I won't call.
Got your note.
I need time to evaluate our situation, and decide what I want.
We'll talk when I get back.
Please understand.
Love, Victoria

She hit SEND, and then turned off her smartphone.

Tipsy and sleepy, now, she placed the smartphone on the nightstand and laid down on the bed where the night was grim and where she'd never felt more alone.

Still wrapped in the damp robe and towel, and lying on the bed, the telephone woke her. She turned slowly, and blinked back at the telephone's red light. Her hand lifted toward the nightstand and hit the empty wine glass, almost knocking it over, and then pulled the receiver to her ear.

"Madam, your colleague is here."

"Debora?" she said, her memory as foggy as the lake air.

"Yes, Ms. Debora has arrived."

"Right…"

"Shall I send her up?"

"You said you'd find her another room."

"I tried…I'm sorry."

Shit.

Her svelte legs swung over the side of the bed and her soggy hair fell from the towel. She finger-combed and twisted the wet locks into a loose knot, closed the cotton robe and tightened its belt around her waist. She swayed to the side table, and caught a glimpse of herself in the bedroom mirror. She moved closer to the blurred image, blinked to focus and wiped the smeared mascara from her eyes. A knock on the door triggered her reflection to change from irritation to charming colleague. Then a second knock came, and she opened the door.

"Why don't I have my own room?" Debora wheeled a suitcase past her, and stopped at the foot of the double bed.

The room closed in on Victoria, then shifted. She leaned against the doorframe as if fixed to the threshold, paralyzed in place. She stared at Debora for a long while until the conversation of other hotel guests filled the hallway, confirming the small hotel was indeed full, and that she had had too much Prosecco. She stepped back, and tightened the cotton robe across her breasts. *I'm not jumping for joy either.*

Debora rested against the bed frame and squinted her eyes. "Are you drunk?"

"No." The Prosecco's effect wrestled with her tongue.

"Trust me, I know drunk, and you are."

"Even if I were, it's none of your business."

"We've got an early morning appointment with the Damiani Group. Remember?" Debora rolled her eyes.

"Of course I remember."

"Well, we'll make a fine team."

"Us...a team? You wouldn't recognize a team if it tackled you to the ground." Victoria eyed Debora's lace dress. She was tall and pretty.

"That's not true." Debora's face softened. "I was captain of the soccer team in school."

Victoria needed a friend to talk to. She wished she could trust Debora to be that friend. Or was that need the result of too much alcohol? "I meant to tell you earlier that you look nice."

With a light touch of her finger to her chin, Debora tilted Victoria's head back, and looked into her eyes. "You haven't eaten anything, have you?"

Victoria shook her head.

Debora went to the night stand, and picked up the phone. "I'm not going to let you ruin tomorrow for us."

"I'm fine." Victoria sat back on the bed.

"No you're not, and Fausto will blame me if things go wrong. You're his *Signorina can't do anything wrong.*"

"Who are you calling?"

"Room service. *Sì…buona sera…*I'd like an order of grilled cheese and prosciutto sandwiches, a side of fried potatoes and a liter of still water."

"I love grilled cheese. Ask for ketchup…for the fries."

Debora rolled her eyes, again, and spoke into the phone. "And ketchup." She set the phone in its cradle. "You want that side of the bed?" She pointed at the mattress, and slipped off her heels.

Victoria nodded and lay back on the pillow.

"Hold on. Your hair is wet." Debora walked in her bare feet across the wood floor to her luggage. She pulled out a blow drier from the neatly packed suitcase, and plugged it in. "Drop the towel from your head."

"Why are you being so nice to me?"

"Drop it." Debora flicked on the blow dryer and ran the forced air over Victoria's damp hair.

Victoria closed her eyes, and relaxed as Debora's fingers and the warm air caressed her hair and scalp, and soothed her nerves. "I thought you hated me."

"It's not you. I don't like anyone."

"You have to like someone."

"I like myself. I can always trust myself, and my grandmother."

"What about your mom…your dad?"

Debora sat silent for a moment, and then said, "Dad is only around when he's not in rehab. And mom…well she's got her own issues."

"I'm sorry…I didn't know."

"Why are you sorry?"

"Not liking anyone sounds lonely."

"You like people and you're nice to them. But who's lonelier, you or me?"

Is it that obvious?

"You care too much. Sometimes it's okay NOT to give a shit."

"I was pretty good at being selfish, you know."

"And then you met Alvise…and gave everything up. I could never love anyone that much."

"He's special…I just didn't expect to…"

"Become a mom."

"Thor is a beautiful boy…but yes…of course…he wasn't in my plans."

"So leave. He's not your son, and you're not married yet. It's easy. Get on a plane and go back to Hollywood."

"So you can have my job?"

"I don't want your job. I'm only working there to save enough money to start my own business."

"What business?"

"Wedding planner in Venice. I'm taking night classes at the European Design Institute, and a web technician is building my website."

"Does Fausto know?"

"No, and you're not going to tell him."

Victoria shook her head. "I think that's great."

A knock on the door brought Debora to her feet. She moved across the bedroom to the door. The waiter stood on the other side, and entered when she opened it. He brought a tray and the smell of melted cheese and fried potatoes into the bedroom with him. He set the tray on a small coffee table, took a smaller tip from Debora's hand, and left the room.

Victoria propped a pile of pillows behind her heavy head. "Do you wonder why we don't get along?"

Debora moved the tray to the foot of the bed, and handed Victoria half of a grilled sandwich wrapped in a paper napkin. She filled two glasses with still water, placing them next to the fried potatoes on the tray, and then sat on the bed. "I told you, I don't get along with anyone."

"Does it have anything to do with me being American?" Victoria nibbled on her sandwich, and then popped a potato fry in her mouth.

"It does if all Americans are so perfect at everything."

"I'm not perfect."

"Well you walk around with an air of someone who can do anything."

"Don't mistake wanting to be perfect with being perfect. There's an endless void between the two." Victoria moved over a little, and made more room for Debora to stretch out on the bed. The walls twisted and slanted around her. She put her sandwich down and laid her head back on the pillow, and urged the room to stand still. She closed her eyes. After a long silence, when being with Debora felt more secure, she said "What you said earlier… about me leaving..."

"I was just blabbering off at the mouth."

"You didn't put the idea in my head. Since Thor arrived, I've thought about it more often than I'd like to admit."

"I have a bad habit of saying things when I shouldn't."

Victoria turned her eyes to Debora's and saw the sincerity that they'd never shown her before. Yet, even as her desire to tell Debora that Thor wasn't Alvise's son was about to take over, she forced herself to withstand the temptation. "They make a mean grilled cheese here."

"Want another?"

Silently, she refused. She sunk back into the tuff of pillows, and turned her head slowly. She looked up at Debora looking down at her. Her expression was sweeter than she'd ever seen it. She fought to keep her eyes open. "You don't have to feel terrible about not liking me. Lately, I don't like myself."

"Let's get that damp robe off of you, before you fall asleep." Debora disappeared into the bathroom, and returned carrying a dry robe.

"Actually, you're very sweet." Victoria sat up, again, and wiggled out of the wet robe. Dropping it to the floor, she wrapped herself in the dry one, and pulled the bedcovers up around her. Her head sunk deeper into the pillows, and she pulled the covers up and over her shoulders. Her eyelids closed.

Chapter 28

FASHIONABLE IN HER blazer, t-shirt and tailored cropped trousers, Victoria forked over the sliced strawberries from the fruit plate and picked at the brioche. Debora, wearing a tight navy knit dress, sipped her espresso. The salty smell of the bacon tomato frittata the owner's son had insisted they try sent Victoria's stomach churning. She took another sip of cappuccino and pushed her chair away from the linen-covered table—*Toscanini's table*—she had been told. The proprietor's kind son confirmed that many Italian and European dignitaries had stayed or eaten at their quaint, lakeside hotel, restaurant and garden. Victoria knew little about Arturo Toscanini or his music career, but she shared the orchestra conductor's taste for this lakeside table and the stunning scenery. Shaded by a lone oak tree at the lake's edge, the table, more secluded than the others, gave them an unobstructed view of the lake and the 17th century Borromeo Palace perched on Isola Bella: *the pretty island.*

Victoria glanced down at her purse, and the light blinking on her cellphone. It was Alvise calling, again. It was his third call that morning. She hadn't answered any of them. Her hungover head, and heavy heart, wouldn't let her talk to him or face their future. Not yet. She was working. Her private life would wait. She reached into her purse, and pulled out a blister pack of Ibuprofen pills. She popped two pills in her mouth, and washed them down with a gulp of water.

The waiters chattered in the far corner of the garden and tended to a few other guests, while a uniformed crew prepared the patio for a wedding reception. She leaned back in her chair, and closed her tired eyes against the sunlight filtering through the oak leaves above. She listened to the quiet rhythm of the lake, and wished her headache would disappear.

"We're meeting the Damiani Group there this morning, right?" Debora lit a cigarette, and adjusted her dark sunglasses.

Victoria opened her eyes, and looked across the lake and at Isola Bella. She nodded, and turned to Debora. "I'm not criticizing you for smoking." *God knows I'm getting used to Italians doing so.* "But how can you smoke so early in the morning?"

"How can you not?" Debora held the cigarette away from her face. The smoke twisted in curls toward the sky.

Victoria frowned and reached for her iPad, and then opened the Damiani Group webpage. "I'd like to see ring settings like this one." She showed Debora a glossy photo of a round solitaire diamond clutched by four white-gold prongs.

"Don't you think the shop could use something a little less classic?" Debora flicked the cigarette ashes onto a mosaic dish.

"Fausto wants classic engagement ring settings…but he did give me some leeway." Victoria glanced down at her left hand, and at the Buccellati ruby and diamond engagement ring. Less traditional than a solitaire diamond, she loved its uniqueness. Yet somehow, now, it looked different to her. Was uncertainty changing her viewpoint about her engagement ring, too? On Christmas Day, when she had slipped it onto her left hand, and then said yes to Alvise, she was confident and secure about her future with him. *Where has my faith in us gone?*

Debora tilted her head up, blew a ruffle of smoke through her lips and studied the iPad screen. "I like that one…the diamond snake band."

Victoria looked back at the iPad screen. "It's not bad…but it's not a classic setting."

"Not everyone likes twin-sets and pearls." Debora took another puff of her cigarette. "I'd wear it."

"You're right, not everyone is boring-old ordinary. We'll ask to see it."

They rose from the famous conductor's table and left the garden restaurant. Draping her silk scarf around her neck and against the cool breeze, Victoria left Debora to finish her cigarette outside while she stopped by the front desk.

"Good morning." Victoria placed the room key on the counter.

"*Buon giorno.* I see you have a late check-out."

"Yes, we'll be out most of the morning. But we'll pick up our things before we catch the train back to Venice."

"No problem. The ferryboat will be at the pier in a few minutes," he said. "The first stop is Isola Bella . . . is that where you wish to go?"

Victoria pulled her purse over her shoulder, tightened the belt around her jacket and nodded. She lowered her sunglasses across her eyes, and exited the hotel. Eyes to the pavement, she turned down the cobblestone path and joined Debora. Together they followed the lakeside route toward the pier.

Boarding the ferryboat, and disappointed to see the vessel brimming with mainland tourists, they made their way through the crowd, avoiding elbows, shoulders and backpacks, and searched for unoccupied seats. Seeing there were none, they climbed the metal stairs to the top deck, and claimed a place under the cloudless sky, and away from the crowd.

Debora lit another cigarette, and Victoria studied the magnificent mountains and their reflection upon the lake. She exhaled a dose of apprehension, and shut her eyes. Chin tilted up, she let the sunshine comfort her bones and soften the early morning chill. The warmth pulled her mind back to days spent on Southern California beaches. She longed for those less complicated days.

The ferryboat's horn tore through the breeze and startled her thoughts, and pounded her head. She opened her eyes and looked sideways over the railing. Down on the dock, a young mariner was untying the heavy burlap cord from the mooring post. The boat engine churned, rattled, and the floor their seats were resting on vibrated. Slowly, the vessel pulled away from the dock. Victoria let out a quiet sigh, and focused on nearby Isola Bella. Soon they would be there. Then, a quick loud whistle came from the deck below. The engine churned and rumbled, once again, and the boat jerked to an ungraceful stop, tossing them forward in their seats. Then the boat reversed, and pulled back to the dock.

Irritated, and anxious to get on with her day, Victoria bounced to her feet, and watched a blur of white fluff and pastel chiffon rush across the dock. *Of course*, she thought. *How could the captain deny a bride and her entourage of bridesmaids and photographers the opportunity to board?* She slipped back into her seat, and felt anxiety rise from her core, and then stop in her throat. Would she ever see her own wedding?

"This lake is getting added to my Best Wedding Destinations list." Debora stretched her neck, puffed on her cigarette and watched the bride board the ferryboat.

Victoria sat quietly, turned her face up to the sun, and waited for the boat to leave the pier.

In the distance, Isola Bella's majestic gardens and tiered botanical terraces raised high above the lake fit its wedding cake description. *It's such a suitable location to view engagement rings*, she thought, *it's almost cliché*. But the tranquil island's centuries-old trees and plants made Victoria feel irrelevant, as if standing in time's shadow. Symbols of longevity and love, engagements and weddings surrounded her, making her wonder: *Is this beautiful island boasting about its past or challenging me and my future? Can this noble place sense my fear and uncertainty? Or is it taunting and criticizing me for my indecision?*

Victoria and Debora disembarked on the heels of the slow throng of passengers, skirted their way around them and hastened down the dock past a wall of clipboard carrying tour guides, and up the stone path. They stayed far from the chattering drove assembling to visit the island, and the wedding entourage which had quickly staked out their ground in the first sun-filled garden they came upon. They headed past the lush green grass, and then up the grand Baroque Palace's exterior staircase.

At the entrance, a Jewelry Trade Show greeter checked their names off a list, and handed them a brochure with a photograph of loose diamonds dripping across the cover. Dressed in a black jacket and pants, a young man escorted them up the winding staircase, and past armed security guards. Victoria and Debora followed their escort and the sound of live chamber music to the *Sala di Napoleone.*

Tall pink walls, red velvet curtains and ornate white and gold rococo embellishments made up the room. In the center, beneath the grand crystal chandelier, stately glass jewelry showcases sat in a disconnected circle. One showcase held jewelry made with pearls—black, white, gold and pink. Another displayed rings, pendants, bracelets and earrings set with rubies, sapphires or emeralds. A third showcase held the diamonds. Stylish men and women who looked as if they'd been dressed and coiffed by Italy's best designers manned the showcases, and spoke in hushed voices to their International clientele. A man in soft gray pin-stripes smiled a noble grin, and nodded in Victoria's and Debora's direction.

"Ready?" Victoria took a deep breath.

"Let's do it," said Debora.

"Buon giorno...benvenute nella sala di Damiani." The man held out his hand.

"It's lovely to be here." Victoria took the man's hand and shook it. "We're from Venice. We have an appointment."

"We're expecting you. A coffee before we begin?"

"No, grazie," said Debora.

"No thank you. We've just had breakfast," said Victoria.

"Then let's get started. Please, have a seat." The salesman gestured toward a side table and velvet covered chairs. He waited for them to be seated, and then took a seat of his own. "Your email said that your store carries fine Italian jewelry, but not the Damiani brand."

"Not yet," said Victoria. "But we'd like to carry your brand, too. We admire the craftsmanship and quality Damiani offers."

"Thank you. But maybe you're not aware that few stores which are not owned by Damiani carry our jewelry. Why should your store represent Damiani? What is special about you and your store in Venice?" The man in gray pinstripes clasped his hands, and held onto his noble smile.

The chair creaked beneath Victoria's weight. She'd been sent there to purchase jewelry, not be interviewed by the suppliers. She turned to Debora who raised an eyebrow and turned her gaze to the showcase of diamonds. Determined to make the deal, Victoria cleared her throat, and called up all her confidence. "Our shop has been family owned for three generations, and got its start by the present owner's grandfather in the 1920s…right around the time your company started making jewelry. We respect tradition, exclusive design, and our clients expect quality. All those things are found in your jewelry."

"I see you've done your homework." A woman wearing a navy blue suit and a tight ponytail with blonde highlights stepped closer, and stood next to Victoria.

"I have…we have." Victoria looked up at the woman, and then glanced at Debora.

"That's right…we have," said Debora. "If I were getting engaged, I'd insist that my fiancé give me one of your rings."

"Not only that, Damiani jewelry is *Made in Italy.* That's important to our clients. Being in Venice, many of them come from around the world. What better way to advertise outside of Italy, than to have…let's say an American business woman return from a vacation in Venice, with or without a fiancé, wearing one of your rings. She returns to work and, even before she pulls out her smartphone to show her colleagues photos of Saint Mark's Square or the Rialto Bridge she's showing them her beautiful Italian Damiani ring. There already jealous that she got the romantic trip to Venice, now she's got a fabulous ring, too. So when it's their turn to choose or give an engagement ring or treat themselves to something luxurious, they're going to remember that ring. They'll remember Damiani."

"Well." The attractive saleswoman smiled. "With a pitch like that, I might just hire you to work for me."

"You hire for Damiani?" Victoria blushed.

"Actually others do that for me."

"She's the company's C.E.O.," said the salesman.

"And they make you work trade shows?" said Debora.

"No." The C.E.O. laughed. "I have a house nearby. I stopped by to see how things were running." She turned to the salesman. "We'd be pleased to have their store carry our brand. Why don't you show them what they came to see?"

"Thank you." Victoria stood, and shook her hand.

The C.E.O. took her hand and gave it a solid shake. "*Il piacere è mio*…the pleasure is mine. I was being sincere. If you're ever looking for a job, contact me." She reached into her pocket, pulled out a business card and handed it to Victoria.

"I will. Thank you." Pride spread across Victoria's face.

Debora stood up, too. "If you're ever in Venice…our store is under the clock tower."

"I'll be happy to stop by. Now, I must be on my way. *Arrivederci.*" The C.E.O. turned to the salesman. "*Buon lavoro*…I'll see you back in Milano."

"Wow." Victoria whispered to Debora.

"It's not every day that our C.E.O. brings on a new client… or offers one a job. You certainly impressed her." The salesman stood, and stepped behind the diamond showcase. "Now, I understand you're looking to increase your shop's engagement ring collection, yes?"

"That's right. We'd like to see your classic mounts," said Victoria. "Our higher end clients prefer traditional."

"But we do have a younger clientele who likes innovative design, too," said Debora. "I like your Eden snake-band with diamonds collection, very much."

"I'll show you our best classic and innovative. All our solitaires carry the Damiani guarantee. Each ring is engraved with the Damiani name." The salesman spread a black velvet cloth on the glass case.

"Are your gems 'conflict free'?" said Victoria. As the words fell from her lips, she looked down at her own engagement ring, again. Could she say that her ring was conflict free? Perhaps the stones were but, since she'd said yes to Alvise's marriage proposal, her life had been one conflict after another.

"I'm glad you asked. Not everyone is concerned with how the gems are mined. But, yes. All our gems comply with the United Nations resolution regarding their origin and process." The salesman set out three solitaire diamond engagement rings with four, six or eight prongs—all holding a one to two carat diamond set in white gold. On the opposite side of the velvet cloth, he displayed two snake band versions—one in white gold and encrusted with diamonds, the other in pink gold with diamonds positioned to represent snake eyes.

"May I try it on?" Debora's eyes sparkled. She pointed to the diamond encrusted snake band.

"Please, do," said the salesman.

Debora slipped the ring on her finger, and Victoria's attention shifted to her vibrating handbag. She pulled back the leather flap, and eyed her smartphone—a fourth call from Alvise, one from her mother—no doubt returning her call from the night before—and a text message from her former boss, Chloe. She let the phone vibrate until it stopped, and turned back to the diamonds. She stood and perused the showcases, and welcomed the salesman to follow her.

"I think it's best to start with these three solitaire engagement rings. Their simple lines and pure diamonds are what most women today want. And like Debora said, the Eden snake band will satisfy contemporary tastes." She moved down the showcase, and thought about the women who would one day wear these stunning rings. *Will their hearts leap, like mine had, when the partner they love more than anything in the world slips one on their finger? Will they be as convinced as I was that their union will be perfect, and ignore the rule that, sooner or later, compromise would drop anchor in their relationship?* She stopped and studied the simple white and gold wedding band sets, and wondered if these brides-to-be would see that loving and being loved brings on life-changing complications. If so, would they still say yes? *If I knew then what I know now, would I have said, yes, to Alvise?* "Add this collection of wedding band sets. They will never go out of style." She moved to the rare gems showcase. "I especially like these."

"The Belle Époque pavé ruby, emerald or sapphire bands?" said the salesman.

"Yes. They're exquisite, and they can be worn as an engagement ring, wedding band or commemorative gift. Please add one of each, including one with all diamonds to our order." *Together, they'll make a beautiful Damiani only display in one of our front windows.*

"Excellent." The salesman followed Victoria around the showcases, and typed the order on his handheld computer.

"Debora. Anything else you think we should add?" said Victoria.

Debora removed the Eden snake band from her finger, and handed it back to the salesman. She stepped to the opposite end of the diamond showcase, and leaned over the collection of solitaire diamonds. "Diamond stud earrings are always fashionable."

"I absolutely agree." The salesman carried his handheld computer, and followed Debora.

"Pick a pair you think would sell well, and we'll add them to our order," said Victoria.

Debora smiled, and pointed to a pair of two carat total weight diamonds in a four prong white gold setting. "These…every woman needs a pair of these."

Victoria joined Debora at the glass counter. "Wow! They are gorgeous." Then, turning to the salesman, "We'll take a pair of these for the store, too. And, *that* will do it for our first order."

"*Benissimo*...I'll send the order through immediately. It should ship out next week." The salesman extended his hand to Debora, shaking it, and then did the same with Victoria.

"Grazie," said Victoria. "It's been a pleasure."

"Arrivederci," said Debora.

Their job done, they left Napoleon's posh quarters, and exited the palace.

"It sure is fun shopping with someone else's money, isn't it?" said Victoria.

"Makes buying expensive stuff easy. We're done, right?"

Victoria nodded.

"I'm going back to the hotel, get my stuff and spend the rest of the day on the mainland. Want to join me?"

Victoria shook her head. "You go on. I'll meet you at the train station."

"Okay. See you later...and...thank you. I enjoyed working with you today."

"We did good together."

Victoria strolled down Isola Bella's gravel paths, beneath the towering trees, and through the meticulous grounds until she came upon the *giardino all'italiana*—the baroque Italian-style garden on the lower terrace. She made her way past the potted lemon trees and clipped boxwood hedges, and sat on the marble bench tucked in the hold of an evergreen shrub. Alone, the quiet garden to herself, she hoped the other island visitors might linger where they were a while longer. The serene surroundings calmed the anxiousness that had returned, but not her tears.

Can I make room in my life for Thor, forever?

Perched on the marble slab, she cried and sobbed. Pools of tears spilled down her face. She dug into her purse, pushed aside her wallet and make-up case, and felt for a tissue, but came up empty handed.

Would it be selfish to deny Alvise his desire to be the boy's father?

She moved her hand to the side pocket and lifted a Kleenex packet—with it came her cellphone. She sighed. No more calls or messages from Alvise. "Can my heart survive without you, Alvise?"

Discarding the tissues for the smartphone, she wiped the back of her hand under one eye and then across the other. She blotted the tears from her cheeks, and then read the message she'd received earlier from Chloe:

Darling!
I've missed you, too.
Fine jewelry, really? How bourgeois.
You must be miserable.
Tell me you'll catch the next plane back to L.A.
Come work for me.
Fabulous things happening at the agency.
Finally, I can offer you that Junior Agent position.
Hollywood trumps fine jewelry!
Let me know. These job openings don't last long.
Kiss...kiss, Chloe.

"Damn it! Why now?" Clenching the cellphone in one hand, she slung her purse over her shoulder and jumped to her feet. Cursing under her breath, she hastened across the grass to where a low-lying marble wall met the lake. She leaned across the marble divide, and eyed the steep drop. Waves crashed and splashed against the embankment, turning sprays of water into pale rainbows.

Is Chloe's message a sign? Should I go back to Los Angeles? Maybe marrying Alvise is not written in the stars. Maybe my destiny isn't in Italy or with him.

Her courage swelled, and she leaned further against the wall. She held on tight to the worn marble with one hand, and lifted her cellphone with the other. She looked long and hard at Chloe's photo and phone number, and then took a long deep breath. There was one way to find out. She'd call Chloe.

Boing! Boing! Boing! An incoming call rang. The screen photo switched from Chloe's to her mother's.

"Mom." Her voice trembled.

"Victoria…I saw your call yesterday. Sorry I couldn't answer, I was with patients all day, and when I was finished with them it was in the middle of the night in Italy…too late to call you. But, I've been meaning to call you all week. Did you see the photo of the dress I sent you? I know Anna will be wearing olive green. Do you think burgundy is too dark?"

"It's good to hear your voice, Mom." Victoria tilted her head back, and tried to keep the tears from spilling from her eyes and down her face.

"Sweetheart, what's wrong?"

"There's something I need to tell you."

"Are you alright?"

"I'm fine…in fact in the last few hours I've been given two fabulous job offers."

"Congratulations."

I'd congratulate myself too, if the rest of my life wasn't in such turmoil.

"Did something happen…something between you and Alvise?"

"Kind of." Victoria lifted a tissue from the packet in her purse, and wiped her wet eyes, and then her nose.

"Tell me, my dear. I'm listening."

"Please understand why I didn't tell you this sooner. I didn't want to worry you…not until we knew more. To make a very long story short, a woman Alvise had a brief relationship with had a son. She died and her friend brought the boy to Venice, saying he was Alvise's son."

"Oh my goodness."

"His name is Thor, he's from Sweden. And he's five years old. He's been living with us for the past few months."

"A child has been living with you for months, and you didn't tell anyone."

"People here know…and Jackie."

"But you didn't tell your father or me."

"Mother, please. I need you to listen. Alvise and the boy had a DNA test and the results…"

"He's Alvise's son?"

"No…but we haven't told anyone that. He doesn't have anyone else…"

"He must have a biological father somewhere."

"That's what I said. But no one seems to know who that is."

"What are you going to do?"

"Alvise wants to adopt him."

"What do you want, Victoria?"

Victoria hesitated a moment, and then said "I don't know if I'm up to it…or if I want to. I came here to build a life with the man I love and, instead, I found a ready-made family. Alvise and I are still getting to know each other. I'm afraid if we adopt the boy…"

"So you *are* considering adopting him?"

"That's where I'm stuck…at considering. I can't get past, considering."

"Do you get along with the boy?"

"I do."

"Honey, this is very complicated. I wish I could make the decision for you. But I can't. I understand how you could be unsure about bringing a child that isn't your own into your life."

"Then you don't think I'm a terrible person? It's okay if I'm unsure about adopting him? It's okay if I don't even know if I want my own children?"

"For Heaven's sake, Victoria. This is the twenty-first century. Women today have choices. No matter what, the decision to have or not have children is yours. Today's women take their time and build lives before contemplating whether or not they want to have children. And many more live happily without becoming mothers."

"So it's okay that I'm not sure?"

"It's fine."

Victoria listened to the long silent pause.

Then her mother said, "I went through a similar…well similarly difficult period when I was your age."

"You didn't want to have children…you didn't want me?"

"Well, not exactly. Oh, dear. I never thought I'd talk to you about this."

"Mom, this is important. I'm asking for your help."

"Okay…but it's not easy…this is not the type of thing a mother should tell her daughter…not right before she's getting married."

"It is if that daughter doubts whether or not a certain marriage is right for her."

"Are you saying that you don't want to marry Alvise?"

"I'm saying that I'm confused. I'm trying to sort things out. I don't want to make a choice I'll regret."

"Well, I'm not proud of this."

"I won't judge you, Mom. I promise."

"When you were in kindergarten I came very close to leaving your father."

"What? Why?"

"I hear judgment."

"That's surprise. Not judgment. Please, go on."

"I thought I was in love with another man. He was an artist I met at an exhibit in Laguna Beach. He was younger than me and totally wrong for me."

"Does any of his stuff hang on our walls at home?"

"That's irrelevant, now."

"That means yes."

"What I'm trying to tell you is that I was about your age, and I had a small child and a growing psychiatric practice. It got to a point where it felt like too much. I wanted more freedom, and this artist had nothing but freedom. We were going to travel—live a Bohemian life."

"Poor Dad."

"Yes, you're right. Your father didn't deserve that treatment. Fortunately, when I was about to leave our marriage, I realized the love affair was more about my insecurities, and my fear of not being able to do it all, than it was about my feelings for the artist. My selfish, and somewhat immature, actions had nothing to do with your father. He's the only man I truly love or want to be with. And I couldn't walk away from you, my precious daughter, either. We were and are a family. I was lucky your father understood what I was going through. He took me back, and he forgave me. As far as I know, he never got even by having his own affaire."

"It's hard to believe that you thought you couldn't do it all, Mom. My entire life, you've been doing it all."

"That is why you have to believe you can do the same, and more, if you choose to. Victoria, marriage is a series of problems and misunderstandings that, with a little luck, turn into comprehension and compromise. It doesn't matter if you live in Los Angeles or Venice, Italy. The only caveat is that you love Alvise. If you do, and if he loves you the way I think he does, then bring back that high-spirited woman I raised. Face the challenge, and then make it work."

Victoria's breath halted in her chest. "I need a few days."

"Dear, you need to let me know whether or not to order my dress for the wedding."

"I will." Victoria hung up the phone, and kept her heart from jumping to her throat.

She trusted Alvise more than anyone else in her life, leaving all she had to be by his side. She had risked her heart and, until Thor came into their lives, never doubted her decision, because she loved him, and knew he loved her. Now, she grappled to find that inner strength, and prayed she'd make the right choice.

A deep sigh pulled her shoulders forward. She needed to walk. She followed the path through a wrought-iron gate, down marble stairs worn by centuries of footsteps, and onto the sun drenched terrace at the island's edge.

The concierge looked up from a stack of ledgers and paperwork. He nodded to Victoria.

"May I have the room key?" Victoria smoothed a curl off her face. "I'll run up and get my things."

Holding the room key by its burgundy tassel, he handed it across the reception desk. "Your colleague said she packed up your bags. So Housekeeping made up the room. You'll find your things there." He turned back to his paperwork.

She twisted the silky key fringe around her index finger, looked passed the concierge, and up at the wall clock. *I better hurry or I'll miss the train.*

She turned the key and, as if intruding on someone else's bed-chamber, cautiously opened the door. The room smelled fresh, clean and without a hint of their presence in the air. The bed had been fitted with fresh sheets, the prosecco bottle, dirty dishes and the ice bucket removed, and the parquet floor swept. Clean towels were on the towel rack, and the courtesy basket had been replenished with soap, shampoo and cream. Except for her suitcase standing next to the armoire, there was no hint that she, or anyone else, had slept there the night before.

She crossed the room and opened the French doors. The sun was slipping behind the mountain top, brushing the sky purple, and illuminating the first evening stars. She stepped onto the balcony, and glanced at the garden and at the happy bride and groom, and their wedding guests leaving the lakeside reception. "Should that be us?" she whispered to herself.

Waiters moved about in the garden below, clearing the wedding luncheon debris from the gravel pavement, rearranging café sized tables dressed in fresh white linens. Candles flickered on the clothed tables as if sending signals to the zillion stars quivering in the early evening sky. The patio heaters glowed below, and Victoria buttoned her jacket against the cool summer breeze. Listening to the lake fold against the shore below, she closed the terrace door behind her, grabbed her suitcase, and left.

The train pealed through the Piedmont mountainside toward Venice. Lush forest landscape and a cloudless night sky ran outside the *fast-track* train windows as if rushing Victoria to face her responsibilities and approach Alvise about their future. She sat next to Debora, and said goodbye to the picturesque lake and its charming islands, and thought about the things she couldn't change. She watched the train steward wheel a cart of drinks and snacks down the corridor, guessing that a cold drink might help her find the right words. A glass of white wine for Debora, she opened a palm size pack of peanuts as the train neared the medieval town of Brescia, and then ordered a second Coca-Cola before they'd left the foggy Lombard plain. Hours into their journey, at the Desenzano Del Garda station, Victoria felt a tug at her heart when a woman in jeans and Superga tennis shoes carried a sleeping child and stuffed toy animal aboard the train. Gently cradling the boy, the woman sat down without waking him, and then arranged the soft red ladybug like a pillow under the child's head. Victoria sighed, realizing life the way she had imagined it with Alvise would never be. She pulled out her smartphone, and tapped out a message:

> I arrive at the Venice train station in an hour. I'll see you at home.

She hit SEND, and felt her heart swell.

Moments later his reply read:

> An hour is an eternity. Will be waiting.

She set the smartphone on the pulldown seat-back table in front of her, and dropped the empty foil peanut sack into the seat-side waste bin. She dusted the salt from her hands, and then brought the plastic cup to her lips and swallowed the last sip of Coca-Cola. Turning to the window, she wiped her hand across the mist on the glass. Outside, the night was as dark as tar.

"You're quiet." Debora leaned forward and popped a few salted peanuts in her mouth, and chased them down with wine.

Nervousness seeped into Victoria's smile. "Important decisions need to be made." Victoria leaned her head against the high-back leather seat, and looked into the night.

Chapter 29

VICTORIA LEFT THE Santa Lucia Venice train station, and rushed through known passages and alleyways, and up and over foot-bridges, but the familiar route gave the impression of being longer now—the distance seemed further. She hurried to be with Alvise, to clear things up, explain everything away.

She charged across the long campo, past packed bars and university students spilling noise and beer onto the sidewalk. She wove in and out of the thick crowd, and around young lovers kissing beneath the campo's two trees. She turned the corner and raised her eyes, looking past the yellow glow of the street lamp, toward their home. The new shutters Alvise had installed were closed tight. She looked at her watch. It was ten o'clock. *He said he'd be home.* She swung open the wrought-iron gate and cringed when the heavy metal frame smacked the yellow stucco wall, dropping a chunk of fresh plaster to the ground. She stepped over the plaster, and rushed through the courtyard fumbling with her keys. The front door unlocked, she entered their warm home—soft music played upstairs.

"Alvise...Thor?"

She climbed the stairs, and followed the scent of sweet tomato and basil sauce into the kitchen. Skillfully stacked logs burned and glowed in the belly of the brick pizza oven. A thick dust of white flour separated rising pizza dough balls from the marble counter. She smiled when, to one side of the sink, she saw a shiny stainless steel dishwasher filling the space that, days before, had been occupied by a double-door cabinet. In the middle of the kitchen, a candlelit table had been set with their mixed-matched china.

"Is anyone home?" She called out. She left her suitcase in the corner, and followed the classical music coming from the living room. There, two glasses of red wine, a basket of freshly baked rosemary focaccia, and a plate of sliced salami and cheese sat on the coffee table. She set her purse on a side chair, and heard giggles coming from behind the sofa. "Okay, either we have some very kind robbers in the house...who brought us a new dishwasher... or..."

"Surprise!" Thor and Alvise jumped out from behind the sofa. Dressed in a white t-shirt, black sweat pants, and an oversized bowtie dangling from his small neck, Thor ran toward her—a pressed dishtowel draped over his forearm. "I'm the maître d' and he's your date."

"You make a fine maître d'." She pulled Thor up in her arms, and gave him a hug. "But I don't remember being asked out on a date."

"You're getting married...he doesn't have to ask," said Thor.

"A man should always ask the woman he loves out on a date...even when they're married...even when he brings home a new dishwasher." She instructed Thor with a kiss on the cheek, and then placed him back on his feet, on the floor.

Alvise stepped closer to Victoria, wrapped an arm around her waist, and dipped her back in a Tango move. "Would you like to have dinner with me, every night, for the rest of our lives?"

Thor giggled, again.

"Well, now that we have a dishwasher." Victoria laughed.

"*Amore*, you might think I don't see things or listen to you. But I do, always."

She let Alvise kiss her neck, and then she pushed herself upright, and stood back up. "Thank you. It's a much appreciated surprise. But it's late, and someone needs to go to bed."

"No…I have to serve your dinner." Thor frowned.

"Mr. Maître d', you've done a beautiful job of setting the table, and putting out a snack for me. I'm certain the pizza will be delicious. Still, I hope you don't mind if I dine on the cheese and focaccia. I'm not very hungry."

"Thor already ate his pizza. So I'm good with a little salami and focaccia."

"Then it's time for bed," said Victoria.

Thor stalled his bedtime by peeking at a paper bag sticking out of her purse.

"It's an apple strudel. But it's for tomorrow."

"Can't I have some…?"

Victoria's eyes widened, her mouth set in a hard line.

"*May* I have it for breakfast?" Thor gave her a lopsided grin.

"Yes, you may." Victoria kissed his head. "Now off to bed."

"*Buonanotte*," said Alvise.

"Good night." Thor pouted.

Victoria watched the small child turn his back on her. "Remember to brush your teeth."

"I already did." Thor dragged his feet and the dishtowel out of the room, and down the hall.

"And I gave him a bath, and got his clothes ready for tomorrow," said Alvise.

Victoria nodded, her lips turned up into a smile. She slipped off her shoes, and put her feet up on the sofa.

Alvise handed her a glass of wine, sat on the sofa next to her, and moved her feet to his lap.

She sipped the wine, sank deeper into the soft cushions and closed her eyes to the feel of Alvise's strong hands massaging the arch of her foot. "That feels divine."

"How was the trade show?"

"We got the Damiani deal."

"I never doubted you would."

"And I got two job offers."

"From?"

"The C.E.O. of Damiani. It's a great opportunity, for someone who lives in Milano."

"And the second offer?"

"That one came from Chloe."

"Your old boss?" His forehead creased, and his face turned pale.

Victoria nodded.

"When did you talk to her?"

"I didn't. It came via text. She offered me the Junior Agent position."

Alvise held her foot in his hands, and stopped massaging it. "Why would she think you would take it now?"

"I don't know." *Something I said in my text to her, maybe?* She placed the wine glass on the coffee table, and filled her cheeks with air and then blew it through her lips. "I mentioned that I missed the glamour of Hollywood."

Alvise dropped her foot on the sofa, and stood. "Do you miss it?"

"At times I do."

Fear veiled his face, and he nibbled on the inside of his cheek. "Are you considering taking the job…going back to Los Angeles?"

Victoria sighed and reached for her glass, and gulped a mouthful of dry red wine.

"Listen, if I have to, I'll continue to tell you for the rest of your life, as much as I care for Thor…if you don't…if you can't make him a part of us, then, whatever you choose, I choose you. Vittoria, I will always choose you."

"Why?"

Alvise moved to the floor and sat in front of her, he took her hands in his. "That's what love does. It makes you need someone. And you're that someone for me. Without you, I'd be lost." He sat on the sofa and next to her.

Victoria's eyes filled with compassion. Right from the start he had stolen her heart. She'd shown him her best and worst parts, and he accepted them.

"Victoria, I'm sorry, but I don't really understand. Where is this uncertainty…this fear coming from? Or is it that you've had enough and just don't…*love* me enough?"

"I've never doubted my love for you."

"Then give me a reason why you doubt *us* so much?"

"It's not us, it's me. I've asked myself a million times if I could be happy as his mother, and make you both happy, too."

"Thor and I are happy. We're ecstatic to have you in our lives. Don't you see the way he looks at you? Don't you see the way I look at you? We'd both be miserable without you."

She'd been so busy worrying about failing as a mother, and therefore fearful she'd regret adopting Thor, that she'd been blind to Thor's feelings toward her. How many more times would Alvise have to tell her that he loved her to convince her to stay? Not long ago, she'd truly believed that their love had been written in the stars. Wasn't it time she stopped questioning the path destiny had placed in front of her, and simply follow it? She turned her back to his chest, and leaned her head against him. "When Thor came to stay with us, I wasn't prepared to be his mother. I wasn't prepared to be anything but that career woman who'd met her dream man, and flew off to Italy to live her fairytale. Instead, I had to confront difficulties I never dreamt I'd be faced with. Thor was one of those. It's taken me a long time to recognize his love, too."

He wrapped his arms around her. "Then stay."

She pulled away from his chest. *He's everything I could want from a partner. So how could life with him be bad?*

"*Vita mia,* there's nothing here that can't be fixed."

Facing him she said, "I'm sorry for having been so difficult, and if somehow I've fractured even the tiniest piece of our love. I do love you, Alvise."

He took her in his arms and gently kissed her again and again, and then once more.

She pulled her lips from his, wiped a tear from her cheek, and smiled. "Well then, if we're going to adopt our boy, you need to tell me what the attorney said."

He pulled her close, again, and hugged her tight. "Since Thor has no one else, I can keep my foster parent status. If his biological father were to show up, which is improbable, the attorney said we could argue that he abandoned him. We can start the adoption process as soon as we're married."

"Thor needs to know that you're not his biological father."

"Can't that wait?"

"Sure, until we find the right time, and the right words."

"Mamma Vittoria." Thor stood in the doorway, rubbing the sleep from his eyes.

Victoria pushed herself away from Alvise, and the soft sofa pillows. Her face flushed. "Thor? I thought you were in bed."

"I was, but I couldn't fall asleep."

Victoria sat up and scooted over. She pulled the boy up on the sofa.

Thor tucked his feet up off the floor, and laid his head on her lap. "What's a biological father?"

Alvise's jaw tightened. He glanced at Victoria, and covered Thor with a plaid throw. "Remember when we got that blood test?"

"Yeah." Thor looked at Alvise.

"We did that to understand if we have the same blood type... to see if I'm your biological father."

"Do we?"

Alvise shook his head. "No…we don't."

"That means you're not my biological father. But you're not my real mother…even if I call you Mamma Vittoria."

"That's right. Your mom, Zinnia, is your biological mother." Victoria caressed a wisp of blond from the boy's forehead.

"Who is my biological father?"

"We don't know," said Alvise.

"No matter who that might be, we want you to stay with us," said Victoria.

"But first, people who make decisions like this for children must decide," said Alvise.

"Why do we have to ask them?"

"I wish we didn't have to. I wish it were that simple," said Alvise.

"What if the people say no?" Thor's eyes popped open and wide. He sat up straight.

"Let's not worry about that," said Alvise.

Victoria sighed, kissed the boy's cheek, and hugged him tight. *Yes. What if they say no?*

Chapter 30

THEIR WEDDING DAY arrived. Victoria, wide awake before the seven a.m. wake-up call, lay in the hotel bed thinking how perfect the wedding rehearsal and dinner had been. She had never been so in love, so happy, so convinced that Alvise was the man for her, and so anxious for good fortune to show her the way to the future.

Rolling out of bed, she went to the second floor window and drew back the velvet drapes. She swung open the windows, pushed on the shutters, and looked outside. Cloudy, gray skies . . . puddles on the pavement . . . a constant drizzle misted her face.

"Jackie, wake up . . . It's raining."

Jackie pushed back the heavy bedspread, tripped to her feet and joined Victoria at the window. "It'll be great for your hair. Mine will look like hell."

It'll stop—it's still early. Victoria shut the window, took a deep breath, and commanded herself to stay calm. "I'm going to get in the shower. You're going to do my makeup, right?"

"Yes, dear . . . I'll order breakfast."

"I'm not hungry." Victoria moved to the mirror, plucked a few bothersome eyebrows, and then set the tweezers on the dresser.

"Not even coffee?" Jackie moved to the nightstand, and picked up the telephone receiver.

"No coffee for me."

"Since when?"

Victoria didn't answer. Recently, the smell of coffee turned her stomach.

"Look at me." Jackie set the receiver back down, and scrutinized her friend from across the room. "Are you pregnant?"

"Shhh…everyone in the hotel will hear you."

"Well are you?"

"There's a chance I am."

"Aren't you on the pill?"

"I was…but I haven't had a period for two months. So I stopped taking it."

Jackie ran toward the bride, and hugged her. "Does Alvise know…your mom?"

"No, no one knows. *I'm* not even sure. I did one of those at-home pregnancy tests, and it came out negative."

"Then you're not pregnant."

"You'd think. But, it's weird. I feel pregnant."

"What's pregnant feel like?"

"Look at my boobs…they've never been this…plump."

"So you're just gonna wait?"

"If I don't get my period in another week, I'll do another test and then go to the doctor…that's what the pharmacist said I should do."

"Then why not tell Alvise?"

"Because…" Victoria had wanted to tell him—each day for the last few weeks—but instead she waited, and hoped her period would come. "We're supposed to be adopting Thor, now, not having a baby of our own."

"I'm sure he can handle both."

I'm not sure I can. Victoria went back to the window. Lightening ran across the sky and thunder rattled the thin plate-glass. Then, as if the gods had tightened their mighty arms around the bulging clouds, a wall of water came crashing to the ground. The wedding day forecast was as uncertain as her predicament. Victoria wanted to share her thoughts with Jackie—not because they made her happy, but because saying them out loud would free her from being the only one to know the truth. *She's my best friend. Best friends give good advice.* "I'm not sure I'm ready to have a baby."

"Well, if you are pregnant, you don't have a lot of choices." Jackie stared at Victoria's back from across the room.

Victoria turned around, and faced her friend's astonishment. "Are you saying I shouldn't have the baby?"

"That's not my decision."

Victoria swallowed hard, and looked up at her bridesmaid's expression which appeared more like that of a courtroom judge. "Please, don't look at me like that. Okay, I hate myself for having considered that option…for a nanosecond. But I could never do that to Alvise or to our child." Victoria turned back to the window, and watched a sopping wet delivery man rush a florist box across the campo and disappear through the hotel entrance. *Our bouquets.* She stared out the window, at the puddles on the pavement that swelled like the tears in her eyes.

"Come on. Don't cry. Today is your big day. Fifty-fifty you're not pregnant, and if you are…it's *not* a problem. For God's sake…

you're marrying the man you love in a couple of hours." Jackie slumped on the foot of the bed.

Victoria left the window, and then dropped into the upholstered side chair, and cried. She pulled a tissue from the box on the end table, and wiped the tears from her face.

"You could light a candle in church today, and pray that you're not a failed contraception statistic." Jackie moved to the chair opposite Victoria.

"This is not funny." Victoria giggled through her tears.

"I'm not joking." Jackie lowered her eyes, placed her fingertips on her temples, and massaged with small circular movements. The room fell silent around them, until she dropped her hands to her lap, and looked at Victoria, once again. "I'm sorry, but I have to ask you this."

Victoria looked down at the tear stained tissue she was shredding to bits. "What?"

Jackie let out a breath, and sat up straight. "Are you sure you want to marry Alvise?"

Victoria's expression relaxed a little, her tears were gone. "I've never been surer."

"Then swear," Jackie jumped up from the chair and went to the nightstand. She grabbed the Holy Bible from the drawer, and held it out to Victoria. "Honest to God...put your hand here, and say you love Alvise."

"Geez, Jackie. We're not in court."

"Well, do you?"

"Yes!" Victoria jumped to her feet, threw her hands to the ceiling. "I love Alvise."

"And you want to spend the rest of your life with him."

"I swear. He's the only person I want to marry. I love him more than anything or anyone."

"Then tell him you think you're pregnant. And stop micro-managing every detail of your life. Let shit happen."

"I do. I'm the definition of *shit happening*."

"So then stop worrying, and stop trying to plan and control everything for fear you'll make a mistake."

"Well listen to you…Miss *I trust men as far as I can throw them*."

"I'm getting better at that. You'd be surprised."

"Yeah, right…anyone I know?"

"Eddie."

Victoria's jaw dropped. "My cousin Eddie?"

Jackie blushed and nodded.

"I tell you my secrets…I go on and on about my problems… and never give you time to tell me this wonderful news. How long has this been going on?"

"Not long enough." Jackie smiled. "We were going to tell you, right after the ceremony."

"Well, I'll be damned…I'm so happy for you." Victoria threw her arms around Jackie. "Wow!" She went back to the window. Looking up at the sky, she ignored that the gray storm clouds had turned black. *You're right. We're both lucky women. Why am I so afraid?* "What sane woman wouldn't want to marry someone like Alvise?"

"Exactly." Jackie glanced at the clock radio. "Now, let's get ready."

Victoria walked to the mirror, and studied her flushed face, her red eyes, and sighed. "You've got some magic to make here."

The girls showered, washed and styled their hair, creamed and perfumed their skin, polished their nails to perfection, and concentrated on forgetting Victoria's dilemma. They took turns looking out the window, only to see the rain pour down harder, and then harder.

Victoria held one eye wide open, shifting her gaze up and down between her image in the mirror and the collection of lipstick, eye shadow, blush, and mascara scattered across the vanity table. Jackie brushed the last stroke of fawn-colored shadow on Victoria's closed eye and then reached for the blush.

"Don't make me up too much...and don't put too much blush on me," said Victoria.

"You want to do it?" Jackie held her makeup brushes in the air.

"Sorry . . . I want to look natural, but striking." She tilted her head back, making highlighting her cheekbones easier.

"I can't work miracles."

"Thanks, just what I want to hear today."

"Come on . . . I'm kidding. You look beautiful...must be that maternal glow."

Victoria held her head still, and rolled her eyes to Jackie's. "You can't say a word about this to anyone."

"I *won't*...more blush . . . and *there*. What do you think?"

Victoria tilted her head sideways, and then moved her face mere inches from the mirror. She studied the soft colors on her eyelids, the thin brown liner that followed the curve of her eyes, and the pastel color on her cheeks and lips, and smiled. "No one will ever know I was crying."

"Now let's get that veil on you."

"Wait a minute." Victoria went to the telephone, dialed, and waited for Rose to answer. "Mom, I'm ready."

After a few minutes, Rose tapped on the door, dressed in a burgundy taffeta cocktail dress, a cascade of her coiffed gray hair peeking out from beneath a wide brimmed hat, and a simple rose corsage already pinned to her matching clutch. The flowers had been delivered to her room, and she was carrying Victoria's bouquet of white peonies and pale English roses in one hand, and two similar nosegays in the other.

Victoria saw serenity on Rose's face. She knew her mother had worried about her from the time she and Alvise had left Los Angeles. Neither of them could have known whether Victoria would be happy in another country, another culture. Since Rose had arrived in Venice, Victoria let her see that she had adapted to her new world, and that she moved and mingled with the locals. Now, there was something else Rose should know.

One at a time, Victoria took the bouquets from her mother's hands and, adoring their delicate fragrance and the florist's fine craftsmanship, carried them to the dresser and carefully set them down. She turned away from the flowers, and slipped her hands deep into the pockets of her robe. "Mom, before we go to church I need to tell you something."

Jackie raised her eyebrows.

Victoria gestured for Jackie to finish putting on her own make up in the bathroom, and waited. When she heard the bathroom door close, she said "Mom, thank you for supporting me. I know you might be concerned about me stepping into a prefabricated family."

Rose moved to the vanity and set down her burgundy satin clutch. "As much as I miss you and would love to tell you to pack your bags and come home, I must tell you how proud I am of you. You've faced and overcome more challenges in the last few months than some people face in a lifetime. Raising your own children is one thing, but another woman's child is a whole other situation."

"Thank you, Mom. We're filing for adoption next week, once our marriage license is registered." Victoria sat down on the vanity stool, her back facing the mirror. "Fingers and hearts crossed we get approved."

Rose looked at her reflection in the vanity mirror, and straightened her hem. "I don't see why they'd deny you. You're already doing an outstanding job of being parents to Thor. He charmed the socks off your father and I. Did you see him extend his little hand and shake ours at the rehearsal dinner last night?"

"I did."

"He's smart and very well behaved. I'm sure his mother had something to do with that, but I see your touch there, too."

Victoria smiled wide. *Hearing that from you means the world to me.* She stood up from the vanity bench, and softly wrapped her arms around her mother.

Rose sighed, and gave her daughter a tender tweak on the cheek.

"I love you, Mom."

"I love you, too." Rose stepped out of Victoria's embrace, and pulled a lace handkerchief from her purse. "It's your grandmother's. A little good luck token never hurt a bride."

Victoria wrapped her arms around her mother again, and placing a gentle kiss on her cheek, she took the square of lace from Rose's hand. She felt happiness percolate from her pores and saw tears of love well up in her mother's eyes.

"I carried it on my wedding day." Rose dabbed at her tears. "My only advice is…love Alvise with all your being."

I already do. Victoria's smile was brilliant. She stepped back, and raised a finger to her mother's cheek, and delicately smudged away the lipstick imprint her kiss had left there. "Mom, just one more thing…there's a chance I might make you a grandmother… sooner than I would have planned."

"You mean…?"

Victoria shrugged her shoulders. "It's early, but can a woman know…just feel pregnant?"

"Absolutely…without a doubt a woman can know." Rose tilted her head, and studied her daughter's face. "I knew when I was only four weeks pregnant with you. But I had to wait two more months for a doctor to confirm it."

"Are we done with the tears and ruining our make-up?" Jackie returned to the room.

"Yes. No more tears." Rose smiled, and wiped the dampness from her eyes.

"Are you ready for the veil?" said Jackie.

Victoria nodded, and sat down, this time facing the vanity mirror. A lump of emotion swelled in her throat as her mother and best friend placed the pearl headband on her hair and then arranged the veil around her loose low-sitting chignon. "Now help me step into the dress."

"You look splendid." Rose adjusted the off-the-shoulder lace cap sleeves, and the sheer ivory chiffon that lined the back of Victoria's dress. She gave herself a final quick check in the mirror, and clasped her clutch off the vanity.

A knock came on the door, and Jackie opened it. "Wow…you look gorgeous."

"*Grazie*…so do you." Ivana stepped into the room, her bridesmaid dress a shade darker than Jackie's pistachio silk and as flattering on her blossoming maternal figure. "Shall we go?" The men and the photographer are waiting in the lobby. And the tide is rising fast."

Down the corridor, Victoria smoothed the pearl and lace work on her gown's Juliet bust line, nodded to her mother and took her bouquet from Jackie's hand. She stood still as her bridesmaids straightened her gown's train and then, one hand on the brass rail, followed them down the stairs and into the marble lobby. The soft pink, damask covered walls made a perfect backdrop for their flowers and their dresses. Camera bulbs flashed at them like an opening night filled with paparazzi, but instead came from the hired photographer, family and friends.

"Dear sweet, daughter." One hand on his heart, Michael Greco stepped forward, and took Victoria's hand with the other one. "You're breathtaking."

"Dad, you look so handsome. Is that a new tuxedo?"

Michael nodded. "I would've worn the old one, but your mother insisted."

Victoria straightened his bowtie and then kissed his cheek, and saw his eyes tear-up. "Dad, please don't cry…you'll make me start, again."

"I'm so proud of you, honey. More importantly, I'm so pleased to see that you're happy."

Victoria squeezed her father's hand, and extended her other hand to her grandmother.

"I see your mother gave you the handkerchief." Eunice took her granddaughter's hand, the one holding her old handkerchief, and kissed it. "Hold onto this handkerchief for *your* daughter or your daughter-in-law. My mother gave it to me when I left England. It brings good luck."

"I will Grand Mom. Thank you." Victoria adjusted Eunice's simple rose corsage. Repining it to her grandmother's gold brocade jacket, she felt a strong hand touch her shoulder. "Eddie!" She fell into her cousin's arms. "I thought I'd see you in church."

"I wanted to kiss the bride before she got married." Eddie, dressed in a dark tuxedo, too, hugged his cousin. "You're gorgeous…and so is your bridesmaid." He pulled Jackie to him, and gave her a kiss on the lips.

Victoria's face glowed. "I'm so happy for you two."

"Okay…enough hugging and kissing." Ciano looked dashing in his black tuxedo. "We need to go. The tide is rising. If we don't hurry the water taxi won't be able to pass under the bridges, and we won't get to the church."

Victoria looked through the lobby windows. The rain poured down, and her heart sank. She couldn't reach the water taxi, much less the church, without ruining her gown. "I've heard the

Venetian saying *a wet bride is a lucky bride*. But this is crazy...I need to change."

"Make it quick." Ciano frowned. "The tide doesn't wait for anyone."

Victoria lifted the front of her gown and rushed back upstairs and, with help from Jackie and Ivana, stepped from her dress with great care, leaving only her veil in place. She slipped on a pair of sweatpants, a borrowed button-down flannel shirt from Eddie and a pair of Jackie's low heels, and zipped up the wedding dress in its bag.

Back in the lobby, she handed her dress to Eddie and her shoes to Ciano. Trying to stay as dry as possible, the wedding party ran to the water taxi, while the doorman carried an enormous rainbow striped umbrella over Victoria's veiled head.

Crammed with the others inside the humid cabin of the water taxi, Victoria rode the choppy waters to the church. Heaven's clouds burst and the relentless downpour sounded like rocks hitting the boat's fiberglass roof. Through the wet, fogged up windows, she watched sheets of water ricochet off the buildings that lined the canals and batter the empty sidewalks. The storm had confined people to stay in and she wondered if Alvise and the other guests would make it to the church on time.

Once they had docked along the church-side canal, she, Ivana and Jackie remained seated as the others stepped off the boat and into the church. When Ciano and Eddie got Rose, Michael and Grandmother Eunice settled, the bride and bridesmaids followed them into the vestry. The priest greeted them, his face amused at the bride's casual appearance.

"You can use this room to change. There's no rush…when you're ready, ring the bell on the wall." The priest pointed to a brass bell, and gave Victoria a kind look. "The groom is already in church—he's a little soggy, but anxious to see you. I'll tell him you're here."

Grateful for his kindness, she waited until the priest, Eddie and Ciano disappeared through the church passageway, to turn to Jackie and Ivana. "This wasn't how I imagined showing up at my wedding."

Victoria undressed, and Jackie and Ivana shook the last beads of water from their tea-length gowns. They held up the wedding dress, more wrinkled than the first time Victoria had put it on, and helped the bride step back into the chiffon.

Debora, wearing a fitted black dress and Chanel red lipstick, stepped into the vestry from the church. "The candles are lit, the guests are all seated, and the church looks almost as ravishing as the bride." She stepped into the heart of the room, and fiddled with the bride's lace neckline and then fluffed up the gown's train. "Thor has the rings, which are securely tied to the pillow, and Susanna has the basket of rose and peony petals…and the handsome groom and his mother are waiting. So everyone and everything is ready…how about the bride?"

Victoria nodded. Her chiffon skirt rustled as she turned toward Debora.

Debora rang the brass bell on the wall, alerting the priest that the bride was ready.

Victoria exited the vestry, stepping out into the campo. Standing in front of la Chiesa di Santa Maria dei Miracoli—the church of Saint Mary of the Miracles—and as if miracles do happen, she sighed. The billowing rain clouds had stormed away leaving behind the crystal clear sky and bright sunlight to warm the air.

This will turn out right after all, she thought.

Michael Greco's tall, dapper figure was by her side. "Ready?" He extended his arm to escort her.

"Thank you for all this, and for being here." She smiled and held onto her father with the same hand that clutched her grandmother's "something old" lace handkerchief. "Jackie...Ivana?"

Ivana blinked back tears, and smoothed her dress over her baby bump. "Damn hormones."

"At least you have an excuse." Jackie laughed and sniffled, and clutched her flowers.

"Follow me." Debora led the wedding party down a dry red carpet that, as soon as the storm had passed, had been extended across the wet campo toward the main entrance.

Standing at the doorway to the small 15th century jewel, Victoria peeked past the heavy velvet curtain that framed the entrance. Old English roses and pale peonies trimmed the pews and the main alter. Their soft color warmed the cool gray-white marble interior, and their delicate perfume spilled out to where she stood. The restless congregation's chatter competed with the sacred sound of the antique pipe organ, while fashionable guests and the more modestly dressed uninvited took their seats. She smiled at the Venetian custom that welcomed those without invitations to enter the church, and partake in the happy event. Unaccustomed to brides being seen before they entered the church, she nodded sweetly, modestly at the local parishioners, mothers of the other gondoliers, and those who came for a glimpse of the American bride who had stolen the heart of their handsome gondolier.

Victoria felt her heart leap and her breath pause when the pipe organ began reverberating *Pachelbel's Canon in D.* She pulled her father closer, felt his hand squeeze hers, and his tender kiss on her forehead. When they stepped up into the doorway, she saw her Alvise. Dashing and handsome in his black tuxedo, standing midway down the aisle with his mother, he was smiling back at her. Commencing down the aisle, she followed Thor and Susanna, and her bridesmaids, and stepped over the rose and peony petals that Susanna had scattered here and there. On her left, in a pew at the back of the church, Cinzia and Paola, and the ladies from the rowing club gathered. Cinzia waved with one hand and, holding up a smartphone with the other, videoed Victoria and her father as they walked by. Further ahead, and on her right, Victoria smiled at Alvise's sister Gina, and her husband Alberto. Gina's cheeks flushed with cheer, and her peacock-blue dress and feather fascinator matched Alberto's tie, and contrasted the wedding color scheme to perfection. Uncle Fausto wore an everyday suit and tie, and stood in the pew in front of Gina and Alberto, and next to Bruno. The father-of-the-groom looked uncomfortable in a tuxedo, and his broad smile showed the pride and the joy he felt inside. Victoria turned her gaze back to the opposite side of the aisle, and saw Barbara and Amber, her former colleagues from the talent agency. Barbara wore lace, and had R.S.V.P.'d for one. Amber wore black, and stood next to the man she'd brought to the company Christmas party—the same man who had irritated

Victoria that evening by repeatedly calling Alvise, Arturo. Chloe, her former boss winked and smiled, and stood in front of them, and next to Howard Woodcock. Tan and fit, they made a stunning couple. She wore a red cocktail dress—no doubt Valentino. He wore a custom-fit suit.

Victoria smiled at her Hollywood friends, and thought about the text message she'd sent Chloe soon after she'd returned to Venice from Lago Maggiore. She'd thanked her for the job offer, and then refused it. A few weeks later, when she sent Chloe a wedding invitation for two, the R.S.V.P. came back with Howard's name on it, too. A separate note, handwritten by Chloe, said that Howard's wife Emilie had filed for divorce. He'd agreed and they'd settled on good, but expensive, terms, and then he asked Chloe to marry him. Chloe added a line to her note that said she hadn't answered him yet.

When Alvise saw Victoria, his breath stilled for a moment in his chest, and he resisted the urge to move toward his bride and kiss her on the lips. Instead, he locked his gaze on her as she sauntered up the aisle toward him. His heart jumped and tumbled when she left her father's arm and put her hand on his. He lifted her other hand to his lips and kissed it, never taking his eyes from hers.

Anna, striking in her olive-green dress and pill-box hat, held on tight to his other arm, until he moved away with the utmost care and, stepping around his mother, walked his bride to the foot of the steep altar where Jackie, Ciano, Ivana, Eddie, the children and the priest waited.

Throughout the ceremony, Alvise watched his radiant bride hang onto each word the priest spoke and relish the ritual of their union. He concentrated on her kneeling, standing or sitting with him, next to him. The choir sang Schubert's *Ave Maria,* and he stood and waited while Victoria gracefully crossed the church and placed a bouquet at the altar of the Virgin Mary. Her eyes dampened when they exchanged their identical gold bands and confident "I do's", and he reached for his handkerchief and dried the moisture from her cheek. When, at last, the priest said "*Puoi baciare la sposa* . . . you may kiss the bride," he did, long and sweet, and the congregation's delight erupted into applause, and cries of *"Viva gli sposi!"* touched the church's vaulted ceiling.

He held her hand as they exited the church, and showers of good cheer and fists full of rice and pasta shells fell upon them. The small campo scarcely held all the well-wishers and made the bombardment of hugs and kisses delightful. Anna approached the bride and groom. She kissed her son's cheek, and then faced Victoria, her hand still on Alvise's. "You're a beautiful bride, Vittoria, and a good woman. My son is a fortunate man."

"Hearing that from you means a lot to me, Anna. I'm as fortunate as you say he is."

"Take this." Anna handed Victoria a small velvet pouch, its drawstring pulled tight.

"What is it?" said Victoria.

"Open it later and you'll see." Anna kissed the bride's cheek, and smiled at the groom. The crowd swarmed around them, urging the bride and groom toward the dozen or so shiny black gondolas lined up and assembled in the canal. Victoria's smile widened, and Alvise couldn't help but be proud of his colleagues who had far exceeded his expectations. The first two spectacular vessels—decorated with intricate gold-leaf carvings, draped in red velvet and hand-embroidered Burano lace, and adorned with splendid floral chests of roses and peonies—were each manned by two gondoliers dressed in formal white uniforms, red sashes tied around their collars and waists.

Under Bruno's frenetic direction, the bride and groom—looking more aristocratic than would real nobility—boarded the first gondola and filled the loveseat. "Where are the *damigelle*… bridesmaids?" Bruno hollered from canal side, over the thick crowd and into the campo. He waved at Ivana and Jackie as they hurried through the crowd. They stepped into the gondola and sat facing the radiant couple, much the same way one would sit on a horse drawn carriage. "*Adesso i bambini*…the children are next." Bruno lifted Thor off the stone pavement, and set him down in the boat. "Sit there, on the stool next to Vittoria." Susanna followed next. She fluffed the skirt of her ivory chiffon dress, straightened the pistachio colored sash, and then scooted onto a black lacquered stool next to Thor.

"You're so pretty, *Zia Vittoria*." Susanna caressed the delicate chiffon and beadwork on the bride's dress.

"Thank you, Susanna. You're beautiful."

"My Mamma is the prettiest bride ever." Thor tugged on his tuxedo jacket, and then reached up and kissed Victoria's cheek.

She returned Thor's kiss on the cheek, and then whispered "Don't tell the groom, but I think you're the most handsome man here."

"I heard that." Alvise gave a quick astonished laugh, and tickled Thor until he giggled, too.

"Papà, you're *bellissimo*, too."

Alvise gave the boy a hug, and carefully sat him back on the stool. He took his bride's hand in his. "You know we're sitting in a very special gondola."

"The wood carving and gold-leaf detail work *are* extraordinary," said Victoria.

"It's black like all the others. So why is it special?" said Thor.

"Because it's *bellissima*," said Susanna.

"It has escorted visiting heads of state and titled blue bloods, including a Prince and a Princess," said Alvise.

"Our wedding gondola is the same gondola that a princess rode in?" said Victoria.

"You're sitting in the spot where Lady Diana sat," said Alvise.

"Really?" Victoria smiled, and straightened her gown around her feet.

Ivana nodded. "It's true. I've seen photos of them in this gondola."

"That makes me your official *lady in waiting*." Jackie chuckled.

Victoria couldn't feel more special. She steadied a natural pose for the photographer, while Jackie and Ivana, and the children waved to the people who had gathered atop a nearby bridge.

His attention pulled to the second deluxe gondola, Alvise squeezed Victoria's hand lightly, and then nodded in its direction. Their mothers were seated in the love seat, chatting like old friends, while her father boarded the gondola, and Bruno directed Eunice to a more comfortable side chair. The other guests, seated in the remaining gondolas, looked more concerned with how the gondoliers tilted their vessels to pass under a low bridge and whether or not the boat would flip, sending them all for a swim.

"Aren't you going to open my mother's gift?" Alvise pointed to the small velvet pouch on Victoria's lap.

Victoria laid her bouquet on the loveseat, between them, and pulled open the sack's drawstring. She turned the velvet pouch upside down. Out fell a brass key. She shook her head, and the corners of her mouth turned up. "It's the extra key to our house."

Alvise smiled, and kissed his bride. "All she needed was time."

During the wedding ceremony, the tide had continued to rise. Now, it wasn't cooperating with the procession or permitting the gondolas an easy exit from the small canals. The talented gondoliers tilted, maneuvered, skulled and rowed the full vessels, instructing the passengers in broken English to sit still and not jeopardize the balance of their boats. Bruno, having only manned and never ridden a gondola, refused to ride in the ceremonial gondola with his wife. Instead, he, Ciano and Eddie boarded the boat carrying the photographer. From there, Bruno shouted and directed the procession. "You wait, the *gondole di lusso* go first." He scolded the gondoliers carrying the wedding guests in their boats, ordering them to let the wedding party's two deluxe gondolas lead the procession. Then, when Howard Woodcock stood up to photograph the wedding party's gondola, Bruno yelled, "Mister... you...*stai seduto, va' a remengo...ti spacchi la testa sul ponte.*" Howard, not understanding a word of Italian, smiled and snapped his camera at Bruno, too, and then sat back down moments before the back of his head met a low sitting bridge.

The parade of gondolas entered the Grand Canal and approached the Ponte di Rialto. Tourists lined the rim of the bridge—the wedding party too splendid to ignore—and their camera lights flashed and popped in clusters, forming a scintillating arc above. As the procession journeyed back through the smaller canals, Victoria smiled sweetly at the applause coming from people crossing over smaller bridges and walkways. Alvise obliged their welcome calls of "*Baci, baci*" by kissing his bride.

Straight in the middle of their glorious parade, the gray sky rumbled, once again, and thunder drummed its warning. Raindrops fell here and there, sending circular ripples across the water's glassy surface. Less than ten minutes away from the Bridge of Sighs, Alvise whistled up to his colleagues, and called out to the other gondoliers rowing behind them, too, "*Voga via…* or we'll never make it to the Bridge of Sighs." Like runners off starting blocks, the caravan sprinted forward. The gondoliers rowed harder, faster, and whisked the wedding party and guests down the canal. They had to reach the *Ponte dei Sospiri* before the storm arrived, or the rain and high tide would force them to take another route.

The gondoliers continued to row as hard and as fast as the tide washed into the city. The stronger and longer their strokes, the heavier the rain came down. Umbrellas popped open and covered the bridal party and their guests, and the tide hit its peak.

"Don't slow down now." Alvise shouted at their gondoliers.

Two final bridges separated the wedding caravan from the Bridge of Sighs. One by one, Alvise's colleagues tipped and tilted their boats, passing under the low lying bridges, and then raced their gondolas ahead.

Jackie turned to Ivana. "What's the Bridge of Sighs?"

"It's a beautiful bridge that connects the Doge's Palace to what was once the prison."

"Why is it called the Bridge of Sighs?"

"The legend says that during the Venetian Republic, when criminals were sentenced in the Doge's Palace and then sent across the enclosed stone bridge to the prison and their fate, which was often death, they sighed as they passed the stone grate windows and had their final look at Venice and at their freedom."

"In America we'd call that The Green Mile."

"Is that a place in America?" said Ivana.

"It's a movie…about death row," said Jackie. "Alvise, why is a death row bridge so important for us to get to?"

"There's another legend that says lovers sitting in a gondola shall be granted eternal love *only* after kissing beneath the Bridge of Sighs and as the bells in the Saint Mark's bell tower toll." Alvise looked at his watch, and then peeked out from under the umbrella. The rain had subsided, again. He handed the umbrella up to the gondolier, and then took Victoria's hand in his.

"This legend of yours, does it say anything about healthy babies being born to lovers who kiss beneath the bridge on their wedding day?" Victoria took Alvise's hand in hers, and placed it on her stomach.

His jaw dropped open, and tears wet his eyes. "No. But we can start a new legend." Bending at the waist, he laid a gentle kiss on the ivory chiffon covering her stomach. In the distance, the bells in the Saint Mark's bell tower rang out, and their gondola slowed to a near standstill. He sat up, again, lifted his eyes to the marble bridge towering overhead, and then set them back on his bride.

Victoria lowered her eyes from the bridge to Thor, and caressed the boy's cheek. She turned her brilliant smile on Alvise. Their eyes met, and she linked her hands behind his neck. "We made it," she said, and then kissed him beneath the Bridge of Sighs.

About the Author

Marie Ohanesian Nardin writes for news outlets and travel media magazines in the U.S.A. and Italy. Born in Los Angeles, California, she lives in the Venetian countryside with her husband—a third generation gondolier—their two daughters, and their Labrador. *Beneath the Lion's Wings* is her debut novel. Marie thanks you for reading *Beneath the Lion's Wings*, and would greatly appreciate you leaving a review on the retailer's website where you purchased her novel and sharing your thoughts about the book with friends and family. To stay informed about Marie's upcoming book events and projects, she invites you to visit her website: www.MarieOhanesianNardinAuthor.com

Printed in Great Britain
by Amazon